Rob May studied English at Lan
illustrator for Super Maths Worl
He is the author of *Dragon*
Sirensbane, a series of fanta
Moonheart – adventurer, gamble

Rob's other works include the *Alien Disaster Trilogy*, a science fiction adventure, and *Girl Under the Gun*, a modern thriller. He lives in Warwickshire, England.

To Mel

Best Wishes

Rob
#WPLondon 15

Books by Rob May

The Kal Moonheart Series
Dragon Killer
Roll the Bones
Sirensbane

The Alien Disaster Trilogy
Alien Disaster
Moon Dust
Lethal Planet

The LJ Hardwick Series
Girl Under the Gun

DRAGON KILLER

ROB MAY

Firebound Books

Published in 2013 by Firebound Books
ISBN: 978-1-5054-0473-9
Copyright 2013 Rob May
Cover illustration by Lin Hsiang

CONTENTS

PART ONE: THE ASSIGNMENT

PART TWO: THE QUEST

PART THREE: THE GAME

PART FOUR: THE DUEL

PART FIVE: THE DRAGON

PART ONE

THE ASSIGNMENT

I.i

The Forest

Kalina Moonheart lay back in the wet grass and raised her arm to shield her eyes from the light. She stretched out her limbs and offered herself up to the warmth of the Sun. It was early summer, and the surrounding ash and oak had only recently burst into leaf. Kalina smiled as she watched two wood pigeons fussing about their nest high up in the trees. Other than the sound of the birds' wings beating, the forest clearing was silent.

She closed her eyes. The Sun still glowed red through her eyelids. Her skin prickled; tomorrow it would be sore, but she didn't care. Right now, everything was perfect.

She must have dozed for a while. A shadow fell across her face and woke her up. Deros was standing there, his bare chest shining with sweat. He was holding a heap of colourful wild flowers.

'You're blocking my sun,' Kalina scolded him, but with affection in her voice.

'I brought you something,' Deros said, kneeling down beside her. 'Poppies, dandelions and ... mouse-ears, I think. And these ones are – I'm not quite sure what these are ...'

She propped herself up on her elbow to look. 'They're *snapdragons*.'

Deros gave her a worried glance. 'Snapdragons?' It was bad luck to pick snapdragons. 'Do you think that *he* will know?'

Kalina laughed and put her hand on his arm. 'I really, really doubt that a simple village boy picking flowers will be at the top of that monster's hit list. But let him come – right now! – if he really cares.'

She had addressed her final words to the sky, but it remained blue, clear and empty.

'Don't say things like that!' Deros said after a few moments of silence. Then he cracked a grin. 'Don't say that I'm simple.'

They both laughed. Kalina pulled Deros close. As she did so, there was a *thwack* and a whirring sound from off in the trees. Then there was a close-up *thunk*. Deros turned pale and looked confused.

'Kal,' he said. 'I ...'

He looked down.

She followed his gaze.

There was an arrow head sticking out of his belly.

I.ii

The City

The iron midnight bell rang out across the city: a muffled monotone knell that made the night's last stragglers walk just that little bit faster home. Kal's eyes snapped open at the sound. She shook her head. *That dream again.* A memory, really, but it didn't trouble her so much these days. *It all happened six years ago!*

She looked out over the rooftops. Kal was high up on top of the Basilica, in the shadows of the colonnade that encircled the dome. From up here she could see everything: the brick and terracotta buildings, bleached by the moon; the pale stone monuments and temples; the tall-masted ships in the docks; and surrounding it all – even the harbour – the towering ringwall: sixty feet high and twenty feet wide to keep monsters out of the city.

This was her new home. She had left her old life behind her, a thousand miles to the north. She was a different person now; she had lodgings here (a small room), friends (well, acquaintances) and skills that could make her money (so long as the law allowed). She also had a wealthy patron, and tonight she had a job to do that she needed to be getting on with.

Kal shook her head to dismiss her thoughts. It was time to go. With practiced ease she traversed the roof of the Basilica and hopped into the branches of the giant cypress tree that grew in the cemetery. From the tree it was an easy jump down

5

the cemetery wall, but from the wall it was an eight-foot leap to the roof of the old bath house. Kal made the jump without a second thought, and even landed quietly. She had done it hundreds of times before.

The bath house was almost a ruin. As she navigated its crumbling roofs, she could hear the cries of children from inside. So they were still using the old building as an orphanage. This crazy city was rich enough to do everything except look after its most vulnerable. Kal promised herself she would drop off a donation later, if the night's work went well.

She dropped down to ground level in the far corner of the bath house. Across the courtyard, one final obstacle stood before her: a ten-foot-high brick wall. There were, truth be told, any number of routes she could take over or around the wall, but Kal had always preferred the direct approach. She thumped her right fist into her left palm; the fingers of her leather gloves were stitched with a layer of tough elastic *cuchuck* – a rare substance imported from the far-off Junglelands. She had coughed up a great deal of gold for a very small supply. Her boots were soled with it, too.

She hopped on the spot for a second, then sprinted at the wall. The grip her gloves and boots provided was only temporary, but it was enough to boost her high enough so that she could grab the curved tiles that decorated the top. Her fingers only barely touched them; without the cuchuck she would surely have fallen back down. As it was, Kal was able to hoist herself nimbly up until she was crouched atop the wall, surveying the other side.

Gardens and pathways lay before her, monochrome in the moonlight. This park was part of the wealthy quarter of the city; it would be empty at night, and the entrances guarded. Kal's unconventional approach, however, ensured there would be no witnesses to her arrival. She dropped down off the wall and slipped along a tree-lined avenue – a shadow dressed in soft black leather. Only the statues – life-size marble representations of long-dead gods – saw her pass.

6

And in the very centre of the gardens: the one who had killed them all. Kal's route took her around the perimeter of the park, but even so she couldn't help but glance over her shoulder at *him*; the only god who still terrorised the world's dreams; the ancient winged beast whose unruly spawn still haunted desolate lands.

The last god standing.

The first monster.

The Dragon.

I.iii

Arcus Hill

The massive marble statue depicted *the Dragon* rearing up on his legs, wings spread wide. Before him was a muscular youth, naked and armed with a bronze spear. It was here, a thousand years ago, atop the highest hill in the city, that *the Dragon* had battled and eventually killed the god Arcus – the final god to fall beneath his savage jaws. But even in death, Arcus still managed to hold on to some residual power; his tomb – buried *somewhere* beneath the hill – had proved over the centuries to be a powerful deterrent to evil. And as such, this square mile of volcanic rock was crammed with an abundance of temples, shrines and statues ... and, of course, the mansions of the powerful and prosperous.

Arcus Hill. Home to rich merchants, richer politicians and those who sat upon chests of inherited wealth. The man Kal was after tonight probably fitted into all three of these categories. The only *other* person Kal knew who lived up here was Zeb Zing, the owner of the Snake Pit, the unruly downtown gaming den – the largest building in the city that wasn't a temple of some sort. Kal liked to joke sometimes that it was *her* temple. At least the gods of luck and fate that she worshipped there were still alive and kicking, and sometimes they even answered her prayers.

On any other night but tonight she could be there right now. Still, it was relatively early and this job shouldn't take too long; she had almost arrived at her destination. Some of the larger mansions on Arcus Hill had frontages directly onto the park. From the cover of a low yew tree, Kal staked out the building opposite. A guard was pacing up and down in front of the gate. At the sound of a distant bell, one that marked the half hour, he left his post and disappeared off into the trees of the park. Kal knew that he had a secret appointment with a girl he had flirted with earlier that day at a local tavern. Too bad for him the girl wouldn't keep her promise. Kal smiled to herself – *it wasn't as if she could be in two places at once*.

When the coast was clear, Kal dashed to the gate. In seconds she was over. Avoiding the portico and the main doors, she made for some steps that went down to a basement-level passage and the servants' entrance. Kal let herself into a kitchen where she paused for breath and listened out for any signs of life. It was silent. Idly, she lifted the lids of some of the earthenware pots. In one she discovered an interesting cheese, so she took a nibble.

Then suddenly she paused, the flavour of the cheese still on her tongue. She was not alone in the kitchen.

Kal peered into the shadows by the opposite door. The moonlight came in through a small window high in the wall and barely lit the kitchen. But something was there, watching her, panting heavily. The light glimmered off a pair of eyes that were just a couple of feet off the ground. Kal looked away quickly.

'Hey boy, it's alright,' she whispered, keeping her voice level.

The shape in the shadows growled. It padded forward, revealing itself to be an enormous wolfhound. Kal wasn't going to be able to make friends with *this* animal; most likely it had been trained to defend its turf. So she dropped to her knees, met the dog's gaze, and offered out her hand.

'Come and get me, then,' she said softly.

The wolfhound pounced. Kal twisted her wrist and the dog's jaws clamped down on her forearm. She wore steel vambraces beneath her leather, which blunted the dog's bite. With her free hand, Kal drew her shortsword from its sheath at her back. With one arm still in the dog's jaws, she twisted around, mounted its back and gripped its head between her knees.

Then she brought the pommel of her sword straight down on the back of the dog's neck, knocking it out cold.

'Naughty boy,' she chided, extricating her arm from the animal's mouth. She wiped the slobber off on a tablecloth.

Kal left the kitchen and found some stairs leading up to the ground floor. She found herself in a circular antechamber, the kind built to impress visitors to the mansion. Thick candles burned in sconces around the walls. The floor was tiled red and white, and in the centre was a column topped with a marble bust. Kal took a moment to examine the sculpture; at least now it wouldn't be too difficult to identify the man who lived here if she found him in the company of others.

She continued deeper into the house, creeping down a corridor laid with a deep-pile carpet that muffled her steps. *Sometimes they just make it too easy*, she thought to herself. Kal stopped outside a door that was slightly ajar, light emanating from the room within. She peeped carefully through the crack. It was a book-lined study. A man with his back to the door was sitting at a large desk piled high with books, maps and documents.

Kal could tell from the shape of his bald head that she had found her target. Slowly, she drew a throwing knife from her boot.

I.iv

Corruption

The man at the desk was holding a document up to read when Kal's knife passed over his right shoulder, skewered the parchment, and pinned it to a painting on the opposite wall. He did a remarkable job of maintaining his composure as he rose from his leather chair and turned to face her.

'I have a message for you, Senator,' Kal said amiably as she entered the room. 'Your home isn't secure from assassins.'

The bald man smiled weakly as he tried to control the anger that nevertheless revealed itself clearly in his eyes. He was young, despite his lack of hair, and dressed richly in a red velvet tunic and a black woollen mantle stitched with gold thread. 'Who are you?' he hissed, raising his hands cautiously, palms out, in a submissive gesture, 'and *what* do you want?'

Kal ignored the questions. 'Do you know what the punishment for corruption in the Senate is?' she asked him instead. 'I guess you must. Exile from the city; expulsion into the Wild. How do you think you'd manage spending your nights in a cave in the Endless Forest, instead of in here with your books?'

The senator regarded her warily. 'If you want to accuse me of something, maybe you should take your complaint to the Senate. Do *you* know what the punishment for breaking and entering a senator's home is?'

Kal was browsing the senator's bookshelves, brushing her fingertips along the leather spines. 'The kitchen door was open,' she said dismissively. 'I've not done any breaking yet. You have an impressive library, Senator.' She picked out a heavy tome bound in deep red leather. '*Calling the Dragon*. Wasn't the author of this book beheaded in Satos Square? I think I was there that day.'

'I wouldn't know,' the senator shrugged. 'I've not read it.'

'A bit harsh, beheading, if you ask me,' Kal went on, thumbing through the pages of the book. 'But I suppose the last thing we need right now is someone encouraging a dragon to visit the city again.'

The senator sagged noticeably. 'I'm just a collector of rare books,' he sighed. 'What do you want me to do? Burn my library?'

'No,' Kal told him. 'Words are just words; a book never harmed anyone by itself. In fact, I'll do you a favour and take this one off your hands; my shelves are a little bare at the moment.' She gave the senator a serious look. 'No, Senator, what I want you to do is to stop accepting donations from – and lending your ear to – the people who supplied you with this book. The Dragonites are a dangerous cult, and religion and politics have never mixed that well in this city.'

He looked at her suspiciously. 'Is that all you want me to do?'

'Yeah,' Kal said with a smile. 'What did you think I was going to do? Carve a permanent warning into that shiny head of yours?'

The senator actually laughed in relief. Then his expression froze.

Kal turned around, following the senator's stare. A man stood in the doorway of the study. He was tall, bearded and wore a coat of boiled leather scales. His dirty boots and cloak suggested that he had travelled a distance to get here. When he saw the book in Kal's hands, he drew a wicked-looking two-handed longsword: it was plain and notched, but had a gleaming sharp point.

Kal threw down the book and reached for her own weapon.

This was an unwelcome complication, but she fought to stay calm and in control.

'Another dog to deal with,' she muttered.

I.v

Swords

Kal and the intruder faced-off across the study.

'Who is this girl, Raelo?' the newcomer asked the senator.

The senator reassumed some of his authority. 'Nobody – a thief; get her!'

The man lunged at Kal with his sword. She hopped back to avoid its deadly point. Kal's own sword was only two feet long, but it was razor-sharp along both edges. It was no good for deflecting a heavy blade, though, and she would need to get up close to her opponent to do any damage.

Raelo cringed as the intruder swung his sword in a wide arc that swept a whole row of books off a shelf and onto the floor. Kal was forced back again. Her elbow knocked against something hard: a tall iron floor-standing candle holder. She grabbed it and flung it at her opponent. As he struggled to shove it to one side, Kal moved in for the kill. But her blade snagged on the interlocking scales of the man's armour, and she realised that she had missed her chance.

The big bearded man brought his sword down awkwardly in a close overhead chop. Kal twisted away and the sword ran down her left side, peeling away her leather and scraping over the steel bands that she wore underneath. She panicked slightly and threw herself down onto the carpet, then rolled underneath the senator's heavy oak desk.

The fallen candle holder had set fire to the study's thick

curtains, and the senator had taken off his mantle and was desperately trying to beat the flames out with it. Kal leaped to her feet on the opposite side of the desk to the big swordsman; this time she had her shortsword in one hand and *Calling the Dragon* in the other. Her opponent kicked at the desk, trying to shove it towards Kal and pin her to the wall, but she jumped up onto it as it moved, hurling the book before her.

The man instinctively batted it away with his sword, but the action left him exposed for a fraction of a second. Kal hadn't stopped moving; she sprang off the desk and fell upon her opponent, her blade held low and pointing upwards.

This time she didn't waste her opportunity; her narrow point slid easily beneath the scales of the man's armour and entered his heart.

He hit the ground dead, with Kal sat astride his chest.

She exhaled in relief and turned to look at the senator, a wild grin on her face. 'I told you that book was dangerous!'

Raelo was standing in the middle of his ruined study, clutching the smoldering remains of his woollen mantle. 'You *killed* him,' he gasped.

'I saved him from a slow death in the torture chamber,' Kal said. 'He was a Dragonite, I take it?'

Raelo nodded.

'Better run to the Senate and beg for their protection,' Kal advised him. 'The next man the Dragonites send here won't be so eager to help you.' She searched through the dead man's belongings and pulled out a money bag. 'There's about two hundred gold crowns in here,' she said, her eyes lighting up.

'Take it,' Raelo sighed, 'and I'll make an effort to forget your face, let alone the fact that you broke into my home at all. Give me a few days to prepare my excuses and I'll go and try and explain this mess to the Senate.'

'That's so very considerate of you,' Kal drawled, taking her leave. 'You'll make a smart politician yet.' She went back downstairs and let herself out the front door. The senator's guard was returning from his illicit night time rendezvous in the park. Kal gave him a friendly smile as she passed by.

The next morning, the nuns and monks who ran Arcus Hill Orphanage would wake to find that a package had been left on their doorstep. Opening the leather bag (that was stained with what looked like blood) they would find a sizable amount of money. They would be delighted, and would immediately begin writing a list to take to the markets: the children would not go hungry for weeks now.

Twenty gold crowns was a generous donation indeed.

END OF PART ONE

PART TWO

THE QUEST

II.i

Prey

Deros tried to stand, but his muscles failed him. Kalina got to her feet to help him. Another arrow hissed by; she looked around desperately to try and see where the danger was coming from. A hundred yards away, across the meadow of wild grass, four figures had emerged from the trees. Her first thought was, *Hunters?*

Deros had seen them too. 'Run, Kal,' he said between gasping breaths.

Two of the figures were wearing helmets; one had a round shield also, and a sword. *Soldiers?*

With fading strength, Deros pushed her away. 'Run, Kal!'

Without him? 'No,' she said, and moved to help him up again. Then she saw what the newcomers really were: not hunters, not soldiers – *not even people.* They were about five feet tall, with long, barrel-shaped torsos and short legs. Their skulls were flat and elongated, and thick back hair sprouted from the gaps in their piecemeal armour.

Goblins!

Kalina took one last look at Deros; the light was leaving his eyes as he implored her to go. She turned tail and ran for her life, not looking back.

She crashed through the forest undergrowth, the soles of her bare feet tearing up on the carpet of thorns and brambles. There was only one way she could go, and that was down. The forest hugged the sides of a valley on the lower slopes of the Starfinger Mountains, and the paths and game trails were almost vertical in places. She was aware of movement among the trees all around her; it seemed like there were more than four goblins in the vicinity – an entire raiding party must have crossed over the mountains.

Not only that, but she caught the harsh smell of smoke in the air. Something was burning.

She knew the forest as well as any trapper or woodcutter; Kalina had spent every one of her eighteen years within twenty miles of the village at the bottom of the valley. She charged down a trail that only last week she had quietly stalked along. That day, armed with sticks of charcoal and a roll of paper, she had spent hours trying to get close enough to sketch the red deer she loved so much.

Today, *Kalina* was the prey. She took a shortcut through a dense hawthorn thicket, almost taking her eye out on some protruding branches. Every fibre of her body screamed at her to go back for Deros, but what could she possibly do? Even if he was still alive, she could hardly carry him: Kalina was five-foot-eight and slightly built; Deros was six-foot-two and weighed almost half as much again as she did. And it wasn't as if she could beg for the goblins' mercy either; they might walk on two legs and scavenge weapons and armour from men, but everyone knew that they were animals really – predators. They lived to kill.

And so she plunged on through the forest in a state of panic and distress. Eventually she came out of the trees and onto the edge of the ridge that overlooked the village ...

... what was left of the village.

Every building was burning. The logging sheds were now enormous bonfires; the stables and fish stores pumped out thick black smoke that carried a sickly, deathly smell. The slate roof of the schoolhouse had fallen in, and living, dancing flames engulfed the rest of the timber and thatch homesteads. The Green Beck, the quick stream that cut through the valley, reflected the flames, putting Kalina in mind of molten iron running from the blacksmith's furnace. Only the wheel of the sawmill, slick with water, still turned, as if oblivious to the fate of the rest of the village. The once-white shrine to Mena was now black.

She dropped to her knees in horror, her thoughts turning to one thing only: *where were the villagers*? Where were her friends and neighbours? Had they already run? Were they already dead? There was no sign of life anywhere in the stricken village.

As the smoke billowed and drifted, she could make out one large, still black shape at the heart of the destruction. The more she stared, the more the shape appeared to suck the light and movement out of the chaos that surrounded it. Whatever it was, it was coiled around the spire of the shrine. Only when it finally moved did she realise what she was looking at.

The creature extended two enormous bat-like wings and raised its sleek, scaly head. It cried out: a harsh, scraping *kyyyrrrrk* like a thousand crows all screaming in unison

Kalina almost fainted.

He had come!

II.ii

Breakfast

The horrible sensation of falling jerked Kal awake. She lay in bed thinking over her dream for a few minutes, then steeled herself to face the morning routine. After five more minutes of putting it off, she flung off her feather-filled blanket and jumped out of bed. Kal's room was in the attic of a four-storey brick residential building on the corner of Satos Square, in one of the busiest quarters of the city. She went to the window bay, pulled open the drapes and stood there, naked, looking down at the activity below. The bustling market had taken over the square; the sound of voices haggling and the smell of spices and cooked meats filled the air. The clock tower in the centre of the square revealed that it was gone eleven o'clock. Kal smiled to herself; the market would soon be winding down.

Across the square, a guard patrolled the terrace atop the city watch headquarters. He raised his hand and waved at Kal when he spotted her. She replied in kind and stepped away from the window. She went and put a pot of water sweetened with sugar on the gridiron over the charcoal fire, and while that was heating up she set about her exercises.

Kal dropped to the wooden floorboards and performed twenty slow push-ups. When she could barely lift herself another inch off the ground she rolled over and started straight leg lifts instead. The pain in her stomach muscles was acute but strangely satisfying. Finally she got up off the floor and stood below the two butcher's hooks that she had installed in the thick wooden beam that ran overhead. She jumped up and gripped the hooks – which were set two feet apart – and pulled her body up until her head almost touched the beam. Muscles screaming, she then lowered herself slowly down again. She managed to do this ten times before falling to the floor and collapsing, breathless.

Self-inflicted torture over, Kal went over to the copper basin in the corner and quickly washed herself down with plant soap and a sea sponge. She examined her reflection in the full-length mirror that was propped against the wall; she wasn't as thin these days as she used to be – good food and city-living had filled her out a bit, but exercise and muscle kept her figure lean. Kal wrapped herself up in a linen robe and moved on to her next task: breakfast.

She dipped into her store of roughly-ground roasted coffee beans and threw a handful into the pot on the fire. She left it brewing while she cracked three eggs into a deep iron skillet. And while they were cooking she cut two thick slices of rye bread and set them to toast. Kal hummed to herself tunelessly as she beat the eggs up; subconsciously timing it all so that the coffee frothed, the eggs scrambled and the bread started to char at almost the same moment. She raked over the hot coals of the oven and took her food to her small table to eat.

Kal's table was littered with the fallout from last night's adventures: two throwing knives, a pile of ivory gaming tokens from the Snake Pit (where she had stayed until almost dawn) and the book from Raelo's study. Kal cleared a space for her food and sat down. She ate her toast and eggs with one hand, and used the other to flick through the pages of *Calling the Dragon*.

As she had suspected, every chapter of the lavishly inked and illustrated work was filled with rambling superstitious nonsense – the incomprehensible ravings of a madman. Not one of the hundreds of suggested methods of luring a dragon, let alone *the Dragon*, matched up with any of Kal's experiences. She wondered if the author had ever even *seen* a dragon, let alone bound one to his will.

Kal slammed the book shut. The Dragonites would be of little threat to the city if this was the kind of drivel they believed in.

The clock outside struck noon. Kal took one last gulp of her coffee; it was black, bitter and delicious. She had better get dressed; the man she liked to refer to as her *patron* would be up and about by now.

It was time for her to report in.

II.iii

Sir Rafe

Amaranthium: the largest city in the world. Over five million people found shelter within its sixty-foot-high walls; and two million more risked a life just outside the walls, working the ring of farmlands between the city and the Wild. Kal Moonheart was just one of those millions, and today no one paid her much attention as she fought her way through the midday crowds. The thoroughfares were packed with men and women from all walks of life: traders and actors, labourers and civil servants; priests, sailors, beggars and scholars. Travellers and refugees from all over the world had been stirring this dense melting pot for centuries.

Kal was dressed aggressively in black knee-high boots, black cotton trousers and a white open-necked silk shirt. Her only embellishment was a black leather choker around her neck. She walked with her head held high, her gaze focused on an indeterminate spot in the middle-distance. It was a ploy Kal often used; she was seemingly oblivious to anyone in her way, and people naturally stepped aside as she bore down on them. It didn't always work, though: Kal shoulder-barged a man carrying a bundle of firewood and sent him sprawling to the pavement.

'*You* need to watch where *I'm* going!' she scolded him cheerfully, not stopping to help.

Visitors to the Basilica on top of Arcus Hill had to tackle

first the forbidding zig-zag of the Godstair. This steep ascent had the effect of weeding out the serious from the merely curious, and Kal soon left the bustle of the city far below her. A thousands steps later, she stopped for a breather in the shadow of the Basilica's cool limestone walls. It was a hot spring day; Kal had broken a sweat already. At least it would be nice and cool when she reached her eventual destination: the crypts.

She entered the Basilica. The public rotunda beneath the enormous dome was a vast open space, home to Amaranthium's twenty-four gods. They stood on plinths in a circle, the symmetry of the Basilica offering prominence to none and equality to all. As always, Kal tried not to draw attention to herself by rushing straight down to the crypts, so she took the time to wander from god to god as if paying her respects. She knew all their names – everyone did. Here was Whalo, lifting his seashell aloft; Arcus with his spear; Mena and her cloven feet ... Once they had all walked among men. Now, of course, they were all dead.

Kal was examining the statue of Banos when someone stepped up beside her. She didn't look around; the last thing she wanted was to get to know any of the other regular visitors. Nevertheless, the newcomer made a move: 'Is my lady an admirer of brave Banos?'

Kal sighed and turned to see who had spoken. A stranger in polished plate armour stood beside her. He wore a deep blue surcoat embellished with a spiral of stars threaded in gold. He was handsome enough, with a broad friendly face and combed-back blond hair.

'If I *see* your lady,' Kal replied, 'I'll be sure to ask her.'

He gave her a genuine, unaffected smile. 'My apologies! Perhaps you are a follower of Draxos instead?'

Kal had to laugh. *Draxos!* The black sheep in the pantheon: ugly and twisted and always up to no good. His only redeeming feature was that in the end, when *the Dragon* came for him, he died defending his brothers' and sisters' children. It

26

was a bittersweet tale that Kal actually enjoyed.

'Perhaps I am!' she teased him, her eyes scanning the rotunda. A white-robed priest had entered and was making his way to the central rostrum; the hourly invocation was about to begin.

'They say you should try to emulate the life of the god you most admire,' Kal's new friend reminded her. 'Banos was a great knight as well as a god: the bravest warrior, undefeated in combat until ... well, you know. My name's Rafe, by the way.'

Kal accepted his gloved hand. '*Sir* Rafe?' she asked him.

He shook his head. 'No, sadly. Just Captain Rafe for now. Although, that is a shortcoming I hope to soon address. Did you know that Banos himself set down three heroic feats by which one could rise to knighthood? They are still enshrined in our law today.'

Kal was curious, despite herself. 'Go on then. What are they?'

'The first heroic feat is to wrestle a god to the ground.'

Kal smiled. 'I think you've missed your chance there – by about a thousand years.'

Rafe was enjoying himself, making the most of his opportunity now that he had a girl's attention. He counted the knightly feats off on his fingers: 'The second is to reach to the peak of the Improbable Mountain.'

'You don't look the suicidal type to me.'

'I actually suffer from a great fear of heights,' he admitted with a straight face. 'So then the only option left to me is the third feat. To join Banos in the ranks of knighthood, I must prove myself as both a warrior and a defender of the city; I must *slay a dragon*.'

Kal touched Rafe lightly on the arm. 'Well good luck with that,' she said. 'I'm sorry, I have to go. It was nice meeting you!'

Rafe looked disappointed. 'You didn't tell me your name!' he called after her.

She left him standing there next to his idol. As the priest began to address the large crowd that had gathered, Kal slipped away and made for the stairs that led down to the crypts. The invocation was not something that she ever cared to stay and listen to. The people of Amaranthium did not *pray*; their dead gods could no longer hear them. Instead, they *pleaded* ...

'Winged Shadow,' the priest intoned, 'deliver us from your wrath and fire ...'

II.iv

The Forgotten Tomb

The priest's drone faded away as Kal moved through the crypts. Passing by the elaborate effigies and oversized sarcophagi of self-important senators and nobles, she entered the ossuary: a dark maze of corridors and chambers, the walls of which were lined from floor to ceiling with the bones of the Basilica's priesthood. There was no glory or even recognition in death here: a priest was granted just one hundred years of time to himself in his or her own wooden coffin, before being moved, bone-by-bone, to fill the gaps in the ossuary walls. Jawless skulls looked down on Kal as she passed by; pillars of tibia and fibula held up torches that lit her way.

Eventually, she arrived at an unlit part of the crypts, where Amaranthium's forgotten line of kings and queens rested. Kal took a torch from a skeletal hand, and plunged into the darkness. She passed by the life-size effigy of King Aldenute, whose suicide five hundred years ago had precipitated the formation of the Republic. Kal counted off Aldenute's ancestors as she went by (they all looked the same to her) until she eventually arrived at the king's great-great-great-great-great-grandfather.

This particular old king stared ahead impassively as Kal stepped around him to get to the door of his tomb. She took a small key from the pouch at her belt and inserted it into what appeared to be a narrow crack in the stone door. The key turned smoothly; the lock was well-oiled. Kal pulled the door open and slipped inside the tomb. Someone had left a candle burning on the stone coffin within; it lit up what was essentially just a natural granite cave.

Kal pulled the door shut behind her and locked it. She shivered; whether from the chill damp or from the fact that she had just locked herself inside a tomb, she couldn't say. Still, she was almost there now. She extinguished her torch in a nearby pool of water and took up the candle. At the back of the cave was a narrow tunnel which twisted and turned deep into Arcus Hill until Kal had lost all sense of distance and direction. Finally, though, she emerged ...

... into a much larger cave. Stalagmites as tall as she was rose all around her, and the roof of the cave was lost in darkness. A ring of lanterns surrounded a long, low stone table in the centre of the cave. Rugs, furs and old leather-upholstered chairs were scattered inside the circle of light. And in one of the chairs, next to a warm brazier, sat Kal's patron: Senator Benedict Godsword – the wealthiest man in Amaranthium; Commander of the Senate Guard; the King Without a Crown and Keeper of the Sword of Banos.

'Hey, Mooney,' he said as he saw Kal approach. 'How did it go last night?'

Kal slumped down in one of the other chairs and put her boots up on the stone table. 'You were right,' she said. 'Raelo had a copy of *Calling the Dragon*. He was being groomed by the Dragonites. I took care of it, though; he's not going to be a problem anymore.'

Benedict was an unkempt man in his late thirties. He wore a shabby blue fur-trimmed doublet and two days' worth of stubble. He put down the wooden bowl of noodles that he was eating from. 'Nice work, Kal ... as always. Have you got the book with you?'

Kal shook her head. 'I sold it in Fig's Rare Books on the way over.'

'Kal!' Benedict sighed. 'If it falls into the wrong hands ...'

'The last time I brought you a dangerous – but valuable – document, you threw it on the fire,' Kal reminded him. 'Besides, I read it. It was a load of old nonsense.'

Benedict shrugged. 'Fair enough.' He tossed a leather pouch over to Kal, who caught it in one hand.

She looked inside; it was full of ivory discs, each inscribed with a denomination and etched with a twisting serpent design.

'Count it if you like,' Benedict said.

Kal briefly weighed the pouch in her hand. 'It's good,' she said, getting up to leave.

'Kal, wait. Sit down. There's something else.'

Kal dropped back into the chair. Benedict rolled a glass bottle to her over the top of the stone table. She uncorked it and took a swig. Kal wasn't usually one for afternoon drinking, but what the hell.

'I have another job for you,' Benedict told her. 'Well, more of a mission really; a quest if you like. But it pays well: more than I've ever paid you before.'

'I'm listening,' she said cautiously.

Her patron took a gulp of his own beer and looked her in the eye. 'Good, because I'm in trouble, Kal, and you might be the only person who can help me.'

II.v

Gold

Benedict stared at the neck of his beer bottle as he spoke. 'You probably wonder where I get all my money from these days, considering that all I seem to do is drink, gamble and chase women.'

Kal shrugged. 'That's none of my business.'

'I've made a few investments over the last couple of years – spent the last of the family fortune and acquired a few ... assets ... here and there. Strictly off the records, if you know what I mean. One of them is a gold mine; it's on an island off the coast of Balibu. It's an almost bottomless seam, and so deep that the heat down there makes it impossible for people to work. So now we use goblins.'

Goblins! Kal didn't know what was worse – goblins this close to civilisation, or goblins being put to work mining gold.

'They're perfect for it, really; they don't steal the gold because they have no idea how much it's worth; and if they do ... well, they'll happily trade it back for a dead chicken.'

Benedict drained his beer. 'But anyway, six weeks ago, there was no gold to be had when my ship from Balibu docked here in the city. Two weeks later, there was a message from man out there, the governor, saying that all contact with the island and the mine had been cut off. And *this* week, the captain of my ship informed me that there was no more news from the governor because *the governor had been killed.*'

Benedict paused to let this sink in.

'Okay,' Kal said, 'so you want me to head over and see what's going on?' *Fine*, she thought; Balibu was a fun place, and there was a large gaming house, *the Crocodile Casa*, that she had always wanted to check out.

'If it was just a matter of a murdered governor, I could send the Senate Guard in to investigate,' Benedict said. 'But Kal, there's more: the governor wasn't stabbed, shot or even poisoned. His smoking skeleton was found in the burned-out ruins of his villa. And there are other rumours flying around too: strange cries and sounds coming from the island, livestock going missing ... and the locals claim to have seen a large black shape that blocks out the moon and stars.'

Kal considered this in silence for a few moments.

'So if you do accept the quest,' Benedict said, 'you might want this.' He placed a shortsword in a black leather sheath on top of the stone table. Kal took it; the hilt and pommel were plain, but when she drew the blade she drew breath.

'This is ...' she began, turning the blade to inspect it. In the torchlight it had a silvery sparkle.

'Yes, it is,' her patron said. 'Well, it wasn't doing much good just hanging in my vestibule. I had a smith shorten the blade for you. There was enough left over to make a nice dagger, too.'

He tossed the dagger over. Kal was lost for words. 'I don't know, Ben ...'

'Come on, Kal, you're the only person I can ask and you know it. After all, you killed a dragon once; you can do it again.'

END OF PART TWO

PART THREE

THE GAME

III.i

Mena's Mirror

Kalina was rooted to the spot in shock and horror. The creature flapped its wings lazily and glided down from the spire of the shrine, landing in the burning ruins of the manor house. Ash and cinders swirled up around it as the great beast clawed about in the debris. Kalina stared in rapt fascination: a dragon! Perhaps not *the* Dragon, the god of all monsters, her rational mind told her, but *a* dragon nonetheless. Her eyes scanned the mountain peaks on every horizon. Did one dragon presage the flights of thousands that, according to legend, heralded the end of the world?

The skies were clear, but she could hear other noises in the forest: the yelps and howls of the goblins behind her. She was going to get caught or killed if she didn't move. Reacting on instinct alone, she launched herself over the edge of the ridge. The slope down to the village was almost vertical. She slid the first few yards, but soon lost her balance and found herself rolling over and over on her side. Thorns and rocks stabbed and knocked her; she banged her head, hit her hip hard, and seconds later felt her shoulder rip open. A breathless panic overtook Kalina as dirt and dust choked and blinded her.

Then she hit the bottom. She scrambled to her feet as goblin arrows dropped all around her. They were on the ridge above her now, hooting and barking. Kalina stumbled onwards blindly, across a scorched field and towards the village.

The dragon raised its head as it saw her coming. It flexed its wings and screamed at her. It was as big as a two-storey house, with glossy black scales and teeth like swords.

Kalina plunged onwards regardless, vaulting a stone wall and racing through the burning village. The dragon was less than fifty yards away now, and it turned its whole bulk to face her. She coughed and spat as she ran through the smoke. She had to jump over a charred corpse that was lying face-down on the ground. Forty yards now, but the dragon couldn't wait: it lifted itself off the ground with a slow flap of its wings, and glided down to get her.

Kalina rushed forward and met the dragon eye-to-eye. Then she jumped ...

... and dived into the deep cold water of the Green Beck. The dragon's shadow passed above her, but all sound was immediately wiped out by the water. She sunk in silence, then the swift current caught her and bore her away. Kalina held her breath, opened her eyes and kicked like a frog, driving her body down into the darkness at the centre of the riverbed. She fought on until her lungs screamed for air; then she fought on some more.

Three long minutes later, her head breached the surface. She had left the village at least a mile behind her, around a bend in the river. Now she was in a different world: here it was just another quiet, sunny spring day. A herd of deer watched her from the bank as she floated past. Downriver, the Green Beck joined the long Cold Flow. Kalina's first thought was that she could stay in the water and let it carry her a thousand miles to Amaranthium, far away from dragons and goblins.

Away from her village, from the people she knew and loved. *Away from Deros.* She had left him dying in the meadow on the mountain slopes. Dare she go back and try to find him? Did she even have a choice? How could she go back on the promises they had made there as they had lain together in the grass? *She couldn't!*

She forced her aching body into action and made for the

shore. Where the two rivers met, a tangle of willows covered an outcropping of land. Kalina knew this place; she had been here before. The low, twisted trees would provide more than just shelter and cover; they would also provide sanctuary. The willow grove was the home of the forest god, Mena.

A tunnel of spiralling roots and branches led to a circular depression in the earth with a small pool in its centre. Above was a domed roof of woven willow limbs that, save for one small round *oculus*, completely blocked out the sky and sun. The shaft of light that fell through the hole in the roof reflected off a large oval mirror that was held upright by a lattice of branches. Catkins grew all around it, framing the shining surface with a floral border of red and yellow.

Kalina stood before the mirror: Mena's mirror. In the days when the gods were alive, Mena had lived here and stood before the mirror, too. The forest god was cloven-hoofed and bestial, but her reflection revealed the golden-haired, beautiful woman that she really was. As Kalina looked at her own image, all she saw was a wet, cut and bruised, skinny adolescent with watery-blue eyes that were too big and too far apart, and a tangled mane of dirty reddish-brown hair.

She knelt at the foot of the mirror. The villagers were not generally inclined to pray to the old gods – no one believed that the gods could actually hear them – and Kalina was no exception. Instead she was looking for something. An old legend had resurfaced in her mind: it was said (in fireside tales) that the weapons of the gods could not only slay dragons, but could fell the largest of them with just the barest of touches.

She sifted through the collection of objects piled around the mirror that had been left here by visitors: carved wooden animals, bronze jewellery, brown wreaths of winter holly, a bowl of nuts. *Honestly!* What was she expecting to find – a magical sword? Kalina looked back up at the mirror: the creature that stared back at her appeared to be laughing and sobbing hysterically at the same time, a mixture of blood and tears streaming down its bruised face.

III.ii

The Swordfish

Kal leaned against the bulwark of the *Swordfish*, chomping on an apple as she watched the crew prepare to make sail. She was wearing a loose long-sleeved shirt and a wide-brimmed floppy hat: ideal clothing for avoiding both the sun and the stares of lecherous sailors. Tossing the apple core into the harbour, she noticed one final passenger making his way up the gangplank: a man dressed in full plate armour, struggling with two bags full of swords, spears and other things that rattled and clanked.

'If you fall into the water, don't expect me to dive in and rescue you,' Kal shouted. 'I didn't pack my can opener.'

The man gave her a broad smile of recognition as he stepped on board. 'It's easier to wear my armour than to carry it,' he explained. 'And no true knight would even think about leaving it behind.'

'You're not a knight yet,' Kal reminded him. 'What are you doing here, Rafe?'

'Senator Godsword is sending me to Balibu to investigate the death of the governor. What are *you* doing here, er ...' He looked at her expectantly.

'Kal,' she introduced herself. 'I'm going on a bird-watching trip.' She didn't want to reveal her own association with Benedict Godsword just yet. 'Here, let me help you with those,' she said, relieving him of one of his bags.

'Thanks, Kal. Let's go and dump all this stuff in the captain's cabin.'

She raised an eyebrow. 'The captain's cabin?'

'Of course. As a representative of the Senate, I'm entitled to make full use of the captain's quarters for the duration of the voyage. I trust that he's already prepared them for my arrival.'

Kal looked over to where the captain, a fat muscular man with a collection of evil scars and a peg-leg, was sharing a lewd joke with two equally dangerous-looking members of his crew. 'I think you'd better follow me,' she told Rafe.

She led him through a hatch and down to the cargo deck. Near the stern of the ship was a curtained-off area with two hammocks, one hung above the other. 'I'll take the top,' Kal said. 'I don't want you falling on top of me, especially if you sleep in your armour.'

Rafe wasn't happy. 'But there are other people down here ... and a strange smell. And probably rats, too.'

Three sailors were sat around an upturned crate throwing dice. They stopped what they were doing and turned to stare at Rafe.

Kal put a hand on his shoulder. 'Don't worry,' she said. 'If any of these rapscallions so much as touch you, I'll make sure that they regret it.'

The sailors laughed and returned to their game. Rafe threw down his bag of weapons with a huff.

They were back up on the main deck when the *Swordfish* passed through Amaranthium's seagate. It had been more than a hundred years since the city was last struck by monsters from the deep, but still the massive gate only opened once a day for an hour at noon. The *Swordfish* was just one of around thirty vessels that headed out under oar in single file, passing a similar-sized line of incoming arrivals on their port side.

Kal was apprehensive as they struck out into the

unbounded, uncharted Silver Sea. Beyond the secure city walls, whether on land or at sea, anything could happen in what was commonly known as *the Wild*, and it often did. Rafe didn't seem as worried, though; rather than nervously monitoring the horizon like Kal was doing, he was scribbling intently in a leather-bound notebook.

Kal tried to take her mind off thoughts of sea serpents and kraken. 'What are you writing?' she asked Rafe. 'Your journal? *Sunday the tenth: met a girl*,' she imagined out loud. '*Unfortunately, she's out of my league.*'

Rafe laughed. 'No. We've got two weeks to kill. I'm going to try and finish my epic romance, *The Song of Banos*. I've written three hundred stanzas so far.'

Kal sighed. She looked over to where the captain was patrolling the deck, supervising the raising of the small schooner's sails. 'Hey, Dead Leg,' she shouted. 'What can we do to help?'

The captain stumped over to them. 'The bilges haven't been cleared for three days. You did a good job sorting that mess out last time you were on board with us, Kal.'

'In that case, I think I deserve a promotion,' she countered.

Dead Leg grunted. 'Fine! *You* can scrub the decks instead.' The captain then turned to Rafe and gave him an evil leer. '*You*, sir, are on bilge duty.'

Rafe looked aghast. 'No,' he spluttered. 'The Senate ... I represent ...'

'The pumps are blocked, so you'll need to go and grab a bucket,' the captain ordered. 'Make your way to the very bottom of the hull, near the foremast. The smell will guide you.'

Rafe staggered away. 'And take your armour off,' Dead Leg called after him. 'The bilgewater will do more damage to it than troll blood!'

'I think I'd *rather* fight a troll!' Rafe moaned.

III.iii

Brimstone

One hundred and fifty feet up the *Swordfish's* mainmast, Kal looked out from the crow's nest. The empty sea stretched out for fifteen miles in all directions. It was the thirteenth day since they had left Amaranthium, and so far Kal had spotted a pirate gang (which they had managed to outrun) and a school of hydra (which they had followed for a while). Now she was looking out expectantly for something else.

And there it was! A low line of dark green on the western horizon. There were few mountains near the coast around Balibu: just miles of endless mangrove swamps and mahogany forests under a sweltering tropical sun. Kal was cool under her hat, but down on the deck the crew were bare-chested and sweating as they hauled on the rigging.

She leaned out over the basket and called down 'Land ahoy!' Nobody noticed. The boatswain was ordering the crew around and commanded all of their attention. Only Rafe, who was halfway up the mizzenmast, heard her. He was hanging from the end of a spar, untangling some of the sails, and was quite a sight, clad only in a headscarf and a loincloth. 'What did you say, Kal?'

She cleared her throat. 'Land Ahoy!' she croaked.

Rafe gave her the thumbs up and dropped down so that he was hanging from the spar by his legs. He cupped his hands to his mouth and bellowed: 'LAND AHOY!'

*** *

The *Swordfish* tacked along the coast for the rest of the afternoon, and evening was falling by the time they reached the port of Balibu. The town had a seawall like Amaranthium, but it was wooden and strung with colourful lamps. The seagate was left open: either the locals didn't fear an attack from the sea, or perhaps they didn't think that a shut gate would make that much of a difference.

Kal gripped the rail as they sped towards the dock. Dead Leg appeared on deck at the last minute and gave calm orders that all but the topsails were to be struck. 'HEAVE-TO!' the boatswain shouted, with an edge of panic in her voice. Rafe looked terrified as the crowded jetty got nearer and nearer. Dead Leg, however, remained calm through it all; he gave Kal a wink and nodded at two of his sailors. They threw out the anchors at the last possible moment and the *Swordfish* slotted neatly sideways into a gap between two smaller brigs. Water slopped all over the jetty, causing a man to spill a basket full of crabs, but otherwise the thrilling manoeuvre was executed perfectly.

The crew waved Kal and Rafe off as they descended the gangplank. Rafe, dressed once more in his armour, turned back to face the ship, gave a theatrical bow and raised his sword in salute. The crew whooped their appreciation. Kal waited patiently for him to finish taking his leave. The night was warm and balmy, and the docks were busy: fishermen finishing up their day's work mingled with the emerging nightlife. Music and singing could be heard emanating from several of the dockside taverns.

Kal looked out to sea. The moon lit the horizon, but there was no sign of Benedict's island gold mine. It must be farther out than she imagined. As she looked around, her eyes fell on a colourful mural painted on the side of a nearby inn: a grinning skull-like feminine face surrounded by flowers. Vuda; the god of dark magic. Kal felt a chill run down her spine.

'Where are you going to be staying?' Rafe asked her.

She shrugged. 'I don't know. I was going to play cards until dawn at the Croc, then hire a boat in the morning to take me out ... ahem, *bird-watching.*'

Rafe looked at her like she was mad. 'Really? Well, I have a whole floor to myself at the Discovery Inn. They have big copper baths full of steaming soapy water. I also heard that they serve up a mean seafood platter. Why don't you join me for supper? The Senate is paying.'

Kal thought about it for at least a second. 'Okay,' she said.

Kal took her glittering knife blade and pried open another oyster shell. She devoured the meat greedily, the salty liquor dribbling down her chin (which was, up until that point, clean and scrubbed after a hot bath) and almost spoiling her plain grey woollen dress.

She noticed Rafe's eyes on her, and deflected his gaze with a question: 'So who do you think killed the governor, then?'

Rafe spread his palms. 'Senator Godsword thinks that a dragon killed him.'

Kal acted like she was surprised. 'A dragon? Why would a dragon want to kill the governor of Balibu?'

'The Senator told me he's worried the Dragonites might have finally discovered the secret to summoning and controlling dragons,' Rafe said. 'Godsword and the governor were good friends, apparently, so he's taking the governor's death as a personal threat: it's no secret that Godsword wants to stamp out that crazy cult.'

Ben and the governor would have to be close, Kal thought, *for the governor to overlook Ben's gold shipments.*

'Well,' she said, 'you might get your shot at a knighthood after all. What's your plan?'

'I might have a walk up to the governor's burned-out villa later,' Rafe replied. 'You know ... to look for clues.'

'Sounds exciting,' Kal said. 'Maybe I'll tag along.'

The cook, a fat black man in a greasy apron, came over and interrupted them. 'More shrimp, my friends? They've been out of the sea no more than a couple of hours; it would be a crying shame to put them on ice.'

Kal nodded eagerly, and the cook filled her plate.

'Do you ever stop eating?' Rafe asked in astonishment.

'You never know where your next meal is coming from,' she answered through a mouthful of shrimp.

'Why are you here, Kal? I don't think it's for bird-watching. What is it that you really do?'

Kal decided to be honest. 'I'm a freelancer,' she told him. 'I investigate things and sort stuff out for people who may not want to go through the official channels: the opposite of you, I guess! But that doesn't mean I do anything wrong or immoral; I just try to fix up complicated situations.'

Rafe nodded. 'I see. A problem solver, huh?'

Kal gave him a wolfish grin. 'More like a problem *exterminator.*'

The governor's villa – or what remained of it – stood on a low hill overlooking the harbour. The second storey had completely collapsed, and only a few scattered piles of fire-blackened bricks gave any indication that there was ever a building here at all. The governor's charred skeleton was lying on its back in the middle of the terrace garden, its arms above its head and its jaw wide open as if frozen in a terrified scream.

'He doesn't look like he died a happy man,' Rafe commented.

'No,' Kal agreed. It was after midnight, but the tropical heat was still oppressive. Kal had changed into a loose shirt and leather skirt, but still she couldn't shake off the prickle of a sweat. She sniffed the air; behind the heady smell of the surrounding jasmine trees and fever grass, there was a hint of something else that Kal recognised ...

'Brimstone,' she said.

Rafe looked around as if expecting to see a dragon right there behind him. 'Brimstone?' he said. 'I guess that proves it then: a dragon did this.'

Kal knelt down in the rubble. 'Not necessarily.' She picked up some broken pieces of terracotta. 'This fire was *set*.'

Rafe came over. 'How can you tell?'

She held up three of the broken pieces, and fitted them together to make a small globe. 'I've seen these before. Filled with petrock and brimstone, they make a very effective *fire-bomb*.'

Rafe drew his sword suddenly. Kal looked at him in alarm. 'Someone is coming,' he said. 'More than one person: a large group.'

Kal drew her shortsword; the moonlight glimmered as it caught the edge of the blade. 'I don't hear any –'

A group of figures stepped into view from out of the shadows of the ruins, surrounding Kal and Rafe. A dozen black-clad men, their faces wrapped in headscarves that concealed all but their eyes. They all carried swords of various lengths and styles.

'Keep your back to me,' Rafe whispered to Kal. 'Let them come to us.'

Kal wasn't happy. Her natural reaction in a big fight would be to start causing chaos; make herself a moving target and stir up some confusion. She didn't have time to argue, though – the newcomers charged in to attack.

Luckily her instincts were faster than her thoughts. She twisted her body to avoid the strike of an assailant who had appeared in front of her. In the same movement, she whipped her own blade around in a wide semi-circle, forcing her attacker back. She over-extended herself, though, and he lifted his sword for an overhead blow that Kal surely wouldn't have chance to avoid ...

... but then he stopped, sword held high. His belly had split open following the scratch that Kal had given it. The man stood still in confusion as his hot, steaming innards slithered down his legs. Then he collapsed in a stinking pile on the ground.

The next attacker tried to reach Kal by thrusting his sword across the body that lay between them. Kal had found the flow of the battle by now, though. Her body and mind were loose and relaxed, ready to take advantage of her enemies' mistakes. In an easy, unhurried movement, she sliced her opponent's sword arm off at the elbow. He screamed and fled into the darkness.

Kal looked around for the next attack. It didn't come; the ruins were silent once more. She turned around and found Rafe standing over a pile of at least five bodies. His armour was splattered in blood, and his face and hair were dripping red with it too. He looked more like a terrible demon than a heroic knight.

'My hero,' Kal said with a smile. She wiped the blood from his eyes. 'Now let's see who these fellows are.'

She went and ripped the headscarf off the body that was the least mangled.

Rafe gasped when he saw the face beneath. 'Good grief!' he exclaimed.

Kal leaned in for a closer look. 'Well,' she said, 'that's something new!'

III.iv

The Croc

Rafe stared down at the face of their fallen attacker. 'Sorcery!' he exclaimed.

Kal looked even closer. 'Let's not jump to conclusions,' she said. 'Maybe it's a mask.' She took her knife and poked about the face – jabbing around the eyes and under the lips.

'It's not a mask,' she said eventually.

The face was ashen grey, with watery yellow eyes and a flat nose. The ears were large and bat-like, but what had made Rafe react was the teeth: the canines were pointed. Not filed down to a point, but elongated like the fangs of a wolf.

'He looks like a cross between a human and a goblin,' Kal said. 'What do they call them in the old legends – *hobgoblins*?' But they both knew that was impossible; there had been many reports of assaults on humans by goblins – and even on goblins by humans – but no offspring had ever been produced.

'Whatever it is, it's a monster,' Rafe said. 'Monsters inside the walls! And you know who commands the monsters.'

As if in answer, the horizon suddenly lit up. Far out to sea, an orange glow flickered for an instant, then died.

Rafe named his nemesis through gritted teeth. '*The Dragon!* I have to go and rouse the guard.'

Kal put a hand on his blood-soaked steel-plated shoulder. 'Wait,' she said. 'The local militia are lazy drunkards, who right now are most likely sleeping with their arms around a bottle of rum. They aren't going to appreciate being dragged out of bed just because you saw a strange light out to sea.'

Rafe tried to pull away. 'I have the authority of the Senate behind me! They'll do what I tell them. I need men on the walls, I need a chain of water buckets ...'

'Rafe, please.' Kal tried to calm him. 'People have been seeing things and jumping at shadows for weeks out here now, and yet the town is still standing. We need to separate the rumours from the facts before we raise the alarm.'

Rafe stopped. He ran his hand anxiously through his long hair. It came out bloody. 'So where do you suppose we go to look for answers?'

Kal smiled. 'As it happens, I know just the place. But first, we have to get you cleaned up.'

The Crocodile Casa was a narrow, low wooden building near the docks. The interior (including the card tables, chairs and the long bar that took up all of one wall) was all constructed from bamboo, while fig trees, vines and bright red and yellow jungle flowers provided the decoration. There was a pungent cloud of spicy smoke in the air that mixed with the more natural – but altogether more unwelcome – scent of body odour.

The gaming den was crowded. Kal felt Rafe bristle beside her. 'Relax,' she said. 'Remember the story of Banos and the King of Thieves?'

'Of course. Banos disguised himself as a robber and lived among the thieves for a year,' Rafe recalled. 'He waited patiently for the perfect opportunity to kill the king.'

'Right. Well think of this as your latest chance to emulate your hero. Be patient. Play the part. Let's go and get a drink.'

Kal led Rafe to the bar. The man behind the counter looked up with a bored expression that didn't change when his eyes met Kal's. She and Rafe had dressed plainly and concealed their weapons. Kal ordered three glasses of sour mash bourbon. She gave one to Rafe, sunk one straight away, and took the other with her as she crossed the busy room to the opposite wall, where a girl sat counting gaming chips behind a caged-off enclosure.

'You'd better tell us what games are running before we decide how many chips we'll need,' Kal said to the girl.

'Sure thing, Miss,' she replied. 'We got tables over by the door that you can join for five crowns. Over in that corner are the twenty-crown tables, and we have some fifty-crown and hundred-crown games running up the top end.'

Rafe stepped up to the slot in the cage and slid some gold over to the girl. 'Let's play some cards then! Give us five crowns worth of chips each.' He turned to Kal. 'My treat. And you can keep whatever you win.'

Kal laughed. 'You already treated me to dinner!' She was surveying the noisy action. 'I think I recognise some of the players at the top table,' she said to the cashier. 'Who's the big guy with his back to us?'

The girl glanced around and leaned closer to the bars of the cage to reply. 'That's Gron Darklaw. He's a strange one, Miss. Hasn't been coming here long. Buys his chips with chunks of raw gold. Drinks and drinks, but it never shows, except that it seems to make him bet more fierce, like. But he tips us well. He talks of wanting to be our next governor, too.'

'Interesting,' Kal said. 'Is that a hundred-crown table too?'

The cashier shook her head. 'It's a private game. They're playing with around a thousand crowns each.'

'Give us a thousand chips each too, then,' Kal said, 'and we'll go and see if they'll let us join in.'

Rafe choked on his bourbon mid-sip. 'Senator Godsword's funds don't stretch *that* far, Kal' he spluttered.

She gave him a sharp look that said, *I told you not to mention the Senate in here*. Then she pulled a piece of paper from the pouch at her belt and handed it to the girl behind the cage.

They had to wait a few minutes while the Croc's owner was called over. He looked at the note for a time, then at Kal, then finally nodded slowly. 'If Zeb Zing at the Snake Pit says you're good for it, then that's fine by me. She's an old friend. In fact, she often tells me about you, Kalina Moonheart.'

Kal enjoyed the expression on Rafe's face as the cashier pushed over two-thousand-crowns-worth of green and black clay chips.

There were six players at the top table. A dark-skinned girl with long black hair looked up as Kal and Rafe approached. She was either the world's most conspicuous pirate, or just simply enjoyed dressing like one: she was sporting a red head-scarf and a fitted white shirt with a wide black belt. 'Hi, Kal,' she said. 'Take a seat.'

The man next to her – a little fat man in a shabby merchant's coat – sighed. 'Oh no, Dragon Killer's here!'

'Hello, Lula. Hi, Vanrar,' Kal said.

The big man named Gron Darklaw looked up from his cards and stared suspiciously as Kal and Rafe took their seats. He had a massive build – muscular, not fat – and Kal reckoned he would be almost eight feet tall if he stood up. Shaggy black hair tumbled around his shoulders, and his eyes were pools of darkness.

'Why do they call you Dragon Killer?' he growled in a low, flat voice.

III.v

High Stakes

'Why do they call me Dragon Killer? Maybe you'll find out tonight.' Kal had sat down on Gron Darklaw's left, between him and the fat merchant Vanrar. Opposite her, across the red baize of the round table, Rafe had found a place between the pirate Lula and another fellow. Under Darklaw's implacable gaze, Kal silently arranged her chips into neat piles.

When she had finished, Darklaw passed Kal the deck. She accepted it with a polite nod and then proceeded to riffle and cut the cards with practiced skill. She dealt out two cards to each player and the game resumed.

Kal's own cards were the Three of Swords and the Seven of Pentacles. She folded them without a second thought, and settled down to watch the game and the players. Kal's approach was to sit quietly and let the action, and the conversation, come to her.

Rafe had no such restraint, and was already making moves and making friends. After winning a handful of small pots, he turned to his neighbour, Lula. 'Is it true that Balibu is being terrorised by a dragon?' he asked her.

'It *is* true,' Lula said. 'I've seen it myself. I was out in my skiff a few nights back and I saw a flash of dragonfire on one of the small uninhabited islands out to sea. I sailed in to see what I could see, and all of a sudden it came right at me: an enormous black winged beast! It scraped the top of my mast,

I swear. I couldn't get back to shore fast enough!' Lula emphasised the end of her story by firmly placing a stack of ten chips in front of her with a thud. It was a strong bet.

Gron Darklaw had been listening silently. Now he took a long sip from his goblet of red wine and spoke. 'Dragons will fight tooth and claw to defend their nests. You were right to back down.' With both hands, Darklaw pushed forward three tall towers of twenty chips each. It was a massive bet of three hundred crowns.

Lula swallowed hard and threw her cards away. Darklaw dragged down the pot with a cruel smile.

The game continued, and an hour later Darklaw finally broke one of the other players completely in a hand that played out right down to the last chip. Darklaw's clutch of wands beat his opponent's three knaves and, as the poor man staggered away from the table, Darklaw was stacking up a pile of chips worth almost three thousand crowns.

Kal was doing well, and with careful play had almost doubled her own stack. But she was losing chips rapidly to Darklaw, who would often jump in to punish her bets with massive raises that she could never justify calling. He was staring at her now in a predatory way, his large tongue licking the rim of his goblet. Kal turned away and looked over at Rafe, whose fortunes had risen and fallen several times over the evening.

'A long-enough lance would bring a dragon down,' he was telling Vanrar the merchant, 'but even better would be if you could lay your hands on one of the weapons of the gods. A dragon would happily lay down and present its neck to you if you wielded, say, the Blade of Banos.'

Vanrar smiled as he glanced at his cards and made a small bet. 'Oh yes, the Blade of Banos. The last time I was in Amaranthium and made Senator Godsword a reasonable offer for that old thing, he claimed to have lost it! But as far as killing dragons goes, the gods didn't have access to half the exciting war machinery that we do now. A ballista could put a bolt through that dragon's neck before it could cough up even a puff of smoke.'

Gron Darklaw made a raise, which Vanrar called without much thought. Lula, who had the deck, dealt out three cards on top of the table, the highest of which was the Queen of Cups. 'Are you not afraid,' Darklaw asked the merchant, 'that killing one dragon will prompt an attack on humanity by all the other dragons in the world, as well as all the terrible beasts – goblins, trolls and the like – that dragons have dominion over?'

'You mean like what the Dragonites are always banging on about?' Vanrar said as he made another bet. 'Oh no, of course not! That's all just foolish superstition, if you ask me. The Dragonites would have us burn humans alive in the streets as sacrifices to appease *the Great Big Dragon in the Sky*, or whatever they call him. When I think of a dragon, I don't think of some divine beast that we must all tip-toe around and be in awe of; I think of the holds of my trading ships stuffed with gleaming claws, shiny scales and succulent dragon hearts that will sell for millions!'

Darklaw had called the bet, and Lula dealt another card onto the table. Vanrar took one more look at his own cards then pushed the remainder of his chips forward. 'So no, Mister Darklaw,' he said, 'I am not afraid of dragons.' When Darklaw called the bet, Vanrar proudly turned his cards face-up: a queen to match the one on the table, and a king. 'I have a pair of beautiful queens. What do you have?'

Darklaw turned over his cards, one by one. The first showed a picture of a blue and gold creature, talons raised and tail coiled around a sword blade. The second showed a similar creature in red and silver, this one holding a pentacle in its claws.

'I have a pair of beautiful dragons,' he said with a wicked grin.

By five in the morning, the Croc was almost deserted, but still the big game went on. There were now only four players left, Darklaw having cleaned out one more player, and Kal having won such a large pot off another that he had picked up what remaining chips he had left and fled the table.

Darklaw now had around four-thousand-crowns-worth of chips piled in front of him. Kal wasn't far behind, but Rafe and Lula's best efforts had left them with slightly less chips than they had started out with. Vanrar had gone broke hours ago, but still hung around to watch the game. He had taken the job of dealing for them, as a way of still being part of the action.

Kal was drinking water; Darklaw was still supping from his goblet of wine that he must have had refilled tens of times throughout the night. Yet he was still the same immobile looming presence, and hardly any more communicative. His bets became larger and more frequent, and although he was losing as many hands as he was winning, he was still stacking up the chips through sheer aggression.

He made another strong bet: four hundred crowns – an amount that would feed a local fisherman and his family for a year. The cards on the table showed two kings and a three. Kal had nothing in her own hand – just two random high cards – but she had to pick a spot to make a stand, and this could be it. She pushed forward a stack of twenty high denomination chips. 'Two thousand,' she announced, then sat back and fixed Darklaw with an inscrutable gaze.

He stared back at her for a good minute, a pained expression on his face. His long fingernails clacked a rhythm on the edge of the table, until finally he scowled and threw his cards forward, relinquishing the pot to Kal. The hand had tipped the balance, and Kal now had the most chips on the table. Darklaw was finally pushed to make a stab at conversation.

'Where did you learn to play cards, Moonheart?'

Kal avoided his eyes. 'My mother used to play a great deal

when she was pregnant,' she replied without further explanation.

Rafe laughed. Vanrar dealt everyone new cards and the game went on. Kal made an opening bet, Lula and Rafe folded – they had been playing it very safe for the past hour or two – but Darklaw made his usual big raise.

'I have been playing for most of my life,' Darklaw told Kal, 'but only recently for such high stakes. It is my desire to prove myself at every aspect of life in this town, now that I have made my home here. I have built my own sailboat too, with my own hands.'

Kal smiled to herself. *Was he trying to impress her now?* She called his raise, and Vanrar dealt out three cards on the table: the Four of Wands, the Six of Swords, and finally the Dragon of Cups. The picture showed a green beast curled around a golden goblet amid a pile of coins and treasure.

'You'll be running this town next,' Kal joked as Darklaw counted out a new bet. Could she push him into opening up any more?

'Where I come from,' he said, ' – far from here – I did indeed hold a position of authority: over fighting men, and also over the economy, such as it was, of my village. It would indeed be an interesting challenge to rule over a town such as this one. The soldiers and the fishermen here have for too long had an easy life in this peaceful place. Perhaps I will put myself forward as the new governor.' Darklaw made his bet: two hundred crowns.

Kal thought for a bit, then called the bet. Vanrar dealt out the next card: the King of Wands. 'Where is your village?' Kal asked Darklaw. 'Would I know it?'

Darklaw treated her to a slow smile. 'No,' he said simply, and pushed out a bet of six hundred crowns. Rafe and Lula were watching with interest. The pot was over a thousand crowns by now; larger than the amount of money that they had each started out playing with.

'If I call, will you tell me?' Kal teased. Darklaw remained

impassive. Kal called anyway, and Vanrar dealt the final card: the Eight of Pentacles.

Darklaw barely glanced at the card. He wasted no time in making another punishing bet: a thousand crowns. Kal sat deep in thought, weighing up Darklaw for a long time. 'What have you got?' she asked him. '*Three* dragons this time? Two in your hand to match the one on the table?'

Darklaw sat as still as a statue, his dark eyes staring back at Kal threateningly. Did he want her to call or fold? Kal couldn't tell, but it really didn't matter: she knew what cards *she* had, and Darklaw had come too far now to back down. Kal pushed her entire stack of chips forward – a wall of coloured clay worth more than three thousand crowns.

'I bet the lot,' she said. 'You don't have the dragons.'

But Darklaw also shoved all of his chips forward with one massive forearm, and with his other hand slapped his cards down face-up: the Dragon of Swords and the Dragon of Wands. Then he drained his goblet of wine in triumph.

Kal sat still for a second. 'Oh, you do have them,' she said calmly. She turned over her own cards: the Five and Seven of Swords. 'Well I have a chain.'

Darklaw's eyes widened in shock. His fist clenched around his goblet as if he would crush it. Rafe laughed in relief and Lula stood up and clapped. Vanrar confirmed the win: 'Four, five, six, seven and eight: Kal wins ... a pot of over eight thousand crowns!'

The fat merchant gave Darklaw a mocking grin. 'Dragon Killer strikes again!' he said.

III.vi

Hot Water

Kal woke up with her mouth tasting like a troll's toilet. Where the hell was she? The bed she was lying in was large, soft and luxurious, and a warm orange glow filled the room. She was still dressed, though. Kal turned her neck stiffly and found herself looking at the slim, brown bare back of the girl lying next to her. Lula? She groaned. Turning the other way, she could see Rafe sprawled out on the sheepskin rug at the side of the bed. The Captain of the Senate Guard was clad only in his smallclothes, with a garland of flowers around his neck.

The orange glow was the twilight filtering through the mottled glass windows of the Discovery Inn; they had slept all day. Memories of the night before started to return: after Kal's big win they had stayed at the Croc downing glasses of rum mixed with coconut milk and pineapple juice. At dawn, the owner had kicked them out and so Kal, Rafe, Lula and the merchant Vanrar had taken their party to the streets. They had banged on the doors of several dockside bars and taverns demanding more rum. Then there had been the street dancing ...

Lula was getting dressed, pulling on her pantaloons and boots. She tied her long black hair back in a ponytail and hitched her cutlass to her belt. Kal rose too and padded over to the door to show her friend out. 'See you at the docks after dark then,' the pirate girl said. 'And make sure you get a good breakfast; you've got a twenty mile row ahead of you!'

Kal made a face, and shut the door of the suite as Lula bounded off downstairs. Kal turned and started picking up Rafe's clothes off the floor, kicking him in the ribs as she did so. 'Hey, sleepyhead. Time to get up!'

Kal stuffed her mouth with a forkful of bacon and eggs. 'Darklaw pays for everything in lumps of gold,' she mumbled as she ate. 'If there's a mine on that island, and he's got access to it, then that means he has an almost unlimited flow of money. That has to be why all last night he was talking up the dangers of disturbing the terrible dragon that's supposedly nesting there. Rumours like that keep curious people away. I'll bet that it was him who got those hobgoblin freaks to burn down the governor's mansion.' She paused to take another mouthful. 'I wonder if paying or bribing his way into a position of power here in Balibu is his ultimate goal, or just the first part of some deranged plan?'

Rafe was slowly nibbling on a mango. His appetite was not the equal of Kal's. 'Maybe you're right,' he said. 'I'm just a soldier, not a detective. But Kal – you don't have to deal with this anymore; that's my job. Why don't you go home? You're rich now! You could buy a small house on Arcus Hill with what you won last night!'

Kal shook her head. 'I'm not rich,' she said. 'Only a fraction of that money is mine to keep. I have backers who each take a percentage of my winnings. But they cover my losses too, so it's their risk, not mine. Not that I often lose, of course ...'

Rafe was intrigued. 'Oh? So who are these mystery backers then?'

'Well, you might know one of them. Benedict Godsword.'

Rafe frowned. 'Benedict ... Senator Godsword? Is that why you're here, Kal? Did he send you too?'

'Yes. That's how I know there's a gold mine out there somewhere. It's Benedict's. Well, it was.'

She watched Rafe try to process this information. 'The

senator has a gold mine? I didn't know about this! But there's no record of … if he's hiding it from the Senate, then that's illegal …'

'Rafe,' Kal said. 'It doesn't matter right now if that mine belongs to the Senate or to Benedict or anyone. If Gron Darklaw's controlling it and killing people to hide it, then we have to stop him, right?'

Rafe nodded slowly. 'You'd risk your life for Benedict Godsword?'

'Yes,' Kal said simply. 'I *owe* him my life.'

She drained the last of her giant mug of black coffee. 'But that's a story for another time. Come on, let's get going.'

They stood side by side admiring the sloop. The headsail was grey, the mainsail deep red, and the cedarwood boards were stained a deep black. It was thirty feet long and expensively detailed: the wheel and rails were padded with leather, and the cleats, lanterns and other fittings were a polished silvery metal.

'That's a man's boat, alright,' Rafe commented. 'Why is the bottom made of metal?'

'The hull,' Kal corrected him. 'I don't know.' She peered into the clear water that was lit by the harbour lights. 'It looks like it's made of platinum. Who would build a boat with a platinum hull?'

'Someone who was very rich and wanted everyone to know it,' Rafe said.

They left Darklaw's boat and continued along the wharf. In the distance, smoke could be seen drifting in front of the stars. Kal saw Lula hurrying towards them through the crowds. She looked serious.

'Vanrar's warehouses have burned down,' Lula said when she reached them.

Kal swore. 'Where's Vanrar? Is he safe?'

'It's too late, Kal,' Lula said. 'He was in the warehouse when it burned. He's dead!'

Kal swore again. *Darklaw!* It had to be. The big man hadn't been impressed with the merchant's lack of respect for his dragon stories. Darklaw was a bully alright, and of the worst kind: one who would not only indirectly threaten people, but also act to keep them in line.

'Let me guess,' Kal said, 'people are saying a dragon did it?'

'That's the word on the street,' Lula confirmed. 'There was a flying shadow ...'

Kal shook her head. *Smoke and mirrors!* What was actually real in this town?

'We need to get to that island and sort this out once and for all,' Rafe said. 'Lula, take us to your boat.'

Lula pulled herself together visibly. 'Yes, sir!' she snapped.

Lula's boat was a small two-seater canoe. Kal made Rafe sit in the aft, and she sat opposite him in the bow.

'Thanks, Lula,' Kal said, as they pushed off from the jetty. 'Remember, if anyone asks about us, we've gone back to Amaranthium!'

'Take care, Kal!' Lula said. 'Look after her, Rafe. I need to know there's going to be more nights like last night to come. But without these sort of mornings after, of course!'

Rafe grunted in reply as he pulled on the oars. With a flash of her gold hooped earrings, Lula vanished from sight. Rafe rowed in silence as they slid through the water, under the watchtower and out through the seagate. The night was moonless and the water was calm. With luck, they would make it to the island in around six hours.

Kal doubled-checked her equipment. She was wearing a rough grey linen dress, open-sleeved and cut to the knees. She also wore her steel vambraces, and her leather boots and cuchuck-stitched gloves; she might need the grip if they went rock-climbing. Her knife was at her belt and her shortsword strapped across her back. What else did she need? Nothing: all she had to do was make sure she had a blade for Darklaw's neck.

After a time, Kal took over the oars, and when they were far enough from the town, they put up the small sail. There was a warm westerly breeze that would help them on their way. Kal made sure that Rafe was happy keeping the canoe on port tack with the sail held on a diagonal, then she tried to find a comfortable position in the cramped hull to lie down. 'Wake me in an hour,' she instructed, and laid her head on a coil of rope.

It only seemed like a moment later when Rafe tapped her on the leg. 'An hour, I said,' Kal complained.

'That *was* an hour,' Rafe grinned. 'I would have given you a few more minutes, but your snoring was frightening the fish. Come on, change over!'

Kal took up the oars and resumed the slow, heavy rhythm. Under both oar *and* sail they were cutting briskly through the water. The night was pitch black, and the lights of Balibu had faded behind them. The God Star burned brightly in the northern sky, though, so Kal fixed their course by that. Rafe watched her row. He was also dressed in loose, light clothes: a vest and breeches torn off mid-thigh. He had insisted on wearing his blue silk surcoat over it all, though: the spiral of stars that decorated it would mark him out as an official representative of the Senate should they need to talk their way out of trouble. In case talks broke down he had also brought a bag of various weapons, as well as his lance.

'You're quite strong for a girl,' he said as he watched Kal.

'Shut up and get some rest,' she rebuked him. 'You're on again in an hour.'

Rafe lay back and draped his hand over the side of the canoe, letting his fingers trail through the dark water. 'It's warm,' he noted. 'The water is really warm.'

'The sea holds the day's warmth,' Kal explained, but she took a moment to test the water. Rafe was right – the water was unusually hot.

'Can dragons breathe fire underwater?' he asked her seriously.

Kal laughed. 'Have you ever seen a dragon breathe fire?' she asked him.

'Not yet!'

'Well, I would worry more about working out how they manage to do that at all, rather than sweating the details.'

Rafe fell silent. Kal continued to row. Maybe she had offended him, but she couldn't think of anything to say. *Conversation Killer*, they should call her. She concentrated on pulling and lifting the oars. The physical exertion was making her hungry – not just for food, but for action. The nervous thrill she felt on the eve of an assignment was like the excitement of sitting down at a card table, but magnified many times over. Rafe must have noticed Kal grinning to herself; his own smile had returned.

A school of large fish had started to follow the canoe. Rafe let them nudge at his fingertips. 'I could just reach down and grab one,' he said. 'We could cook it when we get to the island.'

'They're sharpfins,' Kal said. 'They could reduce your arm to bone in less than a minute.'

Rafe jerked his hand out of the water.

'But it's okay!' she said brightly. 'They only go after blood and shiny things!'

Three hours later, Rafe woke Kal for the last time. 'I'm done!' he said. He had already taken down the sail. 'You can take us in.'

She looked out to sea. Ahead of them, looming out of the darkness was the island. It was about five miles across, and at its centre a triangular mountain rose out of a surrounding girdle of trees. Kal could see the starlight glittering on the surf that was breaking on the beaches.

Dragon or Darklaw, she thought, *Whatever you are, I'm coming for you*!

III.vii

Black Sand

Kal seemed to a have drawn the short straw when it came to the final stretch of rowing. The ebb and flow of the tide meant that for every ten yards she pulled them closer to the beach, they were dragged back out five. Coral scraped the bottom of the small canoe, and twice they got stuck. Rafe used his lance to free them from the reef, but Kal could tell that he wasn't happy using his weapon as a punt. Eventually, though, they made it, speeding towards the shore in the wake of one of the gentle rollers. Rafe leaped out as the canoe hit the sand, and dragged them clear of the water.

Kal disembarked and Rafe easily pulled the empty canoe up the beach towards the shelter of the mangrove trees. Kal followed after him, kicking sand over their tracks to hide any trace of their passage. They had seen no other vessels or lights on the island on the voyage over, so with luck nobody knew of their arrival. At the edge of the trees she crouched and scooped up a handful of sand. She let it sift through her fingers: it was fine, black and sensuously soft. She frowned; warm water and black sand ... what did that signify?

She turned and followed Rafe into the gloomy darkness of the mangroves. The low trees grew close together, their roots twisting around each other in the swampy ground. Rafe had found an elevated spot of dry mud and had already covered the canoe in leaves and driftwood to hide it. Beneath the shelter of a large flat-leaved saltwine bush he had laid out a blanket and was unpacking their food.

'Dried beef – come and get it!' he said. 'Or there's fresh crab if you think we could risk some cooking.' He pulled a large red crustacean from under the blanket and held its wriggling legs out to Kal.

'He looks delicious,' she said. 'We should be alright if we dig a hole to hide the fire.'

They sat together on the blanket and ate the soft white meat on toasted bread. Through a gap in the trees they could see the mountain, a looming black void against the star-strewn night sky. Their plan was to get a few hours' rest and then explore the island at dawn, starting by following the coastline and looking for signs of other ships coming and going. Somewhere there was a natural harbour near the mine entrance, and Kal was convinced that they would find evidence of Darklaw visiting the island.

'Where did you get your knife?' Rafe asked her. Kal was cutting bread with it; the blade glimmered in the firelight.

She had noticed him eyeing her weapon several times since they had met. She handed it over. 'It was a gift. Have a look: it's not magic or anything.'

Rafe weighed it in his hand. He looked almost disappointed. 'It's bloody sharp, though,' he noted.

'It needs to be,' Kal said. 'This bread's bloody tough –'

She froze. Something was flying by, its massive silhouette visible in flashes through the branches of the trees. Kal and Rafe drew back under the cover of their bush as the shape passed almost directly overhead. When it did, they could see exactly what it was: the snub-nosed snout, the thick neck and bulky tubular body, the black wingspan that was fifty feet across, the sinuous tail that followed in its wake. It glided past without a sound.

Kal stood up and watched it slowly circle around the mountain. It caught an updraft and, with a lazy shake of its wings, shifted its course and made for the face of the mountain about half way up. It disappeared into shadow where there must have been a cave entrance.

She felt a shiver of fear run down her body. So there *was* a dragon on the island after all. Kal had a horrible feeling of being in the wrong place at the wrong time. Darklaw she could have dealt with, and she had already survived one encounter with the strange hobgoblin creatures. But a dragon? Did she really want to go through all this again?

She looked at Rafe. He was standing behind her, staring up at the mountain, an awed expression on his face. Kal realised that it must have been the first time that he had seen one of the winged beasts. 'It's actually here, Kal!' he said. 'A dragon! They must have really done it: the Dragonites, they finally found a way to summon one. You know what this means – this is just the beginning of the great war between monsters and men, a war that will be the stuff of legends.' Rafe could hardly contain himself. 'And we're going to be part of it. They'll be writing songs about us, Kal. In a hundred years' time, *we* will be the heroes, and people will talk about *us* the way that *we* talk of the gods.'

Rafe was breaking Kal's heart. 'The Dragonites can't summon dragons, Rafe,' she insisted. 'They're just a noisy cult. I've read their stupid book, *Calling the Dragon*; it's all nonsense. Arcane rituals and human sacrifice – what self-respecting dragon would take any notice of that?'

Rafe looked affronted. 'So why *is* the dragon here?'

'I don't know!' she said, throwing herself back down on the blanket. 'Maybe it just wants a nice warm place to nest and raise a family. When it gets light, we'll go and take a look in that cave. Maybe you can ask it. But don't expect it to leave without a fight; I've seen how stubborn dragons can be.'

Rafe rejoined her on the blanket. 'Lula told me you've tangled with dragons before.'

'It was a long time ago.'

I still dream about it every night!

Rafe leaned closer. 'Can you kill them?'

67

'They're clever,' Kal warned him. 'Cunning even. But their brains aren't any bigger than ours; it's their thick skulls that take up most of the room in their head. If you're smart you can *trick* them.'

'Then we can take it down, Kal, between us! Two brains against one. Benedict will have to knight us both: Sir Rafe and Dame Kalina!'

Dame Kalina! Kal had to laugh. She returned her companion's gaze. Rafe had changed somewhat in the three weeks that she had known him: his pale skin had tanned, and his blond hair – once straight and silky – had now turned wavy and tangled by saltwater, and was tied back from his face with a leather thong. But he hadn't yet lost his optimism and enthusiasm. 'Why do you want to be a knight so bad, Rafe?' she asked him.

'There hasn't been anyone knighted in Amaranthium for over five hundred years,' Rafe said. 'Feron Firehand killed the West Wind Dragon in the Palace Plaza, right in the middle of the city. He severed its head in one blow with the Blade of Banos.'

Kal nodded. 'King Aldenute knighted him. That must have been just before the revolution.'

'Yes. When the king died, Firehand kept the peace. He rose above the violence and settled conflict and dispute on both sides. He was Lord Protector for three years and was a powerful voice in the formation of the Republic. He was tough, principled and fair ... and he was my ancestor, Kal.'

'Quite the role model,' Kal said. 'It's a pity that if you do slay the dragon, he won't be around to appreciate it.'

Kal mentally kicked herself. *Stop saying things like that!*

'You're here, though,' Rafe said quietly.

They sat together in silence for a moment. 'Although,' Rafe said with a grin, 'right now I'm not in *that* much of a hurry for dawn to come so that we can go and meet this dragon. I wish we could stay here for a while longer. No, forever ... forever under the stars.'

On impulse, Kal leaned forward and kissed Rafe on the mouth. He responded instantly with surprising force. Kal gasped as he took her in his arms and put her down on her back on the blanket under the saltwine bush. Her mind emptied – all thoughts of dragons, knights, hobgoblins and villains falling away as she surrendered herself to purely physical instincts.

She arched her back as Rafe's hand found her thigh.

END OF PART THREE

PART FOUR

THE DUEL

IV.i

Refuge

Kalina stepped out into the clearing. It was raining, and the water set rivulets of mud and dirt streaming down her body. She stood staring at the spot where three days before she had lain with Deros. He had promised her that morning that her life was about to change forever, and it had. Except that now it didn't look as though she was going to spend the rest of it as a woodcutter's wife.

She blinked back bitter tears. The grass where Deros had fallen had been sluiced clean by the spring rain. There was no body, no blood – just some crushed wild flowers: poppies and dandelions, and the snapdragons that Deros had fretted over. *She had laughed at him then.* Kalina crushed the flowers beneath her bare feet in anger. She should be miles away from here by now, yet she couldn't bring herself to leave without learning *why* the man she loved had been killed, and his body taken away.

Kalina wasn't a stranger to monster attacks – her own parents had been killed in an unfortunate incident with a troll when she was ten – but for a dragon and a tribe of goblins to destroy a village ... that was unheard of. Was it possible, she wondered, that someone in the village had somehow provoked the attack? The eighty villagers she thought of as her extended family were a diverse crowd, with no shortage of secrets and history between them. They were orphans and widows, runaways and outcasts, retired adventurers and exiled politicians. For many years, people had tended to converge on the village, find a job that needed doing, and then maybe – if they fitted in – think about putting down some roots. Kalina couldn't remember a time before the village was named *Refuge*.

Smoke was still rising from down in the valley where the village nestled. Kalina steeled herself. Was the dragon still there? Was *anyone* but her still alive? She had to know. She had to take one last look.

She moved silently through the trees; not even the deer and birds reacted to her presence. Kalina had stitched together some animal furs and skins she had found in the willow grove at the river fork, and she had smeared mud and dust over her naturally pale skin. Her camouflage was essential: there were goblins in the forest, still.

Lying on her belly beneath the wide fronds of a fern, Kalina spied on a pair of the creatures. These goblins weren't armed and armoured like the group that had chased her down to the village three days ago; in fact, they appeared to be female. They wore skins around their waists, but their breasts were bare. They were collecting sticks of dry wood from the forest floor, communicating in grunts and whistles as they did so. If the goblins were here, then the dragon must be around too; she knew that much from the old stories. Every dragon commanded its own army of goblins, trolls and other monsters. Would the rest of the dragon's horde be coming down from the mountains any time soon? Kalina shuddered at the thought; she really, really shouldn't linger here long.

When the forest was still and empty once more, she slipped away, keeping to the dark shadows between the trees, heading down the slope towards the village. Dusk was making it difficult to see. *But what I can't see, can't see me*, she reasoned. But what use was reason now? Only last week she had been telling her young pupils in the schoolhouse about how goblins all lived in underground chambers that their dragon masters had gouged out of the rock for them; they could probably see quite well in the dark. Kalina had gotten all *her* facts from the schoolmaster who she worked with; he had filled her head with countless old stories and legends. She wondered if his specialist knowledge had been enough to save him from the dragon attack.

She avoided the well-trodden paths and took secret shortcuts through tangled groves and past secluded pools. Eventually she could see the ridgeline through the trees, and she followed it until she came to the Overlook, a pointed finger of limestone that jutted out over the valley. She went down on her hands and knees and crawled to the edge.

What she saw below took her breath away. The village had been completely wiped off the map. No trace remained of any of the fifty or so buildings that were once there – not even one burned-out shell. Instead, in the centre of a mile-wide field of ash, was an enormous smoldering bonfire. Goblins were busy to-ing and fro-ing between the edge of the nearby trees and the smoking heap, which was piled up to the height of a three-storey building. Kalina could see they were bringing more wood to throw onto the bonfire.

No, not a bonfire …

In a shallow crater-like depression on top of the mound of timber, Kalina could see movement. A black man-sized shape was scrabbling atop a pile of still corpses. It moved awkwardly, stretching out its limbs, its neck, tail and wings.

Not a bonfire … *a nest.*

Kalina hissed between clenched teeth. The dragon was using the village and the villagers as a source of fuel and food for its young. Where was the parent now? Probably out hunting in the surrounding countryside; there was enough wood and wildlife nearby to raise a whole litter of juveniles to adulthood.

She was aware suddenly of how exposed she was out on this promontory. *I shouldn't have come back. There's no helping Deros, or any of them now. I need to run far, far –*

A dark shadow fell over her. Kalina felt the rock she was crouching on shudder, and heard the crack of heavy wings battering the air. She was buffeted forward several yards; her feet stumbling out into nothingness. She tried to grab at the sky with her fingers as she began to plummet.

Then she was caught in mid-air. The dragon's clawed toes wrapped painfully around her body like a gibbet. Kalina was still speeding through the air, but this time on a new trajectory: directly towards the nest. At the last moment, the dragon beat its wings and rose up, releasing its hold on her. Then she was falling again, this time head-first, arms flailing.

Fifty yards below her, the hungry juvenile opened its jaws.

IV.ii

Ashes

Kal's eyes flicked open. She could taste fear and bile in her mouth; was that from the dream, or because of the day ahead? The mangroves were black against a pink sky: dawn had arrived – time to get on with it! Removing Rafe's arm from around her waist and getting to her feet, she gulped down water from one of the skins that they had brought with them. Then she went and refilled it from the swamp, and poured the greeny-brown sludge over the ashes in the fire pit. Next, she set about stirring it all up with a stick.

When Rafe awoke he was greeted by the site of Kal rubbing mud and ashes into her body. It covered her face, arms and chest; she looked like a grey ghoul.

'You look beautiful in the mornings,' Rafe said with a grin.

Kal flicked mud at him. 'Rub some of this in,' she ordered. 'Dragons can't smell you if you're smeared with ash. It overpowers their senses.'

Rafe did as he was told. 'Yes, *my lady.*'

Kal smiled despite herself. She couldn't deny that she *was* his lady now. She moved behind him and started helping him apply the mixture to his back. 'When we get to the cave, don't run in swinging your sword,' she said. 'Let me call the shots.'

'I'm yours to command,' Rafe said, holding up an arm to let Kal work mud and ash into his armpit. 'But I think it's about time that you shared with me all that you know about dragons.'

Kal bit her lip. 'There are reasons I don't talk about it, Rafe. For a start, I'm not proud of what I did to that poor creature. And if the Dragonites ever found out what I know ...'

'Come on, Kal, you can trust me,' Rafe said. 'I'll swear by Banos and all the other gods that I'll not tell anyone.'

Kal sighed. She *could* trust Rafe, more than she had ever trusted anyone for a long, long time. She wasn't entirely comfortable with that feeling.

'Alright,' she said, pulling her dress on over her grey skin and throwing the coil of rope over her shoulder. 'I'll tell you everything as we walk. Let's go!'

'I grew up in a small village in the Wild, a thousand miles north of Amaranthium, at the foot of the Starfinger Mountains,' Kal revealed as they splashed inland through the swamp. 'It was a nice quiet life; I lived in a room above the schoolhouse, and taught the younger children. Told them stories mainly; the schoolmaster who took the older class taught me pretty much everything you could possibly want to know about dragons.'

Rafe raised an eyebrow, as if to say, *That's your story?*

'Everything he told me was wrong,' Kal amended wistfully.

They stopped abruptly when Kal held up a hand; she had seen something moving in a clearing ahead of them.

'It's okay,' she said after a pause. 'It's just a big bird.' She moved forward, surprising the bird – a large blue and green Balibu snakeneck – causing it to flee the clearing with much flapping, splashing and rustling of branches.

'I heard that dragons often use birds as spies –' Rafe began, then he caught Kal's look. 'Oh, okay. Forget everything I've heard, right?'

Kal smiled and nodded. They had come to the edge of the trees and were now at the foot of the mountain. The lower slopes were formed of smooth, gently-sloping dark grey rock.

There wasn't much cover. Kal pointed to a valley-like fissure in the rock that snaked up the mountain. It seemed to lead in the general direction of the cave they had seen the dragon fly into.

'I used to spend a lot of time in the forests around the village,' Kal went on as they climbed 'Walking, sketching and painting ... escaping for time alone with the boy I was going to marry ...' She looked back to gauge Rafe's reaction.

His expression was unreadable. 'What happened to him?' he asked, as casually as he could manage.

'Goblins killed him. Six years ago – when we were both eighteen. Goblins came down from over the mountains without warning. They killed almost everyone I knew. I was then chased out of the village by a dragon.'

'Dragons and goblins!' Rafe exclaimed. 'Our dragon here must have sent those half-goblin, half-man monstrosities – the ones that waylaid us at the governor's villa.'

'Wrong again, lover,' Kal chided him. 'Dragons don't have any control over goblins. Or trolls. Or any other kind of monster for that matter. They're solitary beasts really; they certainly aren't interested in raising some sort of apocalyptic army like most people seem to think.'

'Then where did –' Rafe began, but Kal cut him off by pointing out to sea. A small grey-and-red-sailed sloop was hugging the coast.

'Whatever's going on here, it looks like Gron Darklaw isn't afraid of the dragon. He must have found a way to get to the gold in the mine. Either the mine's abandoned, or maybe he's made some kind of deal with the goblins who used to work here. Hell, he might be even treating them better than Senator Godsword's men ever did.' Kal was still angry at Benedict for revealing he had goblins labouring in his mine.

They hurried on up the ever-steepening slope. It was tough going, and after a while they stopped to rest, concealing themselves in the shadow of a large basalt slab. Hot wind was blowing down from the mountain: wind that carried the sickly smell of brimstone. 'So anyway,' Kal said, 'I hid out for days in a den in a clump of willows. But I didn't dare go far from the river or the forest because the dragon was always there, always overhead, circling and watching. I couldn't think of anything but to creep right back to the village and look for any other survivors. That turned out to be the stupidest thing I ever could have done ...'

Rafe looked into Kal's ash-and-mud-smeared face. 'Not stupid!' he argued. 'Brave. You killed a dragon to avenge someone you loved. That's so very brave and noble of you, Kal. I'm slightly in awe of you.'

Kal smiled sadly. 'No, Rafe,' she said. 'I didn't kill the dragon for revenge. I killed it to *survive*.'

Kalina tumbled through the air and landed hard in the nest. Her shoulder exploded in pain and she was stabbed and cut in a hundred places by the sharp wooden wreckage and branches. Her breath was forced out of her, and she could only gag in horror as she opened her eyes and saw the young dragon hopping excitedly in front of her. It struck out at her instantly with razor-sharp jaws that clamped around her forearm and bit deep into her flesh. Kalina pulled away instinctively and felt the horrific pain of tearing flesh.

Please let it end quickly, she prayed. The juvenile put a heavy clawed foot on her stomach to hold her down. The tremendous heat from deep within the burning heart of the nest forced Kalina to squeeze her eyes shut. The last thing she saw was the bloody and charred remains of the faceless corpses that surrounded her.

Then the weight and pain lessened unexpectedly. *Oh no. Don't toy with me. Please don't.*

She opened her eyes. The young dragon was standing before her, frozen in position. A sword blade was protruding from its chest.

As the dragon fell limply to the side, Kalina tried to make

sense of the figure standing before her brandishing the enormous sword. He was dressed in tattered, blackened clothes, and a thick layer of grey mud and ash covered his face and clumped in his hair. But there was something familiar about his stance; something that Kalina had seen every day for the past couple of years.

Refuge's schoolmaster had stepped in to save her ...

'Ben!' she gasped.

IV.iii

The Cave

'Wait a minute,' Rafe said as they clambered up the rocky mountainside. 'Ben? Do you mean Benedict?'

'That's him,' Kal said.

'Senator Godsword?'

'The very same.'

'Benedict Godsword used to be a village schoolmaster?' Rafe looked perplexed. 'But he's the richest man in Amaranthium!'

'This was *before* he came into his inheritance,' Kal laughed.

'But ... the story goes that he was out adventuring during those years, making his fortune ...'

'Teaching can be a great adventure,' she mused. 'Shush now, we're almost at the cave.'

They had found themselves under a wide stone plateau that ran under the bottom of the cave like a shelf. Kal looked for a way up, but there was no obvious route. But the texture of the rock here was pitted and lumpy like coral; Kal reckoned that she could climb it.

'Wait here,' she instructed Rafe. 'I'm going up for a look.'

'Be careful,' he said, letting her climb up his body to get past the shelf's overhang. Kal climbed using mainly the strength in her arms, jamming her fingers into the depressions in the rock, and placing her cuchuck-soled boots on whatever convenient flat surface she could find. She felt strong and secure, but she was aware that if she fell she would probably bounce past Rafe and roll half a mile back down the mountain.

She looked down and gave him a reassuring smile. Then, without warning, the mountain shuddered, causing Kal's legs to slip out from under her. Her left hand left the rockface, leaving her hanging by just three of the fingers of her right hand. Far above her, up above the cave, a spurt of bright orange and yellow flame burst from the peak of the mountain, blasting fifty feet into the air. Then almost as suddenly as it had begun, the shaking ceased and the flame died away. Kal found her footing again and gripped the rock as tightly as she could.

'Kal!' Rafe shouted. *Don't shout, you idiot!* Without looking down, she waved a dismissive hand at him and continued her climb. They had seen a similar flame two nights back as they stood amid the ruins of the governor's villa. She had wondered back then if it was some kind of warning aimed at them. Had they been spotted now, or did the flame carry some other significance? She tried to put it out of her mind so that she could concentrate on her ascent.

Ten long minutes later she made it to the top. She gripped the edge of the shelf with the fingertips of both hands and slowly raised her upper body until her eyes could see over. The sun was shining from behind her, flooding the massive cave with light. Kal could see almost every detail of everything in there.

Her eyes widened. What she saw was hundreds of armed men lined up in ranks beneath the outspread wings of the dragon.

She could barely take it all in at once. Her arms were crying out in pain from the effort of lifting her head, but she forced herself to remain still while her brain clarified what her eyes were telling her. Firstly, the armed men were not *men* at all; they were the tall warriors with the brutish faces that she and Rafe had encountered back on the mainland: hobgoblins! And secondly, the dragon ...

... was a dragon formed from canvas stretched over a

wooden frame. A dragon with swords for claws and lanterns for eyes. With ropes for ligaments, pulleys for joints and sails for wings. It loomed silently over the mass of troops. They stood with their back to it, focusing their attention instead on the figure who was passing in front of them, inspecting the front rank. This one towered over even the tallest of the soldiers, and his great bulk was covered in a frighteningly-styled harness of black and gold armour. The edges of the overlapping plates were curved and pointed: decorations, Kal figured, that would also serve to deflect and entangle weapons. The helmet was magnificent, a roaring dragon head with red jewels for eyes. Kal couldn't see the face behind the long gold teeth, but she had no doubt as to who it was.

She allowed her complaining muscles to relax, and she made her way carefully back down to Rafe.

'Did you see the dragon?' he asked her.

'No,' she said between breaths. 'Gron Darklaw. He has an army of hobgoblins ... or whatever those strange half-man, half-goblin creeps are.' She wiped the sweat from her eyes. 'And also a big flying machine. That's how he managed to convince everyone that there's a dragon on the island.'

'A flying machine?' Rafe said. 'I don't understand.'

Kal tried to explain. 'Like a big black dragon-shaped kite, with a seat in the head for a rider. They must glide on the hot winds and heat from the flames. It looked like an amazing contraption.'

Rafe seemed angry at this news. 'What *is* Darklaw up to?'

'I can guess,' Kal said. 'With a combination of gold, soldiers and a secret base that no one dares approach, Darklaw's dreams of becoming governor of Balibu are all too likely to come true. The gods know why he wants it so bad, but that's not our problem. We have to get back to the mainland and warn people.'

'Wait a minute, Kal,' Rafe said, grabbing her arm as she turned to head back down the mountain. 'You want to leave?'

'I'm not taking on an army,' she shrugged. 'I may be

foolhardy, but I'm not suicidal.'

'Warning the town isn't going to do any good,' Rafe argued. 'You said yourself that the garrison is a load of drunks and layabouts. Balibu is Darklaw's for the taking, whether we warn them or not.'

'So we leave town before things kick off. Get back home and let Ben and the Senate muster the legions to take care of it.'

'*Or*,' Rafe said, 'we take out Darklaw right now. An army is useless without a leader.'

Kal sighed. *You proud fool.*

'Believe me,' she said, 'I'd love to gut Darklaw as much as you would, but fighting my way through a thousand armed freaks to get to him is not part of my job description. We both came to find out what was going on here, and now we know; so come on, let's get going while we still can.'

She started off down the slope, but Rafe remained behind, He was staring up at the very peak of the mountain, where steam was drifting out in the wake of the flame. 'There might be another way in,' he said. 'The kind of secret sneaky way that you like. And if we sort this out on our own, Kal, then the secret of the gold mine won't reach the ears of the Senate. I know that you'd hate it if all this wealth got confiscated by a load of greedy politicians.'

Kal paused in her descent. Rafe knew her weaknesses as well as she knew his.

'I came here to slay a dragon, Kal,' he said as she came back up to rejoin him. 'Gron Darklaw is my dragon now.'

IV.iv

The Blade of Banos

Ben reached down and pulled Kalina up by the hand. She screamed as her arm bent at an unnatural angle. The schoolmaster let go and took her by the other arm instead. With Kalina in one hand, and his massive sword in the other, he slid and skidded down the side of the dragon's nest. The roiling smoke that swathed around the base of the bonfire hid them from goblins in the immediate vicinity, and from the adult dragon circling above them, too. They heard its terrible shriek and the thunder of its wings as it sought them out.

Kalina's legs shook beneath her as Ben dragged her through the ash. The dragon flew low overhead, hunting for them in the smoke. She could see the hunched, shambling shapes of goblins all around them. She was hurting all over and was about to vomit when Ben stopped moving and flicked up a heavy trapdoor with the point of his sword. He lowered Kalina down and jumped in after her. When he pulled the trapdoor shut and drew the heavy bolt across, they found themselves in total darkness.

Kalina crumpled and lay in a ball, moaning and groaning despite herself. She could hear Ben moving about in the darkness knocking things over. There was a flickering light, and she could see him stirring up what looked like a copper bath full of hot ashes. He lit a lantern from the embers and hung it from a hook in the beams above them. Kalina noticed that they were surrounded by ale kegs and stacked wooden furniture. She guessed that they were in the cellar of the village inn, *The White Horse*.

She hauled herself over to a straw-packed mattress in the corner. Ben stowed his sword in an empty barrel and came over to inspect her wounds. He touched Kalina's arm, causing her to cry out. 'Your shoulder's dislocated,' he said. 'Might as well fix it now if we're going to fix it at all.' He took her wrist and held her arm out at a right angle to her body. As Ben started twisting slowly, Kalina felt a wave of nausea wash over her; she turned her head and was sick onto the flagstones. She had barely finished spitting when she heard a solid *thunk*.

'That seemed to work,' Ben said. 'Give me your other arm.' Kalina gasped as Ben poured half a bottle of clear spirit all over the bite wounds on her forearm. When he was done, he sat back and took a long swig from the bottle himself. 'That's the strongest zalka I've ever drunk,' he said, wiping his mouth with the back of his hand. 'Want some?'

Kalina shook her head, then collapsed into an unconscious daze.

She woke up some time later. It could have been hours. Ben was sitting in a chair nearby, drinking from a different bottle. He looked as tired and filthy as Kalina felt herself. She noticed he had bandaged up her arm with a relatively clean rag.

'Hey Mooney,' he said with a faint smile. 'You obviously didn't get my note then. School is closed for the foreseeable future.'

'Ben,' she groaned. 'Is there anyone else alive?'

He shook his head. 'No. And I've had a very good look. Where were you hiding?'

'In the forest, but I didn't dare go far. The dragon was always out and about hunting. What about you? Have you been hiding down here the whole time?'

Ben drained the last few drops of liquor from his bottle. 'I was out fishing when I saw the goblins heading down to the village. I should have run, but no; I came back, too.'

'What for?'

Ben nodded at the sword sticking out of the barrel. 'Family heirloom,' he said. 'I'm nothing without it.'

Kalina remembered the times she had seen Ben charging around the schoolhouse, whirling the sword above his head, enthralling the children with stories about old gods and old kings.

'The Blade of Banos,' she said. 'Right. Well, you did always say that only the weapons of the gods can kill dragons.' She recalled all the other toys and props that had filled the classroom. 'It's too bad I dropped and smashed the Stone of Draxos the other week; we could have teleported right out of here.'

They both froze as a heavy thump shook the cellar. They could hear the dragon roaring directly above them, and other screams and howls that could only have belonged to the goblins.

'What are we going to do, Ben?'

'We'll just have to make a run for it when we get the chance,' he said. 'The ash will help. I found out that dragons are blind to you if you're covered in it.'

Kalina felt a small spark of hope. 'Really? You never mentioned that in all your dragon stories.'

'The stories were all wrong, Kal,' Ben said. 'I found that out the hard way. You should have seen me screaming and shouting at the dragon, thinking that I could *talk* to it, but it just screeched and flapped at me like a wild animal. I dived into an ash pile to avoid being fed to its baby. That was a lucky escape.'

Like a wild animal ...

'Ben,' she said, 'the goblins ...'

'I know, I know,' he said. 'They're not the dragon's minions at all; it's the other way round. When I followed the goblins down into the village, I saw *them* setting the fires. *They* lured the dragon here with fire, Kal. *They* built the nest and the dragon brought its egg down from the mountains. Now it will render this region desolate for miles in all directions. It's the ultimate weapon, and somehow the goblins know exactly how to control it.'

Kalina stood up slowly. 'It doesn't sound like they do anymore, though,' she said. She limped over to the trapdoor. 'Just a quick look,' she promised when Ben rose to his feet nervously. She drew back the bolt and lifted the trap a fraction of an inch. Outside it was chaos: the dragon was tearing its nest apart in a destructive fury, its thick tail whipping up clouds of smoke and ash. Goblins were trying to flee, but the dragon had turned on them, lurching from one corner of the razed ground to the other to cut off their escape. Kalina watched in fascination as the creature simultaneously crushed two goblins to death in each of its claws, while tearing the head off another with its jaws.

And forgotten amid the mad frenzy of destruction, covered in an ever-thickening layer of ash, a still, black winged shape lay crumpled up in a pool of dark red blood.

Kalina pulled the trap shut and turned to Ben. 'We might be stuck down here for a while,' she said.

IV.v

Invasion

Kal scrambled up the final slope. Five thousand feet above sea-level, the summit of the mountain was a flat, circular plain about a hundred feet in diameter, as if a conical peak had once been lopped off by a destructive giant. There was not one, but several fissures in the black rock of the mountain, from which columns of grey steam drifted upwards into the still, blue sky. The smell of brimstone made Kal want to gag, and it was very, very hot: standing between the mountain and the brutal sun was like being caught between a hammer and an anvil.

Looking back, Kal could see the faint green blur of the mainland on the northern horizon. While she waited for Rafe to join her, she walked slowly round the edge of the summit and looked down on the opposite side of the mountain to which they had arrived. There was a natural harbour below, formed out of two massive arms of rock that threatened to touch, but allowed just enough room that a skilfully navigated vessel might be able to slip through. She couldn't see Darklaw's sloop, but there were five larger galleys moored up. A cleared channel led inland through the swamps, and a series of locks and gates rose to where a scattering of wooden structures at the foot of the mountain marked the entrance to the gold mine.

Rafe caught up with her. 'So if it's not magic then,' he asked her, 'what *is* it made of?' He was still thinking about the story that she had been telling him on the climb up.

'Bloodsteel, or so Ben told me,' Kal said. 'The gods apparently had a forge at the very top of the Improbable Mountain, and they made blades from the red ore they mined there.'

Rafe whistled. 'The Blade of Banos! What I wouldn't give to fight with it.'

'It's too old and brittle now,' Kal said. 'I wouldn't trust you with it, the way you fight. You'd probably break it on a hobgoblin's collar bone. Forget about the sword and let's see if we can find a way down into this mountain.'

They approached the largest of the fissures. As well as the steam, a hot wind was blowing up out of it too. As they stood there contemplating the void, the mountain trembled, and tongues of flame briefly licked at the air above the hole. They didn't spurt as high as the ones Kal had seen earlier when she was climbing to the cave, but they were hot enough to cook anyone who got too close.

Rafe gave her a nervous look. 'Maybe this wasn't such a good idea ...'

'It was a *great* idea,' she told him as she took her rope from her shoulder. 'Did you notice how the flames formed *above* the hole; the gases must only ignite when they hit the air. I bet that we will be safer down there than up here. Give me your rope.'

Kal tied both of their ropes together with two overhand knots, looped them over a solid rock, then let both ends drop down into the darkness. She took two small items out of a pouch at her belt and handed one to Rafe. He examined it carefully; it was a steel tool forged in the shape of a figure of eight.

'Loop the rope through like this,' Kal instructed, 'and then hook it to your belt. The friction will slow your descent.' With a torch in her left hand, she hopped backwards into the fissure and started walking confidently down the sheer rockface. 'Hold the rope here by your hip to control your speed,' she called up to Rafe, 'and don't let go!'

A hundred feet down, Kal found a ledge that was safe enough to stand on. When Rafe eventually made it down too, she tugged on one end of the rope. The other end shot upwards, passed around the anchoring rock at the top, then fell back down into her hands. She wiped the sweat from her brow and smiled at her companion. 'Ready to do that again?' she asked as she looped the rope around a new anchor.

Rafe didn't look quite so anxious this time. 'Of course,' he said. 'I was just getting used to it.'

Kal kissed him before she dropped down deeper into the dark mountain.

At the bottom of the next descent they found themselves at a junction of several tunnels and chasms. They shouldered their ropes once more and decided to explore the route with the gentlest gradient. A hot wind blew in their faces as they walked, and it threatened to extinguish their torch. The rock was almost too hot to touch; they could feel its heat through their boots. Kal was sure that she heard voices being carried up on the wind, too. After another couple of spots where they had to use the ropes, she reckoned that they must be approaching the level of Darklaw's cave. But they could hit a dead end or too narrow a gap at any moment; there might not be a way through after all.

Kal didn't want to think about that. There was no way back up if they ran out of options. But then the hot air and vapour had to be coming from somewhere down below, and if nothing else then surely they would eventually find the tunnels of the gold mine at the foot of the mountain.

'Talk to me, Kal,' Rafe said as they picked their way through. 'What happened next with the dragon?'

'Let me concentrate on where we're going,' she said. 'Do you want me to twist an ankle? I'll tell you all the stories you want when we get home.'

Rafe carried on regardless. 'Oh, so you'll still want to know me when we get back then? I don't have such an exciting life back in Amaranthium, you know. Organising guard duty rosters, mostly.'

Kal stopped and sighed. She turned around and faced him. 'You'll be a hero when we get back!' she said. 'And of course I'll want to know you. You'll be the first person I'll call on if my loft gets infested by trolls.'

Rafe laughed. 'I'm qualified for that! Me and some lads in the Guard once had to chase off three sea trolls that had tunnelled into the city. Now that *was* an exciting day!' He noticed something over Kal's shoulder. 'Kal, look,' he said. 'There's light ahead.'

She smothered the torch and they both waited in silence while their eyes adjusted. Sure enough, there was a flickering glow coming from further down a tight, narrow tunnel. Kal led the way on her hands and knees. She thought she could hear the voices nearby. The glow was shining up through a crack in the floor. She lay down and put her eye to the crack. Below her was a cave that was flooded with torchlight.

Rafe shuffled up beside her. 'It's him!' he breathed after taking a look.

They could see down into a cave that had been carved and flattened to make it more habitable. Animal skins were spread over the floor, and torches were set in alcoves in the walls. A large wooden table took up most of the space in the centre of the room, and a detailed map had been rolled out across its surface. Gron Darklaw, still in his black and gold armour, laid his helmet down on the corner of the table and addressed the soldier – one of the half-man, half-goblin brutes – who was with him.

'The Senate have sent a replacement governor; his ship is due to arrive at noon tomorrow. Take a squad of some of the most restless men and intercept the ship *here*.' – Darklaw indicated on the map with a thick finger – 'Kill everyone on board and then set fire to the ship. The new governor may have brought his family – women and children. I know how depraved some of the men are, Gurik; this job should quench their appetites for the time being.'

93

The hobgoblin named Gurik nodded. 'Yes, Sir,' he growled.

Darklaw scratched his chin as he thought aloud. 'When the town council gather to discuss the tragic news, I will offer them my services: money to build defences, and troops to protect them from the dragon that they think is terrorising Balibu. It will be an easy, bloodless invasion. Do you think the men will be able to restrain themselves? I am sure that in time I will be able to find some discreet outlets for their vices.'

The hobgoblin made a noise that might have been a grunt or a laugh. 'They want to fight most of all, Sir,' he said.

Darklaw's finger traced the coastline around Balibu. 'And they will. It won't be long before the Senate sends an army to take back the town. The peninsula will force any army to pass through *here*. A spot like that will cost them ... what do you think, Gurik? Ten of their men for every one of ours?'

Gurik laughed for sure this time: a horrible croaking cackle. 'Yes, Sir!'

'Good!' Darklaw seemed pleased with his plans. 'Go and prepare the men.'

The hobgoblin saluted and left the cave through a thick iron-banded wooden door that covered the entrance to a tunnel. Darklaw remained standing before his map. Kal and Rafe watched as the big man looked slowly around the room, making a strange sniffing noise; his broad, flat features taking on a bestial aspect.

'You can come out now, Dragon Killer,' he said. 'I can smell you and your mate.'

IV.vi

Forever Under the Stars

Darklaw looked up. Kal jerked her head back, but not before their eyes had met. She couldn't help but gasp: the last time she had looked him in the eye, over the card table, she remembered his eyes being a deep black. But now they were a bright gleaming yellow.

Darklaw immediately left the cave below. It was barely a minute later that Kal and Rafe heard smashing and pounding noises, as if someone was breaking through the rock with a pickaxe. 'We can't run or fight in these tunnels,' Kal told Rafe. 'We'll just have to try and talk our way out of this.' Rafe nodded in agreement.

The rockface ahead of them collapsed and sunlight came streaming through to their hiding place. Kal and Rafe crawled the last few yards towards the light and stepped out into the open. Small goblin workers wielding hammers and tools stood aside to let them through, and Kal and Rafe found themselves at the back of the enormous cavern that housed Darklaw's flying machine. The canvas and timber dragon loomed over them, and all around it were hundreds of Darklaw's larger hobgoblin soldiers. They sat in alcoves around the edges of the cave and stood around in groups, paused in the middle of weapon training exercises. They perched on wooden scaffolding and in the framework of the dragon itself. And in the centre of the cave, waiting to meet his new guests, was Gron Darklaw himself.

He sneered at Kal and Rafe. 'I might have guessed that you would find your way here,' he said in his deep growl. 'You've had a small taste of my wealth and gold, and now you've come for more, is that it?'

'We're here on behalf of the Senate,' Kal began. 'We can negotiate a peaceful solution to –'

'As Captain of the Senate Guard I challenge you to single combat,' Rafe interrupted. 'If I win, then we walk out of here alive.'

'I accept,' Darklaw replied instantly.

Ten minutes later, Kal and Rafe were in Darklaw's armoury. He had graciously allowed Rafe to choose whatever arms and armour he required before their fight. Rafe seemed genuinely grateful, but Darklaw's supreme confidence was eating at Kal's nerves.

'You're taking an awful risk, doing this,' she told Rafe as she adjusted the straps on a breastplate for him. 'We know relatively nothing about this Gron Darklaw. We don't know how well he fights.'

Rafe shrugged. 'I know how well *I* fight. Darklaw probably *imagines* he fights better then he actually does, just as he imagined that he was the greatest card player in town the other night at the Croc. That's his weakness, Kal: he wants to be this amazing fighter, general, governor, sailor, gambler ... but he's reaching too far. I knew that he wouldn't be able to refuse the ultimate test of valour, especially when I challenged him in front of his men. He's made a big mistake agreeing to take me on.'

'Maybe ...' Kal was conflicted. She wasn't the greatest judge of character, but was Rafe? 'I just hope that you're right. There: you're all set.'

Rafe stomped about and swung his arms to test his range of movement. A forty-pound suit of armour, its weight spread evenly, was not much of a hindrance to a fit, strong man like

Rafe. 'It's fine,' he said. 'It's not my own suit, but it will do the same job. I'm not the sentimental type!'

'Really?' Kal said, 'So you won't be needing this then.' She held up Rafe's blue Senate Guard surcoat.

He bent his head to allow her to put it on over the armour. 'This is different,' Rafe said. 'Armour is armour, steel is steel, but this shows that I represent the Senate; that my cause is just!'

Kal handed him something else. 'And what about this? What does this represent?'

Rafe was thrilled with the offering. 'I may wear the armour of sub-human monsters, but I now carry the weapon of the gods,' he said, strapping Kal's dagger to his belt on his right side. He attached his own steel sword to his left side and was ready for action.

'Let's get this over with then,' Kal said.

Escorted by guards, they walked hand-in-hand back down the sweltering tunnels to the giant cave. More and more hobgoblins had filled the space now, as well as many of the smaller regular goblins; short shambling primitives, milling around half-naked as was their wont. One of them carried a stone pitcher and gold goblet across the cave to where Darklaw was waiting. The big man took the drink and then sent the goblin away with a pat on the head that looked almost affectionate.

Darklaw had moved over to the mouth of the cave, where the low afternoon sun glinted off the black in his armour and set the gold in it on fire. The crowds formed a semi-circle around the shelf of rock that jutted out from the cave entrance. Darklaw had created an arena with a deadly drop-off at its edge. Kal frowned as they pushed their way through the mass of goblins and hobgoblins; was there a reason for this, or did Darklaw simply have a flair for the dramatic?

Rafe walked right up in front of Darklaw and gave him a cordial nod. Darklaw grinned, took a slug of his wine, and beckoned another goblin. This one came over staggering under the weight of a giant scabbard. Darklaw took up the fifty-inch bastard sword in one hand and made a show of inspecting the blade. Kal half expected him to lick it.

'So we face one another once again,' Darklaw said to Rafe, belatedly returning the nod. 'But this time the stakes are rather a lot higher than those at the card table.'

'*All or nothing* will be the motto on my crest after this,' Rafe managed to retort.

Kal could hardly bear it any longer. She sat with her head in her hands between two of the toes of the wooden dragon. 'Why are you doing this?' she muttered.

Rafe didn't hear her, but Darklaw did. 'Why am I doing this?' he said, looking over to her. 'Some would consider it an honour to be invited to fight with a representative of the almighty Senate. A man of my standing is rarely afforded such respect.'

Kal looked up sharply. *Was that it?* Was this fight yet another feather in Darklaw's cap; another rung in the ladder of greatness. Or did she detect a bitterness behind his words. *Did he have some grievance with the Senate?*

There was no time to think any deeper on it, though. The two men stood twenty paces apart, facing each other with swords drawn. Rafe was tall, but Darklaw had at least an extra two feet on him. 'To the death then,' the giant confirmed. 'If you want to run ... well, you'll need to sprout wings.' Darklaw had put on his golden dragon helmet. 'Whenever you are ready, Captain.'

Rafe had also donned a helmet, a plain bascinet with a visor. 'I'm ready –' he began.

Darklaw wasted no time in charging forward across the cave floor. Rafe barely had time to raise his sword. Their blades met with a thundering metallic crash. Darklaw held on to his, but Rafe's went spinning out of his hand. Rafe fell to the floor to avoid Darklaw's follow-up blow, and rolled across the cave, his armour clattering, to where his sword had landed.

He jumped to his feet as Darklaw reached him again, and this time he managed to deflect his opponent's blow with the flat of his blade, using his body weight to lean into Darklaw's attack and to force his sword aside. As the giant struggled to regain control, Rafe brought his sword down hard on Darklaw's right flank, smashing away the tassets that connected to the bottom of his elaborately-fashioned breastplate. Darklaw kicked out desperately and caught Rafe in the chest with one of his pointed sabatons. Rafe fell onto his back, the wind knocked out of him.

Instead of continuing his assault, Darklaw turned and walked calmly back to his goblet and pitcher and poured himself another drink. He gulped it noisily, blood-red wine dribbling down his chin. Rafe just stood with his hands on his knees trying to catch his breath. Barely a minute later, Darklaw broke the period of respite and advanced slowly on Rafe with his bastard sword raised high, like a serpent ready to strike.

Rafe wasn't ready yet; he backed away from Darklaw, getting dangerously near to the edge of the rock shelf before he finally put up his sword and got back into the fight. This time Darklaw's attacks were less urgent than before, and Rafe was able to match him blow-for-blow. But Kal could see that Rafe was giving up ground to Darklaw's implacable advance. When Rafe was almost at the edge of the rocky plateau he hesitated, and Darklaw's next blow tore his sword from his grasp again, this time sending it flying out over the edge and down the mountainside.

Rafe didn't waste time regretting the loss of one of his weapons. He went down on one knee, pulled Kal's knife from his belt, and stuck the bloodsteel blade deep into Darklaw's side where his armour had been torn away. Darklaw seemed hardly to feel it, though; he kept his own sword moving in a practiced series of strokes, finally bringing it down on Rafe's arm, chopping hand and dagger away at the wrist.

Kal rose in horror. Rafe howled in pain and shock. Darklaw

kicked Rafe's legs out from under him and pinned him to the ground with his foot. He placed the point of his sword over Rafe's chest, over the spiral of stars on his blue surcoat. He paused there for a moment, then moved the blade down until it rested over Rafe's belly instead.

'I yield,' Rafe groaned. 'Mercy.'

Darklaw shook his head. 'You won't find that here,' he said, and drove his sword deep into Rafe's stomach.

Then Darklaw turned away from Rafe and walked to the back of the cave, clutching his wounded side. He passed Kal, who ran to where Rafe lay. 'Give the girl a minute with him, then lock her up below,' Darklaw ordered as he passed his troops. Then he was gone, taking his pitcher of wine with him.

Kal kneeled beside Rafe and removed his helmet. He looked up at her with stricken eyes. 'He got me, Kal,' he choked. 'I'm going to die.'

She looked at his awful wound. 'I know,' she said, taking his hand. 'It's alright.'

The crowd of hobgoblins were getting closer, curiosity and hunger in their eyes. 'Don't let them take me,' Rafe pleaded.

Kal took the fallen dagger from the cave floor. She brushed Rafe's hair out of his eyes as she placed the tip of the dagger over the pulse in his neck.

Rafe tried to smile. 'I told you we should have stayed hidden in our camp in the swamp ...'

... forever under the stars. Kal swallowed a sob as she drove the dagger home.

A look of fear and confusion passed across Rafe's face. Kal put her lips to his.

'You'll always be my knight,' she told him as he died.

END OF PART FOUR

PART FIVE

THE DRAGON

V.i

Departure

Darthon Twill, miller.
    Alfred Bone, innkeeper.
    Tarla Yarrow, cordwainer.
    Kalina put down the pencil. Was that it? No, there was one more ...
Deros Brown, woodcutter.
    She closed the book and put it away. That was all of them: the eighty adults and children who had lived and worked in Refuge, and who had been slaughtered by goblins as food for the dragon. The book would have to stand as the only memorial to them and to the village.

    Kalina got up and stretched her legs; after three days underground her injuries troubled her less, but the confinement was almost too much to bear. She was thankful that their food supply was about to run out; they had no excuse to stay here any longer. She started filling a leather satchel with what little they had remaining: a stale loaf, some hard strips of bacon and three overripe apples. In the corner, Ben was doing his best to empty the cellar of what was left of the spirits.

    'Enough, Ben,' Kalina said. 'I want to walk out of here *with* you, not carrying you.'

    'It's no good,' Ben slurred. '*The Dragon* has been hunting down my family for hundreds of years. He wants to eat me then fly off with my sword and drop it off in some fiery mountain somewhere. Why else is he still here, Kal?'

What in the world was Ben talking about now? 'It's *a* dragon, not *the Dragon*. And it's still here because it's got nowhere else to go. Or maybe it can smell our scent around the nest and figures we couldn't have gone far. Either way, it's an animal, Ben; a dangerous wild animal ... It's not your mortal enemy. You're getting mixed up with the stories that you tell the children. Come on; smear on some ash!'

Ben heaved himself out of the chair and joined Kalina at the copper bath. In silence they both rubbed and smeared the foul mix of mud and ash over their faces and under their collars and sleeves. Kalina had found some dirty work clothes and a pair of boots stashed in the cellar. She and Ben looked like a pair of matching twins: refugees from some terrible disaster.

Ben strapped his scabbard and massive sword to his back. Kalina carried the supplies. As they double-checked everything they became gradually aware of a noise: a low rumbling *thrum* that rose and fell at regular intervals.

'Is that me making that noise?' Ben said, looking around.

'No,' Kalina snapped. 'Be quiet and stay still.' She went to the trapdoor and slid the bolt as quietly as she could. Lifting it carefully, she looked out.

The night was black: pitch-black. There were no stars in the sky ...

... except that she wasn't looking at the sky. She was staring up at the underside of the dragon's wing. The beast was right on top of them, its enormous body resting on the ground, as big as a hundred bales of hay. The *thrumming* noise was louder, matching the rhythm of the dragon's breath. *It was snoring.*

Kalina silently beckoned Ben and lifted herself up out of the cellar. When he climbed out after her he almost didn't notice the dragon at first. Then he did a double-take and fell over in shock. Kalina put her hand over his mouth and helped him up.

They crept quietly, inch by inch, alongside the dragon's body towards its neck, to where they could get out from under its wing. The animal's torso swelled with each breath, and the inch-thick scales glimmered as the faint moonlight hit them. There were oily patterns in the scales, Kalina noticed, like in a starling's feathers.

She paused at the top of the wing, where one long clawed thumb protruded from the point where the outer-wing swept back along the dragon's body. The long tapering neck was curled around on itself, and the dragon's head was directly in front of them. The head itself was bigger than a shire horse, the jaws like a cave. The dragon's breath was hot and strangely sweet. The leathery ears were long and pointed, but the eyes were comparatively small ... and they were open.

Each eye was about twenty inches across and round, like a buckler: a deep orange colour with a thin vertical slit-like pupil. Kalina and Ben held their breath and stood as still as rabbits caught in the gaze of a hawk. Was the dragon looking at them? It was hard to tell. It was still snoring. As they watched, a long and supple tongue slid out from between its teeth and wiped across its left eye.

Kalina started to breathe again. It must be asleep still. She started to move away, but Ben held her back. He put his hand on the hilt of his sword and nodded at the dragon's eye. Kalina shook her head emphatically. How fast did Ben imagine that he could deliver a killing blow, before the dragon woke and took them out with one lazy flick of its wing?

Besides, this close-up the sleeping dragon looked less like a monster to her now, and more like a natural wonder. To be so near to such a deadly predator left Kalina with a heart-stopping sense of awe. Could she even blame it for trying to feed her to its young? 'Fly away back across the mountain,' she mouthed to the dragon. 'There's nothing for you in these lands but trouble and death.'

Kalina lingered as Ben walked away as fast as he dared. Eventually, she too turned and left the beautiful creature behind. Five minutes later she had left the village of Refuge behind her, as well.

She would never return.

V.ii

Lake of Fire

Kal woke up feeling sick and confused. Had they drugged her? She couldn't remember much past being dragged away from Rafe's body. Now she was naked, lying under thin sheets in a hot room. The sheets were pure white silk, the bed heavy dark wood, and the room tastefully decorated with solid furniture, red wall hangings and white wool rugs. But behind it all was bare rock; she was still under the mountain.

She swung her legs off the bed and looked around. There was no sign of her old clothes or weapons. On a nearby dresser was a small wooden box. She opened it ... then quickly shut it when she saw what was inside.

There were two thick wooden doors in the room. She opened one and came face-to-face with a guard stationed in the tunnel outside. His yellow eyes dragged themselves down her body with undisguised fervour. Kal slammed the door in his face and leaned back against it; but the guard made no attempt to enter.

She tried the other door; this one led to a small tiled chamber with a sunken bath. It was full of hot steaming water, and there were towels, soaps and pots of oils standing by ready to be used. Kal lingered by the door for a time, silently cursing at the situation that she found herself in. Then she stepped down into the bath, cursing again at the needling heat, until her whole body was submerged. She held her breath, squeezed her eyes shut and put her head under the water ... and tried as hard as she could to empty her mind.

An hour later, pink, scrubbed and oiled, Kal prepared to face up to the trap that she was caught in. In the wardrobe next to the bed she had found an exquisite and expensive black dress. Looking at her reflection in the full-length mirror in the wardrobe door, she had to admit that she had never been dressed quite so well in her life. The dress was satin and sleeveless – cut square and high at the front, but open at the back. It fitted closely to her stomach with barely enough material spare to pinch. The dress was gathered at the waist and fell to just above the knee, and was slit to the thigh on the right side. Kal's expression was one of controlled fury as she attacked her shoulder-length reddish hair with a fine-toothed bone comb. It was either wear the dress or face her enemies naked.

She went back to the box on the dresser and flipped the lid again. Inside was a heavy gold and silver necklace adorned with diamonds. There was a note with it, written in an elegant hand: *Wear this to dinner. GD.*

The man's audacious presumption angered Kal no end. Nevertheless, she estimated the necklace to be worth at least a thousand gold crowns, so she draped it around her neck and fastened the clasp. There! Ready to take on this monster at his own game, whatever his game may be. She slipped on the only other items left for her in the room – a pair of simple leather sandals – and opened the door to confront the guard once more. This time he stood to one side and gestured down the passageway. She walked past him, feeling the heat of his gaze on her bare shoulders.

The tunnel led downwards, deeper into the root of the mountain. A hot wind blew in Kal's face; it was like walking into the mouth of hell. Guards were posted at intersections along the way to prevent her from straying from the path. She caught glimpses of activity and heard a jumble of sounds:

shouting, clanking and banging, and the *woosh* and *thunk* of some kind of heavy machinery. At one junction, she had to pause at some tracks to let a minecart past. It was full of sparkling rocks. The gold mine, it seemed, was in full operation.

But the route that she was on was for her alone, and soon she had left the noise behind her. It got hotter and hotter until Kal could almost bear it no longer. Then the tunnel opened out and the oppressive heat lifted slightly. Kal's breath caught in amazement. She was at the entrance to a circular cavern that was around two hundred yards wide. The roof was high, but was spiked with stalactites, some of which were over twenty feet long and almost low enough to touch. But what had taken her breath was the lake that filled the cavern: a lake of red molten rock. Flames flickered on its surface, shining orange bubbles rose and popped, patterns of black crust constantly formed and dissolved, and a shimmering heat haze hung over the whole expanse.

Kal squinted to see better: there was a narrow natural bridge that led out across the lake to a small island at its centre. A boat was moored up at the island, too. But how? Then she realised: it was Gron Darklaw's platinum-hulled sloop. So that was why he had built it; only the super-resistant precious metal would enable a vessel to float in lava.

She stepped out onto the bridge. The intense heat forced her to walk fast. When she was halfway across she could see what was waiting for her on the island: Gron Darklaw was there, standing next to a table that was set for two. Next to a domed silver food cover were two goblets and Darklaw's ubiquitous pitcher of wine. The man turned to face her as she stepped off the bridge, his yellow eyes gleaming in anticipation. He had dressed in a fine black tunic, black hose and boots, and had made some attempt to tame his wild hair; it was slicked back and greasy, and Kal could see the pointed tips of his ears poking out.

Darklaw attempted a warm smile. As his cruel lips parted, Kal could see his teeth clearly for the first time: they had been roughly filed down, but the vicious incisors were still prominent. How could she have not seen it before; *he was one of them* – a monster, a fusion of goblin and human, just like the army he commanded.

The big man pretended to ignore her gaping stare. He was holding two blades: Kal's shortsword and dagger. 'This one gave me quite a nasty bite,' he said, tossing the dagger into the lava lake. 'I had to stitch myself up with a needle and thread.' He threw the shortsword in after it. Kal watched with silent regret as the ancient weapons floated for a moment on the lava's crust, then sank out of view.

Darklaw moved to the table and pulled out a chair for her. 'Your mate fought bravely and with honour,' he said, 'but the fighting is over now, and I won. So come, let us put it all behind us and eat.'

Kal sat down rigidly in the chair, saying nothing. The table was positioned at the centre of the island, giving some respite from the heat. There was a knife and fork set before her, but the blade was small and blunted: a fish knife. Still, it would serve better than her fingernails ...

Her goblet was filled. Darklaw poured some for himself and tipped it down his throat. He refilled his glass before taking his place opposite Kal. She noticed him wince slightly as he sat, his hand moving to his injured side. 'Drink!' he ordered. 'To my victory yesterday. And to the future.'

Kal brought the goblet to her lips reluctantly. She took a sip then spat it out straight away. *The wine was sugared!* What a surprise: Darklaw's tastes ran vulgar. She tipped her goblet over in protest. Darklaw's brow creased somewhat, but he plunged ahead and on to the main course. He lifted the silver food cover and revealed two barbequed silvery fish lying side-by-side on a bed of seaweed. Sharpfins: their long jaws gaping open, revealing rows of tiny razor-sharp teeth. They were garnished with lemons and onions and a sweet-smelling sauce. Kal wanted to grab one of the fish and ram it down Darklaw's windpipe, but her body was telling her to eat. The fish looked delicious.

'There are thousands of sharpfins in the waters around the island,' Darklaw said proudly. 'I have been encouraging them to breed by scattering extra food among the corals. Live food of course; the sharpfins only swarm together to hunt. I find them a useful extra ring of defence, and they also provide me with plenty of meat to feed my army.'

Kal looked Darklaw in the eye. 'Did you bring me here just to talk about your pets?' she spat with barely-concealed hatred.

Darklaw slowly shook his head. 'No, I brought you here to make you an offer. But first, I will tell you my story ...'

V.iii

The Tribe

'I was born thirty-eight years ago, in a small village called Fugrun, five thousand miles west of here, in the very heart of the Dark Tundra. It was a brutal life; the winters were harsh, the summers bone-dry, and the wild animal threats numerous. I was taught to kill a sabre wulf with my bare hands when I was eight; every child was, for our own protection. My father was the village chief, and I spent most of my nights having to listen to him implore our god, Zug, to keep the cold away, to keep the goats safe, to aid the hunters ... my father prayed all day and all night.

'I used to lie on the roof of our hut, wrapped in the pelt of the sabre wulf that I had killed, just to get away from the sound of my father's voice. I would watch the moon and the stars. Zug was said to push the moon across the sky at night. But I started to question the convictions of my father and the rest of the village elders. The stars moved also as I watched them; did Zug push them around, too? There were an awful lot of them. My father would deflect my questions about Zug with ever-evasive explanations. Things came to a head one terrible winter when my father decreed that five of our best hunters were to be sacrificed in order to persuade Zug to melt the snows. It was the first time that I ever killed a man.

'I strangled my father with my bare hands whilst the rest of the village watched. I was fourteen years old.

'Under my strict rule, the Dark Claw tribe saw out the winter and thrived again in the spring. We then found ourselves in the unusual position of having a stockpile of surplus goods; the neighbouring villages that we traded with could not keep up with our new regime. They were still held back by their time-wasting superstitious rituals. There was only one thing for it: on a moonless night, I led a band of my best men into the next village and slaughtered their elders. We showed no mercy and killed half of their warriors. To those remaining I offered a choice: submit to my rule, or die by the sword. My tribe gained many new warriors, wives and livestock that night.

'By my twenty-fourth year, all the villages in the Dark Tundra were under my control – over a hundred of them. My horde numbered almost five thousand fighting men. I formed a brotherhood of my twenty best warriors, bound to me by the promise of an equal share of all the gold and all the best horses, goats and women. Together we ruled over all ten thousand habitable square miles of tundra.

'We turned our eyes then to the mountains in the east. There was good building stone and precious gems to be mined from them. My father and all the old chiefs and elders had warned us to fear the *gruken* – those you call goblins – who dwelled under the mountains. They were Zug's evil minions, we were told. But my years in the saddle, carving out an empire, had taught me many things about life in this world. The bones and skulls of our ancient forebears are scattered and buried all over the tundra. I had seen skeletons of all shapes and sizes in my travels; enough to deduce that we were once one tribe, divided at some time in the distant past, and then moulded over the aeons by the differing conditions of our respective habitats.

'So we joined our gruken cousins to the tribe; traded food and wood with them for stone and gems. We learned the secret passes through the mountains; we had conquered a once-impassable boundary ... and then reached another: the sea.'

Gron waded into the swirling grey surf. He scooped up a handful of seawater and tasted it with his tongue; it was salty, unlike any water he had ever tasted before. He turned back to where his wife and child were standing just out of reach of the tide, and made a show of grimacing, spitting and wiping his mouth. They both laughed.

Next to him, one of his sworn brothers fingered a long length of seaweed. 'Do you really want to conquer a land of wet grass and fish?' he asked his chief.

'No,' Gron replied, looking out across the ocean to where the sun was rising. 'I want to conquer the horizon.'

'But it was to be another couple of years before I got my chance to cross the ocean. I was standing in the foundations of the stone hall that we were raising on the site of my old village, when a messenger arrived to say that a *ship* full of strange men had landed at the coast. I immediately hurried east to meet these newcomers. This historic first contact between my people and *humans* was marred somewhat by skirmishes that left many dead on both sides, but when I arrived the captain was more than happy to cease hostilities and talk.

'He was a man as different to me as I am to a gruken; a man of smooth features and slim limbs. I wondered how long ago it was that *our* ancestors had been split by the sea and changed, century by century, into the two different men that now stood talking on a stony beach. He told me stories of the power of the Senate, the splendour of Amaranthium – the Endless City – and the might of the legions. My thoughts shifted from dreams of conquest to the desire to travel to these strange new places, to learn the ways of *civilisation*.

'With half his crew dead, the captain was effectively stranded. So we made a bargain: we would sail together, back across the ocean. I took half my brotherhood with me, as well as my wife, my small son, and twenty more of my strongest and cleverest men. We also took goods for trade: chests of diamonds and gold, hand-woven carpets and casks of fermented mares' milk. My men were just as happy at sea as they were in the saddle, and so a month later we arrived at the westernmost port of the Republic: Balibu.

'This all happened just over ten years ago. Balibu was a small town, but to my eyes it was a wonder. My men were even more excited than I was: they had been promised a tour of the dockside attractions by the sailors, with whom they were now firm friends. My wife was impressed by the hot sun and warm winds.

'The governor of Balibu received us in the inner ward of the fort where the Senate garrison was housed. I stood proudly before him, my men and my family at my side. He listened to the captain's story; he inspected our gifts and had them carried away; but when I stepped forward to speak, the governor held up a hand. I stopped, not because of the man's hand, but because of the fifty crossbows that were aiming down from the battlements that enclosed us.

'The governor then condemned us as monsters. He decreed that we were servants of some god he named *the Dragon*, and that clearly we had been sent on a mission to infiltrate his town and destroy it from within. I had barely time to comprehend what I was hearing: even the rulers of the civilised world appeared to be victims of delusion and superstition! In fury and anger, I moved forward again. The governor made a signal with his hand, and the air was suddenly filled with the twang of crossbow bolts ...

'Six hours later, under the cover of darkness, I crawled out from under the pile of bloody bodies. My own body had been pierced in many places, but I was still alive. I bade farewell to my dead men and my dead wife and child, and then disappeared, bleeding, into the hot night. I was alone in a strange and unfamiliar world. My authority and ambition had been stripped away, and I was lucky to be left with even my life.

'For five years I wandered the length and breadth of the Republic, earning my living through fighting, manual labour and gambling. I grew my hair to hide the shape of my ears, filed down my teeth and discovered that the juice from a certain plant could temporarily alter the colour of my eyes. I travelled from Balibu in the west to Zorronov in the east; from the Starfinger Mountains in the north to the Auspice Islands in the south; and everywhere I went I saw people clinging to their ancient dead gods, living in fear of the terrible *Dragon* that haunted their imagination. I was sicker than ever of this new world and soon longed for home.

'One long summer I apprenticed myself to a boat-builder in the Auspice Islands. In my spare time I worked on a vessel that would be sturdy enough to carry me home across the ocean: an oversized kayak with watertight compartments fore and aft. The boat-builder thought that I was mad to attempt a single-handed crossing, but I promised him that he would not hear the last of me. And so began three gruelling months alone at sea, eating raw fish and drinking a mixture of seawater and rainwater. Alone with my dark thoughts, I vowed that I would return to Balibu with my tribe to deliver my vengeance. If the people lived in fear of a dragon, then a dragon they would get …

'He is here now – and his name is Gron Darklaw!'

'You are one of the few people who have shown me no fear, Kalina Moonheart. You and your captain; I will honour him with a statue in the centre of Balibu. As for you, I told you that I have an offer to make. I will not try to hide the fact that you impress me: you fight well; you gamble with cunning and control; you have an adventurous spirit, daring to come here despite the warnings; you are young, fit and healthy …

'If you accept, I would make you my wife!'

V.iv

Promises

Kal stopped chewing halfway through a mouthful of fish. Despite the heat of the lava chamber, a trickle of cool sweat ran down her neck. 'No,' she replied. 'Never.'

'No?' Darklaw stood up and loomed over Kal, his fists on the table. 'Why not? Kalina, I would raise a palace for us over the ruins of the governor's villa in Balibu. You would want for nothing! I would even let you fight by my side. I would *want* you to fight by my side.'

Kal spat out her fish and stood up to look Darklaw in the eye. 'I could never marry a killer,' she said.

Darklaw looked surprised. 'You are a killer, too!' he said, leaning closer.

'I only *kill* killers. You kill anyone who stands in your way. You killed Vanrar the merchant; he was a friend of mine. And you're sending a ship out today to murder the new governor!'

Darklaw shrugged and waved the accusations aside. 'Pah! Merchants and politicians are warriors of a sort, too; it is just that money and influence are their weapons, not blades. I heard that Vanrar had a business rival poisoned once. I have heard many worse things about senators.'

'What about the new governor's family? You told your men to kill them, too.'

Darklaw scowled. 'If people insist on bringing their family and children into battle; well, then their lives are forfeit. That is a lesson that I have learned myself; one that will forever pain me.'

The big man turned away abruptly from the table and went to the edge of the lava lake, where he stood staring out into nothingness, one hand clutching his stitched-up side. Kal sighed. She couldn't decide if she felt revulsion or pity for the man. She walked around the table and cautiously approached him. It would be so easy to spring forward and push him into the lava. Could she do that to him? She had done worse things to people ...

She stepped up behind him and placed a hand on his shoulder. 'Gron,' she said, 'call off the attack on the governor's ship. Send your army back home. Come with me to Amaranthium, and I promise ...'

'You promise what?' Darklaw said, turning his head towards her. There was both pain and hope in his voice.

'... and I promise that I'll make sure you get a fair trial. I know people high up in the Senate ...'

Without warning he lashed out with his powerful arm, sending Kal flying backwards across the island so that she landed painfully on her back with her head out over the edge of the rock. She felt her hair singeing from the heat of the lava that bubbled just a few feet below.

Darklaw advanced on her with tears in his eyes. '*Damn the Senate to hell!* Your promises are worthless; the Senate is a nest of vipers that will most likely betray us both. And I will never submit to any authority. I take what I want, and I want you. If you will not be mine by choice, then I will take you by force!'

Kal struggled to her feet and ran and put the table between them. She hurled the silver domed food cover at him as he advanced on her; it bounced harmlessly off his shoulder. She took up the silver platter that the fish had lay on and tossed it at him like a discus; Darklaw swatted it away with his forearm.

Then he grabbed the heavy wooden table in both hands and hurled it away to one side. It hit the lava and burst into flames.

Kal took the opportunity to lift a chair by its back and smash its legs in Darklaw's face. It barely slowed him; he advanced on her with a mad fury in his eyes. As she retreated, Kal tripped on the uneven ground; she was forced to scuttle backwards on all fours like a crab. She reached the narrow bridge that spanned the lava, and kept backing onto it. She didn't dare take her eyes off Darklaw – if she ran and he threw something at her as she retreated, she would end up taking a very hot bath.

Darklaw stood and watched from the island. He took deep breaths to bring his body back under control. When Kal reached the opposite shore of the lake, she stood and stared him down. 'You're insane!' she shouted across the lake.

He just stood there, glowering at her. Kal shrugged and turned to leave ... and found that two guards had come down the tunnel to the chamber and were standing right behind her. One grabbed her by the wrists, and the other took her ankles. She hung between them, twisting helplessly.

'Take her away,' Darklaw commanded. 'And chain her up this time.'

The guards took Kal back up the tunnel. It was humiliating, being carried swinging between them like a carcass. She hissed and spat, but her captors ignored her. They passed the door to her previous luxury prison and took a turning that led them nearer to the noise of the mine. Some goblins carrying pick axes shambled past and looked at Kal blankly. Those poor, small creatures had a dumb animal look in their eyes, but it was relatively friendly compared to the cruel aggression that she saw behind the eyes of the bigger hobgoblins.

The next people they passed were a group of soldiers going in the opposite direction. 'You coming?' one of them asked the pair carrying Kal. 'Ship's leaving any minute to go get this new guv'nor. Should be fun!' One of Kal's guards grunted an affirmative. 'Just give us five minutes and we'll be there.' None of the others seemed surprised that they were hauling a prisoner down the tunnels. Perhaps this was normal routine around here. Where were they taking her?

It turned out to be a small chamber that had a stone block at its centre. Chains and manacles were bolted to the ground at all four corners. Other than that, the space was bare; just four walls of roughly hewn black granite. Kal noticed blood stains on the ground, though. A chill ran through her that turned to panic.

'No,' she gasped, struggling harder. If they managed to shackle her then it would all be over.

She twisted and writhed as the guard at her head clamped one manacle over her left wrist. The rough iron was tight and bit into her skin. The guard at her feet secured her right ankle. Kal tried to kick out with her left foot, but the hobgoblin just laughed and slapped her leg away.

But Kal was more flexible than either brute suspected: she lifted her hips and rolled back on her shoulders as much as the chains would allow, bringing her free left leg up past her head to smash into the jaw of the guard who was trying to chain her other wrist. He let go of her right arm and she reached quickly down to where her dress gathered at her waist ...

... and then brought the concealed fish knife up and into his brain via his eye socket. As the dead guard fell away, the other one moved in to try and take Kal's weapon away from her. She looped the chain that trailed from her left wrist around his neck and yanked it tight. He fell to his knees, choking. As he struggled for air, Kal reached down his body and pulled the sword out of the scabbard at his belt. There was no room to swing it, so instead she slid the blade along the chain down to the guard's neck and started sawing away. It was hard work killing him, but eventually he stopped moving. Kal threw down the sword and lay back on the stone block in exhaustion.

The fish knife proved to be a useful tool when it came to unlocking the manacles. Once she was free she rubbed her wrist and ankle. Both were sore, but at least the skin had not broken. She was going to bruise all over after banging herself around on the stone block, though. Kal smiled grimly as she buckled the guard's sword belt around her waist over her torn satin dress. *Oh well. It had turned out a lot worse for those two.*

She armed herself with two long daggers, which would serve her better in a fight than the guards' longswords. She tried on their boots but they were far too big, and their heavy leather jerkins would just weigh her down. So in the end she left dressed as she had arrived: but this time ready for both dinner *and* for war.

The mountain trembled again as Kal stalked the tunnels; the hot wind sucked back momentarily, then blew harder, pulling at her hair and dress. *You should have killed me instead of trying to woo me, Darklaw*, she said silently. *I'm going to put an end to you and your invasion.*

But this time I promise you that you're not going to get a fair fight.

V.v

The King Without a Crown

Kalina and Ben walked at a relaxed pace along the rushing waters of the Green Beck. If it wasn't for the sleeping dragon that they had left three miles behind them, they could have been on a quiet moonlit stroll. The only sounds came from the river and from the crisp night breeze that blew upstream and shook the leaves in the forest around them. They had not seen or heard any signs of animals: no owls hooted, no foxes or rabbits ventured onto the path. The forest was usually teeming with life, even at night. Now it felt abandoned.

Ben was beginning to sober up. He looked like he was about to throw up in the forest undergrowth, so Kalina directed him to the river. 'The last thing we want is the dragon getting a whiff of your last meal,' she told him.

'I'm sorry,' he said when he had finished. 'I swear that after this I'm never touching another bottle again. I'm a terrible drunk.'

'Don't be too hard on yourself,' Kalina said. 'You were never drunk when you were teaching the children. What you do in your spare time is nobody's business.'

Ben smiled. 'Thanks, Kal. You always did see the good in everyone.'

'I saw the good in you when you plucked me out of the dragon's nest,' she laughed. 'With your legendary sword! What were you babbling on about back in the cellar? About *the*

Dragon hunting you and your family?'

Ben sighed. They walked in silence for a moment, then he seemed to make up his mind about something. 'Do you remember any of the things I told you about my life *before* I arrived in Refuge?'

Kalina nodded 'All that exciting stuff about you being the son of a fortune teller and a thief lord?'

'Yes,' Ben said. 'Well ... none of it was true.'

'I never thought that it was, Ben! I didn't care, though; nobody asks questions about anyone's past in Refuge. Hell, I think I was the only person living there who wasn't trying to put some old secret life behind them.'

'I know that,' Ben said, 'but I thought a crazy lie might help disguise an even crazier truth. Kal, my family does have a secret; one that drove my father to an early grave.'

Kalina was intrigued immediately. 'This sounds like one of the stories you tell in class. Are there gods and monsters involved?'

'Of course. How did you guess? It was my father who filled my head with all those old stories of Arcus, Draxos, Pescipus, Mena and the rest. My father ...' Ben paused for effect '... told me that he was a descendant of Banos himself.'

Banos. The warrior god. Together with his close friend Arcus, the two immortals had waged war on the armies of monsters for centuries. They defeated the three hundred trolls of Hagaroth without any help from others; they snatched the Eye of the Titan from the Chasm of Bad Blood; they saved the world on countless occasions in times of war ... and provoked many a conflict in times of peace. They were the last gods to fall finally to *the Dragon* a thousand years ago ...

... and between them they fathered scores of long-forgotten children, thanks to their relentless assault on the virtues of adoring mortal admirers. So Kalina wasn't particularly impressed by Ben's claim. 'Banos wasn't exactly fussy about who he got it on with, Ben. I've met sheep who can claim to be his direct descendants, too.'

'Were any of these sheep descended via the Godsword line of kings and queens?'

Kalina whistled quietly through her teeth. *That was different. That would change everything.* 'Are you certain?' she asked.

'Well I haven't got a crown-shaped birthmark, if that's what you're asking,' Ben said, 'but I do have this. Take a closer look.'

He handed her his massive sword. Kalina didn't have to draw it from its scabbard to realise that it was heavier than the prop that she had always assumed it to be. She drew the blade an inch and felt the edge.

'And you let the children play with this?' she said, sucking her bleeding thumb.

'Only if they behave. It's the real thing, though: the Blade of Banos. It's bloodsteel; the gods forged it out of the hardest ore from the highest peak of the largest mountain in the world: the Improbable Mountain. Banos passed it down to the daughter that he gave Queen Oulia. King Aldenute killed himself with it five hundred years later. His descendants have continued to pass it down through the generations, despite living simple lives far removed from gods and monarchs. My father gave it to me the day he died.'

Kalina was amazed. 'But Ben, that would make you –'

'It makes me nothing, Kal. We have a republic now; I have no more right to wear a crown than you do. It was something *else* that my father died trying to find. My great-great-many times great-grandfather King Aldenute was the richest man in the world, but the last thing that he told his family was that he had hidden his vast wealth where his enemies would never find it.'

'Did you ever find out where?' she asked Ben.

'The sly old fool said that he said he had hidden it with Banos himself. But everyone knows that Banos is the only god who *doesn't* have a tomb; it's a mystery where his remains lie! My father eventually decided, for some mad reason, that

Banos was frozen in ice in the Askulin Glacier. He came back from *that* adventure with a minotaur horn stuck in his chest. Before he died, he made me promise to continue the search ... and I did, Kal, for a while at least. But eventually my dreams of riches faded, and the simple life of a schoolteacher started to look more appealing. I'm thirty now; too old to be exploring ruins and climbing mountains!'

Kalina smiled and handed Ben back his sword. They walked in silence for a while. Ben's story had taken their minds off the dragon for a time, and Kalina was encouraged to see that they were almost at the juncture of the Green Back and the Cold Flow. She let her thoughts drift to other old stories and legends, anything to distract her mind from recent events. Every mile they travelled took them further and further away from the dragon and closer to the safety of ...

She stopped suddenly in her tracks. Ben almost walked into her. 'What's wrong?' he asked.

'I know where it is,' she said. 'The tomb of Banos.'

Just at that moment, something stepped out onto the path in front of them. Ben drew his sword from its scabbard. The creature on the path froze when it spotted them. It was an albino deer, probably ignored by the herd and left behind when all the other animals had fled the forest. Kalina and Ben relaxed and the deer bounded off down the path.

'You were saying –' Ben began.

Before Kalina could reply, a familiar sound tore through the still night air: a screeching *kyyyrrrrk* that battered their eardrums. Back in the direction of Refuge, something had stirred.

'Oh no, no, no,' Ben moaned, holding his weapon out in front of him, point down like he no longer wanted it. 'I told you that it was after me and the sword!'

The Blade of Banos glittered in the moonlight, except for some dark spots where the bloodsteel was dulled by stains. An odd tangy smell hit Kalina's nostrils.

'It's not the sword it can sense,' she told Ben. 'It can smell the blood of its young on the blade.' She took the sword out of Ben's loose grip and hurled it into the river.

'Now run!' she ordered.

Kalina sprinted off along the path. Ben snapped out of his daze and tried to catch up. 'Run where?' he shouted after her, breathlessly.

'I know a place!'

They ran downriver at full pelt for half a mile, and made it to the grove of willow trees just in time. Kalina and Ben collapsed in the damp dirt at the foot of Mena's Mirror just as the dragon landed on top of the willows. The trees bent and creaked, but the branches were woven together too tightly for the dragon to get its claws down to them. It continued roaring and flapping around outside for some time.

Ben sat with his head in his hands. He looked defeated already. 'What are we going to do, Kal?' he said. 'Trees aren't going to protect us for long.'

Kal knew that they were doomed, yet for some reason she was calm. Maybe the terror had run its course. Maybe the sanctuary of Mena had a soothing influence.

'You're right,' she said, 'and we're not going to be able to sneak out of here either this time, that's for sure. Ben, you need to think back over everything you've ever read or heard – try and remember anything from history or legend that might be relevant. There must be something in one of your old stories that can help us.'

Kalina couldn't believe what she was considering, but it was do-or-die time now.

'If you ever want me to show you where your ancestor is buried, then I need to know how to kill this dragon.'

V.vi

Sabotage

The black rock tunnels were tight and suffocating. Kal's mouth was bone-dry; the last time that she had tasted water on her lips was when she and Rafe were climbing the mountain. Gron Darklaw's sharpfin supper had been succulent, alright, but heavily salted. She tried hard not to think about what it would feel like to gulp down cold clear spring water; dreaming of it would just make her feel worse.

And now she was lost. The twisting, turning tunnels all looked the same. There was noise and heat coming from all directions. It had been impossible to remember the route the guards had followed when she was being carried along, hung between them like a piece of meat, her nose sometimes scraping the ground. Somehow she had to find a way to stop Darklaw's men from sailing off to murder the new governor. But how was she going to do that? There was no time to make her way back to the mainland to warn anyone. She could think of only one thing that would cause the hobgoblins to call off their attack.

She had to do what Rafe tried and failed to do; she had to kill Gron Darklaw.

If she could ever find him! Kal continued on, taking the passages that led down deeper into the mountain. If Darklaw wasn't still on his little island, then maybe she could sail his boat out to the swamp. Or if the boat wasn't there, then there was that main tunnel up from the lava lake that all the other routes branched off from. Kal stopped for breath at a Y-shaped junction and brushed her damp fringe out of her eyes. If, if, if! But in her favour was the fact that Darklaw didn't know that she was coming. A surprise blade in his back would take him down easy enough!

A stinging hot wind hit Kal from out of the left passage. She could hear echoes of shouts, and the clamour of machinery, as if there was a large open space down that way. She could also detect a faint pale light. Kal decided to take a look. What she discovered at the end of the tunnel wasn't another big cave or chamber, but an immense shaft.

The gold mine was more than a hundred yards across. Far above, several shafts of sunlight filtered in from cracks in the mountain. The natural light was barely enough to reach down to Kal's level, though, and below her the shaft disappeared into a darkness that was scattered with pin-prick flashes of torch-light. The walls of the shaft were smooth dark granite, criss-crossed with grey seams of quartz that caught the sun and glittered.

On Kal's side of the shaft, a wooden scaffold hugged the wall; an intricate lattice of ladders and platforms that was crawling with short, hunched goblins on their way up and down the mine. They ignored Kal as they trudged to work. Were they happier now under Darklaw's regime than under Benedict's? Did they even know or care that the mine had changed hands?

As Kal watched the goblins, she noticed that the scaffold served another purpose: it supported a network of metal pipes that were attached to the underside of the wooden boards that the miners walked along. The pipes were about eighteen inches thick and ran in and out of caves and tunnels in the walls of the shaft; in other places they were bolted vertically to the rock; and here and there Kal spotted cast iron junction boxes where three or more pipes intersected. She put a hand on the pipe that ran along the wall on her level; it was hot to the touch, too hot to rest her palm against for more than a second.

The pipework seemed new. Was this some innovation of Darklaw's? Further along the scaffold she saw a goblin at a junction box turning a heavy iron wheel, like the sort found at the helm of a ship. As the goblin turned it one way, a hissing head of steam was released from a pipe above the goblin's head. As he then put his weight into turning the wheel back the other way, a loud clanking sound started up. Kal looked up and saw the arm of an enormous crane swing out over the shaft. A wide platform was descending on chains. As it passed her, Kal could see that it was empty now, but would no doubt return filled with rocks. It seemed that Darklaw had harnessed the heat of the mountain to mine deeper and more efficiently than ever before.

Kal could only shake her head at the intellect and innovation that was wasted in a man like Gron Darklaw; a man who in other circumstances would have been an asset to the Senate ... to humanity, even. Instead he channelled his keen mind into plans of death and destruction.

When the goblin at the controls had moved on, Kal ran along the scaffold and past the control wheel, until she came to a new tunnel that led away from the shaft and back up into the mountain. This one had a track for minecarts, so surely it would lead her back to more recognisable territory, if not directly to the mine entrance. There was a cart waiting, linked to the tracks by a long chain. A metal pipe also ran up the side of the tunnel, and there was another control station with levers as well as a wheel. So the goblins no longer had to *push* the minecarts – perhaps Darklaw's new regime wasn't entirely to their detriment after all.

Kal laughed to herself as she briefly considered riding the cart up the track, but that would surely throw the only advantage she had – that nobody knew she was loose – out of the window. Even so, she couldn't resist a peek into the cart. It was loaded with fist-sized chunks of quartz that sparkled with gold. She took one and weighed it in her hand. The concentration of gold looked unusually high – maybe as much as half the weight of the rock. Idle thoughts crossed her mind: could she somehow complete her mission *and* escape the island with a few chunks of quartz? Ben would never have to know ...

She kicked herself mentally and hurried on up the tunnel. What good was gold to anyone if you were dead? Kal tried to put all thoughts of gold and riches out of her mind and attempted to focus on finding Darklaw. Soon enough she reached a wooden bridge where the minecart track passed over a wide thoroughfare below. Gron Darklaw and a squad of his hobgoblin soldiers had just passed underneath. He was briefing them as they walked; as they continued up the main tunnel, Kal could just about make out talk of map coordinates and schedules. Two of the men were rolling barrels of pitch along behind the rest of the squad.

When they had disappeared out of sight, Kal prepared to drop down off the bridge and follow them. But she couldn't help thinking of what she had seen back in the gold mine. *Don't think about it*, she told herself. *It's a stupid idea!*

But what if she couldn't create a chance to kill Darklaw? What if she just had to abandon the plan and run? She was only one person against an army after all – so why shouldn't she take the easy option?

Kal cursed under her breath as she made a final decision. 'Sorry, Ben,' she muttered under her breath as she turned and ran back down the track to the shaft.

Ten minutes later, Kal came back up the track with a heavy sack over her shoulder. When she reached the main tunnel again she dropped down from the bridge and stashed her load in the shadow of a fold of rock. *Now to take care of Darklaw.* She needed to get close to him, but not so close that he could smell her this time. Just close enough to put a dagger in his back, and then make her escape amid the confusion that would hopefully follow. Kal slipped off her sandals to silence her approach – she often went barefoot, so her soles were toughened – and then hurried up the tunnel.

She found Darklaw and his men in a cavern that opened out onto the swamp. The slight hint of a breeze that brought in the rotten egg smell of the mangroves was a welcome relief. Three small galleys, their low masts almost scraping the cavern roof, were docked in deep rectangular channels that had been cut into the cavern floor. Kal dropped behind a stack of barrels and spied through the gaps. Darklaw was about thirty feet away with his back to her. It was a fair distance for a knife throw: any further and a quick and clean kill would be impossible.

The big man was still wearing his black tunic and hose from dinner, but he now carried his cruel bastard sword at his back. His squad stood rigidly to attention in front of him, their unruly wildness held in check by Darklaw's commanding presence. They stood in silence in front of the ramp up to one of the galleys, waiting to board. Darklaw's next-in-command looked nervous; he was looking anxiously around the cavern as if waiting for someone. A small rumbling tremor hit the mountain, but the men were so used to it, and so disciplined, that they ignored it.

'You are two men short, Gurik,' Darklaw growled. 'Who is missing?'

'Fug and Jeg, Sir,' the hobgoblin replied. 'They were last seen taking a prisoner –'

Kal's window of opportunity was about to slam shut if she didn't act now. In one movement she stood up from behind the barrels and let fly with one of her daggers, almost falling forward as she put her weight behind the throw. She knew her aim was good as soon as the dagger left her hand: the eight-inch blade was heading straight for the back of Darklaw's neck. There was no time for him to avoid it ...

... except that he did. At the last moment he casually tilted his head to one side, and Kal's dagger flew past and instead struck the one called Gurik right between the eyes, killing him instantly. Darklaw didn't even turn around as he proceeded to issue orders to his men. 'Seal the exits!' he barked. The hobgoblins started to run in all different directions at the same time Kal did. Three blocked her escape into the swamp; on impulse she ran over to the nearest galley and prepared to dive into the dock.

Kal pulled up short so fast that she fell onto her back. *It was a dry dock.* The gates out to the channel through the swamp were closed – if she had dived she would have cracked her skull on the rock ten feet down. When she picked herself up and turned around, she found the squad of troops surrounding her in a wide semi-circle. Darklaw himself stood with them, a grim look on his face.

He drew his bastard sword, the same sword that had felled Rafe. 'It pains me to say it,' he sighed, 'but there comes a time in every relationship where you just have to cut your losses and put an end to it.'

'Didn't you notice that's what I've been trying to do!' Kal shot back.

One of the soldiers came hurrying over. 'Sir, we found this hidden just down the tunnel.' He dropped Kal's heavy sack at Darklaw's feet.

Darklaw's yellow eyes narrowed and he hissed. 'You would not only kill me in cold blood, Moonheart, but you would steal from me, too! That which I would have gladly given to you freely! I misjudged you: you have no honour, no shame and no pride. I was a fool to pursue you!'

Kal spat at the floor between her and her nemesis. As if in answer, the mountain began to shake once more.

Darklaw was so incensed that he couldn't even speak. He kicked at the sack and spilled the contents all over the cavern floor.

But it wasn't gold-flecked rocks of quartz that spread out between Darklaw and Kal, but variously-shaped pieces of cast iron: levers and handles, wheels and bolts.

Darklaw's face froze in surprise as he stared at the debris. The mountain continued to shake.

'What have you done?' he said to Kal in a low voice.

'Ended your invasion,' she replied as the ground buckled beneath them and chunks of rock began to fall from above.

V.vii

Flames

The dragon landed at the edge of the treeline. With its jaws it gripped the trunk of a thick oak, then wrenched the ancient tree back and forth until its roots were pulled from the earth. The dragon then smashed the whole tree down, breaking it in two. Holding it in place with a foot, it attacked the branches with its teeth, ripping them from the trunk four or five at a time.

Kalina watched the show from just inside the entrance tunnel to the willow grove. 'What's it doing?' Ben asked from within.

'Gardening by the looks of it,' she replied. 'Unless dragons eat leaves and twigs. You tell me, Ben.'

'I'm pretty sure that they're carnivores,' Ben said dryly as she rejoined him in the earthy hollow under the canopy of trees. 'In the stories I tell, they are usually partial to human flesh. Cooked human flesh.'

Kalina sat down on a thick willow root opposite him. 'Got any more ideas?' she asked.

Ben shook his head. 'The most recently-recorded dragon attack was when the West Wind Dragon attacked the city, and that was five hundred years ago. Feron Firehand killed that one ... again, with a weapon of the gods. The very same weapon, as it happens, that *you* tossed in the river half a mile back.'

Kalina waved away Ben's complaint. 'I'm sorry, alright? But what's done is done. You know what they say: you can't put the milk back in the cow.'

She got up and paced around what was once the home of the forest god Mena, but was now their prison. 'It's a shame that Mena didn't leave any weapons lying around for us to use. Just this big old mirror. Maybe we could try running outside holding it aloft.' Kalina gave a harsh laugh. 'If we're lucky, the dragon will be scared off by its own reflection.'

Ben watched her as she fidgeted about. 'You're in a strange humour, Kal. What's got into you?'

'What's got into me? Nothing, apart from the fact that almost everyone I know is dead, and here we are trapped by a dragon that's hell-bent on revenge. If I don't laugh about it then I'll probably just break down and die.'

Ben shrugged. 'Well, the mirror trick might do the job for all I know. I've got a thousand stupid stories and legends in my head, but it turns out that none of them are worth a damn in the real world. It's probably just as well that the Godsword line of kings ends with me here, where nobody's around to see and write or sing about it. If we escaped to Amaranthium then we'd probably just die with everyone else when the dragons, goblins and trolls finally take the city. Oh well, civilisation has had a good run. Nothing lasts forever, and two thousand years is more than long enough.'

'I'm not giving up!' Kalina hissed between gritted teeth.

There was a flapping of wings close by and they both flinched as something heavy crashed down on the roof of woven willow branches above them. It wasn't the dragon this time; they could hear the monster hit the ground nearby. A minute later the willows bent again as more stuff crashed down on them.

'It's dropping logs and branches,' Kalina realised. 'It's building a new nest right on top of us!'

She turned to Mena's Mirror in desperation. It was said that the bestial forest god saw her inner beauty when she looked in it: the mirror was supposed to reveal the truth about everyone. But all Kalina could see in it was a frightened man and a dirty, wild-eyed girl. She lashed out with her fist and punched the glass, but the only thing that broke was the skin on her knuckles.

She sucked at the blood thoughtfully for a few minutes. Ben just sat with his head in his hands.

'I've got a plan,' she announced eventually.

They worked methodically on Kal's plan for the rest of the afternoon. She gave Ben the easy and trivial jobs whenever she saw him dithering anxiously behind her. As they worked away, so too did the dragon, flying back and forth, piling trees and branches above and around them. Kal sent Ben down the entrance tunnel of spiralling branches several times to make sure that their exit was kept clear. As evening fell, and the light from the tunnel faded, she had him build a fire in a circle of stones.

'Just be careful,' she warned. 'We don't want to help the dragon and light this bonfire for it.'

Ben struck his flint against his steel, scraping off tiny glowing slivers of hot metal that rained down on the dry kindling. 'I don't think that it needs our help,' he said. 'The West Wind Dragon set half of downtown Amaranthium ablaze with just one breath, remember?'

'I can't quite recall what I was doing that day,' Kal said sarcastically. 'Come on, Ben; knowing what we know now, it was probably someone else who started the fire to lure the dragon, and not the other way round. I'll believe a dragon can breathe fire the day I *see* a dragon breathe fire!'

'Let's just hope that it's not today,' Ben said gloomily as he went back to twisting the thinnest willow branches together to make strong inch-thick cables.

They ate a final meal of old bread and bacon. Ben had mixed up a mushy paste of herbs to garnish it, but they still found themselves having to swallow hard to force it all down. As they sat and ate in silence, something dripped from the roof of branches and landed on Kal's arm. It was a clear amber liquid. She licked it; it was sticky, sweet and oily. She summoned up some saliva and spat the taste away.

'Now I know what dragon pee tastes like,' she said.

After they had eaten, Kal was making some last minute checks when Ben broached a subject that he had evidently been dwelling on all day.

'The tomb ...' he began.

'What?'

'The resting place of Banos ... you said you knew where it was. If you don't tell me now, Kal, then I might never know.'

Kal laughed. 'You *know* the answer, Ben. You've just never put two and two together.'

Ben shrugged and spread his hands.

'You know *everything* about the gods, Ben. Come on, where is Whalo buried?'

'In Brightfish Bay, with his wife, Vuda. What's that got to do with anything?'

'And Lumatore?'

'They built a mausoleum at the bottom of the Canyon of Bones. She lies there with Draxos, her husband. I can see what you're getting at, Kal, but Banos never spent longer than a night with a girl, let alone ever got around to marrying one! He spent his whole life in the saddle, riding from battle to battle with Arcus, getting mixed-up in whatever conflict they came across, and stirring up trouble when there was none to be found. Arcus was just as bad; he never married either –'

Kal raised an eyebrow. Ben's face lit up as the realisation hit him.

'Oh! Of course! It's so obvious, really. I guess they were too busy having fun to stop and marry each other.'

'Find Arcus,' Kal confirmed, 'and that's where you'll find Banos, too.'

'You're right,' Ben said. 'And no one ever figured it out

because nobody has actually *seen* Arcus's tomb; he was buried deep under the rock of the hill where he fought his final battle against *the Dragon*. But my ancestors must have found the tomb and buried Banos alongside him! Kal, we have to get to Amaranthium! We have to go to Arcus Hill and find the *Forgotten Tomb!*'

Kal was pleased to see Ben in a better mood, but he seemed to have forgotten their current predicament. 'Let's worry about that later,' she said as she dragged a long, twisted willow root into a new position. 'We have a dragon to deal with first.'

By midnight they were as ready as they ever would be. Kal could hear the dragon shuffling around on top of the nest above them. She put her hand on Ben's shoulder as they prepared to leave the safety of the willow grove. 'Just don't look back, okay? Run to the river and stay underwater as long as you can as you go downstream. Hopefully, the dragon won't chase you if it's after me.'

Ben nodded nervously. 'Are you sure that there's nothing I can do?'

'You would just be in my way,' Kal said. 'Besides, someone has to stay alive to tell our story. That's what you're best at, Ben. Make me look good, okay?'

They grasped each other's wrists in farewell.

'Let's do it!' Kal urged before they could change their mind. They both ran, side-by-side, down the natural corridor of branches and roots that had been shaped by a god's hand centuries ago. Next, they passed the jumbled piles of new debris that the dragon had dropped around the grove. Finally, they made it out into the open, and Ben shot off to the left. Kal heard a splash as he hit the water.

She ran forward as far as she dared, then turned right and circled back to the entrance tunnel. It was enough: the dragon roused itself from the top of its mountain of branches and, with one powerful flap of its wings, dropped down to the ground just yards from Kal. She tripped and stumbled as she ran – what was once a field of grass was now littered with a layer of leaves and small twigs that had blown off the dragon's pile. Kal rolled, sprang to her feet and got back under the cover of the tunnel entrance.

Then she turned to face the dragon. It had paused not thirty yards away, standing on its powerful legs, its wings spread wide: a black shadow against the deep blue night sky. Its neck dipped down and it brought its small bright eyes on a level with Kal. It cocked its head this way and that, as if suspicious somehow that she wasn't running for her life.

Kal backed slowly into the tunnel, waving her arms in front of her. 'Come on!' she shouted. 'Come and get me!'

The dragon didn't move, except to fold one massive wing in on itself, bringing its claw to its head as if to scratch an itch. Kal clenched her fists; her fingers were slick with sweat. She wiped her eyes with the back of her hand. No – it wasn't sweat. It was more of that oily substance that she must have picked up when she rolled in the leaves. Kal noticed that all the nearby twigs, leaves and branches were covered in it too; a shiny film that glistened in the moonlight. *What was it?*

The Dragon was now scraping its bony claw over the carapace of scales that armoured its head. A quick rhythmic flicking motion; *skkrrt, skkrrt, skkrrt.* Was it trying to communicate something? Was it sending out some kind of signal? The dragon took a long deep breath. Was it –

Bone and scale – *flint and steel*! Kal threw herself to the ground as the first sparks showered from the dragon's armour. The oiled leaves on the ground burst into flames almost instantly, and when the dragon exhaled, a wide cone of furious fire ignited the ground between it and Kal. She covered her head with her arms as her clothing was set alight.

The dragon advanced. The flames started to jump between all the trees and branches piled around.

The bonfire had been lit.

V.viii

Open Wounds

Darklaw lunged at Kal, but the cave floor buckled beneath him and he fell to his knees. The whole mouth of the cave collapsed in on itself, plunging them all into darkness and cutting off their escape into the swamp. The only thing that Kal could see was the faint red glow opposite from the tunnel that she had arrived up. In the near total darkness she leaped forward and climbed over Darklaw's kneeling bulk to get past him. He grunted and flailed his arms as she placed her foot on his face and vaulted over his shoulder.

As she stumbled for the tunnel, Kal heard the ripping sounds of tearing wood as the galleys were crushed by the crumbling cave; she heard the screams and shouts of the hobgoblins, and the sickening sounds of hard heavy rocks landing on soft fleshy bodies. She made it to the tunnel and picked up her pace, running deeper into the convulsing mountain.

Prior to her attempt on Darklaw's life, Kal had returned to the gold mine and closed, then crippled, all of the escape valves in the network of pipes. The pressurised super-heated vapour that, for centuries before Darklaw's arrival, had been venting safely through the island's crevices and fumaroles, was now trapped underground by the very machinery that was put in place to control it. As it drew up its power to break free again, it rocked the mountain by its very roots, like an angry behemoth shaking the bars of its cage.

As Kal ran, she saw the short goblin mine-workers running in all directions. Did they know of ways out, or were they panicking like doomed rats aboard a sinking ship? Should she follow them, or stick to her own risky escape plan? Kal decided to keep running.

A voice shouted from up the tunnel behind her: 'Moonheart!'

She skidded to a halt and turned, if only just to make sure that Darklaw was too far away to catch her.

He was standing almost out of sight at a crossroads further up the tunnel. 'Come with me!' he urged. 'I know the way out of here!'

Was he serious? 'No!' she replied, almost screaming over the noise of the earthquake. 'Not with you! Never!'

'You'll die here if you don't!' he shouted. 'You beat me, Moonheart! You won! Now let us leave together and I will come with you to the city and submit to their justice. I will save you now if you will speak in my favour. You promised that you would!'

'You should have accepted my offer back then,' Kal told him. 'I don't give second chances!' She turned her back on his reply and ran on. Darklaw's curses echoed off the tunnel walls, but he didn't follow her any further.

When she reached the lower cavern it was hotter than ever, and the lava lake was bubbling and frothing like a saucepan brought to the boil. Kal had to jump and skip as she crossed the narrow stone bridge, the lava spitting and sloshing around her feet. Darklaw's platinum-hulled sloop was still there, but the lava was now rising and spilling over the edge of the island: there was a six foot gap between Kal and her escape ticket. She didn't think – she just ran as hard as she could and launched herself at the rail of the small boat. Her elbow hooked around it and her knees banged into the metal hull as she raised her legs to keep them above the level of the lava. Kal screamed in pain, and then screamed again in exertion as she forced her muscles to pull herself over the rail and out of danger.

The lava was rising rapidly. From where Kal lay in the bottom of the sloop, she could see the deadly stalactites in the cavern roof looming closer and closer. She scrabbled to her feet and grabbed the long platinum pole that Darklaw must have used for punting across the lake. She didn't need it, though; the boat was caught in a current that had appeared from somewhere and had now created a lava flow from one side of the cavern to the other. Kal peered through the heat haze ahead of her and saw what was happening: as the lava level rose, it was spilling over the gate of a lock that must have been the means that Darklaw brought his boat in and out of his lair. Kal held on tight to the lip of the cabin hatch as the sloop plunged down a six-foot drop and entered a subterranean river where the hot lava was mixing with swamp water and creating foul-smelling, scalding clouds of steam.

She wrapped herself up in the sail that lay folded up next to the mast at the bottom of the boat. The heat was still almost too much to bear, she had no idea where the hell this ride was taking her, and she could hardly get any oxygen to her lungs – but at least she hadn't been boiled alive yet.

When the pressure lifted, Kal threw back the damp sail. The boat had left the mountain and was passing through a deep and narrow canyon in the rock. The sides of the canyon were shaking, splitting and shifting, and the space between them was just ten feet wide; if the sloop wasn't scraping along the left wall of the canyon, then it was scraping along the right. Still, she was still moving in the right direction as the water surged forward, pushed out of the mountain by a tide of lava. But when Kal glanced back, she saw that the lava was hot on her heels, rising ten feet above her, filling the canyon from side to side …

Kal closed her eyes. *I almost made it!*

Ten seconds later she opened them again. She was still alive. What was once a wave of red molten death was now a solid grey cliff of billowy undulating rock. The lava had cooled and hardened, apparently satisfied with chasing her out of the caves. The sloop was free to slip easily out of the canyon and into the sea, where the current caught it and dragged it parallel to the coast. The mangroves and mountain came into view, and Kal was presented with a vista that was both silent and still; under a hot sun and a clear blue sky was a beautiful tropical scene that belied the turmoil taking place underground. Kal could just about make out the tiny shapes of the goblin workers spilling down the slopes, along with a handful of Darklaw's soldiers. But as she watched, bursts of orange flame began flowering over the mountainside, starting at the base and spreading upwards.

Then with an ear-splitting *boom*, the top of the volcano exploded.

'And did Mister Darklaw die in the volcano?'

Kal nodded and kissed the forehead of her child.

'Yes, Darling. Bad Mister Darklaw died instantly when the mountain fell on top of him. It was a quick and painless end. He didn't suffer. He didn't feel a thing.'

Kal struggled to get the sloop under sail as soon as possible. Behind her a three-hundred-foot fountain of lava spewed from the top of the volcano. Rivers of the stuff were running down into the swamp, sending up toxic clouds of greenish steam. Fist-sized projectiles were falling out of the sky and splashing all around the boat. Kal yelled as one hit her on the shoulder while she was concentrating on slotting the mainmast into its socket. She picked it up; it was a lightweight black rock that was pockmarked with air bubbles. She kicked it overboard.

More and more rocks were raining down on Kal when she finally caught some wind and started to move clear of the eruption. Tiny pieces of sharp volcanic glass were now showering her as well, forcing her into the cover of the sloop's small cabin. But taking one last look back, she saw that she was not out of danger yet ...

A great black winged shape was gliding above the lava flows and heading in her direction. So that was Darklaw's escape plan, to ride to safety in his flying machine! As Kal watched, the wood and canvas dragon was hit by a barrage of hot rocks that ripped through its wings and set them on fire. *Ha!* Darklaw didn't have Kal's luck when it came to making an exit.

Her laugh stuck in her throat. The flaming dragon was falling out of the sky sure enough, but it was closing in on her position, getting closer and closer every second. The same wind that was filling the sails of the sloop was also bringing her enemy directly to her. She could now see Darklaw at the controls of the dragon, desperately working the levers that pulled the ropes that moved the wings. For one heart-stopping moment it looked as if he was intent on smashing the great machine into the boat, but then at the last moment Darklaw yanked the controls back and the dragon sailed overhead, missing the top of the sloop's mast by only a couple of inches.

Kal watched the winged-contraption as it finally smacked down onto the water, ceasing to be a life-like monster, and becoming instead just a sinking mass of wood and material. She almost didn't register the *thunk* as something heavy fell from the passing dragon and hit the deck behind her.

She threw herself to the deck just in time as Darklaw's bastard sword sliced through the air above her head. As the giant advanced on her in a rage, Kal reached up and pushed the boom that held the mainsail in position; it swung around and knocked the sword out of Darklaw's hand and sent it to the bottom of the sea. Kal scrabbled up on top of the roof of the cabin and tried to put the mainmast between herself and her foe. She had no weapon; she must have lost her second dagger during her escape. Darklaw didn't let up his attack; he jumped up onto the cabin roof and advanced on Kal with his arms outstretched.

'Stop! Please!' Kal cried, almost in tears. She was exhausted and in no fit state to fight anyone, let alone the muscled beast that stood before her.

Darklaw was unheeding and implacable, though, his features twisting in anger and hatred. He wrapped both of his huge hands around Kal's throat and lifted her off the deck by her neck. 'Die!' he roared. 'Just die!'

Kal could feel the gold and silver necklace that Darklaw had given her pressing into her neck beneath his grip. His yellow eyes bore into hers as if he was determined to bear witness to her final moments. Kal knew that she had taken her last ever breath; she couldn't move her tongue, swallow or even force her lips to speak.

But she could still *think*. And moments before her body gave up the will to live, she remembered ...

She brought her right knee up and into Darklaw's side, opening up the wound that Rafe had made with the Blade of Banos. Darklaw screamed in pain as the stitches split. He dropped to his knees, but still he didn't loosen his grip on Kal's neck. However, when she felt her feet hit the deck again, Kal put her hands on Darklaw's wrists, returned his intense stare, then pushed with her thigh muscles and twisted her body to the side. It was enough – together they fell from the deck of the boat and into the hot sea.

They found themselves suspended in a silent blue world, locked together and sinking slowly to the sand below. A torrent of thick blood gushed from Darklaw's side and hung in the water like a dark ribbon, but if he knew that he was finished then he was determined to take Kal down with him: his hands remained clamped to her neck. She sensed movement in the water around them, but her oxygen-starved brain was shutting down and her field of vision was shrinking to a narrow tunnel, down which Darklaw's yellow eyes glared back at her. The only thing keeping her conscious was the sharp pain of the links of the necklace as they bit into her neck.

Kal's hands had lost their grip on Darklaw's wrists. Her fingers were turning numb and her arms felt like they belonged to someone else. With one final supreme force of will, she concentrated on flexing her triceps and pivoting her arms at her shoulders. She reached back behind her neck, fingers fumbling at the clasp of the necklace.

When it came undone, it slipped from around her neck, and so did Darklaw's grasp. His body was sinking suddenly away from her. The last thing that Kal saw before the darkness took her was Darklaw's expression of furious anger turn to one of desperate terror as the circling sharpfins closed in on his bleeding body. Then he was lost amid the feeding frenzy as several dozen of the razor-toothed predators fought for their share of his flesh.

The ribbon of blood soon turned into a heavy all-enveloping cloud.

When Kal came to, she was lying on her back on the deck of the *Swordfish*. She felt someone's lips on hers, and when she opened her eyes she saw her friend Lula smiling back at her. Dead Leg, the captain, was standing over her, too, a broad grin on his face.

'Kal!' a voice shouted from just off to one side. 'You're alive!'

Lula helped Kal sit up, and she turned to see another familiar face. 'Ben!' she gasped, coughing up seawater at the same time. 'What are you doing here?'

'I left the city a few days after you did,' he explained. 'The Senate was looking for someone to take on the job of governor temporarily and, well, I fancied a holiday and the chance to keep an eye on my gold mine ... so here I am!'

Kal laughed and gave Ben a wet hug. Far out to sea she could see a haze of smoke hanging over the island.

'So?' Ben asked as Kal rested her tired head on his shoulder. 'Can I go and get my gold back now? Did you kill the dragon?'

'Yeah,' Kal sighed. 'I got him.'

V.ix

Smoke and Mirrors

The Dragon roared and advanced on Kal; she could hear its feet thumping on the ground as it stomped towards her. She screwed her eyes shut and tried to block out the pain of the flames that ate at her back. What else could she do? She had attempted to roll out the fire, but the dragon's flammable, sticky secretion was not just all over her body, but all over the leaves and branches on the ground, too.

The plan that she and Ben had spent most of the day working on had failed in an instant. The dragon had a better trick up its sleeve than Kal did. It had prepared its own trap and sprung it with a spark struck from its scales, and with one breath had ended Kal's wild hopes of ever killing it.

Something heavy pressed down on her back. At least for a brief moment the pain let up as the flames that were ravaging her body were extinguished. Kal braced herself for the bite of the dragon's jaws, but instead she heard a sharp voice at her ear –

'Get up, Mooney. You're no good to me dead!'

It was Ben. He had returned, soaking wet, from the river and flopped down on top of her. As the dragon bounded closer, they both rose and stumbled through the burning debris towards the heart of the willow grove. As they ran down the tunnel of twisted roots and branches, Kal tore away her smouldering, smoking clothes.

She could sense the dragon hot on their heels. The tunnel was just wide enough to allow its head in, and the dragon's neck was just long enough for it to reach all the way down. Its advance down the tunnel was heralded by the sharp cracking of twigs and branches.

Kal and Ben made it to the open space that was the god Mena's sanctuary, at the very centre of what was now the dragon's nest. The domed ceiling of knotted willows was obscured by a haze of smoke that was filtering in from the nest's burning extremities. Ben ran across the earthy bowl in the hope that the dragon wouldn't be able to stretch as far as the other side, but Kal flung herself down in the very centre of the depression and turned to face her enemy.

It came at her relentlessly; its giant head emerged from the tunnel, and when it opened its jaws they filled almost the entire sacred space under the willows. The dragon's teeth were glistening like oiled swords, and its breath was hot and sweet. Kal sprawled in the dirt before it, half-naked and defenceless, a perfect offering to the creature that most men believed to be spawned from the dragon god himself.

But not Kal. To her, the dragon was simply a dangerous animal that needed to be put down.

But first it needed to be *snared* ...

Her hands felt around beneath her and found the end of a rope of slender entwined branches. She heaved on it and the rope lifted out of the dirt where it had been partially buried. The other end of the rope was knotted around a peg that had been hammered into a knothole in a trunk at the edge of the grove. As Kal gritted her teeth and yanked the rope as hard as she could, the peg popped free.

It had been securing another rope, one that held in place the thickest and longest of all the willow roots. It had taken all of Kal and Ben's strength to bend it back on itself, and now that it was released, it whipped through the smoke-filled air and slammed into the back of the dragon's neck with enough force to pin its head to the ground. If the dragon had been any smaller, then the blow would surely have broken its vertebrae, or even severed its head.

But if the dragon had been any smaller, then Kal wouldn't have needed to turn the willow root into a *guillotine* ...

The entire length of the foot-thick root was bristling with glittering shards from the broken mirror that Kal had jammed into splits in the wood. The jagged glass hit the dragon from behind, sliding beneath the overlapping scales and cutting deep into its flesh. The animal screeched in pain and surprise, its small brain unable to comprehend where the attack had come from. Instinctively, it tried to pull back and retreat from danger.

Except it couldn't move. Kal had ensured that the ends of the branches and roots that made up the entrance tunnel had been rearranged so that they all pointed inwards. The dragon had been able to slide in easily enough, but when it tried to pull out, the scales of its neck were caught in a hundred places. It was trapped.

Kal felt focused and determined as she reached for the final item that she had half-buried in the earth: a twenty inch-long shard of glass, the largest one that had fallen from the mirror when she had smashed it. The dragon was stunned and confused, and made no move to bite her as she stepped forward and moved slowly around its jaws to stand just to the left of its head. The creature watched her approach, somehow conveying a stricken and terrified expression with one unblinking orange eye.

'I'm sorry,' Kal told the dragon. 'But this isn't your time any more. You need to go now ... go back into stories and legend.'

She gripped the deadly shard with both hands and speared the dragon's eyeball, pushing the point deeper and deeper into its skull with all her strength until she found the brain.

The dragon died quietly, but not cleanly. Blood, gelatinous eyeball fluids and brain juices all sprayed out and washed all over Kal, painting her red, yellow and black from head to toe. She remained calm and still as the torrent bathed her, while in her head a strange transformation was taking place. For the first time in days, as she stood over the dragon's body, she was experiencing a profound feeling, one she had last felt when she lay in the forest meadow with Deros, just before her life was upturned. Now – as then – she felt careless, safe and free, with her whole future ahead of her.

Except that now she would never be Kalina Brown, village schoolteacher and woodcutter's wife. That life was closed to her forever.

From this moment on, she would always be Kal Moonheart, *Dragon Killer*.

THE END

Kal Moonheart returns in

ROLL THE BONES

An immortal killer stalks the streets of Amaranthium, leaving a trail of mutilated corpses in its wake. A week before the summer elections, Kal Moonheart is called before a clandestine gathering of the city's elite, and charged with ending the murders before a terrible secret can come to light – one that threatens to shake the Republic by its very foundations. As Kal hunts the killer, her courage, loyalties and heart are put to the test, and she must decide if she can trust even her closest friends.

Available now

SIRENS BANE

On a freezing winter night, Kal Moonheart is dragged from her bed by a friend in need. Renowned pirate and smuggler Lula Pearl has been struck with a fearsome curse, and Kal must join her and set sail on their most dangerous voyage ever. On the other side of the world, the Auspice Islands have been overrun by a horde of zombies, led by a man whose terrifying schemes threaten all life both under and above the waves – the almighty sorcerer known as Corus Sirensbane.

Available now

49155706R00096

Made in the USA
Charleston, SC
19 November 2015

The Rise & Fall
of British Eagle

Rob Coppinger

SunRise

SunRise

First published in Great Britain in 2022 by SunRise

SunRise Publishing Ltd
124 City Road
London EC1V 2NX

ISBN 978-1-9144892-4-2

A CIP catalogue record for this book is available from the British Library.

Typeset in Minion Pro and Impact.

Contents

But the cruellest of our revenue laws, I will venture to affirm, are mild and gentle, in comparison to some of those which the clamour of our merchants and manufacturers has extorted from the legislature, for the support of their own absurd and oppressive monopolies. Like the laws of Draco, these laws may be said to be all written in blood.

Adam Smith

PREFACE & ACKNOWLEDGEMENTS

The story of Harold Bamberg and the rise and fall of his airline, British Eagle, is as much a story of powerful people making decisions that benefit them, rather than the wider society, as it is the history of a failed independent company in an industry where so many would fall by the wayside. It is a tale worth remembering and its lessons reverberate to this day.

I'd like to thank my publisher, Malcolm Turner, without whom this book would not have been possible, for giving me the opportunity to investigate this history. I originally set out with the intention of writing about an outsider — because Bamberg was a Jewish German refugee — but I eventually realised that everyone, even the British born, are outsiders when a small wealthy group dominates entire sections of the economy.

A great source of information to paint this picture was my former employer *Flight International* magazine. The reporting by the *Flight* team and their Transport Editor Mike Ramsden in particular, provided a rich vein of material. Ramsden was a hugely respected journalist who passed away in 2019, aged 90. A very special thank you to DVV Media, now the owners of *Flight International* magazine, and its Editor Craig Hoyle for their very kind help providing *Flight* articles from the 1950s, 1960s and 1970s.

Other key individuals in my journey were the former Eagle employees Philip Johns, Eric Tarrant, and David Hedges, whose book, *The Eagle Years 1948–1968*, was a great source of information, and my phone interview with David was very insightful.

While a large part of the source material for this book was from aviation publications, I hope it can be enjoyed by a wider audience, whose interests may also lie in business history or the sociology of the UK, and not simply an enthusiasm for airlines. I also need to thank travel writer and ocean liner expert Chris Frame for his expertise on Cunard, whose acquisition of Bamberg's airline was such a major turning point in the tale. The gamut of personalities in Bamberg's life from Cunard's Sir Basil Smallpeice to Sir Freddie Laker helped to give real colour to the theme of powerful people distorting an industry for their own ends. Laker's story can be seen as a repetition of the Bamberg tale in many ways. It is even more telling that Laker's Skytrain only really took off because of the actions of a President of the United States. Finally, I'd like to thank Eric Tarrant, archivist at www.britisheagle.net. That website was the starting point for my writing journey.

I wrote this book in 2021 at my home in Brittany, France. Looking from the outside into the UK I still wonder how the cycle of a society being organised for the benefit of an elite can be stopped.

Rob Coppinger
Nantes, August 2022

1 An Eagle Falls

The blue and grey medal with its pink ribbon shone against the plush lining of a small box. For a Jewish refugee, who had built a major airline from nothing, a CBE in the New Year's Honours marked the high point of a remarkable career. Still only forty-four years old, Harold Bamberg had left school at seventeen and founded his company with just £100 in capital and a single war-weary Halifax bomber. He had made his first million while still in his twenties, played polo with prince Phillip, and now travelled between his country estate, West End offices and Mayfair flat in a chauffeured Rolls-Royce complete with telephone, dictating machine and the license plate HB 100.

On 13 February 1968, Bamberg took his wife and two children to Buckingham Palace for his investiture by the Queen. It was a cold Tuesday morning, but a warm, proud day for the family of this German émigré. Ten months later his airline, British Eagle International, would collapse. He had survived a succession of governments who thought state run airlines should be protected from free market competition — along with the constant skulduggery of his competitors — but, in the end, Bamberg could not prevent his bankers winding up the company he had built up over a generation. Eagle was the second largest of some 30 British independent airlines, most of which would, ultimately, either fail or be absorbed into one of the state-owned giants.

Such was the support of his employees, that they offered their pensions to keep the airline going, but Bamberg rejected the staff's generous offer. Despite all his efforts and the hard work of his team, He could not fight off the anti-competitive threat of Sir Giles Guthrie and Sir Anthony Milward, the respective heads of the UK government's airlines, British Overseas Airways Corporation (BOAC) and British European Airways (BEA).

Before Guthrie and Milward there had been Rear-Admiral Sir Matthew Slattery, Sir Gerard John Regis Leo d'Erlanger, Sir Miles Thomas and Lord Douglas. These public school-educated, typically Oxbridge graduates had been given control of the UK's flagship airlines and all the government support they needed. British Caledonian Airways' Chairman, Sir Adam Thomson, said in 1990: '[State-owned] BOAC thought they had a God given right to air travel. The BOAC lobby was pretty all powerful.' [1]

In his fight to win, Bamberg would be the first to introduce low fare flights and in-flight catering for premium services. He would also be a pioneer of the low-cost inclusive tours which enabled so many British families to take holidays abroad. As well as London, he operated from Bermuda and the Caribbean, thereby avoiding UK government restrictions and competing with US airlines for the lucrative New York route, but ultimately it would not be enough. Events beyond Bamberg's control — the 1967 devaluing of sterling followed by currency controls and the £50 travel allowance — weighed heavily on British Eagle's fortunes. After 20 years, the changing geopolitical landscape — and the RAF's acquisition of VC10s — would also bring the crucial UK armed forces trooping revenues to an end, hastening Eagle's demise.

Born in Berlin on 17 November 1923 to a German father and a British mother, Bamberg's family were Jews who escaped Hitler's Germany for Britain in 1938 (Hedges, 2021). Finishing his schooling in England, Bamberg joined the RAF in 1941 aged 17; as soon as he legally could. In 1941, while BOAC was still flying its traditional Empire routes, Bamberg was training as a wireless operator and his German speaking abilities would give him a special role in the war.

On 25 August 1941 No 1419 (Special Duties) Flight was renumbered No 138 Squadron. After his training in 1942, Bamberg was posted to 138 Squadron which was stationed at RAF Tempsford near Bedford in southern England. The squadron was still assigned to what was called "special duties". Their role was to maintain communications with resistance groups in occupied Europe and their aircraft would fly into Nazi occupied territory to drop and pick up Special Operations Executive (SOE) agents and drop supplies.

Bamberg would not have known it at the time but the man in whose aircraft he flew, Frederick Handley Page, had started an airline only to have it merged with others into Imperial Airways 16 years earlier. Bamberg's endeavours would eventually suffer a similar fate, but in the 1940s, he and his crewmates were trying to avoid Nazi flak. In October 1942, 138 Squadron gave up the SOE agent transport duties to concentrate on supply dropping. On 9 March 1945 the unit transferred to Bomber Command and undertook bombing operations until the end of the war in Europe.[2] Bamberg survived 37 missions and, as well as his Halifax radio operator function, he had a role in intercepting German radio traffic and replying to it with false position reports. He would be demobbed shortly after the war in Europe ended but as he took off his RAF uniform for the last time, he could not have known that he would soon be flying Halifaxes again in a peaceful role, or that it would be the beginning of 20 years of airline activity.

The Halifax was the second British four-engined bomber to enter service in World War Two. Between 1941 and 1945, the RAF's Halifaxes made more than 75,000 bombing sorties, dropping 231,300 tonnes of ordnance. That was more than a quarter of all the bombs dropped on Germany by the RAF. The first Halifax to bomb Germany took part in a raid on Hamburg on the night of 12–13 March 1941. The missions the Halifax took on were so dangerous that eventually Bomber Command restricted the crews to less hazardous targets over Germany from September 1943.

From 1941, the Halifax shared, with the Avro Lancaster bomber, most of the burden of the nightly bombing campaign against Nazi Germany. The Halifax was more flexible than the Lancaster and it was used extensively on other duties including glider-towing, agent dropping, transport and general reconnaissance work for Coastal Command.[3]

In May of 1943, Viscount Knollys, who had been Governor of Bermuda since 1941, became BOAC Chairman. That very month, Nazi Germany's Ruhr valley, with its vast industry powering Hitler's war effort, had become an important target. The famous Dam Busters raid, Operation Chastise, was launched on 17 May, and that same month Halifaxes were sent by the RAF to destroy the Ruhr's transport hub at Bochum in western Germany.[4]

In the wake of World War Two, three years after

One of Eagle Aviation's ex-RAF Handley Page Halifaxes.

those critical missions, the UK government passed the Civil Aviation Act 1946. This Act would create British European Airways (BEA), an airline that, as the name suggested, would fly UK domestic and European routes. Strangely, the aircraft and crew that would fly for BEA were already fully operational, as the Royal Air Force's 110th Wing of Transport Command. On 1 August 1946, BEA came into being with 21 110th Wing Douglas DC-3 aircraft while BOAC's European division had started its services on 1 January that year with its own 110th Wing aircraft.[5]

After he left the Royal Air Force, Bamberg studied the aviation business as an employee of American Overseas Airlines (AOA), spending some time in the United States. American Overseas Airlines was set up in the 1930s and flew between the continental United States and Europe. This experience with AOA taught Bamberg the importance of marketing. It would be reflected in his decisions on cities he would fly from, to be closer to the customer, and exploiting the glamour, and subsequent media coverage, of flying female models and pop stars.

Bamberg's start was not so glamourous but certainly healthy for his new enterprise, he engaged with the fruit and vegetable businesses of London's Covent Garden. Producers in Spain, Italy and the Netherlands would use Bamberg's aircraft to fly their food into the UK for sale in London. The culmination of his wartime flying, his business experience with AOA and his talks with the market sellers led to him registering his charter airline, Eagle Aviation Limited, in April 1948.[6]

The £100 of capital it was registered with would be £3,700 in 2020 prices. Registered as an Aldermaston based business in southern England, Bamberg had one director, a Walter Lyons. A few weeks later, in May, Bamberg acquired the assets of Air Freight Limited which was based in Bovingdon, northeast of London. Air Freight's assets included a Handley Page Halifax aircraft and Bamberg resurrected that company's name as an associate company in 1952. He would buy another Halifax from its manufacturer, Handley Page in October 1948. It had been built for a foreign buyer and painted red so it was distinctive among what would be a growing fleet of Halifaxes at Eagle Aviation.

While that aircraft was painted red, Bamberg's Eagle Aviation fleet had no specific colour scheme, or livery, to use airline jargon. His aircraft were left unpainted, a livery would probably be an indulgence that Bamberg's start-up airline could ill afford. What they may have had is what is called a cheatline, where the company name, in this case it would have just been Eagle, would be in a coloured strip along the fuselage. Some aircraft did have the Eagle symbol on the vertical tail fin. This symbol was an E with the parts of the E representing the wings

14

and legs of a bird and its head sticking out of the central part of the E pointing in the opposite direction.

In the months after Bamberg registered his airline, the UK government began an investigation which would result in decisions that would help Eagle Aviation, a rarity. On 21 July 1948, the then Minister of Civil Aviation, Lord Pakenham, appointed Lord Douglas to investigate the operation of "associate agreements" and their relation to the Civil Aviation Act (Humphreys, 1973). In 1948, Douglas was a recently retired Marshal of the RAF and he would complete the investigation for Lord Pakenham.

Lord Sir William Douglas of Kirtleside was born William Sholto Douglas on 23 December 1893 in Oxfordshire. He attended the University of Oxford's Lincoln College and in 1915 joined the then Royal Flying Corps and became a fighter pilot. He was awarded the Military Cross in 1916 and the Distinguished Flying Cross in 1917, aged 24. After World War One Douglas became Chief Test Pilot for the Handley Page company before joining the RAF in 1920.

Rising up through the ranks, Douglas became an RAF instructor at the Imperial Defence College and in 1936 was appointed as director of staff studies in the Air Ministry. In 1938, aged, 45, he was promoted to Vice Marshal and became Assistant Chief of Air Staff, responsible for training and equipment procurement. In November 1941, Douglas became head of RAF Fighter Command. In 1943 he was appointed Commander in Chief of the RAF in the Middle East and in 1944, Commander in Chief of Coastal Command. After World War Two, Douglas became Commander in Chief and Military Governor of the British Occupation Zone in Germany and in January 1946 was knighted and promoted to Marshal of the RAF. He was awarded his peerage in 1948 and became the 1st Baron Douglas of Kirtleside. After he completed the aviation investigation for Lord Pakenham, Douglas was appointed Chairman of the recently created BEA. Eagle Aviation would eventually be awarded one of BEA's associate agreements. But what does a former RAF Marshall know about running an airline?

While Lord Douglas' review of associate agreements benefited Bamberg in the short term, the former RAF Marshal was BEA Chairman until 1964 and during those 16 years BEA opposed the independents on domestic and European routes vociferously.

The man who gave Lord Douglas the job was Clement Attlee's Labour government aviation Minster, Lord Pakenham. The second son of the fifth Earl of Longford, Frank Pakenham, as he was then, was born on 5 December 1905. He was educated at Eton and the University of Oxford's Christ Church college. At the age of 25 he joined the Conservative Party but his future wife, Elizabeth Harman, whom he had met at Oxford, persuaded him to become a socialist.[7] In the 1930s, before he entered government, Pakenham was a politics lecturer at Christ Church college.

By 1941 he was personal assistant to the social economist and future Liberal peer of the House of Lords, Sir William Beveridge.[8] Beveridge was an advisor to the cross-party national government of the war years. In 1945, Pakenham was given a peerage by the then Prime minster Clement Attlee, after Labour won the election that year, and he became Baron Pakenham of Cowley in the City of Oxford. Attlee wanted Pakenham in the government and in 1945, he gave Pakenham a job in the War Office, then made him Minister of State for

Germany, and finally appointed him as Civil Aviation Minister in 1948.

Aviation Minister was Pakenham's longest role lasting until 1951 when he became First Lord of the Admiralty, in charge of the Navy. After the Labour party's defeat in the 1951 election Pakenham eventually became Chairman of the National bank in 1955 without any previous banking experience. Upon his older brother's death, he became 7th Earl of Longford in 1961. He would later be appointed to his first cabinet post by Labour prime minister Harold Wilson: Lord Privy Seal and leader of the House of Lords. Known for most of his life as Lord Longford, he advocated the release of child murderer Myra Hindley and campaigned for penal reform. His anti-pornography campaigning was widely ridiculed, especially when he visited strip clubs in Copenhagen, leading to his nickname, Lord Porn.

Longford and Douglas are two examples of people whose impact on the UK aviation was significant yet neither had any industry or aviation experience. Longford oversaw the Civil Aviation Act of 1949 that regulated BOAC and BEA. They would dominate UK aviation for 25 years until British Airways was recreated in 1974. From 1949 until 1964, Lord Douglas would work to ensure his airline attacked the independents' attempts at making inroads into the domestic and European scheduled services as often as possible.

Bamberg would fight BEA's opposition again and again. From that early Eagle Aviation fleet of Handley Page Halifaxes carrying fruit and vegetables Bamberg would challenge the UK and international airline market over the next 20 years with industry and world firsts. He may not have known at the time that his Halifax was built by a company, Handley Page, whose foray into airlines had been short lived. Frederick Handley Page, its founder, was a man like Bamberg, from a modest background whose hard work built his aircraft manufacturing business.

Handley Page's attempt at an airline, Handley Page Transport, was subsumed into Imperial Airways in the 1920s by a Conservative government. In turn, in 1939, the war time cross-party national government led by Conservative politician Neville Chamberlain decided Imperial would become part of BOAC. World War Two allowed another consolidation of UK airlines ensuring the industry's domination by shipping and railway scions. Thirty years later, government action during another Conservative administration would see a final merger of UK airlines.

While the summer of 1948 saw Bamberg's first commercial flight, a cargo of cherries from Verona, Italy to Bovingdon, world events were taking a turn for the worst and relations between the Soviet Union and the UK, France and the US were deteriorating. Three years after the fall of Adolf Hitler's Third Reich, the Western Allies sought to re-establish Germany as a functioning state with a currency.[9] The Secretary-General of the Communist Party of the Soviet Union, Joseph Vissarionovich Stalin, had other ideas and Eagle Aviation would be in the middle of it all.

From 1948 to 1968, Bamberg's airlines participated in history with the Berlin Airlift, the Suez crisis, the Aden evacuation, the first scheduled flights to socialist Yugoslavia during the Cold War, the first civil aircraft landing in Moscow since 1945, and the first scheduled services from South Africa to South America. He had also developed crucial routes from Bermuda, which would be a launching pad for his transatlantic goals, and the Holy Grail of London to New York — then and now one of the world's most lucrative airline routes. Despite all his efforts to make the most of the underserved markets in the UK, in Europe and the West Indies, the long reach of the UK regulator and the shadow of the powerful US airlines made Bamberg's business life a tough one.

To survive, Bamberg agreed to his airlines being taken over by a shipping line, the most famous in the world. And ultimately, he had to make deals with the Devil, the state run, aristocrat-managed BOAC. That did not sit well with Bamberg, and his independent instincts and entrepreneurial spirit led him to quit the cosy confines of the state-owned behemoth. Bamberg's comeback was a success for a few years, he managed to build his airline back up to be a significant player. This was despite being forced to give his Caribbean routes to BOAC and despite BEA literally planning its UK flight schedule to deliberately sabotage British Eagle. Yet, Bamberg still had successes, and not only with airlines: his travel agencies were pioneers of all-new package holidays which were making foreign travel available to the masses.

Ultimately, Bamberg, along with Sir Frederick Laker and many others, was crushed beneath the steamroller of government-owned and government-protected airlines. Only Sir Richard Branson would avoid a similar fate and that was because Margaret Thatcher's government was not going to intervene following their privatisation of British Airways.

The final year for Bamberg as head of an airline, 1968, began with ambitious plans to again fight the government's restrictions and the opposition from the soon to be merged BOAC and BEA. In his New

Year comments for his airline's staff newspaper, *Eagle International News*, Bamberg wrote about ending the ban on his airline flying transatlantic routes. It was a ban that had interrupted a previous 15-year licence that had briefly, until 1976, given his airline access to the lucrative London-New York route. As 1968 progressed the problems began to stack up. On 5 June, Israel attacked its Arab neighbours.

That Six-Day War would drive up oil prices and be one of the many factors that led to the end of Bamberg's airline business. Bamberg had registered his first airline — air charter firm Eagle Aviation Limited — on 14 April 1948, and exactly a month later, on 15 May, the Arab countries surrounding Israel attacked the fledgling Jewish state. Bamberg could never have conceived that this centuries old religious struggle would erupt again in 20 years, and his airline would be another victim of it.

The 1968 New Year's plan was for Bamberg's team to argue at the Air Transport Licensing Board (ATLB) hearings, from 16 January to 8 February, that British Eagle International Airlines should have licences for scheduled passenger services for London to New York, London-Bermuda and the Bahamas to Chicago. Later in the year, Bamberg planned to ask for an all-cargo licence between London and the US eastern seaboard. He wrote in his New Year's address: "The London-New York service is the prime route, and we feel that the ATLB will recognise the need for a second carrier on this route as they did in July 1961" (the year in which Bamberg had won his 15-year licence).

The then newly constituted ATLB had granted the licence for the lucrative London-New York daily service for 15 years, effective from 1 August 1961, to Cunard Eagle. This airline was a merger of Bamberg's then named Eagle Airways and the Cunard shipping line whose Chairman was the 46-year-old, Eton-educated baronet, Sir John Brocklebank.[10] In March 1960, Cunard Eagle came into being with Brocklebank its Chairman, but its propitious start was undermined the following year when the ATLB revoked that licence on appeal from BOAC, only months after awarding it. Troubled from almost the beginning, Bamberg would go his separate way in 1963 and Cunard went through with an equally ill-fated deal with BOAC.

Bamberg explained in his 1968 New Year's address to staff, that he intended to convince the ATLB that the policy of "single designation" (first advocated in 1945 and underlined in 1965 by the then Labour party government's Minister of Aviation, Roy Jenkins MP) was wrong. His optimism, however, was misplaced. and Eagle's application would be refused. Despite this major setback, he was still confidently predicting a profitable 1968, while admitting they would not see as much profit as 1966.

Bamberg told reporters in February of 1968, 'we are buoyant.' The profit (including the sale of 14 of his aircraft) he predicted would be about £250,000, which is £4.4 million in pounds sterling in 2020.[11] Yet, before the year was out, Eagle had to cease trading; a very different picture to the close of 1966 when — three years after leaving the clutches of Cunard, Bamberg had rebuilt an airline which had UK domestic routes and wanted to relaunch transatlantic routes.

By the end of 1966, British Eagle International Airways had carried 944,488 passengers, filling 76% of its passenger capacity and generating a turnover of £15.5 million (£286 million in 2020 Sterling) with an operating profit of £384,000. In comparison, in 1963, Bamberg had carried 153,000 passengers and made a loss of £80,000 (British Eagle, 1968). Interviewed in the 18 April 1968 edition of *Flight International* for the 20th anniversary of Bamberg's airline endeavours, the publication asked if there is one event that "gives you outstanding pleasure?" Bamberg replied: "I think my greatest satisfaction has been to see the rebirth and development of Eagle since that very difficult period in 1963 after the formation of BOAC-Cunard."

While Bamberg was fighting for his airline in the 1968 ATLB deliberations, another government committee was working on a report, commonly referred to as *The Edwards Report*, which would be published in May of that year. The 394-document's full title was: *British air transport in the seventies. Report of the Committee of Inquiry into Civil Air Transport* and the committee's Chairman was Sir Ronald Stanley Edwards. Sir Ronald was Chairman of the pharmaceutical giant, the Beecham Group, and a professor of economics at the London School of Economics. The report would lead to the Civil Aviation Act of 1971 which ended the ATLB and created today's Civil Aviation Authority (CAA).

In the history of UK air transport, government committees had rarely been good news for independent airlines. Edwards' terms of reference were, "To inquire into the ... methods of regulating competition and of licensing currently employed; and to propose with due attention to other forms of transport in this country what changes may be desirable ..." Successive government reports on the airline industry had seen government-forced mergers creating the first British Airways, Imperial Airways, BOAC, British European Airways, British United Airways and finally the second British Airways, which ultimately absorbed British Caledonian.

In June 1968, while the Edwards Report was being debated in Parliament, Bamberg received bad news; the ATLB would not grant licences for scheduled services across the North Atlantic. The ATLB Chairman in 1968, and indeed from 1961 until 1970 was Sir Daniel Jack. The University of Durham David Dale Professor of Economics was awarded a CBE in 1951 and knighted in 1966.[12] His Board's decision meant BOAC would remain the only British scheduled carrier on the North Atlantic for the foreseeable future. BOAC had appealed the Cunard-Eagle transatlantic licence before and now in 1968 it had won again.

In April 1968, Bamberg's British Eagle had 2,500 employees, and a fleet consisting of one Boeing 707-365C, one Boeing 707-138B, five British Aircraft Corporation (BAC) One-Eleven 300s, 12 Bristol Type 175 Britannias, four Vickers Viscount 700s and two Boeing 707s were on order. But, in March 1968, British Eagle's UK government Far East trooping contract ended, as did its migrant contract with Australia's government. Those reversals, including the transatlantic licence denial, would have a devastating impact. The start of October 1968 saw redundancy notices to 418 employees in London and Liverpool Speke and British Eagle's Speke maintenance base was closed.[13]

Despite the problems, British Eagle applied to the ATLB for permission to extend its 14-day holiday flights to the Bahamas to include Jamaica. But, at the beginning of November 1968, the ATLB actually revoked British Eagle's licence for London-Bermuda/Nassau inclusive tours altogether. An inclusive tour was essentially a package holiday, the flight and hotel were included in the price. BOAC had applied for the revocation in July claiming British Eagle malpractice. Still, Bamberg hoped to start a Luxembourg service by year's end, but it would never come. By mid-1968, Eagle was forecasting a loss of more than £500,000 for that year, in part, caused by the Labour government's £50 limit on money taken out of the country for holidays. This policy led to cancellations for British Eagle in its inclusive-tour holiday market of more than £1 million.

Despite this forecast loss, Bamberg had been seeking refinancing and Eagle could have been helped by one of its lenders, Hambros Bank. But the revocation of the Caribbean inclusive-tour licence saw Hambros withdraw its support. As of 7 November, British Eagle International Airlines went into liquidation with debts of some £5.5 million.[14] In a House of Commons debate on 7 November, the then President of the government's Board of Trade, Labour party Member of Parliament for Grimsby, Anthony Crosland, said: "I much regret that one of the oldest and most respected of British independent airlines, British Eagle, with its charter company, Eagle Aviation Limited, has had to cease operations."[15]

What distorted the airline market and would see so many airlines go out of business, including Bamberg's, was the dominant market position of the two state owned airlines, BOAC and BEA. The origins of these airlines dates back to the early 1920s and decisions made by a Conservative government. While BOAC was created through the merger of Imperial Airways and the first British Airways (1935–1940), Imperial itself had been a creation of Sir Stanley Baldwin's Conservative government of 1923 (the Conservative win in the 1922 General Election had relegated the Liberals to third-party status). The Conservative Party went on to spend all but eight of the next forty-two years as the largest party in Parliament, and Labour emerged as the main opposition).

A government committee led by the banker Sir Herbert Hambling was set up in 1923 to examine the airline industry. His conclusion — the need for a merger of many airlines into one — would be repeated in the decades to come to the detriment of the UK airline industry and Bamberg. The anti-competitive, state-directed policy for the aviation industry would repeatedly kill those who innovated and forced the merger of airlines that could have become world leaders. For the UK aviation industry, this act of forced mergers was the original sin the government would repeatedly commit. Why governments accepted these recommendations, and repeated that sin, has origins with the railways and shipping industries whose aristocratic owners saw aviation as a threat.

The Hambling committee sat prior to the second UK national election in 13 months. A year after the 1922 election, another countrywide ballot was held in December 1923. The second election was called by Baldwin because he wanted a people's mandate after Andrew Bonar Law, who had led the Conservatives to power in the November 1922 election, resigned due to ill health. The 1922 election had seen a huge change in the British parliamentary make-up as most of the 105 Irish seats ceased to exist that year. This was because 26 of Ireland's 32 counties had formed the Irish Free State in 1922 after the negotiated withdrawal of the British.

Baldwin's election did not go well, and the majority achieved by Bonar Law was reduced, but the Conservatives still won and implemented Hambling's recommendations: principally that the main UK airlines should be merged and the new entity be given a £1 million (£62 million in 2020 prices) subsidy over ten years.[16] The government accepted the recommendation and in March 1924 Imperial Airways Limited was created. The four companies being merged were British Marine Air Navigation, which operated flying boats, Daimler Airway, Handley Page Transport and Instone Air Line.

Hambling's report stated that the new airline formed out of the merger would be "a commercial organisation run entirely on business lines with a privileged position with regard to air transport subsidies". It also stated: "The government should not exercise any direct control over the activities of the Company".[17] The new Imperial Airways had Sir Eric Geddes as Chairman, Lieutenant-Colonel (retired) Frank Searle as Managing Director, and a former Daimler Airway colleague of Searle's, Major George Woods Humphrey, as General Manager on the Board.

The first British Airways had been formed in November 1935 from the amalgamation of three other airlines: United Airways, Hillman's Airways and Spartan Airlines. The finance came from banking and aeronautical interests closely allied with the railways and coach operators.

On 3 September 1939, fifteen years after the creation of Imperial Airways and just four years after another merger formed the first British Airways, both airlines came under state control. The slow slide to further mergers, justified by the outbreak of World War Two, began soon after British Airways was formed. In 1935, the Interdepartmental Committee on International Air Communications under the chairmanship of the Permanent Secretary to the Treasury, Sir Warren Fisher, was set up to examine UK aviation. It became known as the Fisher committee.

British Airways and Whitehall Securities Director and Conservative party Parliamentarian for Thanet, Harold Balfour, was a prominent critic of Imperial Airways at the time. The Fisher committee recommended in 1936 that British Airways also be given preferential treatment by the government. This policy of giving preferential treatment to airlines whose owners also had links with the Conservative party would occur again 34 years later. But in the 1930s, Imperial Airways was criticised by Balfour and others for its lack of new aircraft and connections with the railways through Railway Air Services, whose personnel were supplied by Imperial Airways.[18]

However, with the strains of World War Two, the outcome was probably not what the boards of Imperial and British Airways had expected in 1936. The two airlines were instead combined into a single organisation for the war effort. Sir John Reith, a former Director-General of the BBC, had been appointed to run Imperial. Reith replaced George Woods Humphrey, a man with 20 years' experience in the UK airline industry. Reith (who applied when he saw the job advertised in his exclusive St James club) would be one of many examples of Establishment individuals with no aviation background being given the leadership of the British airline industry.[19]

Reith was not Chairman of Imperial Airways, which became BOAC shortly after, for very long — he was only in the position until January 1940 when he left to become Minister for Information. During World War Two, BOAC operated under the orders of the UK's Secretary of State for Air, initially as a transport service for the Royal Air Force. Throughout the War they operated transatlantic services plus a network of African and Middle Eastern routes centred on Cairo.

When World War Two ended, however, commercial aviation began to grow exponentially in ways few could have predicted, and Harold Bamberg was one of several entrepreneurs who saw an opportunity to build a new independent airline. Much of that growth was created by remarkable geopolitical events, the first of which became known as The Berlin Airlift.

Avro Tudor C5, G-AKBZ *Star Falcon* of British South American Airways at Wunstorf aerodrome in 1948 during the Berlin Airlift. In the background is Eagle Aviation's Handley Page Halifax, G-ALEF *Red Eagle*. Image from Imperial War Museum.

2 The End of One War

On 24 June 1948, Soviet armed forces blockaded all the routes, road, rail and water, into Berlin's areas not controlled by the Russians, nothing could go in or out with the Russian's approval. Berlin was far from the western Allies' sectors in occupied Germany. The country had been carved into four areas. The Soviet sector stretched from the northwesternmost tip of what was then Czechoslovakia along a meandering line up through Germany to where the German, Polish border meets the Baltic Sea.

Germany's historical capital, Berlin, was nearer Poland than it was the dividing line between Soviet occupied Germany and the German territory controlled by the US, France and the UK. Berlin was also divided into four sectors between the Soviet Union on the eastern side of the city and the UK, France and the US in its West. Berlin's Tempelhof Airport, a monument of Nazi architecture, was in the US sector and on 26 June the US launched Operation Vittles, which the UK joined. The Allies also imposed their own counter-blockade, restricting trade with East Germany.[20] The UK military had its own operation, PLAINFARE, which began on 28 June 1948, and Bamberg's freighters would be a part of it.

The UK-US airlift transported more than 2.3 million tons of freight by almost 278,000 flights from 26 June

1948 to 6 October 1949 for West Berlin's population of more than 2.5 million people. Of this, the British lift carried 542,236 tons, of which the RAF carried 394,509 tons while the remaining 147,727 tons were delivered by Bamberg's Eagle Aviation and the other airlines. Eagle Aviation itself delivered 7,300 tons over 1,054 sorties from 26 August 1948 to 15 August 1949.[21] British aircraft, in total, carried 241,000 tons of food, 165,000 tons of coal and 92,000 tons of wet fuel, which was entirely flown in by civil aircraft.

The British aircraft also carried 35,000 tons of freight, including 12,800 tons of economic goods, and 131,436 passengers out of the city. British aircraft flew more than 32 million miles, consumed over 35 million gallons of Avgas and spent over 200,000 hours in the air. They helped sustain a city of more than two and a half million inhabitants for many months including through the winter.[22] The Soviet Union ended the blockade after 10 months and 16 days, on 11 May 1949. The Allies airlift, however, continued until October with about 1,000 daily landings to ensure West Berlin's warehouses were full in the event of another action by the Soviets.

By late 1948, Bamberg's first Halifax was flying full time to Berlin via Wunstorf, near Hanover in northern Germany for the Allies' air bridge. The demand for airlift was so great that Bamberg bought his second Halifax, the red one from Handley Page, which he named *Red Eagle*. In early 1949 he purchased two more. With a fleet of four Halifaxes, the Allies' air bridge stopover would soon move to Fuhlsbüttel near Hamburg, further north than Hanover. *Red Eagle* suffered a mishap on landing at Fuhlsbüttel when its undercarriage collapsed damaging a propeller, but no one was injured. The cargo was undamaged, and the aircraft was repaired and continued to fly.

With no end in sight for the air lift at the start of 1949, Bamberg had purchased three Avro 685 York aircraft by the start of the year.[23] The Yorks were designed to be transport aircraft with a new square cross section for a larger internal volume and a high wing mounted on a blocky fuselage. While the York used some parts that originated with the famed Avro Lancaster bomber, the tail had three vertical fins, rather than the Lancaster's two, and was powered by four Rolls-Royce Merlin engines.

The Handley Page Halifax had flown before the Avro Lancaster, as the second of the four-engine heavy bombers to enter service with the RAF. As the war progressed, the Halifax became overshadowed by the Lancaster which appeared capable of carrying ever-increasing bomb loads without serious degradation of its performance. Both aircraft had the forward gunner position in a transparent bubble and four engines along with the double vertical fin tail. While the Lancaster became the iconic World War Two bomber, the Halifax would have a secondary role in civil transport and Bamberg's airline was one of several that came to rely on it.

The Berlin airlift was a perfect start for Bamberg, providing consistent work for that key period whenever any business begins, along with a reliable revenue stream and time to plan for expansion into other charter markets. While Bamberg was helping to keep Berlin fed and supplied for any possible future Soviet blockades, the Labour government elected in 1949 was drawing up legislation that would stack the rules against independent airlines for decades to come. The Air Corporation Act 1949 would be given Royal Assent and become law on 16 December, two and a half months after the end of Operation PLAINFARE on 6 October 1949.

The independent airlines were not going to be recognised for what they had done for the Berlin airlift by the Labour government of Clement Attlee. Prime minister Attlee's Air Corporation Act ignored the independents and gave a monopoly of scheduled services to the then state airlines, British European Airways (BEA) and British Overseas Airways Corporation (BOAC). Despite the fact that during the Berlin airlift British airlines had transported almost double the total tonnage of mail and cargo carried by all UK civil aircraft on scheduled services over the previous 23 years; the independent airlines would essentially be ghettoed into the charter sector.

The very month that the 1949 Air Corporation Act became law, Hunting Air Travel lost its lucrative contract with the Overseas Food Corporation to BOAC. Between November 1948 and October 1949 Hunting had carried 2,000 passengers between London and East Africa for the Overseas Food Corporation. What would help the independent airlines, Eagle Aviation included, was where practicality impinged on ideology. The reality was that the government was finding it difficult to raise the capital needed for the rebuilding of the economy in the wake of the devastation of World War Two. The need to fund Attlee's new Welfare State programmes did not help either.

The limits of government spending meant the state-owned airlines could not expand fast enough to maintain all the domestic routes which they had taken over in 1946 and 1947 through the 1946 Civil Aviation Act. Flying in the face of the policy of state-owned airlines exclusively operating scheduled services was the fact that there was more demand than BOAC and BEA could meet. In July 1947, while Operation PLAINFARE was in full swing, the Parliamentary Secretary to the Ministry of Civil Aviation, George Lindren, had said: "It would be at variance with the Act to allow charter companies to run scheduled services where the Corporations were unwilling to do so." But the reality was somewhat different.

The *volte face* less than a year later was possible because of a clause in the 1946 Civil Aviation Act which created BEA. Clause 14, sub-section four, of the 1946 Act, was originally intended to cover the need for either BEA or BOAC to contract out to another airline for a temporary period, or for emergency operations — another Berlin airlift perhaps. So, two years after the Labour government's Civil Aviation Act, a central tenet of it was being undermined by the very same government. The principle of a government monopoly in British scheduled air transport ceased to exist as it allowed, albeit only slightly, the participation of private operators in the provision of regular air services.

By May 1948, the government had decided to allow a number of independent airlines to operate certain regular services as "associates" of BEA. Initially this was only for an experimental period of six months, but this was later extended to two years. It should have been a boom time for the independent airlines: guaranteed Berlin freight charters and domestic UK scheduled services. The independents however did not negotiate these "associate agreements" with the Ministry; the deal was whatever BEA dictated to them. The associate agreements were drawn up by BEA and they alone defined exactly how the services were to be run.

During the initial trial period associate airlines were

restricted to routes on which the demand was seasonal, such as trips to holiday resorts and short-distance ferry services. The Welsh airline Cambrian Airways became the first independent to be awarded a licence for the route between Cardiff and Weston-super-Mare — a route previously closed down by BEA as uneconomic. The parcelling out of these associate agreements, however, would get some government oversight when the government announced that the Air Transport Advisory Council (ATAC), under the Chairmanship of Lord Terrington, was to consider each application for a licence and recommend acceptance.

Lord Terrington would be a dominant figure in aviation regulation until his death in 1961. He remained the head of ATAC and went on to become head of its successor organisation which was created by the 1960 Civil Aviation (Licensing) Act. Like Beveridge, Lord Terrington was a Liberal Party House of Lords member, but unlike Beveridge, was a hereditary peer: the 3rd Baron Terrington (real name Horace Woodhouse). By May 1948, he licensed 20 charter companies to operate domestic scheduled services on 11 routes and inclusive tours on 13.

As if the terms of the agreements were not bad enough with BEA's dictation, the government took the view that the ATAC should have the right to fix the maximum and minimum fares to be charged. It probably helped that BOAC Director Sir Gerard d'Erlanger was a member of the ATAC Council. Worse still, the fares should not be less than those charged by the state-owned airlines — except by agreement with them — which was unlikely. In 1949, with the boost to the UK aviation industry of the Berlin airlift, the ATAC received a total of 231 applications for licences. It recommended that 24 independent airlines should be given BEA associate status for one year for 59 scheduled services and 26 inclusive tours. Fifty-seven scheduled services were approved by the Minister.

The scheduled services and inclusive tours were not enough to help the many independents sustained by the Berlin airlift. In early 1950, Eagle Aviation received its BEA associate agreement for UK scheduled services. It was to operate between Bovingdon and three other destinations, Whitchurch near Bristol, Plymouth on the south coast and Lands End in Cornwall. Eagle had asked for a London, Bristol, Cardiff route but was only given London to Bristol, which made it economically unviable. Lord Douglas' associate agreements were poisoned chalices, politically expedient for the politics of the places BEA had abandoned but its predecessors had served. Bamberg's entry into the scheduled service market ended as soon as it began.

Bamberg had set up a travel agent which would also organise general shipping for freight. Air Liaison Limited would sell tickets and book freight for all the major airlines as well as Eagle. It had been set up in 1948 as an associate company of Eagle Aviation with an office in Birmingham and in Eagle's headquarters in Clarges Street, in the upper-class Mayfair quarter of London. Like Eagle, Bamberg was the Managing Director of Air Liaison. It was a small beginning as a travel agent, a side to the airline industry that Bamberg would later grow into a significant UK tourism market player.

In April of that year, Bamberg moved Eagle Aviation's operating base to Luton, Bedfordshire and its grass runway, leaving Aldermaston airport behind. At the same time, Bamberg bought Luton Flying Club. The clubhouse had a lounge with a bar and a billiards table, bedrooms, offices, briefing rooms and was single storey.

Bamberg hired ex-military pilots and trained his fleet's crews there using a variety of aircraft. In 1953, he sold 50% of the Club to his Deputy Chief Engineer who later purchased the other 50%.

While Bamberg's head office remained in Clarges street, Eagle Aviation would be based at Luton for the next two and a half years. While the Halifaxes had been used for fruit and vegetables and other cargo, it was the Avro 685 York aircraft that enabled Bamberg to move heavy freight, including ships' propeller shafts. One of them alone — flown from Thornaby in northern England to Amsterdam — weighed nine tons and was 19 feet long.

In September, Bamberg expanded his aviation business again buying Trent Valley Aviation which had been operating freight services and scheduled passenger flights from Nottinghamshire in the English midlands. Bamberg relocated the company's aircraft to Luton, one of which was a Douglas DC-3 Dakota. The aircraft's first charter flight for Eagle Aviation was to take Rolls Royce employees on a day trip from Bovingdon to Paris. In October, Bamberg announced that a new associate agreement had been granted. This one was for one year, would start in 1951, and was to fly between Tollerton, near Nottingham and the island of Jersey in the English Channel. Tollerton was, and still is, a rural village surrounded by farmland. Its population was less than 1,500 people.

With the sort of "agreement" Bamberg had been granted it was no surprise that that by 1950 there was growing dissatisfaction being voiced by the independent airlines. They hated the one-year associate agreements they were being given for the scheduled services and inclusive tours. Unsurprisingly, the independent airlines

An ex-RAF C-47 (Dakota) of Eagle Aviation.

were not able to plan ahead with just twelve-month agreements which made it difficult for them to raise capital to finance the purchase of new equipment. The number of applications for associate agreements fell in 1950 to 177.

The ATAC recommended 80 more long scheduled services and 16 inclusive tours and Minister approved 76 of the scheduled service routes, but they were still one-year agreements. Eventually the complaints were heard and the government and BEA agreed to an extension to a maximum of five years. But that was not enough. In 1951 the ATAC reported: "It has... become even more apparent that there is only a limited field in which independent companies can hope to operate associated services economically under the present arrangements... The experiences of the past year suggest to the Council that the independent companies are unlikely to seek an increase in the number of scheduled services under associate agreements with the Corporations, unless they can be given longer tenure and better opportunities to plan their operations on a basis giving more economical use of their aircraft."

In March 1951, British Aviation Services' Silver City airline won a small victory and gained a five-year licence for cross-channel air-ferry services. Finally, an independent airline had obtained the security that most of the privately-owned carriers had been demanding. Silver City had been started in 1946 and its first Managing Director was former RAF Air Commodore, Griffith "Taffy" Powell. He hired ex-RAF people to run Silver City. Following the 1951 electoral victory of the Conservatives later that year the five-year licence was extended to cover ten years. Vehicle-ferry services were the type of activity that by the early 1950s both the Labour and Conservative Parties saw as most suitable for the independent airlines.[24]

In 1951, Bamberg's Eagle Aviation was operating three Avro York transport aircraft, a Handley Page Halifax aircraft and the Douglas C-47 Dakota; having completed the move from Aldermaston to Luton by late August 1950. Bamberg was specialising in heavy freight loads and had transported a second ship's propeller shaft in July 1950 from Amsterdam to Plaisance, Mauritius in the Pacific Ocean. At this time, the Dakota aircraft, however, was not being used by Bamberg, it was being flown by Air Malta for seven months operating a schedule service to Cairo, Catania and Rome.[25] But in 1950 a new major source of income was to arrive for Bamberg — government trooping contracts — charter flights for transporting British soldiers and airmen.

Before World War Two, and for some time after it, troop transport had largely been a sea going exercise, shipping personnel around the British Empire.

Military aircraft had had a growing role but the first public statement about the use of civil aircraft in this role appears to have been in August 1950. The then Labour government's Secretary of State for Air, Arthur Henderson MP, referred to it in a speech at Plymouth. Henderson said that charter aircraft were already carrying Royal Auxiliary Air Force squadron personnel, and other units, to their training camps in different parts of the UK and Germany.

Transporting troops by air was regarded at the time as an experimental, marginal exercise. The vast majority of servicemen were being transported by sea. Henderson told the House of Commons on 6 March 1951: 'I think that it can be regarded as money well spent, not only because of the value of the service received, but also because it has helped to maintain a valuable and considerable potential represented by the civil aviation industry'.[26] Bamberg's relationship with trooping contracts began in October 1950 when Eagle Aviation was chartered by the UK's Air Ministry to fly personnel to Iwakuni, Japan.

Later in 1951 the number of trooping charter flights was increased substantially. The Air Ministry awarded Hunting Air Travel a contract in mid-1951 which was claimed at the time to be the largest passenger contract ever awarded to an independent transport operator. Hunting Air Travel was owned by the Hunting family whose immense wealth came from oil. The contract was for carrying armed services personnel and their families between the UK and Malta and Gibraltar, amounting to 50,000 passengers a year.

The UK held a General Election on 25 October 1951 which returned the Conservative Party and Sir Winston Churchill to 10 Downing Street. Within a month an even larger trooping contract was placed. In November 1951, Airwork, which was owned by aristocrats, was awarded a much larger contract for trooping flights between the UK and the Middle East. It was valued at more than £1.25 million (£40 million in 2020 prices). In the 1950s, Airwork's owners included Lord Guinness, Lord Poole, Lord Vestey and Lord Cowdray, the richest man in Britain at the time.

In 1951, Eagle had more than 12 pilots, new aircraft and 100 staff, and were flying all over the world from Luton, and elsewhere including Blackbushe Airport in Hampshire. Blackbushe exists today and serves general aviation aircraft.[27] Operating mainly from Luton, Eagle Aviation was booming and Japan, Hong Kong, Delhi, Teheran, Bombay, Bahrain and Gothenburg, were all either destinations or waypoints between Europe and the rest of the world for Eagle Aviation. From August, Eagle Aviation had regular contract flights for the Air Ministry.

That year, Bamberg would encounter a man who would not only be a competitor but ultimately suffer the same fate as the German émigré. Frederick 'Freddie' Laker had decided to move out of aircraft parts supply and aircraft sales and into airline services. Laker bought a small airline called Air Charter from Harold Bamberg for £20,000, and was able to use its losses against profits he had made with other businesses and avoid some tax.[28] Laker would be a competitor until 1958 when he sold out to the aristocratic aviation firm Airwork.

Following Bamberg's 1951 sale of his Air Charter business to Laker, Bamberg sold five Avro York aircraft from his fleet to Skyways, which claimed to be the largest European independent airline. Bamberg's Eagle Aviation continued with three Douglas DC-3 'Dakotas'

A Vickers Viking of Eagle Aviation.

(the RAF's name for the aircraft) and three Vickers VC.1 Viking aircraft. Bamberg was also developing a maintenance and repair service after buying in November of that year Aviation Servicing which was based at Blackbushe airport.

Aviation Servicing had been Westminster Aircraft Servicing when its parent company Westminster Airways, also based at Blackbushe airport, had formed it in 1949. One of Eagle's contemporaries, Westminster Airways was started by four members of the House of Commons. When Westminster Airways collapsed, Aviation Servicing was sold to Britavia, having had its name changed in 1951. It continued as Aviation Servicing for another two years until Bamberg renamed it Eagle Aircraft Services. Bamberg would operate flights from Blackbushe for many years.

The start of 1952 saw the end of Eagle's first circumnavigation of the world covering 31,000 miles. On 9 December 1951, a York flew to Iwakuni in Japan and then to Hong Kong where it was fitted with seats.

Two weeks later on 25 December the converted York left Hong Kong with Filipino seamen to go to Brazil. Flying across the Pacific to South America and Porto Alegre in Brazil, the York made the final leg across the Atlantic to complete the circumnavigation, landing in Luton in early January.

In early March, two ex-RAF Dakotas were delivered to Eagle Aviation and another two arrived in April. The fifth year of Eagle Aviation was turning out to be just as successful with the Air Ministry flights, a new market in ferrying student groups to different European cities and taking the Turkish team to the Helsinki Olympics. In August, Bamberg bought two Yorks from BOAC increasing his ownership of the type to six. Freddie Laker leased one of the six Yorks for a month in 1952.

This year would also see the beginning of liveries for Bamberg's aircraft. Several of his fleet, but mainly the Dakotas, were given a white fuselage top and a bare metal underside with a white vertical tail fin. The fin had a British union flag and a red cheatline ran the full length of the fuselage above the windows. A short red cheatline ran from the centre of the aircraft's nose to the just after the first passenger window and showed the name Eagle Aviation Ltd.

That year Eagle Aviation set a record with the longest charter ever caried out by a British operator. The charter covered a distance of 37,000 miles starting with Dusseldorf, then Karachi, then Brazil, via Aden, Khartoum, Kano, Dakar and Natal. From Brazil the flight returned to Karachi and then flew again to Brazil. The two flights were carrying cattle. From Brazil the aircraft went back to Luton. November saw a dramatic departure for Bamberg, he sold his entire York fleet and their associated Air Ministry contracts to Skyways.

The sale was a protest against UK government policy. Despite all the success Eagle Aviation had had, the government policy of ghettoing the independent airlines into the charter market and only giving them the uneconomic UK routes BEA did not want to have to fly was undermining the airline sector. The objections by BOAC and BEA to everything and anything the independent airlines wanted to do was deeply frustrating. The government was no help either and the civil servants were only concerned about BOAC.

The year of 1952 did see the Conservative government introduce its "new deal" for aviation. Under the 1949 civil aviation act, independent airlines had to negotiate an associate agreement with BEA to operate any inclusive tour charters. Inclusive tours means the flight and hotel are included in the one price. The new deal lifted this restriction and the independents simply had to show that any inclusive tour services they operated would not divert a significant number of passengers from existing scheduled services, but they had to apply to the ATAC for licenses. The State airlines, BOAC and BEA, were also prevented from retaining obsolescent aircraft specifically for charter purposes — diminishing their capacity for this sector.

As 1952 drew to a close, Bamberg bought the Blackbushe based Aviation Servicing Company from Britavia. This purchase led Eagle to leave Luton and operate his remaining fleet of aircraft from Blackbushe with a focus on European freight. Crewsair had gone bust about this time and Bamberg bought the liquidated firm's Vickers Viking aircraft. His fleet was growing again and back in double digits.

In December 1952, Eagle Aviation operated two tours for United States military personnel stationed in Europe.

Maybe Bamberg was inspired by the UK trooping contracts but both tours used the Dakotas, aircraft the US, and UK, servicemen would have known well from their war time use for transport. One tour departed from Milan, Italy, Lyon and Perpignan in France, Spain's San Sebastian and Zagreb, capital of Croatia. While Bamberg was making the most of every opportunity and growing his airline, the Soviet Union would deliver another good prospect.

Russian dictator Joseph Stalin died on 5 March 1953. He had dominated the Soviet Union since 1928, when he became Communist party General Secretary following Lenin's death in 1924, and had occupied a large part of central Europe from 1945.[29] Stalin's attitude to Yugoslavia had been hostile even though both countries were officially socialist. The month Stalin died, Bamberg's Eagle was granted a seven-year licence to operate a scheduled passenger service between London (Blackbushe) and Yugoslavia's capital of Belgrade via Munich.

An early industry record for Eagle Aviation, it became the first post-World War Two airline to provide an international scheduled service for both tourists and businessmen with its Yugoslav route.[30] The London-Munich-Belgrade service was also the airline's first scheduled passenger route. Despite the 1949 ACA, the UK state-owned airlines were not the first to fly to the heart of the Socialist Federal Republic of Yugoslavia; a country which would become a popular tourist destination for Western Europeans.

After Stalin's death, the Soviet regime began what it called an "new course," which meant a less belligerent stance towards its neighbours. The normalisation of relations between the Soviet Union and Yugoslavia became a strategic step for the new Soviet foreign policy.[31] For Bamberg, this meant an opportunity that would not face geopolitical interference and in May 1953 Eagle ran a proving flight to Belgrade in Yugoslavia's Serbia with 26 passengers including members of the press, Yugoslav diplomats and travel agents.

The scheduled passenger service between London and Belgrade was another symbol of Yugoslavia's unique status in a continent divided between capitalism and communism; where Belgrade worked closely with Russia's Warsaw Pact nations and promoted socialism but also traded with the West. Eagle used one of its new Vickers Viking aircraft and the flight left Blackbushe arriving in Munich on time later that day where lunch was served. Continuing on to Zemun Airport, now called Belgrade Nikola Tesla Airport, in Belgrade, the flight had taken eight hours.[32]

On 6 June 1953, amid much ceremony, Eagle Aviation started its first scheduled passenger service on what it called its Air Link to Yugoslavia, which it would operate with Vickers Vikings. The Viking had been designed as an interim civil airliner for BEA with up to 21 passengers and four crew including the cabin steward. A twin-engine short-range airliner, the design made use of the outer wings, engine nacelles and undercarriage of the Vickers Aircraft Wellington bomber. The Wellington bombers had been used against German targets in daylight raids in the Balkans in 1944 and 1945.

Aviation journal *Flight* participated in the 6 June Blackbushe to Belgrade inaugural flight and reported on it in its 19 June edition. "At 10.15 the weather promised to be fine as the Viking rose from Blackbushe into a warm blue sky, cleared the London Control Zone, and set course for Munich at 9,500ft. Coastal cloud over

Dover and Dunkirk preceded more scattered cumulus as Roubaix, the Ardennes, and Luxembourg passed below. The typical closely-striped curves of agricultural patchwork — slashed here and there by the NATO airstrips — then disappeared from view as we entered a forest of magnificent cloud formations. As we crossed the Rhine, Stewardess Tuffy — an Australian, previously with T.A.A. — began to serve lunch. Normally, a crew of four will be carried; on this particular trip R/OrT Denby was receiving familiarization training as an additional crew member. Munich was our mid-way stop, after three hours 12 minutes flying time. Here the refuelling and passenger-handling arrangements — a B.E.A. responsibility by contract with Eagle — were supervised by Mr. D. C. L. Oxley, the Corporation's station manager there. Passengers waited in the large, impressive, red stone terminal building as the aircraft chores were completed; a red Swiss Jungmann taxied in and out briskly to contrast with the Skymaster, Viking, Dakota and Convair movements of the big airlines, and at 14:53 hrs *Sir Henry Morgan* took off again, on what was, perhaps, the more interesting leg of its journey. The white-topped Austrian Alps appeared as an imposing backcloth as we approached Salzburg at 11,500 ft. Then we flew on towards Graz between a text-book selection of fascinating clouds above and the awesome close view of the mountains themselves below, including the 9,800 ft peak of Mount Dachstein, to starboard. A starboard turn at Graz pointed the aircraft towards Jugoslavia and the Zagreb beacon, after which came a turn to port and the final long straight leg to Belgrade. We passed over slightly hilly farmland and isolated communities, with here and there the colour-splash of newly built houses and farm buildings, before the ground was masked by a thick layer of strato-cumulus, through which the letdown to Belgrade was made. Final approach to Zemun airport was along the line of the Sava river."

Belgrade airport, located West of the city, had a control tower that sat at one end of a long two-storey administrative building. On top of the control tower was the radar. Next to the administrative building was the large free-standing terminal with a roof whose corners pointed up and outwards.[33] Belgrade airport staff and Bamberg's passengers would have seen a new livery.

Not hugely different to the one adopted in 1952, the fuselage cheatline had a white line added, the fin gained the Eagle symbol or the civil air ensign, and the name on the nose was shortened to just Eagle. The British civil air ensign was an equivalent of the Red Ensign for merchant ships.

In the 1950s, Belgrade was much like many European cities, reconstruction after World War Two saw the rise of residential blocks for high density housing, office blocks and wide streets for the many trams and buses. The flights to the country would contribute to Yugoslavia's economic links with the West that saw its citizens able to buy Western convenience goods; a policy that kept Yugoslavia and the Soviet Union at loggerheads until both these states fell in the 1990s.

While Yugoslavia was ruled by Croatian born Communist party leader and Yugoslav President, Josip Bro (also known simply as Tito, a pseudonym he had adopted decades earlier), with his socialist five-year plans, Bamberg and his fellow independent airlines had already experienced the equally interventionist bureaucratic decisions of UK governments. By November 1953, the Conservative government was raising the levels of borrowing for BOAC and BEA.

BOAC could increase its borrowing limit by 30% from £60 million to £80 million. In sterling today, according to the Bank of England inflation calculator, £80 million would be worth £2.2 billion. BEA also received a nice increase of 75% from £20 million to £35 million; worth £999 million in 2020 prices.

Eagle were known for their friendly cabin crew.

3 Growing Eagle

At the start of the 1950s, Bamberg's Eagle Aviation was still too small to bother the state-run airlines and, while it partially became an associate airline of BEA, most of the routes were essentially uneconomic. While Eagle Aviation had grown, thanks in part to the Berlin airlift, Bamberg's company was still very much a charter freight operation as the decade began. From Aldermaston to Bovingdon, to Luton and then Blackbushe, with a growing, then shrinking, then growing again fleet of aircraft, the relocation to Blackbushe would see the emphasis of the airline change. Passengers would be the new mantra and for this Bamberg invested in Vickers Viking and Douglas Dakota aircraft.

For Bamberg, the 1950s were about developing scheduled services from Blackbushe and operating these alongside the all-important trooping flights. This was going to finally happen in 1953 after persistent lobbying. The associate agreements had been a gaping hole in the principle of the Labour party state airline policy foisted on the independents. The election of the Conservative party in 1951 had at least presented an opportunity to further widen the hole. Two years later, in 1953, that persistent lobbying saw new government regulations allowing the independents to apply for scheduled service licenses. However, the obstacle was that the service could not overlap with a BOAC or BEA service.

In March 1953, Bamberg announced that Eagle had been awarded a seven-year licence to fly a London to Belgrade, Yugoslavia route, via Munich and the first flight took place in May. That summer also saw the first Eagle inclusive tour flights from Manchester and Birmingham to Palma on behalf of Sir Henry Lunn, the UK travel agents. Eagle Aviation's reach would extend far beyond Europe that year. Iraqi Airways had problems with its Vickers Viking fleet and asked Bamberg to help it maintain its schedules, such was the worldwide reputation Eagle Aviation was garnering.

Servicing aircraft was another key part of Eagle's growing business activity, an area of work Bamberg had invested in when he had bought Aviation Servicing in 1952. On 17 July 1953, Aviation Servicing was renamed Eagle Aircraft Services. While it offered third party servicing, its main role was maintaining Eagle's large Viking fleet. Eagle's Chief Engineer at the time was Don Peacock who would go on to found Monarch Airlines which would operate for 50 years from 1967 until 2017 when it collapsed. Bamberg was also getting more involved in aircraft trading, buying and selling them in the UK and abroad. Eagle Aircraft Services was the vehicle for this. In 1953, Bamberg took a bank loan of £420,000 and purchased fourteen Vickers Viking aircraft from the state airline BEA.

For the trooping contract flights these Vikings were given the name Troopmaster and when used on civilian services they were promoted as Mayfair Vikings. Having served Sir Henry Lunn, Bamberg tried to interest the giant travel agency Thomas Cook & Son in package holidays using chartered Eagle Vikings. Having no luck there, he bought enough of a share in the Sir Henry Lunn travel agency chain to become its Chairman and

Managing Director. Early in 1955 Bamberg borrowed more money from the bank and bought Sir Henry Lunn outright.

Bamberg's Eagle Aircraft Services firm converted several of the 14 Vikings to a thirty-seven-seat high-density layout. While Eagle Aviation had carried out the airline's first scheduled service to Yugoslavia, it would be Eagle Airways and the Vikings that would become the purely passenger business. Eagle Airways Limited came into existence on 1 July 1953 and launched a scheduled service to Gothenburg, Sweden, via Denmark. The 29 October saw a Viking fly the first service from Blackbushe. Bamberg's American marketing experience had taught him a few tricks and for the inaugural Gothenburg flight the winner of the 1953 Miss Sweden competition, Ulla Sandklef, was on the flight for media publicity.

The following year, 1954, saw continued advances for Bamberg's growing Eagle empire. On the 1 January, Bamberg submitted an application to the UK government for inclusive tour licenses to Copenhagen, Frankfurt, Lisbon, Nice, Stockholm, Tangier, Vienna and Munich. The success of the Belgrade scheduled service also led Eagle to apply for intermediate traffic stops at Strasbourg, Graz and Linz. Bamberg took every opportunity to expand Eagle's network in the face of BOAC and BEA monopolies on so many routes. At the end of March, three Eagle Vikings and a Dakota were sent to Gibraltar, but not for an inclusive tour. The SS *Empire Windrush*, while bringing wounded soldiers home from the Far East, had caught fire and sunk in the Mediterranean, and the aircraft were needed to bring the troops home. She was the same *Windrush* whose name would become a modern icon for bringing some of the first West Indian immigrants to Britain during the early 1950s. Seventy years later, they are still known as the *Windrush* generation (in 2018 many of the original *Windrush* immigrants were wrongly detained, denied legal rights, threatened with deportation, and in at least 83 cases wrongly deported from the UK by the Home Office). Over two days Eagle operated seven flights to return the troops and ship's crew to the UK. Eagle's help with the servicemen's return led to the airline being awarded a two-year trooping contract for ferrying military personnel and their families from Blackbushe to Rhodesia.

On 1 May 1954, Eagle started another military contract, the Canal Zone Troops Leave Scheme. The Canal in question was Suez, the channel of water that runs through Egypt connecting the Mediterranean and the Gulf of Suez which leads to the Red Sea. A special summer leave scheme had been created to allow all those who were half-way through a year-long deployment to a violent Egypt to take 10 days leave in Cyprus. While two Eagle Viking's were helping besieged soldiers take leave, Bamberg's airline was delivering mail and newspapers in the UK due to a railway strike. Railwaymen in the western region of British Railways had gone on strike in May, the same month the Vikings had started flying to Egypt. Eagle Aviation Vikings and Dakota aircraft were providing an emergency airlift for the mail and newspapers for several weeks with night flights from Northolt northwest of London to Cardiff in Wales and Exeter in southwest England.

In September 1954, Eagle found itself again responding to a demand caused by industrial action. A dock strike had left cargo stranded across the UK with the docks full of products going nowhere. Along with a number of other airlines, Eagle helped transport the goods across Europe from Amsterdam to Gothenburg to Malmo and Paris. The year ended as it had begun, with Bamberg expanding the number of destinations for his airlines. One of his applications was to fly charter flights from Blackbushe to Zurich for the skiing season.

The next year was to feel very familiar with more charter flights, more destinations, more Canal leave scheme work, along with the ongoing trooping contracts, but Eagle was also now involved in air-to-air photography using an Avro Lancaster loaned by the Air Ministry. The aircraft flew at the 1956 Farnborough International Airshow and was even was used by photographers from *Flight* magazine. In 1955 Eagle and a number of other carriers formed the British Independent Air Organisation to lobby government directly on behalf of British independent airlines.

Bamberg was also making the most of the charter market with his outright acquisition of the Sir Henry Lunn travel agency in early 1955. That summer, the Eagle Aviation fleet flew for the Sir Henry Lunn inclusive tour programme and the number of destinations expanded enormously. From Blackbushe, the Vikings, and two Dakotas, flew to Corsica, Klagenfurt, Minorca, Nice, Palma, Turin and Valencia. Tours marketed as Treasures of Italy and Castles in Spain, went to Pisa and San Sebastian, respectively. Bamberg also applied for charters during the winter of 1955 and summer of 1956 on behalf of smaller travel agencies.

Tartan Arrow, See Spain, Co-operative Travel Service, Trans Continental Travel Agency of Jersey, the Workers Travel Association and Wenger Airtours, were the agencies Bamberg submitted charter applications for. The new destinations included, Naples, Cannes,

Basle, Treviso, Bordeaux, Beauvais, Jersey, Perpignan, Barcelona, Milan and the Croatian cities of Rijeka and Zagreb. Wenger Air Tours and the Co-operative Travel Service would become new customers for Eagle. The year saw a new scheduled service too. On 23 May Eagle flew its route proving flight to Innsbruck Austria with a Dakota. The route of the full flight was Blackbushe, Luxembourg, Innsbruck, and return.

In September, Eagle was awarded a £1.25 million two-year contract to transport troops and their families to Cyprus, Gibraltar, Malta, Tripoli, and Fayid in the Canal Zone. The first flight took place in October. Bamberg would secure more miliary contracts in 1956 but this time with foreign governments, France and Argentina. Four Vikings were purchased from BEA, overhauled, converted to the Argentine Air Force's needs, repainted and then delivered to South America. For the French Air Force, it was Dakotas that had to be overhauled.

The "Med Air" contract continued during 1956 and with Bamberg's inclusive tours there were more destinations including Luxembourg, Lyon, La Baule and Zaragoza, Spain. A significant development for Eagle that year was the first international scheduled service from a London airport in direct competition with BEA. On 18 May an Eagle Viking departed from Blackbushe to go to Dinard in Brittany, France to inaugurate this international scheduled service — the first for a UK independent airline. That same month Bamberg secured another trooping contract for West Africa, which previously had been an ad-hoc arrangement. Now it was a one-year contract with a potential 12-month extension.

Almost as glamorous as those destinations, Eagle Airways was involved in film production that year. A Viking bought from Central African Airways was repainted for a fictious airline called Globe Link. The film it was used for, *The Crooked Sky,* would be released in 1957. The one hour 17-minute movie's plot was about a counterfeit ring using an airline to smuggle fake notes into the UK from the United States. The film's two American leads, Wayne Morris and Karin Booth were mainly television actors.[34] The filming took place in the UK at Blackbushe airport.

Even more significant and dramatic than any movie, 1956 saw the rise of a rebellion in Hungary against Soviet Union backed Communist party rule that was brutally crushed. Eagle Airways would help the refugees who would flee Hungary. In June, Hungarians began to protest against the country's regime of the Soviet backed Communist party led by Matyas Rákosi. Moscow had replaced him with Ernő Gerő hoping the protests would end, but they did not. On 23 October 1956, students took to the streets along with workers and the Hungarian army.

As the protests and riots spread, the Soviet leadership agreed with their communist Hungarian counterparts to the formation of a new administration. Its leader would be the more liberal Imre Nagy, a popular communist figure. Nagy wanted to bring in reforms including free elections, the private ownership of farmland, an impartial legal system, an end to Warsaw Pact membership and the total withdrawal of Soviet troops from Hungary. On 1 November, Nagy announced the decision to have free elections and to leave the Warsaw Pact.

Hungary leaving the Warsaw Pact and the total withdrawal of Soviet troops from the country, in the eyes of the Russians, would weaken the defences of their Union of Soviet Socialist Republics. So, Moscow sent its tanks and troops into Hungary to crush the rebellion.[35] The failed uprising and revolution saw thousands of Hungarians flee their country and walking west into Austria. Operating on behalf of the British Red Cross, the first Eagle aircraft to arrive in Vienna was a Viking. It landed on 16 November and flew the refugees to the UK.

Eagle flew regularly between Blackbushe and Vienna or Linz for the next four weeks delivering blankets, food, medical supplies and clothing. Nursing staff were also on the flights to help the refugees. The airlift came to an end on 14 December by which time more than 7,000 people have been evacuated by UK airlines; of which 1,200 were transported by Eagle over 36 flights. While the world's attention was focused on Hungary's rebellion, the leadership of BOAC had quietly changed, an event that would have a significant long-term effect.

In 1956, the leadership of the UK's flagship state-owned airline BOAC changed for the first time since 1940. Bernard Clive Pearson stepped down and on 1 May 1956 Gerard d'Erlanger became Chairman. A Director of the original 1935 British Airways Limited, d'Erlanger had also been appointed to the Board of

Directors of BOAC when it was created 16 years earlier. Pearson, who had been the original BA's Chairman, became the Chairman of BOAC on 1 April 1940 when Imperial Airways and British Airways were merged into the new state flagship airline.[36]

Imperial and BA had been merged under a Conservative government whose prime minister was Neville Chamberlain. In 1956, Pearson would be replaced by d'Erlanger under the Conservative government of Anthony Eden. The significance of this is the fact that Pearson and d'Erlanger represented business interests in rail. The independent airlines meanwhile would see significant investment from shipping firms. The representation of these industries reveals a truth about the business and political machinations that Bamberg and other independents were up against, whether they knew it or not. If they had read the Swinton Plan everything that would happen in the subsequent decades would have been easily understood.

In March 1945, five months before the General Election that year that swept Clement Attlee's Labour party to power, Conservative peer Viscount Swinton, the very first British Minister of Civil Aviation, published his aviation White Paper, known as the Swinton Plan. In 1945, BOAC already existed, and BEA would come to exist the following year. Swinton's plan was to have three state airlines whose investors would underline where the power really lay in the UK airline industry. Swinton's White Paper said: "It is… the essence of the government's plan that those interests concerned in transport by sea [shipping] and by land [rail] should be brought into a real and effective partnership with the organisations which will be responsible for transport by air."

Swinton split the activities of the three corporations into three broad geographical areas. BOAC would be responsible for the North Atlantic and Commonwealth routes, with extensions to China and the Far East. While BOAC was wholly state-owned, shipping companies would be able to be owners of BOAC "subsidiaries" on certain routes and no limit was placed on the shipping firms' participation. Swinton's version of BEA would be partly owned by BOAC, but the other shareholders would be railway companies, sea shipping lines and travel agencies. Swinton's BEA would not have a monopoly and other carriers would be able to develop new routes. Charter services were to be a free-for-all, open competition.

The third state-owned airline, oddly, would be responsible for the development of routes to South America. BOAC would be a shareholder along with the four British shipping companies who in January 1944 had formed British Latin American Airlines Limited.[37] Following their return to government after the war, the victorious Labour party adopted its own BOAC-BEA state-owned airlines arrangement, the leadership of BOAC and BEA still reflected the rail dominance of Conservative party linked airlines.

When Bernard Clive Pearson had been appointed Chairman of BOAC in 1940, the Conservative led national government was appointing someone whose family business, Whitehall Securities, had long standing business links with the rail industry. Great Western Railway and Southern Railway companies were co-owners, with Whitehall Securities, of Channel Islands Airway which became part of the first BA. Imperial Airways also had connections with the rail industry. It had been criticised in Parliament in the 1930s for its connections with the firm Railway Air Services. Imperial Airways' Chairman Sir Eric Geddes and his Managing Director Frank Searle both came from the railway industry.

When Gerard d'Erlanger became BOAC Chairman, after having been on its Board since 1940, his continental family were aristocratic bankers whose own bank was Erlanger & Söhne.[38] They also owned French and German banks and became partners in Whitehall Securities with the Pearsons. The d'Erlanger family's investments through their banks included railway and tramway companies. The d'Erlangers even had a bank called Railway Bank. D'Erlanger's father, Baron Emile Beaumont D'Erlanger, had been Chairman of Channel Tunnel Company in 1911, which like today's Eurotunnel was a cross-channel railway project.[39]

The truth behind the many airline industry deals was that they suited the immensely wealthy railway and shipping families whose ancestors had funded the industrial revolution and built the British Empire. It was events in Europe, however, that would bring more opportunities to Bamberg. As the East-West Cold War grew colder, Eagle would not only land in Belgrade, Yugoslavia, but an Eagle Viking would be the first British civil aircraft to arrive in Moscow since World War Two. From Blackbushe, the flight had taken a party of eleven fashion models to Moscow via Warsaw.

For Bamberg's Eagle Aviation and Eagle Airways, the 1950s were turning out to be a success. The decade had begun with fruit and grown to wider general charter work, trooping flights and inclusive tour charters. Eagle Airways was operating the scheduled services but as Bamberg approached his first decade running an airline tragedy struck. In 1957, British Eagle suffered its first fatal accident in four years of passenger services. Thirty-three people were killed on the night of 1 May when an Eagle Aviation aircraft crashed at Blackbushe airport. It was destroyed while making an emergency return to the airfield having just taken off to fly to Lyons and Idris in Libya.

The UK government's War Office had chartered the flight for troop transport. On 2 May the then Conservative government's Under-Secretary for Air, Charles Ian Orr-Ewing MP announced that a public inquiry would be held. Orr-Ewing was educated at Trinity College, Oxford and he was the seventh generation of his family to be a member of Parliament. He would later become Baron Orr-Ewing of Little Berkhamsted and serve in the House of Lords until his death at the age of 87 in 1999.[40]

The Labour Party, whose policies would always be anti-independent airline, questioned why the state airlines were not transporting troops. Herbert Morrison, Labour parliamentarian for the London seat of Hackney South, criticized the government's "bias against the use of public corporation aircraft." The then prime minister Harold Macmillan said there would be a full public inquiry into the accident and that wider issues would also be examined.[41]

The enquiry found that the crash was caused by pilot error. The Eagle Aviation Vickers Viking aircraft took from Blackbushe at 22:14 hrs local time. Two minutes after take-off the crew reported a port engine failure. The pilot said over the radio just before crash, "I am making a left-hand circuit to come in again." When the aircraft was turning the aircraft was too low and the left wingtip struck the ground and the aircraft crashed inverted into a nearby wood and caught fire.[42] The crash and subsequent fire killed all but one passenger.

The accident did not end the contract Bamberg had with the Air Ministry for the "Med Air" flights and in 1957 Eagle was flying troops to East Africa as well as West Africa. Along with the continuation of the trooping contracts, the year saw Eagle inaugurate new routes to Basle, Hamburg, Ostend and Palma. Manchester became a growing source of passengers for Eagle. While Bamberg had had a maintenance depot at Manchester it was opening a passenger office in the city that led to a high level of demand that summer. This year saw a new livery for Bamberg's fleet. The fuselage top became maroon, not white, the windows had a pearl grey type running over them and the airline name on the aircraft would be either Eagle or Eagle Airways. While the fuselage was maroon, the vertical tail fin was now white.

With Manchester's added demand, Bamberg's 19 Viking aircraft were busy flying from Blackbushe, Heathrow and Manchester with 'high load factors', which means almost all the seats onboard filled with passengers. Eagle aircraft were serving 30 destinations across all the inclusive tours and scheduled services. The growing fleet and destinations led Bamberg to reorganise his companies. First Air Trading Limited was the big change, a new company solely responsible for the lucrative aircraft trading Bamberg had been engaged in for a number of years. The other big change was that Eagle Aviation would formally become the charter and freight firm, while Eagle Airways was the scheduled services outfit.

Another explanation for the reorganisation could have been Bamberg's new horizons, the West Indies and Bermuda. The reason was clear, as David Hedges explained in his book, *The Eagle Years 1948–1968*: "By now it was obvious to all independent operators that the prime domestic and international routes were still reserved for the State Corporations [BOAC and BEA] and if Eagle was to expand further it would have to find a way around the state 'monopoly.'"Bamberg's decision was to form Eagle Airways (Bermuda) Limited.

It was in December 1957 that Eagle Airways (Bermuda) was announced. In the same month, Bamberg formed Eagle Overseas Airways, perhaps a nod to American Overseas Airways where he had worked after the war. Bamberg's Overseas Airways was a market research arm. It studied all aspects of air transport worldwide and the related ancillary services. It would draw up proposals for expansion in the scheduled, charter and inclusive tour markets.

The announcement was that the new airline had been given permission to operate up to 28 services a week from Bermuda to New York and Montreal. Eagle Airways (Bermuda) also announced that it was opening sales offices in New York and Montreal. The year ended with a western hemisphere first for Bamberg's airlines and a total aircraft fleet that had reached 26 aircraft. That Bermuda-New York service was another first of an all-together different kind, the first time a British independent operator was in direct competition with BOAC.

On 28 February 1958, Eagle found itself being praised in Parliament for its cheaper fares. In an air transport development debate, the member of Parliament for Cheadle, William Shepherd, said: "One of the firms which has done more to bring about cheap fares and to bring a new idea to the industry is Eagle Airways, which is perhaps the most enterprising firm in Europe today. It has started with the idea of providing an all-in holiday for almost as low a cost as the price of an ordinary ticket for the air journey. This is an ingenious idea and is an example of how flexible and enterprising a private enterprise company can be. I am convinced that a public corporation would never have conceived this idea. There would have been a dozen reasons why it was impracticable to do it."

By 1958, Eagle Airways had developed a rapidly growing network of scheduled services from London and Manchester and Birmingham to Innsbruck, Luxembourg, Brussels, Majorca and elsewhere. The airline's fleet now had two Viscount 805 aircraft as well as its fleet of 22 Vickers Vikings. The Vikings were used for flights from London to Luxembourg, Innsbruck, Dinard, La Baule, Ostend and Jersey, and from Manchester to Ostend. Services operated with Viscounts were Manchester to Hamburg, Copenhagen, Brussels and Frankfurt and London to Pisa. Eagle used

Eagle engineer working on a Vickers Viking.

Vikings and Viscounts for its Birmingham to Majorca flights. For charter flights and troop transports Bamberg had his company Eagle Aviation.

In mid-April, Eagle Airways' (Bermuda) first aircraft rolled out of the hangar at Blackbushe airport. Above its doors was written "The Bermudan Airline" and its colonial registration. Sunday 20 April saw Bamberg and the Eagle Airways' (Bermuda) aircraft depart for Hamilton, Bermuda's capital city. Prior to their departure, Bamberg held a press conference. He made it crystal clear that the Bermuda airline was about breaking out of the constraints of the British system which gave BOAC and BEA the whip hand. Bamberg's experience with American Overseas Airways would help him in his marketing battle with BOAC and Pan Am in the western hemisphere.

The year saw further progress with the trooping flights. Bamberg still had three Vikings in Nicosia, Cyprus for the Med Air troop flights contract. With the success of the Sir Henry Lunn acquisition Bamberg acquired Poly Travel in early 1958, merging it with the Sir Henry Lunn chain and renaming it Lunn Poly. The summer of 1958 saw Eagle's fourteen-strong Viking fleet operate inclusive tour charters from Blackbushe, Birmingham and Manchester to more than twenty UK and foreign destinations. Dinard, Innsbruck and Luxembourg became scheduled services along with Basle, Jersey, La Baule, and Ostend. In August, Eagle added its first four-engine Douglas DC-6A aircraft to its fleet.[43]

In December 1958, Bamberg set his sights on more international destinations and with lower prices. He applied to the Air Transport Advisory Council for services to UK overseas territories with a ticket price half that of a normal tourist fare. He could do this

A British Eagle Vickers Viscount.

because under international aviation rules the UK overseas territories were deemed domestic destinations and so national rules applied to so-called cabotage routes within a nation's territory. Bamberg was free to propose half-price fares, while the truly foreign destinations governed by international rules agreed between governments prevented this sort of freedom. Bamberg's proposal would come to be known as Very Low Fares.

With the VLF application made in December 1958, Bamberg got his hearing with the ATAC in April 1959. He had made his application with the support of several governments of UK overseas territories, and this helped, but not in the way expected. While ATAC rejected the bid for VLF fares to these destinations, the then Minister of Transport did give one concession. Bamberg would be allowed to operate a service between London and Nassau via Bermuda but only in cooperation with BOAC. This was fraught with difficulty as BOAC was opposed to Eagle being allowed to fly this route. The

VLF fares would be given the name Skycoach and the London to Nassau service would operate once a month with BOAC.

However, a first class and economy service (a misnomer as it was more expensive than a VLF ticket) could operate once a week; again with BOAC. Another issue was that while the ATAC hearing had been in April 1959, the Nassau Skycoach service would not be allowed to start until 10 October 1960. Despite the government's resistance and BOAC's opposition, the 1950s was a decade of steady progress. Bamberg was even able to use his VLF fares before October 1960, a whole year before.

The ever-widening number of destinations both for charter and scheduled services, along with the launch of package holidays and Mediterranean aerial cruises, had all been a great boon for Eagle. While ATAC and BOAC were hostile to Bamberg's efforts, the US authorities were more obliging. Eagle was given permission to fly to Washington and Baltimore and the first flight took place on 19 March. Bamberg also got approval early in 1959 to start flights to Montreal for later that year. His next target was Florida and by June the US authorities had also approved Nassau to Miami flights. By the end of 1959, Eagle had flown more than 15,000 passengers on its new American routes.

Back in Europe, the summer of 1959 saw inaugural flights to Pisa and Rimini for that year's sunshine season. By September, the Rimini flights had been so successful, that the Deputy of the Rimini regional parliament awarded Bamberg a statuette for services to tourism. The company's head office had moved from Clarges Street in Mayfair to Marble Arch House in Edgware Road. Flights from Manchester continued to have good demand but by 1959, most of Eagle Airway's scheduled services were flown from Heathrow airport. This brought the airline into direct competition with BEA, especially with flights to Jersey.

By September 1959, Eagle had had one of its most profitable summer seasons. One good source of revenue did come to an end, a long-term trooping contract for Aden, Nairobi and Nicosia. However, ad-hoc work for the government continued. Overall though Eagle Aviation and Eagle Airways had strong growth. It was not lost on BOAC that in the North American and Caribbean markets Bamberg's share had risen from 6% in 1958 to 10% in 1959. The intervention of BOAC would increase in the coming years.

The month of October 1959 saw an example of the state-owned behemoth's intervention. A shipping company had chartered a flight from Hong Kong to London for its crew but had not taken all of the available seats. Hong Kong was a UK territory at the time and would be until its handover to the People's Republic of China in 1997. As Hong Kong was a UK territory, Bamberg could offer his VLF fares for the remaining seats, all were sold, proving the demand was there.

BOAC strongly objected to this, it had a monopoly on the London, Hong Kong route at the time for scheduled services, but for once there was nothing the state airline could do. Another example of BOAC's growing opposition to Eagle was its objections over a flight from London to Bermuda. A December flight with a mix of Eagle staff and VLF paying passengers proved that the demand for lower fares was there. BOAC objected to this flight too, claiming that such flights would significantly impact its transatlantic traffic.

The 1960s would bring more significant change and more opposition from powerful players. One event that cast a long shadow over Eagle's future was the 1960 merger of two competitor airlines, Hunting Clan and Airwork, creating a more powerful independent operator: British United Airways (BUA). This new, large, independent company, which increased the pressure on Bamberg, was led by Sir Anthony Cayzer, a baronet whose family included Conservative party members of Parliament. While BUA only outlasted Eagle by a few years, its merger with other airlines and its final absorption into the new British Airways of 1973 is a lesson in how Britain really works.

Harold Bamberg's engineers run up the engines on one of Eagle's DC-6 aircraft.

4 Bermuda Triangle

As early as 1957 Bamberg had formed a subsidiary that would have a significant role in not only Eagle's future but also that of the shipping line Cunard. With the UK government setting new limits on routes, Bamberg saw opportunities in the Atlantic and created Eagle Airways (Bermuda) to chase transatlantic routes and services to New York. He would later establish a Bahamian subsidiary that enabled him to start a scheduled service between the Nassau and Luxembourg — highly secretive private banking was one thing Luxembourg and the British West Indies had in common.

On 1 May 1958, Eagle Airways (Bermuda) started a daily New York to Bermuda service using Viscount 805 aircraft.[44] New York was the epicentre of transatlantic passenger demand and that has never changed. Bamberg had started the Bermuda New York route to, again, avoid the many restrictions placed on his airline by the UK government. The Bermudan authorities welcomed the new links to the American mainland and the Caribbean islands would become important to Bamberg, enabling him to expand internationally while evading British legal limits.

From 1958 to 1960, Bamberg's airline increased its passenger numbers from 9,977 to more than 18,000 on the Bermuda to New York service. The British Eagle airliners would land at Bermuda Airport, now called

69

Bermuda L.F. Wade International Airport, with its then squat two-story terminal buildings. Staying in the brightly coloured cottages, tourists could take a horse drawn carriage through the islands' streets of colonial buildings, relax on one of the many beaches or hop between scores of tiny islands.

In 1958, following his successes in Bermuda and the Caribbean, Bamberg saw a new opportunity to legally challenge BOAC on another overseas route, Bermuda to London. Aviation trade title *Flight* magazine noted in an article on BOAC and Eagle that a Bermuda-London route had the island government's support.[45] But the Bermudan government would not make the final decision, that would be the UK government with the help of its Air Transport Advisory Council (ATAC). And Bamberg did not just want to create new routes, he wanted to offer them at very competitive prices.

BOAC had another problem, Freddie Laker wanted to operate a UK to New York service that included two weeks in a hotel for £165 (£3,926 in 2020 prices). Laker's Air Charter airline, which he had bought from Bamberg, was working with UK travel agent Horizon Holidays. The Laker and Bamberg Bermuda to London and London to New York applications were submitted to ATAC with a 1 March 1959 start date.[46] What Bamberg could not have known at the time is that Laker would not be the owner of his own airline the following year. By 1959 he had sold out to Airwork but he remained Managing Director.

Almost two years later, *Flight* magazine's then Air Transport Editor, J. Michael "Mike" Ramsden, reported in-depth on Bamberg's Very Low Fare (VLF) London to Bermuda service. In his article, *Blackbushe to Bermuda* in *Flight*'s 29 January 1960 edition he reported on the resentment in the colony towards London's apparent reluctance to approve new UK-Bermuda services. While the British Colonial Office and Foreign Office (these two Offices would be merged in the 1960s) believed that the existing air services were sufficient, there was finally some movement when two "non-systematic" flights were allowed to go ahead by both the UK authorities and the Bermuda government.[47]

These were not charter or scheduled flights but could carry paying passengers. Both flights used Douglas DC-6C aircraft which took off from Blackbushe Airport, which is about 40 miles from central London (although it advertised itself as a London airport). The first "non-systematic" flight had occurred in the previous December. The second had to wait a month and occurred in January. It was this flight that Ramsden took, a trip that lasted from 9–13 January.

The non-systematic flight was advertised at £124, which is £2,920 at 2020 prices, but considered a VLF at the time. Ramsden reported that there were paying passengers onboard with about 80% of the seats taken. He began the article with the conflict between the Bermuda and UK governments over Eagle's route application. "It is my understanding," said Bermuda government civil aviation Director, Wing Commander E. M. "Mo" Ware, DFC, BSC, AFRAeS, "that this Board thought it in the public interest for Eagle Airways Bermuda to have a licence to operate a scheduled service between Bermuda and London."

Ware went on: "It is embarrassing for the Board, as I understand it, that the UK authorities have so far been unable to decide whether this service can or cannot be operated into and out of the UK." Speaking to the Bermudan government, Ramsden found an administration which did not want to speak openly against BOAC. A senior government official would speak to Ramsden but only on the condition of anonymity. The official said that there was a "very strong desire" to see Eagle Airways Bermuda expand its services.

This was because it would also improve the tourist services to the US. A big problem for Bermuda was that it was cheaper to fly to London via New York than to fly direct, Bermuda to London. The Bermuda government saw Bamberg's VLF as a way to generate, not only an increase in passenger demand from its own people — businessmen, civil servants, families and their distant relatives — but also to encourage UK tourism to the island. "One of our problems," the unnamed the official told Ramsden "is how to sustain the island's tourist business in [the] die off-peak months of December, January and February. The preferable source is Europe, which means largely the UK."

Incredibly, of the 109,515 tourists arriving by air in 1959, less than 2,000 were from the UK. The national carrier, BOAC, was the obvious airline to improve that situation but it had not responded to Bermuda's requests. Instead, routes to and from Bermuda were dominated by US and Canadian carriers because BOAC had at one time pulled out of providing such a service. Being a British colony, Bermuda did not want a vital tourist route, which supported 75% of its entire 1959 economy (£700 million in 2020 prices), dependent on the carriers of a foreign country.

Unsurprisingly, Bermuda had welcomed Bamberg, who was a willing partner, and approved Eagle's proposal. Ramsden's unnamed government official simply said it was a "disappointing situation for Eagle," while Ware would not comment on the official attitude in the island towards BOAC. However, Ramsden did find stronger views about BOAC and wrote: "We heard many criticisms of BOAC. Because this airline is a state corporation it is highly vulnerable (and sensitive) to criticism." The criticism cannot just be levelled at BOAC, it was a government airline and there was Bamberg offering to provide a service which had good demand.

Ramsden reported that Bermudans felt the UK-Bermuda services were "just not adequate." The Bermuda government had spoken to the UK many times about the matter. The British government and BOAC's response was that the route was simply not profitable enough, while the UK-New York route was. BOAC did stop at Bermuda, but only to serve its flights to Caracas, Venezuela and Bogota, Colombia. Unbelievably, along with this limited service, Bermudans found it difficult to get seats. "This is why we welcome Eagle as well as BOAC," the unnamed government official told *Flight*.

Ware emphasised to Ramsden that Bermuda's Board of Civil Aviation had approved Eagle's application for the London-Bermuda service and sent it to London in September 1958. Sixteen months later in January 1960, nothing had happened. One possible reason for this delay was highlighted by Ramsden in his article: the UK government's stated "determination to do nothing that will undermine the position of the state corporation". The UK authorities may also have wanted to sit on the Bermudan application because Bamberg had already successfully won approval for services to Montreal, Baltimore and Washington.[48]

Two months after the non-systematic flights, in March 1960, Bamberg gained allies in opening up the transatlantic routes he coveted. In March 1960, almost months after Bamberg's original Bermudan applications,

Eagle would merge with the fabled Cunard shipping line, who had long sought an entrée into transatlantic air services. That month, Cunard Chairman, Sir John Brocklebank, announced his company would be buying a controlling stake in Bamberg's Eagle Airways. The UK based airline, Cunard Eagle, came into existence on Monday 21 March 1960 with Cunard's Chairman, Sir John Brocklebank, announcing that he intended to buy more than a 50% of Eagle.

This year, Bamberg's fleet livery changed again, and twice in one year. Before July, the colour scheme became a fuselage top that was white with a red vertical tail fin which had a wide black band and a large E. The nose cheatline returned to its previous red but the airline name was in black. From July, after Cunard had bought Eagle, the fin E became the flying Eagle symbol in white, the white fuselage had a red cheatline added and the fuselage now carried, in black, the name Cunard Eagle Airways.

By mid-March, Bamberg had applied to the US licensing authority, the Civil Aeronautics Board (CAB), to change his airline Eagle Airways (Bermuda) to British Eagle International Airways; the new name under which the Bermuda and Bahamas associates would trade. There were no plans for Bamberg's UK companies to trade under the new name.[49] Bamberg did not have to wait long before BOAC started to resist this new entity, Cunard Eagle, and its new routes. The state airline would start fighting back by strongly opposing the Cunard Eagle airline's application to run services from Bermuda to Jamaica and the Bahamas. BOAC's decision to oppose Eagle flights between Caribbean islands also followed Bamberg's considerable success with the Bermuda to New York services which had begun in May 1958.

Despite all of BOAC's politicking between Bermuda and the UK, the investment by the Eton-educated Baron Brocklebank of Greenlands would lead to the now Cunard Eagle Airways (Bermuda) getting approval for its Blackbushe to Bermuda flights. The presence of an aristocrat on the Eagle team had made all the difference and the flights would start on 1 October that year. The partnership of an aristocratic shipping line with an entrepreneurial airline would be viewed as a real threat by BOAC. The signs of an impending London, Bermuda route were spotted by *Flight*. The magazine had speculated that Bamberg's March 1960 acquisition of a Bristol Britannia from Cuba's national airline, Cubana, was for this transatlantic route.[50]

On 5 April 1960, the then Conservative party government aviation Minister, Duncan Sandys MP, confirmed the new London-Bermuda route. Sandys informed the House of Commons of the recent Cunard, Eagle merger and about the latest international developments in air fares. "The Eagle airline, in which the Cunard Shipping Company have acquired a majority holding, will operate services of all classes between Britain and Bermuda, in parallel with BOAC partnership arrangements," Sandys said at the dispatch box.[51] However, "partnership arrangements" was not as fair as it might seem.

Those "partnership arrangements" forced Eagle to share first-class fares, operate the Bermuda service on alternate months with BOAC, and be in a revenue sharing pool with the state-owned airline. A pool was an airline revenue sharing concept. It meant Bamberg had to share his revenue on a pro rata basis with BOAC with the resulting renumeration calculated from the share of capacity each airline operated on those routes. BOAC would always be able to provide more capacity. Commenting on the aviation Minister's 5 April statement to the House of Commons in its 15 April 1960 edition, *Flight* said that: 'Curiously, the BOAC statement which followed the Minister's address to the Commons made no mention of the corporation's partnership [arrangement] with Eagle and Cunard on the Bermuda route'.[52]

BOAC may not have wanted to refer to it because they did not want to be questioned about their intentions regarding this new, stronger, competitor. Despite all the hindrances, in May 1960, the new Cunard Eagle Airways announced a coach class cabotage service to Bermuda from 1 October. A Douglas DC-6C aircraft would be flown monthly for this service which would be in that "pool" with BOAC. Cunard Eagle was also expanding its first-class and economy-class services to include Nassau in the Bahamas.

The start of the 1960s was a time when casino gambling on the islands of Nassau, Bermuda and Paradise grew with the rising tourist resorts. From 1 October 1960, British Eagle also started flying updated 98-seat Britannias from London Airport to Nassau. In a three-class layout, the Britannias had 14 first class, 66 economy and 18 Skycoach seats, the latter of which were for UK residents only. The Bahamas tourist industry promoted the islands as places of endless beaches and night-time glamour. Again, that would be in a pool with BOAC.[53]

Another big change for Eagle after the Cunard merger and route gains was its location. Eagle moved its maintenance and operations base to London Airport, now known as Heathrow, because of the "long haul nature of their operations," according to the 3 June 1960

British Eagle served the London to Nassau route with
98-seat Bristol Britannias. Image: Ralf Manteufel.

edition of *Flight*. In that June edition, *Flight* also reported
that on 31 May, a few days before, all flying had ceased at
Blackbushe. The last of its tenants had relocated, either
to Heathrow or Gatwick Airport in 1960.

The Cunard Eagle merger made such an impact in
the board room of BOAC that just a few months later
BOAC proposed a joint transatlantic venture to Cunard,
but this was rejected.[54] It was not a new idea. In 1946 the
reverse had happened, and Cunard had proposed a joint
transatlantic venture with BOAC to the then aviation
Minister, but that was rejected. The 1960 rejection was
not the end of the matter, however, and about a year
later, Cunard would do a deal with BOAC to Bamberg's
detriment.

But Bamberg had shown that by registering a
company outside the UK an independent airline could
expand its scheduled operations and attract wealthy
investors. Powerful people were against that. BOAC

had a subsidiary in the Caribbean, British West Indies Airways (BWIA) and changes in the region's politics were going to give BOAC a great deal of power. The now defunct Federal government of the West Indies was deeply involved with BOAC in 1960 because the then two-year old Federation had wanted to buy BWIA. In 1956, the British Caribbean Federation Act was passed to federate the ten UK Caribbean territories; Antigua and Barbuda, Barbados, Dominica, Grenada, Jamaica, Montserrat, the then St Kitts-Nevis-Anguilla, Saint Lucia, St Vincent and Trinidad and Tobago.

The Federation was led by an Executive Governor-General, Lord Hailes, who was appointed by the UK government. Lord Hailes was born Patrick Buchan-Hepburn, youngest son of Sir Archibald Buchan-Hepburn, 4th Baronet of the Buchan-Hepburn baronets. Educated at Harrow and Trinity College, Cambridge, Patrick Buchan-Hepburn was a Conservative Member of Parliament from 1931, when he was aged 30, until 1955. In 1957 he was knighted, and Sir Patrick was given a peerage and made Baron Hailes of Prestonkirk in the same year. Earlier in his life he had been personal secretary to Winston Churchill.

On 22 April 1958 in Port of Spain, Trinidad, the inauguration of the federal legislature of the West Indies took place officiated by the sister of Her Majesty Queen Elizabeth II, Princess Margaret.[55] In May 1960, the issue of aviation was so important that the Federation appointed a commission of inquiry into the future of air transport in the territories. The UK government's Colonial Office contributed to the cost.[56] This Federation, which wanted BOAC's BWIA, would go on to oppose an application by Bamberg for a Bermuda to Barbados, Antigua and Trinidad route.

However, the new Cunard Eagle did manage to get approval for one route, it would fly from London to the Bahamas from October 1960. In January 1962, however, the Federation would collapse from internal strife and airline politics was one of the many causes for its downfall. While Ramsden was in Bermuda in January 1960, he was told Jamaica could have the biggest airline in the West Indies if it wanted too. Jamaica's then Prime Minister Michael Norman Manley was in the UK at the time telling the government that they cannot keep pushing BOAC's services on to the Jamaican people.

If the Caribbean colonies' own interests were not encouraged relations with London would become worse.[57] Manley, born in Jamaica in 1924, had attended a local school, St Andrew Preparatory School, and would go on to Canada's McGill University in Montreal. In 1943, he joined the Royal Canadian Air Force attaining the rank of Pilot Officer. Nazi Germany surrendered just before he saw active service. After the war, Manley went to the London School of Economics for a bachelor's degree in government and worked from 1950 to 1951 as a BBC External Services journalist. He returned to Jamaica in December 1951 and became Associate Editor of the socialist weekly newspaper *Public Opinion* before becoming a politician.[58]

Manley had supported the movement for a West Indies Federation and political independence for the anglophone Caribbean but by 1960 he had threatened to leave the Federation which had then existed for barely two years. When it finally fell, Manley was instrumental in the creation of the Caribbean Community (CARICOM), an intergovernmental body which still exists today. CARICOM's states' total population is about 16 million. It oversees a single market between fifteen Member States from a total group of 20 countries including five Associate States. As well as the Caribbean islands its Member States include the South American nations of Guyana and Suriname.

While Manley was agitating for the end of the Federation, Bamberg's run of luck with Cunard was continuing. Fourteen months after securing the Blackbushe to Bermuda route in April 1960, the UK government's Air Transport Licensing Board granted Cunard Eagle a London to New York licence using Boeing 707-465s and Britannias. Cunard Eagle would now compete head-to-head with BOAC. However, although the London-New York licence was granted in June 1961, Cunard Eagle would never actually fly that route.

Flights from London to New York were the red line across which the UK's state-owned airlines and their allies in the government would not allow Bamberg to cross. Less than five months later, the licence had been revoked.[59] Cunard Eagle had invested £6 million (£141 million in 2020 prices) in two new Boeing 707s specially purchased for the route.[60] While Cunard Eagle, even with its establishment leadership, had lost the London-New York route, it offered more seats on the Nassau to Miami route than on all its European scheduled routes put together. With its London to Nassau route, Cunard Eagle could offer a through-route to Miami, but not a direct flight to the Floridian city.

While Bamberg wanted to find a Caribbean path to breaking free, Cunard Chairman Sir John Brocklebank had made ominous sounds about the future of its aviation partnership. "[The] extent of Cunard's investment in air transport and its relations with Cunard's shipping interests will be the subject of close examination."[61]

Brocklebank said the loss of the North Atlantic licence had put the Cunard-Eagle partnership in jeopardy. Despite the New York set back, the first of the Boeing 707 aircraft arrived and was used for the London to Bermuda and Bahamas services from 5 May 1961.[62]

The Caribbean to US mainland market was extremely competitive, Bamberg's airline was up against Pan American, the world's most powerful international airline, as well as BOAC. As 1962 began, Cunard Eagle Airways (Bahamas) operated four flights a day between Nassau and Miami, plus one weekly service. The airline had a daily service from Bermuda to New York, and from Bermuda to Nassau. That year the airline also extended its route network to Jamaica from Nassau. Speaking to *Flight* in November 1961, Cunard Eagle (Bermuda)'s New York based General Sales Manager, Alfred Hudson, said: "Everyone said we hadn't a hope. We went in and fought, and Pan American, Eastern [Air Lines] and BOAC fought harder. This develops the business for everyone."

To help Cunard Eagle compete on price the airline withdrew its International Air Transport Association membership as of 28 March 1962. In theory, this meant Cunard Eagle was free to fix its own prices for the Bermuda to London and Bermuda to New York routes.

When Cunard Eagle's London to Bermuda and Nassau service was extended to Miami, a London bus was driven around Florida for two weeks with two stewardesses on board to promote the new US gateway to Europe. The bus tour resulted in "yards of press cuttings," according to the *Flight* story. Other ideas Hudson and his team had to getting US passengers included targeting golfers and honeymooners. Cunard Eagle promoted its readiness to carry golf bags for just $2 ($18 in 2021 prices, according to the Federal Reserve Bank of Minnesota inflation calculator).

The airline needed a lot more demand, and more routes, because its second Boeing 707 was to be delivered in June of 1962. *Flight* speculated that Cunard Eagle would reapply for its North Atlantic/New York licence.[63] The immediate solution was to start a twice-weekly Boeing 707-420 service London-Bermuda-Nassau, from 5 May, with one flight ending in Miami, the other in Jamaica. After the second 707 arrived, the goal was to make it three weekly flights with two terminating in Miami and one in Jamaica. That was to start on 5 July.

Another possibility was Jamaica's future airline. The island was to become independent of the UK on 6 August that year and its government had put out a tender for airlines to start a carrier for Jamaica. Cunard Eagle was already a flag carrier for the Bahamas and Bermuda, meaning it was registered there and had preferential rights. According to *Flight*, the competition would be between BOAC and Cunard Eagle, whose western hemisphere chief executive, Harry P Snelling, told *Flight* that losing the North Atlantic licence, "could have sunk us, but it didn't, it hasn't and it isn't going to," and the magazine further reported that they intended to re-apply for the licence.[64]

Cunard Eagle were wrong and events beyond Bamberg and his team's control would change things radically. Less than a month later BOAC bought into Cunard Eagle Airways. In one swoop, BOAC had ended the threat of a possible competitor on the London New York route, had gained the Caribbean services Bamberg's team had built up over years and eliminated Eagle from their Jamaica routes. Competition with BOAC on any route ended. The ATLB North Atlantic decision had scuttled Cunard's plans and the shipping firm saw no future in a Caribbean-centric venture with Bamberg.

By June 1962, Bamberg was sat on the board of BOAC-Cunard with managers who had been his sworn competition not so long ago. It was not a situation he could stomach for long. In February the following year, Bamberg would announce that he had bought 60% of the Cunard airline with an option to buy the remaining 40%. The resurrected Eagle airline was to become British Eagle International Airlines Ltd (BEIA), but not until the autumn of 1963.

Flight speculated at the time that Bamberg's Caribbean plans would not be taken any further for the time being. Instead, the renewed Eagle Airways would pay special attention to UK domestic routes. Eagle also possessed licences for Copenhagen, Stockholm, Venice, Dublin and Nice. Bamberg owned the UK travel agents, Lunn Poly, and they were expected to generate new passenger demand. Another source of revenue for Bamberg was the maintenance contracts he had with, of all airlines, BOAC-Cunard and Ghana Airways.[65]

In April 1964, *Flight International* printed its World Airline Survey and it was official, British Eagle International Airlines did not fly to the Caribbean or Bermuda or operate any routes there. Bamberg's days of trying to avoid British restrictions in the West Indies and mid-Atlantic had ended. Instead, British Eagle International Airlines with 940 employees and its head office at Heathrow, flew long haul trooping flights but was essentially now a Europe-only airline. And Sir John Brocklebank was still on the board of directors while also being Deputy Chairman of BOAC-Cunard.

BOAC-Cunard operated from London to Bermuda, Nassau, Jamaica, Barbados, and Trinidad as well as to

Lima, Caracas and Bogota. It also flew New York to Bermuda, Nassau and Jamaica as well as to Antigua, Barbados and Port of Spain on charter to BWIA. For the US mainland it operated routes to New York, Boston, Washington, Detroit, Chicago and Miami. It also had flights to New York from Manchester and Glasgow, as well as London. It had a fleet of 11 Boeing 707 aircraft, two of which had been ordered for Cunard Eagle. British Eagle International Airlines had none.

Ten years after starting his airline, Bamberg was almost back where he had been in 1958 when he started his Bermudan subsidiary. For a brief few months Bamberg's alliance with an establishment shipping line, Cunard, seemed to have unlocked the biggest prize of all, London to New York. In June 1962, two years and three months later, Bamberg had found himself on the board of a BOAC company. His aristocratic partner, Sir John Brocklebank, had sold out to BOAC and its Chairman Rear Admiral Sir Matthew Slattery. Slattery would be replaced as Chairman on 1 January 1964 by Sir Giles Guthrie, Baron of Brent Eleigh Hall in the County of Suffolk.

Harold Bamberg (centre) with Eagle stewardesses.

5 Package Holidays

amberg spearheaded package holidays with trips to Spain and Italy and created the travel agency, Lunn Poly, a brand name that would last until 2004 when it was finally retired by its then German owner. Bamberg's travel agency originated from two successful firms originating in the 19th century, Poly Travel and Sir Henry Lunn Travel. The latter was acquired in the 1950s by Bamberg and the former in 1962. He combined them into Lunn Poly in 1965. The package holidays Bamberg sold allowed him to offer his lower fares and he introduced a hire purchase scheme to make the vacations more affordable for everyday people. It was a bright spot in an otherwise never-ending struggle with the government regulators.

Bamberg's acquisition of the travel agencies was a recognition of the growing popularity of holiday travel and a way for him to guarantee he filled his fleet's seat capacity. Before World War Two the levels of domestic UK tourism had become significant. According to an estimate for 1939, seven million people visited Blackpool, 5.5 million went to Southend-on-Sea and another 1.5 million stayed in holiday camps. In 1941, the UK's population was 48 million. As Europe rebuilt itself after the devastation of World War Two people's lives became more prosperous and this level of domestic travel began to rise again, accompanied with an increasing number of foreign trips.

The popularity of travel for tourism began in the 19th century when the UK transport infrastructure was opening up travel for almost every level of society. The railway network's expansion and greater steamboat availability for faster journey times and lower fares saw more and more UK destinations come within reach of the typical household's budget. Seaside resorts were popular, to some degree because of the lack of pollution compared to Britain's industrial cities. Londoners took trains to Southend and steamboats to Gravesend and Margate for day trips and special excursions. Working class people from the North and the Midlands took boats to Ilfracombe on Devon county's coast. It is no surprise that the UK's railway and shipping interests understood the significance of air travel and were intent on controlling as much of it as they could.

A half century later and international travel was picking up steam. In 1951, an estimated 1.5 million holidays of four nights or more were spent abroad by Britons. This number of holidays increased to two million in 1955, 3.5 million in 1960 and five million in 1965. The airline entrepreneurs made the most of this trend towards foreign travel and did their upmost to enable it. Bamberg and his on-and-off again rival, Frederick Laker, have been cited by travel historians as particularly significant in their contributions to the rapid expansion of UK foreign tourism after the war.[66]

Bamberg was quick to see the significance of leisure travel for his airlines. He had tried to interest the giant travel agency Thomas Cook & Son in package holidays using his chartered Eagle Vikings, but he had no luck. So, just months after his first passenger flights, he bought into Sir Henry Lunn travel agency and finally took it over entirely.

Sir Henry Simpson Lunn, to give his full name, did not live to see the extent to which his travel agency would change people's lives in Bamberg's hands. Lunn died in 1939, aged 80. He had been born in 1859 in Horncastle, Lincolnshire. Raised as a Methodist he was educated at Horncastle Grammar School and would eventually train as a medical doctor at Trinity College, Dublin. He also became a Methodist church minister, being ordained in 1886. Lunn's association with travel really began with his missionary work to India.

While Lunn had to return from the sub-continent due to ill health, it was his religious work that led him to set up his long-lasting travel agency. Lunn first organised the annual Grindelwald Reunion Conferences and then other English church leader gatherings from 1892 to 1896. In 1893, he set up Co-operative Educational Tours. In 1902, he organised his first inclusive tours which went to Adelboden and Wengen in Switzerland. His tours combined winter sports and a religious retreat. Many Anglican churches were established at fashionable winter resorts at the time.

In 1905, Lunn created the Public Schools Alpine Sports Club. With this Club he made large bookings with major hotels and in particular with the Le Beauregard sanatorium. In 1906, he founded the Hellenic Travellers Club with his friend, Liberal party parliamentarian Viscount Bryce of Dechmont, and in 1908 Lunn started his Alpine Sports firm. That same year he formed the Alpine Ski Club, a gentleman's club for ski-mountaineers.[67] All these firms would become part of the Sir Henry Lunn Travel company. Lunn also stood for election to the House of Commons for the Liberal party in 1910, the same year he was knighted by King George V, and he tried again in 1923; both times unsuccessfully.[68]

With the success of the Sir Henry Lunn acquisition Bamberg acquired Poly Travel in early 1962. Bamberg and four other directors from Lunn joined the board of Poly Travel, which continued as a separate company under its own name for a few more years. In 1967, it was merged with Sir Henry Lunn Limited. Poly Travel's origins lie with the Polytechnic Young Men's Christian Institute of the 1880s. That Institute eventually became part of the Polytechnic of Central London in 1970 and the University of Westminster in 1992.

Strangely, a link with the Polytechnic that would become the University of Westminster, continued in the form of a deed of covenant payment of £1,000 a year for seven years. From 1 August 1963 until 1970, Poly Travel paid the Polytechnic £1,000. Its covenant payments outliving Bamberg's British Eagle by two years. It was almost 90 years before that when the seed was sown for the travel agency PTA would become. The Polytechnic Young Men's Christian Institute would create the Polytechnic Touring Association (PTA) in the 1880s. By the time Bamberg bought it, it had changed its name to simply Poly Travel. The event that led to the PTA occurred in 1888 and the man who became the driving force behind what would become Poly Travel was the Polytechnic's Secretary, Robert Mitchell.

Mitchell realised in 1888 that the students had never seen the mountains their geography teacher was teaching them about. He came to believe that travel was a necessary part of education so young men could fully understand what they were being taught. The PTA tours would eventually be sold as opportunities for people to refresh themselves physically and spiritually. Like Lunn, Switzerland was a first destination along with Belgium, for walks through the former battlefields of an earlier

Franco-German war. That first trip took place in 1888 and was for 60–70 people.

The next year, the Polytechnic took a number of parties to the 1889 Paris Exhibition with a tremendous increase in numbers, almost 2,500. The start of the last decade of the 19th century saw Ireland and Scotland added to the list of destinations. In 1891, Mitchell was made the Polytechnic's Director of Education and he personally led many tours. The success of the Polytechnic's trips led to the registration of the Polytechnic Touring Association, a company limited by shares, on 29 September 1911. The PTA would go on to greater success long after Mitchell's death in 1933.

On 1 October 1962, with the PTA having renamed itself Poly Travel some years after Mitchell's death, Bamberg bought the company. In a letter written by Bamberg in 2011 he said: "Poly Travel had 19 branches and we wanted to expedite our national coverage for the purpose of marketing the package holiday … [by working with travel agents] you could buy the hotel accommodation and the airline fee at the point of sale in England … we were able to plan ahead and we could allocate large numbers of seats on the airline and accommodation at the hotel".[69] The industry term for package holidays was "inclusive tours," meaning the flight and hotel were included in the price.

When Bamberg reclaimed his airline from his Cunard business partners in 1963, his travel firms would be key to generate the necessary passenger demand. In early 1963, Bamberg had bought 60% of Cunard Eagle, the company formed from his 1960 deal with shipping giant Cunard. Bamberg's resurrected airline would eventually be legally renamed British Eagle International Airlines Limited by the autumn of that year — but stripped of its former Caribbean and Bermudan routes. British Eagle was now a Europe-only airline — bar its troop transportation contracts with the UK government.

In 1963, Bamberg's resurrected airline was operating charter flights and inclusive tours with daily services between London and Glasgow, Edinburgh and Belfast. A wholly-owned subsidiary of British Eagle, Starways, flew routes to London, Chester, Liverpool and Glasgow. British Eagle International Airlines' international services operated from London, Birmingham and Manchester. From London, it flew to Luxembourg, Innsbruck, Dinard, La Baule, Perpignan, Stuttgart, Pisa and Rimini; from Birmingham it was to Palma; and from Manchester to Nice, Rimini, La Baule and Ostend. The Air Transport Licensing Board had also granted licences for additional routes. These included London to Geneva, Copenhagen, Stockholm, Venice, Dublin, and between Liverpool and Dublin.

In the 1950s one million Britons holidayed abroad, by the end of the 1960s it was 2.5 million. Two years after resurrecting his independent airline as British Eagle in 1963, Bamberg merged his Sir Henry Lunn Travel and PTA firms into one company, Lunn Poly. Bamberg's Lunn Poly was an early tourist trade innovator splitting its leisure and business travel with the high street shops selling package holidays while specialised offices served the business traveller. A year later in 1966, Bamberg brought his travel agencies under one organisation, his Travel Trust group. The group would include Everyman Travel. Together they made the UK's largest private travel organisation with major holiday contracts with Cosmos, Global and Cooks. Travel Trust was able to cater for the complete range of inclusive tour promotions.

When the end came for Bamberg's airlines businesses

in November 1968, the travel agencies continued. When British Eagle ceased trading, his Travel Trust companies made alternative arrangements for customers booked on charter flights with Eagle Aviation.[70] There were two elements to the divestiture of Bamberg's travel agencies, who would the agencies now contract for their flights and who would own the agencies themselves? The former was the quicker and easier decision. While BEA wanted the contracts, unsurprisingly, Bamberg did not choose his state-owned nemesis. Travel Trust had never had a contract with BEA or its subsidiaries, the regional airlines, Cambrian Airways and BKS Air Transport.

Instead, the UK independent Dan-Air won the contract. The good news for Travel Trust's customers would be that prices would not change, and they would be flown on jet airliners, not Bamberg's fleet of older propeller powered Britannia aircraft. Dan-Air committed to completing the Travel Trust Group's 1969 programme with de Havilland Comets and BAC1-11s. The UK independent airline would sign a three-year time charter agreement with Travel Trust out to 1972.[71] However, Eagle's customers would have to take Dan-Air flights from Gatwick and not Heathrow after the Heathrow scheduling committee refused to accept the programme.[72]

Selling the Travel Trust group of companies was the more significant decision, but it would be one the receivers, the bank Kleinwort Benson, would make. There was at least £2 million of airline debt to creditors to pay off. Bamberg's Travel Trust group came close to being bought by the UK government's Transport Holding Company (THC), which owned the Skyways airline and Thomas Cook. Bamberg had been trying to negotiate a three-year time-charter between a resurrected British

Eagle and THC but the government firm balked, and no deal was done.

Eventually, the Travel Trust firms were sold off individually. Sunair bought Lunn Poly for £175,000 and in 1972, Lunn Poly became part of Thomson Travel Group. Lunn Poly's 1960s innovation of splitting its leisure and business travel between its high street shops and specialised call centres was very successful throughout the 1970s and 1980s. By the mid-1990s it had become the largest travel agency in the UK. But with the advent of the Internet, the biggest change in holiday booking habits occurred, probably since the Polytechnic Young Men's Christian Institute created the Polytechnic Touring Association. Lunn Poly, however, continued to be a very successful company and would remain a household name until 2004.

By the mid-1990s Lunn Poly had become the largest travel agency in the UK.

6 Very Low Fare Revolution

B amberg pushed for low fares long before anyone had even contemplated the kind of low-cost airlines that exist today. His actions caused a change in civil aviation law in the UK, as well as fares, and ultimately changed the price passengers paid world-wide with a transformation of the fare structure agreed through the International Air Transport Association (IATA) — the main trade association for the airline industry then and today. On 19 April 1945, IATA was founded in Havana, Cuba as the prime inter-airline cooperation organisation for promoting beneficial, safe, reliable and economic air transport for the world's consumers. IATA then had 57 members from 31 nations, mostly in Europe and North America.[73]

It was on a cold November day, 13 years later, in 1958 that Bamberg's Eagle Airways applied to the UK government's Air Transport Advisory Council (ATAC) to operate very low fare (VLF) services to British cabotage points. Cabotage is simply the airline industry term for flights within a nation's territory.[74] These VLFs were about half the cost of the existing scheduled air fares, and at the time were described as a "bombshell" for the market. Bamberg wanted the VLFs on routes from London to Aden and Singapore, Nassau and Kingston, Trinidad, Kano and Lagos, Nicosia, Malta, Gibraltar, Nairobi and Aden and

Hong Kong. While only Gibraltar is a UK territory in 2022, they were all British territories in 1958.

The market reaction saw Bamberg's competitors, Airwork and Hunting-Clan, announce a scheme that was essentially a replica of Eagle's. Commentary at the time suggested the Bamberg VLF proposal surprised and embarrassed the government, ATAC, and other airlines.[75] The VLF proposals put the government in a difficult situation, demonstrating that the 1952 "new deal" policy, created in response to criticism of the previous Labour government's state-led aviation rules, was not working. Allowing the independent airlines to operate VLF services could severely undermine the competitive position of the state's BOAC and BEA.

The airlines' proposals did involve using aircraft long since paid for, such as the Bristol Britannia. There would be no in-flight catering and squeezing more passengers in with less generous seating would also be required to make the new prices profitable. The degree to which the independent airlines were cutting fares can be demonstrated with the example of their return fare of £245 for Hong Kong, almost half that of BOAC's £415. Another example is Bamberg's similarly aggressive cuts for European fares. For a round trip to Malta, Eagle would charge £19 compared to BEA's £52.

Bamberg did get a hearing with ATAC after his late 1958 application for very low fares, but it was not until April 1959. It would be the longest hearing ATAC had ever conducted, and the Council would not exist for much longer with the Conservative government's Civil Aviation Licensing Act of 1960. Bamberg had gone to the hearing armed with agreements from British colonies for services, but ATAC rejected it all.

The Conservative government's answer to the

independent airlines challenge to its own "new deal" (which the policies of the 1945 Labour government had slightly modified) was to introduce its own civil aviation act. This VLF challenge to BOAC and BEA led directly to the Civil Aviation Licensing Act of 1960.[76] The British Independent Air Transport Association (BIATA), whose members were Eagle and its contemporaries, had been lobbying the Conservative government elected in 1951, but it would be seven years before BIATA made any real progress.

A key BIATA victory was convincing the UK government of a need for a Ministry of Aviation. The aviation work of government had been part of the vaguely named Ministry of Supply. The Minister of Transport and Civil Aviation in 1959 was public school-educated Harold Watkinson MP. Elected as Member of Parliament for Woking in 1950, his engineering background saw Sir Winston Churchill appoint him as Parliamentary Secretary to the Ministry of Transport and Civil Aviation. Watkinson had studied engineering at King's College, London and in another common aviation link, he had worked in shipping, and in ship building, before becoming an MP.[77]

At the August 1959 luncheon of the government's Air Registration Board, which certified aircraft types for their airworthiness, Watkinson told the attendees: "At home... my thoughts are turning very much to the concept of a freer pattern of air transport. This, I think, would be best achieved by the concept of a new, more independent licensing authority. This, of course, would need legislation and no doubt changes in existing legislation. It is, therefore, a matter for the next Parliament".[78]

While the 1960 Civil Aviation (Licensing) Act was

supposed to create a better framework for airlines and that "new deal," all it really did was to create red tape. Watkinson's vision of a "'freer pattern of air transport" would not take shape. The first new hurdle was the requirement for an applicant airline's financial position to be investigated by the Air Transport Licensing Board, which the 1960 Civil Aviation (Licensing) Act would also create. The claim was that an applicant airline was financially and commercially stable and able to operate the service granted to it.

But such an investigation would take time and the inevitable delays in this drawn-out process would be too long for the tour operators. The result was that while the Conservative government claimed to want to help UK airlines, tour operators often opted for foreign carriers. The inclusive tour operator promoter who had to deliver a service for summer and winter season tourists could not wait for the ATLB's decision. Even if it was positive, it would come too late and if not positive, the result would be the same — foreign carriers were hired.

The licensing process now took much longer as each applicant was thoroughly investigated, even well-established operators. Another, probably bigger hurdle, for the applicant airlines was BEA's constant objection to almost all of the inclusive tour licences. The airline claimed "material diversion" of scheduled service traffic for everything. The foreign carriers had an in-built advantage because the UK did not want other countries refusing BOAC and BEA licences, or any other British airline. So, the UK government would readily approve foreign airlines' permits.

The tour operators knew this, and so British tourists flew aboard on foreign aircraft instead of UK airlines simply because of red tape introduced by a Conservative government. During 1962 and 1963, more than one-third of inclusive tour flights between the UK and continental Europe were carried by foreign airlines.

Another response for 1960 to the VLF challenge from the government was to allow additional "third-class'" services to some colonial territories at ticket prices up to 16% below the new IATA tourist fares. The state airlines, BOAC and BEA, could run these third-class services as well as independents. But the passenger bookings had to be pooled, shared out between the airlines, and BOAC had to have 70%. BOAC could see advantages for itself against international rivals in the calls for lower fares. Second class fares were also to see a price cut, again up to 16%, but this was on all routes, except on the North Atlantic.

The price cuts had been possible because of the arguments BOAC had made in September 1959, after Bamberg's VLF challenge. BOAC made its case at IATA's prehearing conference in Honolulu, which dealt with a range of airline issues.[79] BOAC wanted to extend, not the new VLF category, but existing economy category fares beyond the North Atlantic. While the Honolulu hearing was to address fares worldwide it would only agree new fare structures for some regions: they were Europe, between Europe and South America, and between North and South America. As the then Conservative government aviation Minister, Duncan Sandys MP, explained to the House of Commons on 5 April 1960: "This was due largely to the demand for the introduction of cheaper fares, put forward by BOAC, in agreement with Her Majesty's government".[80] However, the conference ended without agreement on fares for the rest of the world. IATA's main conference which followed the

Honolulu event was its 1960 annual meeting held that year in Copenhagen, Denmark.

North Atlantic passenger fares were subject to special rules under an inter-governmental Memorandum of Understanding (MoU) between the US and European Civil Aviation Conference (ECAC) states. The BOAC campaign eventually worked, and economy fares were duly available beyond the North Atlantic. Following this IATA meeting, the UK government gave the green light to UK airlines offering their low fare cabotage services, which would be marketed as Skycoach, because that did not require IATA members agreement. These fares were on the average 27% below the old lowest IATA fares, though they were not as low as the proposed VLF fares, which had averaged more than 40% less.

While the airlines referred to their tickets as low fares or very low fares, they were considerably more expensive than the fares that people encounter with today's low-cost airlines. In 1961, the mean gross weekly earnings for a British man in full-time manual employment in the UK was £15.60, when converted to the new decimal currency system introduced in 1971 for the pound sterling.[81] In 2020 prices, £15.60 would have been worth about £230 today. The UK government's Office for National Statistics' (ONS) data for 1961 shows that the mean gross weekly income for women in manual labour was half that of men's.

While Bamberg's April 1959 bid for VLF routes to British colonies had been rejected by ATAC, despite the said colonies agreeing to Eagle services, the UK government did eventually give a concession. Bamberg was allowed to operate a Skycoach service which it would share with BOAC once a month from London to Nassau via Bermuda. But in return Bamberg had to withdraw all his other VLF applications. BOAC was opposed to it, but it did eventually go ahead in October 1960 — seven months after Cunard had bought Eagle.

Bamberg wanted to introduce his "low" fares on routes beyond France and Spain. In 2001, he wrote: "The Conservative party took the initiative [on VLF], however, it took a further five years to change the system and our application for long haul very low fare services (VLF) was not approved."[82]

In 1960, *Flight* magazine produced a comparison table to show the old fares, proposed VLF fares and the actual IATA approved low fares for a small number of the London originating return flights the UK airlines operated. In 2020 prices, for a return flight to the Bahamas, the lowest former IATA fare was £5,440, the old VLF was £3,297, the new IATA low fare was £4,474 and the Skycoach cabotage fare was £3,815. All of these fares are completely unaffordable for the average British manual worker today and were doubly so for the common working men and women of 1960.

The push for VLF was motivated by the downward trend in air fares. This trend and the lower cost levels that underpinned it prompted Eagle and two other independent airlines, Airwork and Hunting-Clan, to make their respective requests to government for lower fares and this new VLF category. According to *Flight*, Airwork was, "never entirely happy about VLF themselves". Airwork's management may have been concerned about the outcome of these changes for them. Airwork and Hunting-Clan made their own VLF application in February 1959 and their fears were soon justified.[83]

Airwork and Hunting-Clan would merge their airlines in May 1960 as a direct result of the forthcoming

VLF changes and called the new entity, British United Airways (BUA). *Flight* reported that the merger, 'saw the loss of many jobs'. The merger was an outcome of VLF related route politics in Africa, with BOAC at the centre of the negotiations. It was not until 4 October 1960 that the first of the low cabotage air fares were introduced. While those fares hammered out in Honolulu in 1959 were lower, there would be competition to lower them dramatically.

In 1961, the new Scottish independent airline Caledonian Airways made its first charter passenger carrying flight on 29 November from London to Barbados. The new airline offered a London to Bermuda group charter fare of £35 a head in 1961 prices for the off season.[84] In the summer month's that price jumped to £80. According to the Bank of England inflation calculator, that lower fare of £35 equates to £797 in 2020 prices, equivalent to about a year's income for an average male manual worker in 1961. Caledonian Airways would one day be merged with BUA to create British Caledonian Airways.

Africa was BUA's main foreign market and while it employed the Skycoach fare there, the mid-Atlantic was Cunard Eagle's sphere. On Monday, 10 October 1960, a 113-seat Cunard Eagle Bristol Britannia 310 airliner inaugurated the first scheduled Skycoach service to Bermuda and Nassau, but this would be very restricted. Only six such services per year were to be operated, and alternately, between Cunard Eagle and its mortal enemy, BOAC.

Meanwhile, first-class and standard economy-class services would often be operated by both airlines using Bristol Britannias. Just five days after its first Skycoach flight, Cunard Eagle started a non-VLF fortnightly service to Bermuda and the Bahamas on 15 October. That service was to become weekly from January 1961. These new route arrangements would also be subject to revenue "pooling", which simply means revenue sharing. The basis for the pro rata share each airline received from the revenue pool was calculated from the amount of capacity airlines operated on those routes.[85] BOAC would always have the greater capacity and the airlines had to negotiate their pool agreement between themselves. Bamberg's very low fares proposal was a fight with the UK authorities he would not win and another example of the Establishment's readiness to kill competition.

Fly straight
to your winter sports
paradise in

AUSTRIA

LONDON - INNSBRUCK

EAGLE AIRWAYS

7 Bamberg's Contemporaries

There was a multitude of airlines popping in and out of existence in the 1940s, 1950s and 1960s competing with Bamberg's Eagle and British Eagle and often surviving only as associate companies of BOAC and BEA. For almost all of them, there was a slow takeover by the big market players while others simply collapsed. Bamberg's competition were examples of what could have happened to his Eagle and what did happen to his British Eagle airline. He operated in the post-World War Two environment where almost all the airlines of significance before 1939 had been absorbed by Imperial and the first British Airways which became BOAC and BEA.

With the surplus aircraft up for sale immediately after World War Two and an oversupply of pilots demobbed from the RAF, the late 1940s saw about a dozen independent airlines amass some market weight. But 10 years later there were only four of any significance. In 1946, Silver City Airways, Britavia, Air Kruise and Skyways started operating. Hunting Air Travel and Airwork both pre-dated World War Two, the only two. None of these airlines would exist after 1960. The consolidation of the UK airline industry is very much the story of the evolution of Hunting Air Travel and Airwork.

While Hunting Air Travel and Airwork had been in existence before the war they did not start flying charter operations until 1946. Hunting Air Travel was not dissimilar in scope to Airwork, it had its own well-known engineering company, Field Aircraft Services, and another sister firm, Percival, which built training, touring and light transport aircraft. Both firms were well connected and had businesses beyond just the airline, the latter being a lesson Bamberg would take on. Hunting Air Travel was owned by the Hunting family whose immense wealth came from 19th century oil exploitation. Hunting exists today as an energy services provider.[86]

In the 1940s, the Hunting group had strong connections with East and Central Africa, and it also had shipping interests. Hunting Air Travel operated from Luton Airport in December 1945, but did not participate in the Berlin airlift, they had more than enough work flying to and within East Africa. In the early 1950s, its East Africa connections would help Hunting Air Travel win a licence from the East African colonial administration, despite objections from BOAC, to fly expatriates back to England for low fares, as part of the airline's East African Club. The then Labour government's Air Ministry had wanted BOAC to get the licence. Despite the government's disappointment, it did not stop Hunting Air Travel benefiting from trooping contracts and it was awarded several in August 1951.

Hunting Air Travel merged with Clan Line Steamers for £500,000 to form the airline, Hunting-Clan Line Transport in 1953. Clan Line Steamers was a shipping company owned by the aristocratic Cayzer family. In 1953, a Lord Rotherwick, who gained his peerage in 1939 for services to the Conservative party, was Clan

Line Chairman. Lord Rotherwick is the Cayzer family's hereditary peerage, a Lord Rotherwick sat in the House of Lords until February 2022. On Tuesday 1 February 2022, 3rd Baron Rotherwick, Herbert Robin Cayzer left the Lords, and his seat was taken by Viscount Camrose, Jonathan William Berry.

One of the Clan Line Steamers' board members in 1953 was his middle-aged nephew William Nicholas Cayzer. Cambridge-educated William had started work for the family shipping line, Clan Line, in 1931, straight after he graduated from Corpus Christi college, Cambridge and became a company director just seven years later. In the same year that Clan Line bought an interest in the airline, Hunting Air Travel applied to the Conservative government under its "New Deal" for a small domestic and northern European network operating out of Newcastle.

Now known as Hunting-Clan Air Transport, the airline launched its Northern Network in May 1953. By the mid-1950s, Hunting-Clan Air Transport had struggled with its Newcastle based northern network and handed it over to its newly acquired subsidiary, Dragon Airways. The company had more success with its Africa cargo service to East and Central Africa, which had expanded to include Johannesburg in South Africa. By 1958, Hunting-Clan Air Transport had become part of an ambitious shipping consortium, British & Commonwealth Shipping created by the merger of Cayzer's Clan Line with the Union Castle shipping line. The resulting conglomerate owned more than 100 sea going vessels. It was William Nicholas Cayzer, who was a 2nd baronet, who had become Chairman of British & Commonwealth (B&C) shipping. Cayzer gained this position when his uncle, Lord Rotherwick, had died two years earlier in 1958. Cayzer had risen to the position of vice-chairmanship beside his uncle. In 1960, Hunting Clan Air Transport would be merged with Airwork.

Founded in 1928, Airwork operated from its own private Heston Aerodrome in Middlesex until 1935 when it moved to Gatwick airport. Airwork Services was started by Air Commodore Sir Henry Nigel St Valery Norman, 2nd Baronet, CBE and the aeronautical engineer, Frederick Alan Irving Muntz. Sandhurst-educated St Valery Norman died in an aircraft crash in 1943 but the firm would continue under Muntz. He had attended the prestigious Winchester College public school and like William Cayzer was a graduate of the University of Cambridge. Muntz's working life would be entirely in aviation, but he would not lead Airwork once B&C had become the larger shareholding. Airwork's other shareholders included Lord Cowdray, the richest man in Britain at the time, along with Lord Vestey and Lord Guinness.

While Hunting-Clan Air Transport origins were with a family whose wealth was in oil, Airwork Services had avoided being merged into the first British Airways or BOAC partly because of its commercial success. This was largely due to its involvement with the oil industry. Its customers included the Sudan government, Iraq Petroleum, Anglo-Iranian Oil, Kuwait Oil and Britain's Overseas Food Corporation which involved ferrying food from East Africa. Airwork also had a major operation in Ecuador with about ten aircraft flying for Shell and its oil exploration activities.

Like Hunting Air Travel, Airwork's business also consisted of flying clubs, training schools, airport catering, aircraft sales, engineering, worldwide ferrying services and sundry government support contracts.

Contract flying was only a part, albeit a significant part, of its revenues. For the Berlin airlift, Airwork only sent two Bristol Freighters which were able to carry outsize cargo loaded through the large clamshell nose doors but it received trooping contracts earlier than anyone else. In 1949 it began carrying the armed forces' families to and from the Suez Canal Zone under a charter from the then War Office. A shortage of shipping had led to unacceptable delays for family voyages.

Airwork followed the Canal Zone flights with a six-month War Office trooping contract to West Africa in 1949, giving it four to six flights a month. The Air Ministry at the time was extremely interested in farming out trooping flights to independents. When the Conservative government was elected in 1951, like other independents, Airwork benefited from the "New Deal" associate agreements with BOAC and BEA. In the early 1950s, Airwork also benefited from more investment by shipping companies. A Lord Leathers, who was a shipping industrialist, encouraged his shipping colleagues to invest in some of the airlines because of the market synergy for freight services. Airwork, Hunting, Britavia and Skyways all profited with new shipping line shareholders.

Airwork launched a transatlantic freight service in 1955 but the venture did not succeed and was withdrawn after only nine months. In the late 1950s, Airwork held board meetings at the Savoy hotel in London's Strand. Sir Myles Dermott Norris Wyatt was Managing Director and the other board members attending meetings were Lord Guinness, Lord Poole and Geoffrey Murrant. Ex-RAF pilot Gerald Freeman was Airwork's head of acquisition. He had started the air taxi service Transair after the war and it was later bought by Airwork.[87]

Transair started flying newspapers from October 1948 between London and Paris. The airline also made Mediterranean flights. In 1957, Transair was bought by Airwork, and it won the "West Med" contract for flights to Malta, Gibraltar and Libya from October 1957. Despite the fact that Airwork was a successful going concern, it would merge in 1960 with Hunting-Clan Air Transport and it's name would not survive beyond the 1950s like so many of Bamberg's contemporaries. One competitor airline that Bamberg would actually buy was Liverpool based Starways. The year 1950 saw Starways offering its services with a Douglas DC-3 Dakota. The airline specialised in pilgrimage traffic for the Cathedral Touring Agency to Tarbes in France. Like the other airlines, Starways would have its share of licence refusals from the UK authorities in the 1950s. However, it would find work flying for the United Nations to the Congo in Africa before flying UK tourists for Bamberg.

Of Bamberg's contemporaries, Skyways was the closest to the state-owned airlines. It was started by Air Commodore Alfred Cecil Critchley and Sir Alan Cobham, the inventor of air-to-air refuelling whose eponymous aviation technology company exists today. Cobham had joined the Royal Flying Corps, the RAF's predecessor, in 1917, aged 23 and after World War One, he joined the aircraft manufacturer de Havilland in 1921. Cobham became famous for his long-distance flights for Imperial Airways and the government's Air Ministry. In 1926, he was knighted aged 32 and during the 1930s he ran a flying display team before inventing air-to-air refuelling.[88] He started his own company Flight Refuelling Limited in 1934 which eventually became the firm that bears his name today.[89]

Skyways was a charter airline and like Airwork it

often flew for the oil industry. An early contract was with Anglo-Iranian Oil for flights between Iran and the UK. In 1947, Skyways was chartered by BOAC to fill gaps in its schedules and capacity, in particular flights to the Middle east. In the late 1940s, Skyways would benefit from "associate agreements" with BEA providing flight within the UK. The Berlin airlift was another opportunity for Skyways, just as it was for almost all of the UK's independent airlines.

In 1953, an Avro York aircraft operated by Skyways crashed into the Atlantic on the way to the Caribbean. Skyways stopped its Caribbean service and a Skyway's Director, Sir Wavell Wakefield, the then Conservative member of Parliament for St Marylebone, defended the firm in the House of Commons. About this time, Bamberg sold his York aircraft to Skyways, partly in protest at government policy. As 1953 came to a close, it looked like BOAC was going to buy a 25% stake in Skyways. The deal had been brokered between BOAC Chairman Sir Miles Thomas and Wakefield, but complaints from other airlines to the government saw the deal quashed in March 1954.

As the 1950s progressed, Skyways, like other airlines, profited from trooping flights and charter work — both freight and passengers. Skyways close relationship with BOAC did not end. In 1954, the State airline contracted Skyways to fly the corporation's all-cargo services to Singapore. In 1955, like Eagle, Skyways had UK to Cyprus trooping contracts. In 1957, Skyways received a major Far East trooping contract. Skyways purchased Bahama Airways and ended the 1950s much like Bamberg's Eagle, flying between Miami and Nassau and looking for further opportunities in the mid-Atlantic and Caribbean.

A Lockheed Constellation of Skyways.

The State airline was not going to object to the airline of Air Commodore Alfred Cecil Critchley, Sir Alan Cobham and Sir Wavell Wakefield operating in the West Indies. However, in the face of Cunard-Eagle, BOAC bought Bahamas Airways back. Bahamas Airways was one of several branch airlines BOAC had developed in the 1950s including, British West Indian Airways, Middle East Airlines, Gulf Aviation and Aden Airways.

In 1959 the Conservative Prime Minister Harold Macmillan made Winston Churchill's son-in-law Duncan Sandys responsible for the Ministry of Supply with the intention of rationalising the airline industry. Born in 1908, Sandys was the son of a Conservative party member of Parliament and was himself a member, for a South London constituency. The 1960 Civil Aviation Act should have been a time of liberalisation and opportunity but instead it was the instrument with which Eton and Oxford-educated Sandys would aim to reduce the number of British registered airlines. The 1960 Act created the Air Transport Licensing Board

(ATLB) which had substantial powers to tell the airlines what to do. Within 12 months 8 airlines were merged into 2.

With the Civil Aviation Act's outcome of rationalisation rather than the liberalisation the government claimed was the goal, Critchley and Cobham must have decided to throw in the towel. Skyways was divided up with its coach-air operation, Skyways Coach-Air, hived off and the long haul cargo operation being sold to a new airline, Euravia. Sandys wanted amalgamations in the independent airline sector and looked to Airwork to provide a lead.

The Cayzer family were beneficiaries of the 1960 Act's rationalisation. Sir William Nicholas Cayzer (2021), born 1911, would have been a contemporary of Duncan Sandys at Eton and Oxford. The 'liberalisation' that had been expected from the licensing act would actually allow Establishment families to benefit from that airline rationalisation. Airwork had already scooped up a number of operators. Bristow Helicopters was the last to succumb thanks to Freddie Laker. In 1958, Frederick Laker had sold a controlling interest in his Air Charter airline and his Southend-based engineering firm Aviation Traders to Airwork and joined the firm.

In January 1960, and on 1 March, Sir Myles Wyatt, Airwork's Chairman and Managing Director announced the impending merger of his airline group with Hunting-Clan Air Transport. British United Airlines (BUA) was the biggest outcome of that rationalisation and another creature of the Establishment. The combined group included Airwork, Airwork Helicopters, Bristow Helicopters, Channel Air Bridge, Hunting-Clan Air Transport, Morton and Olley, Transair and Frederick Alfred Laker's Air Charter. Morton and Olley was not an airline but two well-known pilots. Captain Olley was based at Croydon and owned by the nationalised British Railways, but his Olley Air Service, a charter airline, did not get absorbed by BEA in 1949. Neither did his former chief pilot, Captain Morton, who had formed his own charter airline also based at Croydon.

The most famous of Bamberg's contemporaries was Frederick 'Freddie' Alfred Laker. Born in Canterbury, Kent in 1922, Laker had had an avid interest in all things electrical and mechanical as a boy and took an engineering evening course at the age of 14. It was seeing Germany's Hindenburg airship and a Handley Page biplane fly over Canterbury Cathedral that led him to choose a future in aviation. At the age of 16 Laker left a state-run school and went to work for aircraft maker Short Brothers in Rochester as an engineering apprentice.

This start with aviation was interrupted when the Short Brothers' factory was bombed in 1940 but he obtained work as a flight engineer for the Air Transport Auxiliary (ATA). The ATA was run by a man who was already a Director of British Airways Limited and would later become BOAC Chairman, Sir Gerard d'Erlanger. Later in Laker's life, BOAC and the second manifestation of British Airways would ultimately bring his aviation career to an end. The ATA ceased to exist in November 1945 and in 1946, while Bamberg was deciding what he would do with his £100, he joined the newly created, state-owned, BEA.

Laker left BEA after a few months and joined London Aero & Motor Services, which operated charter services, but left that within a year to form his own company, Aviation Traders. Buying and selling government military surplus, including non-aviation items, Laker also worked as Chief Engineer for a small charter airline called Payloads. It went out of business, but its owner, Bobby Sanderson, gave Laker the capital he needed to finance his own airline. Laker bought ten Handley Page Halton freighters from BOAC.[90] Within five years, Laker would be buying a small struggling airline from Harold Bamberg called Air Charter which would successfully compete with Airwork and Skyways. In August 1954, Laker's Air Charter was awarded the government's Canzair contract, taking over from Airwork and Skyways, to provide the daily flights. In 1956, Air Charter again won over Skyways for the UK, Cyprus trooping contract. But in the 1950s Laker financially weakened himself with a foolhardy diversion into aircraft development with the failed *Accountant* aircraft. In January 1958, Laker sold Aviation Traders Engineering (ATEL) and Air Charter (ACG), to Airwork.

Signing the deal with Sir Myles Wyatt, Laker was retained by Airwork and became a board member.[91] Laker was quickly bored and went to his boss, Wyatt, for what else he could do for his new employer. Wyatt asked Laker to see how they could acquire Alan Bristow's helicopter company. Airwork's own helicopter firm was a loss maker. Bristow was a tax exile in Bermuda, so Laker took his family to Bermuda for a holiday.

While there Laker and his family were invited to a cocktail party at the home of Taffy Powell who had founded Silver City Airways in 1948, the same year Bamberg got his airline going. Powell would later represent British Eagle in North America after Silver City had been bought by BUA. At that cocktail party Laker would meet helicopter operator Alan Bristow. That meeting eventually led to Laker successfully buying Bristow Helicopters for Airwork in May 1960, and Bristow remained its Chief Executive. Airwork's helicopter operation was subsumed into the Bristow business and the new combined rotorcraft business became profitable for many years to come.[92]

In the same month the newly merged Hunting Clan and Airwork companies became British United Airways, and Laker continued to run the two businesses of his, ATEL and ACG, that had been subsumed into the new airline. As the rationalisation process steamrollered forward, BUA would also swallow British Aviation Services with it its many subsidiary airlines and the British Aviation Insurance Company. Founded in 1930 and still in existence today, the British Aviation Insurance Company was the parent of charter airline Britavia, which had itself absorbed a number of airlines before the 1960 Civil Aviation Act forced a final rationalisation.

One was Aquila Airways, a flying boat airline that operated aircraft retired by BOAC when they ceased their flying boat operations in 1950. Britavia also bought Manx Airlines and the remnants of Blackpool based Lancashire Aircraft Corporation. They were consolidated with Dragon Airways into one unit and operated under the Silver City name as its northern division. Silver City Airways, created in 1946, was another important BUA acquisition. Its first managing director was former RAF Air Commodore, Griffith "Taffy" Powell. Taffy had been Britavia's chief technical officer before leading Silver City along with several ex-RAF people who had served with him in Ferry Command and Transport Command. Taffy retired in 1957 and in the same year Silver City absorbed Air Kruise whose founder, Hugh Kennard, became Deputy Managing Director of Silver

City. Air Kruise had been a neighbour of Silver City at Lympne Airport and had started an air coach passenger service to Le Touquet.

By the late 1950s, Silver City had become a household name by ferrying cars along with passengers onboard its Bristol Type 170 Superfreighter aircraft. Taking a car onboard an aircraft became routine for stars of stage and screen, politicians and sportsmen including David Niven and Stirling Moss. They all used the Silver City air ferry along with Her Majesty Queen Elizabeth II whose Rolls-Royce was flown by Silver City.[93] In 1960, Silver City transported around 90,000 vehicles and 220,000 passengers with 40,000 Channel crossings.[94] It was this year that Silver City was bought by Air Holdings, the parent body of the newly formed BUA. Silver City failed to make a success of its long haul operations, but for domestic scheduled services it had built up an extensive network.

Britavia would be absorbed into the BUA family of companies two years later in 1962. Along with Silver City and Britavia, BUA would also absorb Jersey Airlines and British United Air Ferries (BUAF). The latter would be immortalised in the 1963 James Bond film *Goldfinger*. The titular villain, Auric Goldfinger, would depart the UK from Southend Airport with his Rolls Royce loaded aboard one of BUAF's Aviation Traders' ATL-98 Carvair freighters. However, it was actually Silver City's car ferry service that James Bond author Ian Fleming had referred to in his 1959 novel, *Goldfinger*. In the book, Bond is talking to Goldfinger who reveals that he transports his armoured car onboard Silver City aircraft for biannual golfing holidays.[95]

Jersey Airlines (not to be confused with the Whitehall Securities owned Jersey Airways which predated

World War Two) was a newcomer in post-war Britain. As its name suggests, it flew channel island services, specialising in underserved regions of the UK, often in collaboration with BEA. From peripheral beginnings by 1960 Jersey would be flying 250,000 people a year, despite severing its connection with BEA. It made itself attractive enough that BUA's owner, Air Holdings, came calling in 1962, at which point Jersey Airlines became British United (Channel Islands) Airways.

Two airlines that would survive from the 1940s were Cambrian Airways and BKS Air Transport (BKS stood for Barnby, Keegan and Stevens). Cambrian and BKS both became subsidiary airlines of the State-owned BEA. Cambrian Airways Limited began scheduled services in 1949 and concentrated on serving South Wales and the West of England. A ten-year operating agreement was signed with BEA in 1956 and the State-owned airline acquired a 33% share in Cambrian in 1958. Unlike BOAC's proposed share in Skyways, this investment was not opposed.

Cambrian operated from Cardiff and Bristol to Liverpool and Manchester. The latter was a feeder service for BOAC and BEA. Cambrian would also fly from Manchester and Liverpool through Cardiff and Bristol to the Channel Islands. Another set of services was Cardiff and Bristol to Bournemouth and Paris or Cork to London direct and via Cardiff or Bristol. A five times weekly service from Glasgow and Manchester to Bristol and Cardiff was started on 2 April 1962. Cambrian would finally be absorbed into the new British Airways in the 1970s. BKS Air Transport, which would also be known as BKS Aerocharter, was another of the subsidiary BEA airlines which would eventually be absorbed into the new British Airways. One major independent airline, however, Harold Bamberg's British Eagle, would remain stubbornly outside the fold and would continue to be independent until its bankruptcy in 1968.

As the 1960s progressed, Laker had become BUA's Managing Director but friction between himself and Sir Myles Wyatt was causing problems. In December 1965, Laker left BUA as the airline racked up losses. The government's 1968 Edwards Report was the beginning of a process that would see new life injected into BUA where other airlines were left to fall.

"There were whispers and rumours going around and it didn't have a good spirit or feel about it in those last few months," recalls Eagle radio engineer, Philip Johns. "I think because of that [Edwards Report] that's when clearly, rumours were starting to go around and so forth. After my very buoyant nine years with them there were clearly signs and a change of mood. With the opposition that was going on at the time, both with government and a difficulty to get certain routes and so forth, it just wasn't an easy time."

While the committee that produced the Edwards Report was formed under a Labour government, the then Prime minster, Harold Wilson, called an election in 1970 which he lost to the Conservatives. Edward Heath became Prime minister, and he would set the country on a course to join the then European Economic Community. But, before that, Heath's government would implement the recommendations of the Edwards Report with its own civil aviation legislation. That legislation was the Civil Aviation Act of 1971 which ended the ATLB and created the Civil Aviation Authority (CAA) which still exists today.

One of the recommendations of 394-page *The Edwards*

Report published six months before British Eagle went bust was for debt-stricken BUA and Caledonian to merge as a "second force" airline. But no action would be taken for this second force for almost another four years. By second force it meant another state backed airline, BOAC and BEA being the first force. Like Bamberg's Eagle, Caledonian Airways had been fighting its corner as an independent since its inception in 1961 as the new Scottish private airline.[96] Making its first charter passenger carrying flight on 29 November 1961, Caledonian flew principally across the Atlantic and it's perhaps no surprise that Caledonian's co-founder, John de la Haye, had worked on North Atlantic charters for British Eagle.

On 29 March 1971 the House of Commons held a debate for the Civil Aviation Bill. The Minister for Trade at the time was Michael Antony Cristobal Noble and he made it clear what would happen to Caledonian and BUA. Noble was the youngest son of Sir John Noble, 1st baronet. Noble himself, while a Conservative member of Parliament for Argyll, would become Lord Baron Glenkinglas in 1974 after serving as the Argyll MP from 1958 to 1974. At the debate, Noble said: "What has now been established is that Caledonian/BUA should be the principal independent scheduled airline."[97] How is a government backed airline independent? And when it came to a BUA/Caledonian merger, there was a big problem; BUA was in such terrible debt it could not buy Caledonian. This is why Noble had referred to Caledonian/BUA.

Alan Bristow had replaced Freddie Laker as BUA's Managing Director, and he explained how the reverse takeover (a smaller company buying a larger enterprise) was done in his autobiography. "It became necessary for me to arrange an accommodation with Caledonian Airways, which in effect meant selling the company to Caledonian... I briefly examined the possibility of a management buyout, but we couldn't raise the wind [money]... Caledonian was only a fraction of BUA's size and they couldn't raise the £32 million required to buy out Air Holdings. At Air Holdings Board meetings there were long discussions about how deals might be structured, but none of them stood up to scrutiny. Eventually I suggested: 'Why don't we do a lease-purchase deal?'" Bristow admits that he could not see a conventional viable option and a lease-purchase was the best route simply because that way, "a joint Caledonian-BUA operation has cash flow enough to meet the payments... A deposit of three and a half million was agreed, with sixty monthly payments to make up the balance. At first Caledonian couldn't raise the deposit and talks were broken off, but eventually they managed to find it. We were effectively 'going banker' for Adam Thompson. One of Caledonian's stipulations was that as far as the public was concerned, Caledonian was buying BUA, and it was agreed that no one should talk about the deal in any other terms until after the final payment... In 1970, the company became Caledonian BUA, later changed to British Caledonian, and by 1975 Adam Thompson owned all of it. He defaulted on only one monthly payment; Nick Cayzer called me in to discuss it, and I advised that Caledonian be given a little leeway because I thought they were good for the money."

Bamberg and British Eagle may have been a victim of timing, but why did the Edwards Report, in May 1968, recommend a BUA, Caledonian merger? British Eagle was still operating, and its 1967 financial results had shown a profit. What was it that BUA's owners, the aristocratic Cayzer family, did not like about the idea of BUA merging with German Jewish émigré Harold Bamberg's British Eagle, whose debts were far less than BUA's and which was a similarly sized company? A key part of Bamberg's success compared to the other airlines was that he saw the value in being vertically integrated, meaning he provided the travel agencies through whom people booked their holidays and in turn those agencies booked the flights, chartering Bamberg's fleet. But what had happened to other airlines, acquisition by a bigger player, would happen to Bamberg's Eagle but not in quite the same way.

Harold Bamberg on the flight deck of a British Eagle
Bristol Britannia.

119

8 Cunard Arrives

Cunard Eagle would seem like a perfect vehicle for Bamberg's ambitions with the Establishment shipping company investing in an airline, but the relationship which began in early 1960 became far more complicated. Bamberg found himself rubbing shoulders with British Establishment figures with different ideas about the airline industry. Worse still, Cunard would later agree to a deal with BOAC creating BOAC Cunard which essentially ended British Eagle's existence as an independent airline. It was a sorry chapter in the Bamberg story from start to finish.

In 1960, the Cunard shipping line, seeing competition from transatlantic airlines, bought a controlling share of Eagle Airways creating Cunard Eagle in March of that year. In a business marriage that would help fend off the likes of BUA, Bamberg became the new airline's Managing Director, but not all would go well. Bamberg's Eagle Aviation had been the only one of Britain's big five independent airlines which did not have investors from the shipping industry. Cunard Eagle changed all that when it was born on Monday 21 March 1960. Cunard's Chairman, Sir John Brocklebank, announced an agreement in principle to buy, more than a 50% interest in Eagle.[98]

Cunard was operating transatlantic crossings and feeling the effects of a rapid rise in air travel. That year more than one million passengers had crossed the

Atlantic by air and, like the railway and other shipping firms that had invested in airlines, Cunard saw a metaphoric train it needed to board. By May of 1960 Sir John's shipping line bought the entire share capital of Eagle.

The Cunard take-over also coincided with a move of premises for Eagle. Blackbushe was to be closed to commercial traffic from May 1960 so, in March, Eagle moved its main operating and maintenance base to Heathrow. Eagle had been operating from Heathrow since 1957 and the practical reality was that by 1960 most of the airlines' operations were at London airport, soon to be renamed Heathrow. Bamberg's Eagle would stay at Heathrow for the remainder of his time in airline management.

Electrician, Eric Tarrant, recalled, "I was at Heathrow when it happened [Cunard's purchase]. It was actually a very happy time and morale was very high and, there was clearly a buzz because of the talk of bringing in the Boeing 707. It was quite an exciting time, we felt, to be tied up with Cunard. We did [see a great future ahead] because there was the tie up with the two [Cunard] ships, Queen Mary and Queen Elizabeth. I remember in the radio shop itself we were at that time recrystallising some of the radios to be able to talk to the ships' captains over the Atlantic. That could be relayed to the passengers on the PA."

The Eagle, Cunard tie up came at a time of management turbulence for BOAC. Sir Gerard d'Erlanger, BOAC Chairman since 1 May 1956, had told the then aviation Minister Duncan Sandys MP that, "he would like, as soon as it was convenient, to give up his post as chairman of BOAC, so that he could devote his whole time to his own business."[99] The first half of 1960 had already seen three members of the BOAC Board replaced because of ill health or their appointment period had ended.

To replace them, Sandys had appointed, Chairman of B.T.R. Industries and Westminster Bank director, Sir Walter Worboys; Unilever Vice-Chairman Mr. J. A. Connel and a Lionel Poole, who had been National Union of Boot and Shoe Operatives General Secretary. Sandys also appointed an existing Board member, former civil servant Sir Wilfred Neden, to the position of Deputy Chairman, on a part-time basis. None of them had previous aviation experience. On a full-time basis, however, Sandys would appoint Sir Matthew Slattery as Chairman. Previously he had led the aircraft manufacturer Short and Harland as well as the Bristol Aircraft Company.[100]

Slattery was the privately-educated son of the Irish banker, Henry Francis Slattery who had been Chairman of The National Bank of Ireland for 14 years before Sir Matthew's 1902 birth.[101] In 1916, Slattery, the youngest of Henry's children, joined the Royal Navy at 13, and was educated at the Royal Naval College, Osborne and then the Royal Naval College in Dartmouth. He would become a Fleet Air Arm pilot and rise to the rank of Rear-Admiral by the end of World War Two. His last role for the Navy included Chief of Naval Air Equipment and Director-General of Naval Aircraft Development and Production.

Slattery left the Royal Navy in 1948 to become the Managing Director of Northern Ireland-based Short Brothers and Harland, which was building aircraft for the UK military. He took on the additional role of Chairman in 1952. In 1957, Prime Minister Harold Macmillan appointed Slattery special adviser on the transport of Middle East oil and the same year he became Managing

Director of the Bristol Airplane Company, which had taken a 15.25% share in Short Brothers and Harland three years earlier in 1954.

On 29 July 1960, Slattery started work as BOAC Chairman. He took little time in proposing a joint transatlantic venture to Cunard, but this was rejected.[102] It was not an entirely new idea. In 1946, the then Cunard Chairman, Sir Percy Bates, who died that very year, had proposed it to the then aviation Minister, Lord Winster, but the suggestion was rejected. Slattery would eventually be more successful but first the ATLB and the new aviation Minister needed to look at the possible repercussions for BOAC.

Fifteen years after that 1946 proposal, Cunard had finally achieved its long-standing goal of having an airline business with transatlantic ambitions. Within 14 months the Air Transport Licensing Board (ATLB) would award the new Cunard Eagle the North Atlantic licence its shipping owner had long desired. Unfortunately, it was a misleading start to what would become a very negative intervention by the ATLB and a sorry tale for Bamberg that he would never fully recover from.

In April 1960, *Flight International* reported the ATLB's first job would be to decide between Cunard Eagle and BOAC on transatlantic routes. The ATLB's first Chairman was Liberal Party House of Lords member, Lord Terrington, but he died in January 1961. Lord Terrington was the 3rd Baron Terrington, a hereditary peerage, and his real name was Horace Woodhouse. Educated at New College, Oxford, Woodhouse had been an industrial dispute mediator until he obtained his title from the death of his older brother in 1940.[103] When Terrington died, he would be succeeded at the ATLB by Professor Daniel Jack, a University of

Durham economics professor. Jack would lead the Board until 1970.[104]

In the meantime, 28 July 1960 saw Cunard Eagle Airways Limited come into existence. The new airline set out to make the most of what permissions it already had for transatlantic operations. In April, Cunard had applied to US authorities for an unrestricted charter operation into the USA. While the new management team waited for a decision, the 1960 summer season charters went to New York via Montreal; a route already approved for Eagle. Bamberg and his new Cunard Board members also undertook an extensive transatlantic charter programme.

From June to September Heathrow, Glasgow Prestwick and Shannon in Ireland were linked with Montreal and New York. The first of these charters flew in mid-June. Prestwick alone saw almost 40 charters during that season while the first Skycoach service to Bermuda and Nassau took place in October. Skycoach was the name given to the very low fares that Bamberg had lobbied for, and the government and other airlines had agreed too. Applying for VLF across a range of destinations, the government only allowed a monthly Skycoach service to the Caribbean in conjunction with BOAC with an 18-month delay on its introduction, and it was October before that day finally came.

The fortnightly first class and economy fare (which was more expensive than Skycoach) flights that Bamberg had had to agree too began on 15 October. The new services, along with the monthly Skycoach and fortnightly regular flights, were proving themselves and by mid-March 1961 the first class and economy passengers got to fly every week. Over the months the passenger numbers were encouraging, Cunard Eagle's

A Bermudan registered Boeing 707 of Cunard Eagle
Airways.

share of the market rose by two percentage points
to 12%, equating to 20,000 passengers a year. It was
in January 1961 that Cunard Eagle finally put in its
application for scheduled services from the UK to the
USA and Canada. The flights would be from Heathrow,
Manchester and Glasgow Prestwick to New York,
Chicago, Detroit, Philadelphia, Washington, Baltimore,
Boston, Montreal and Toronto. The ATLB hearing took
place on 18 April with Cunard Eagle putting forward the
argument that the transatlantic sector needed maximum
British participation and so two carriers should be
allowed. BOAC made its case against the argument for
two carriers flying across the North Atlantic, the newly
formed ATLB needed to make a crucial decision.

Although the ATLB under Jack's leadership would
one day contribute to the death of Bamberg's airline
ambitions, its first decision was positive for Cunard
Eagle. In June 1961, Jack's ATLB ruled that Cunard

Eagle could have a 15-year licence for a London to New York service, using Boeing 707-465s and Bristol Britannias. From 31 August 1961 to 31 July 1976, flights were to be once daily for passengers from Manchester and Prestwick to Philadelphia, Boston. Baltimore and Washington. All these destinations were in the US-UK Air Agreement. Cunard Eagle did not, however, get everything it wanted, it was refused rights to operate to Toronto, Montreal, Detroit and Chicago.[105]

This decision was, predictably, met by horror at BOAC. Sir Basil Smallpeice, BOAC Managing Director at the time, wrote in his 1980 autobiography, *Of Comets and Queens*: "The timing [of the ATLB decision] could not have been worse from our point of view. If Cunard were allowed on to the North Atlantic with additional aircraft, it could only be at the cost of traffic that we badly needed in the recession from the beginning." January 1961 saw the start of a contraction in US passenger demand which had started to emerge late in 1960, according to Smallpeice.[106]

A trade recession in the United States had begun in late 1960 which worsened through that winter and by Spring US industry was suffering. Smallpeice wrote that this impacted greatly on the recent American trend of finding sunny shores for a winter break. The recession also meant businesses cut back substantially on the travel budgets. What compounded this situation of widespread belt tightening was the delivery of new aircraft to many airline fleets.

Conservative Minister for Aviation in 1960, Duncan Sandys MP, had appointed the members of the ATLB.[107] It was one of Sandys' last acts as Minister (He would be replaced that year by Peter Thorneycroft MP) and the ATLB would be quite an assortment of individuals with only one member who had any air transport knowledge. He was an A. H. Wilson who had been Deputy Secretary at the Ministry of Transport and Civil Aviation and he was awarded a CBE and made a Companion of the Order of the Bath for his troubles.

The other members, none of whom had any aviation knowledge, were: London School of Economics professor of Statistics, Professor R. G. D. Allen CBE; C. Bagnall CBE, the Managing Director of a Nylon yarn producing firm; E. Baldry OBE, a Senior Partner at Allen, Baldry, Holman & Best chartered accountants; Sir Friston How, a senior civil servant and former Secretary of the Atomic Energy Office, and finally, the West Midland Traffic Area Chairman of the Traffic Commissioners, W. P. James OBE.

The lack of aviation knowledge amongst the ATLB members raised questions over the Board's ability to make any sound judgements, but the powers reserved for the aviation Minister also undermined the organisation's integrity. While the ATLB was supposed to have more independence and power than the Air Transport Advisory Council it replaced, the Civil Aviation Act reserved the important powers over international traffic rights and international fares for the government Minister. The argument was that these involve questions of national sovereignty which could not be delegated. While on the face of it the ATLB was the new authority in town, the Conservative government of Harold Macmillan was ultimately going to pull the strings on the industry questions of import.

If the fact that the aviation Minister, who was now Peter Thorneycroft MP, made the decisions regarding foreign routes was not enough; the ATLB's Constitution also set out criteria limiting any independent airline's right to fly on any BOAC or BEA route. Before allowing any independent such access, the ATLB had to consider, the adequacy of BOAC or BEA services and the possibility of wasteful duplication of, or material diversion from, BEA or BOAC services; and the corporations' financial commitments or commercial agreements, such as pool agreements. There was not going to be any generous handing over of BOAC and BEA business to independent airlines.[108]

As far as the Cunard Eagle, BOAC transatlantic route fight was concerned, the ATLB was really a paper tiger with little or no say in the matter in actuality. BOAC made its determination clear to fight the single June 1961 Cunard Eagle win: "We shall personally appeal against [the ATLB's decision]... as we have the right to do... The Board's decision appears to accept that inevitably there will be diversions... of traffic from BOAC if Cunard Eagle operate successfully... BOAC had understood that it was the intention of Parliament, as embodied in the Civil Aviation Licensing Act, 1960, that this should not occur."

Cunard Eagle was not only facing an appeal from BOAC, in June 1961 BEA was also lobbying the ATLB not to give domestic routes either to Bamberg's airline or BUA, which was then run by Freddie Laker. In May 1961, BEA Chairman Lord Douglas had accused BUA and Cunard Eagle of a "take-over" and that the two airlines were trying to "filch" BEA's business. Laker hit back and said: "BEA's war on the independents in fact started some years ago — behind the scenes — when they successfully persuaded the IATA airlines to offer cheap fares to package-tour operators on their scheduled services"[109]

A decision on the BEA complaint would not be made

until February 1963, but long before then the North Atlantic ATLB decision would be reversed by the new aviation Minster, Peter Thorneycroft MP, who ruled that Cunard Eagle would not be keeping its North Atlantic licence. Thorneycroft's view was that there were, "too many seats chasing too few passengers," over the Atlantic. His decision was reinforced by a judge. When BOAC appealed, Thorneycroft appointed a retired judge, Sir Fred Pritchard, to review the matter.

Held at the end of September in Holborn town hall, BOAC and Cunard Eagle's senior management were grilled by each other's barristers while Sir Fred looked on. Smallpeice wrote of this event: "I was more than a little nervous at being cross-examined by so eminent QC [Queens' Counsel] as Mr Gerald Gardiner (later Lord Gardiner and Lord Chancellor)'. A Queen's Counsel is a lawyer whose achievements in the profession have been recognised by the Crown. Sir Fred's conclusion after witnessing such cross-examinations was that the ATLB board had not exercised their "proper function of furthering the development of British civil aviation".[110]

The decision no doubt cheered BOAC Chairman Sir Matthew Slattery, who may have also known Thorneycroft. In 1945 Thorneycroft was the Ministry of War Transport's Parliamentary Secretary while Slattery had been Chief Naval Representative at the Ministry of Aircraft Production.[111] Sixteen years later, in November 1961, Thorneycroft made a formal announcement to the House of Commons that he had accepted the recommendations of Sir Fred. The ATLB had formally reversed its decision earlier in October, days after Sir Fred's decision; a decision which would lead to the end of Cunard Eagle and paradoxically the resignations of Slattery and Smallpeice.

However, at the time the BOAC management were elated with the decision. Smallpeice wrote in his autobiography that the "outcome was gratifying" and Sir Fred's recommendations established "future guidelines for the Licensing Board. What we desperately needed in 1961 was not just to retain our business, but to increase it". The tactic employed to increase it was one that had led ultimately to BOAC's creation, larger airlines absorbing smaller ones with state help. In late 1961, the scene was set for BOAC to absorb Cunard Eagle, thus increasing BOAC's business.

With the North Atlantic licence lost, Cunard Eagle still had Bamberg's well-established routes from the UK to Bermuda and the Caribbean. The solution in late 1961 was to offer services into the USA from there. Slattery was still concerned that Cunard Eagle could be given a North Atlantic licence again by a future Conservative administration. Cunard Eagle was able to appeal the ATLB's licence reversal, but the result did not change — BOAC had decisively won. Nevertheless, Cunard Eagle's transatlantic charter services continued to thrive and the Cunard network of 17 sales offices across North America helped a great deal. For the transatlantic charter services, most flights were from Heathrow, but Belfast, Manchester and Prestwick all saw activity.

The Caribbean and Bermuda services had also thrived. A now weekly London, Nassau, Miami route fed a Nassau-Miami service which was flying four times a day. Bermuda to New York flights increased to twice daily and off-peak fares were driving the demand. By the end of 1961 Cunard Eagle's share of the East Coast to Caribbean market had increased to 15%. The ATLB decision however, was a deeply damaging one and all the Manchester services were dropped as a cost cutting measure. Eagle had operated from Manchester for eight years and had flown to Bergen, Pisa, Copenhagen, Rimini, Ostend and Hamburg.

The following year, 1962, saw the arrival of the first of two Boeing 707 aircraft that Cunard Eagle had ordered when it was expecting the transatlantic scheduled service licence. Cunard Eagle had been flying Bermuda-New York using Bamberg's workhorse aircraft, the Vickers Viscounts. The 707 arrived on 27 February and started flying on that Bermuda-Miami route on 27 March. The 707, which had a Bermuda registration, was still only flying on an ad-hoc basis when it entered service on the Bermuda-Miami route. Still, this made Cunard Eagle the first British independent airline to operate jet services with fare-paying passengers.[112] Less than two months later, on 5 May, Cunard Eagle's first 707 inaugurated a twice-weekly scheduled jet service from Heathrow to Bermuda and Nassau.

On 5 May, the inaugural flight left London with Bamberg and a Cunard Steamship Company director, Ben Russell, on board. Along with guests there were more than 50 paying passengers on the flight. Now there would be three weekly flights with two ending in Miami and one in Jamaica.[113] Bamberg had also luckily just received a new licence to fly to Jamaica.

Eagle would also be able to find work for the 707 in serving that extension to the existing UK to Caribbean charters. Bamberg also wanted to extend his Caribbean operations to Montego Bay and Kingston and there were even discussions with Jamaican authorities about helping to create a national Jamaican airline, but they went nowhere. These were positives in a year where very little was moving in Bamberg and Eagle's favour.

Despite the ATLB reversal and Cunard Eagle's

cost cutting measures BOAC's Managing Director, Smallpeice and Slattery still had concerns about the Cunard Eagle tie up. During the past 10-years of Conservative rule there had been three different prime ministers and many cabinet changes. What view would a future aviation minister or prime Minister take? For BOAC a partial merger with Cunard removed a powerful rival from the market. The Cunard investment in Bamberg's airline and its initial victory with the ATLB had, for a moment, created a genuine competitive threat to BOAC.

Smallpeice would have a pivotal role in the birth of the long gestating idea of BOAC-Cunard. Little did he know it would also be the end of his career with BOAC although, ironically, not Cunard. Smallpeice, who was knighted in 1961 and made a Knight Commander of the Royal Victorian Order, was born in Rio de Janeiro in 1906, a privately-educated banker's son. He became an accountant and joined BOAC in 1950 as the Financial Comptroller, becoming BOAC's Deputy Managing Director in 1954 and Managing Director from 1954–56.

By early 1962, Smallpeice had seen several advantages in BOAC absorbing Cunard Eagle. First, Cunard had great brand value in the USA along with sales offices in key locations. Secondly, he saw the infusion of private capital into BOAC as highly desirable, partly because private investors' needs could justify the purchase of more efficient Boeing jets and BOAC could escape the long standing rule that they should always give preference to British aircraft.

Cunard Eagle's two Boeing 707 jetliners would be a welcome addition to BOAC's fleet. When buying into British Eagle in March 1960, Cunard had signed a deal for two new Boeing 707-400 aircraft with an option for a third. BOAC had had recent problems with its maintenance staff's trade unions and Smallpeice saw the guarantee of more work for them as a possible solution to those negotiations.

Discussions between Cunard and BOAC went on in secret. Cunard had become fed up with the aviation authorities on both sides of the Atlantic. The ATLB decision was a particularly grievous blow. The passenger rights Cunard was expecting just did not materialise either side of the Atlantic. Secret negotiations between the Chairman of Cunard, Sir John Brocklebank, and BOAC's Slattery were carried out with the intention of merging Cunard Eagle into BOAC. If Cunard thought that this would help it realise its transatlantic ambitions the outcome would demonstrate that nothing of the sort was going to happen.

With Slattery's approval, Smallpeice invited Bamberg and Cunard Director Richard Taylor to the BOAC offices on 27 April 1962. Smallpeice remembers that Bamberg was quiet throughout the meeting while Taylor saw advantages in promoting a company jointly with BOAC, but Taylor probably knew that his boss had already secretly negotiated a deal. Smallpeice recalled that Brocklebank and his board must have approved of the idea as "matters went ahead fairly rapidly". A joint, BOAC, Cunard company would be formed and the contentious issue was how much of the joint venture each side owned. For Smallpeice, Cunard Eagle owning more than 25% was unacceptable.

Brocklebank's board rolled over and agreed to this lopsided joint company on 16 May 1962 in their own office in Regent Street, London. The government was not so impressed by the 25% limitation and Thorneycroft told BOAC that a politically acceptable share had to be at least 33.3%. On 6 June 1962, BOAC and Cunard signed the deal, the split would be 70% BOAC, 30% Cunard. The BOAC-Cunard board met for the first time on 22 June 1962 at BOAC's offices at 157–197 Buckingham Palace Road, London.

By June 1962, Bamberg was sat on the board of BOAC-Cunard with managers who had been his sworn competition not so long ago. It was an uncomfortable arrangement, but the earlier marriage between Cunard and Eagle had also been stormy: the two groups came from very different business cultures and Cunard's management instinctively distrusted their aviation colleagues. Worse still, the new company had no interest in non-Atlantic services despite those routes representing the bulk of Eagle's activity. In Bamberg's view, Cunard had disposed of years of his management team's hard work establishing Eagle as a major international air carrier.

If BOAC-Cunard had achieved one thing, it was to eliminate a competitor, British Eagle, from the airline marketplace. Perhaps that was the plan all along? There were significant differences in opinion of where the strategic focus lied combined with the cultural differences between an Establishment shipping firm and an independent airline. What had always been a potentially difficult relationship was, unsurprisingly, a very unhappy one at managerial level.[114]

As well as BOAC contributing 70% of the capital to the new BOAC-Cunard, the state airline provided eight Boeing 707s to the combined fleet. With the merger, this fleet, rather embarrassingly for Bamberg, included the two new 707-400s originally ordered for Cunard Eagle.[115] They were not all that Bamberg would lose. Cunard also stripped Eagle of its Bermuda and Nassau operations.

Eagle Aviation and Airways were now subsidiaries of BOAC-Cunard and all of their transatlantic licenses had been transferred to BOAC. The Eagle fleet was also dismantled.

Along with the loss of the Boeing 707s, the Eagle fleet had shrunk to eight aircraft, where a few years earlier it had been more than 20. What was left of Eagle was now a UK and Europe operation with some trooping contracts. Morale at the company was at an all-time low. Bamberg's people, aircraft and offices had been absorbed into an entity that had more than 140 sales offices worldwide and half of them had been established between 1958 (19 years after BOAC was established) and 1962.

By September 1961, BOAC's management was expecting a £5 million (£114 million in 2020 prices) operating loss for the 1961/62 financial year. The government was supposed to benefit from an annual dividend of £6 million from its leading state airline and that would have driven that loss to £11 million. In the previous year, BOAC had made a profit of more than £4 million, or about £100 million in 2020 prices.

BOAC had been investing in new jet airliners and retiring its older propeller driven aircraft became a priority for greater efficiency. Smallpeice described how the BOAC board members Sir Walter Worboys and Unilever's J. A. Connel, men with no aviation experience, advised the company to carry on as they had done in the 1950s, but trying to sell more tickets, and making the corporation more efficient to enable it to "ride out the bad weather". It was a counsel of despair, and one victim would be the independent airline and BOAC associate Skyways.

Skyways was a freight airline which Smallpeice

described as supplementing BOAC, not competing with it. They ferried BOAC's engines and carried some of the airline's cargo on the eastern routes, as well as freight for other customers. Skyways' acceptance of its subsidiary role to BOAC would be its downfall. With its larger jet airliners BOAC was increasingly able to carry cargo as well as passenger luggage. And its new aircraft's jet engines did not need as much maintenance as the powerplants that drove propellers. In the spring of 1962, BOAC called in Skyways management and told them it would only need a fraction of Skyways capacity. The independent immediately went bust.

Two months later BOAC acquired Cunard Eagle and BOAC-Cunard was born. With Bamberg's airline absorbed, Smallpeice and his board focused on their global marketplace. The challenges BOAC then faced were manifold: competition in Europe by US airlines seeking foreign revenue while passenger numbers were down at home; a dip in traffic from partner airline Air Canada; a strained relationship with Qantas, and new profitability demands from the UK government. All while BOAC was expected to buy British built airliners when airlines across the world were buying more efficient aircraft from Boeing and Douglas.

BOAC was also weighed down by losses that had occurred long before the Cunard venture. These included a £1 million write off from the four-propeller Avro 688 Tudor aircraft which BOAC inherited from British South American Airways (BSSA) when BSSA was absorbed into BOAC in 1949. Worse still was an £8 million cost for BOAC's fleet of the world's first jet airliner, the Mark 1 de Havilland Comet. The first Comet arrived in 1951 and just three years later in 1954, after fatal mid-flight aircraft break-ups due to a fundamental design flaw, the entire fleet was permanently grounded.

BOAC's fleet of Bristol Britannias had been seriously delayed by technical problems, and the airline had had to spent £5 million leasing four-propeller Douglas DC-7C aircraft in the interim. The Britannias would ultimately cost BOAC up to £22 million and the early disposal of another disappointing British-built plane, the Handley Page Hermes, would lead to the loss of valuable trooping contracts. Because these aircraft had been made largely obsolete by the Boeing 707, their second-hand value was poor, and BOAC had to accept fire sale prices.

With the experience of the Comet, Smallpeice and his team were reluctant to buy the British made jet powered Vickers VC10. It had two versions, Standard and Super. Propelled by four jet engines, Smallpeice feared that the running costs of the VC10 would be unacceptable high. He wanted to buy American Being 707s which, his team calculated, would save the airline £8 million a year.

The BOAC management team highlighted these losses and cost pressures at a time when the government was working on new legislation intended to make nationalised industries profitable. Bamberg had joined BOAC at a moment when the airline's relationship with its master, the Ministry of Aviation, was at an all-time low, not helped by future plans to build a supersonic airliner, Concorde, which BOAC would be expected to buy. The friction resulted in the Chairman and Managing Director being persuaded to resign in what really amounted to dismissal.

Buying Concorde, which would not fly until 1969, was a very distant prospect and not only due to the aircraft's long development programme. In July 1962, Eton and Oxford-educated Julien Amery MP was appointed the

Conservative government's Minister of Aviation. Amery was Prime Minister Harold Macmillan's son-in-law and this new aviation Minister would bring the guillotine down on Slattery and Smallpeice. That July BOAC, was predicting a £5 million operating loss for the 1962/63 financial year, repeating the previous year's bad figures.

Smallpeice and Slattery would submit reports to Amery later in 1962 asking for £70 million (£1.4 billion in 2020 prices) for BOAC. The two of them were also worried about the new legislation for nationalised industries. Amery decided to bring in the chartered accountants Peat, Marwick, Mitchell & Co. to write an independent report on BOAC's finances. In mid-February 1963, two of the accounting firm's consultants went to see Smallpeice who records in his autobiography, "I began to fear that nothing very positive or helpful would come of this inquiry. But it was approaching its end."

As 1963 rolled around Eagle had no major scheduled services and an engineering wing that had been trained in recent years for maintaining the new jetliners — but BOAC had all the jets. Cunard was not interested in its one-time ally, its management only had time for BOAC. Cunard's Directors were unlikely to be aware of the implications of the enquiry by accountants Peat, Marwick, Mitchell & Co. On 14 February 1963, it was announced that Bamberg's time with BOAC had come to an end.

The reason for Bamberg's resignation, after only nine months, was simple — his offer to buy 60% of Cunard's holding in Eagle with an option to buy the remaining 40% had been accepted. On 1 March 1963 he took back control of his airline and on 9 August 1963, the reborn carrier reverted to its previous name, Eagle Airways Limited.

Announcing his re-emergence as an independent, Bamberg said he was extremely pleased that "it will now be possible for me to replan the policy and activities of the company, and to develop it in my own way." After three years, he was once again master of the airline he founded in 1948. *Flight* stated that it was "believed that Mr Bamberg made the purchase from his own resources, and it is probable that he would have repossessed 100 per cent had he been able to do so."

The price paid by Bamberg for the 60% in 1963 was not disclosed but *Flight* explained that it had been "unofficially said" that Cunard paid about £1 million (£23.5 in 2020 prices) for Eagle. Based on that, *Flight* estimated that Bamberg had paid about £250,000 (£5.3 million in 2020 prices) for his 60% because it had been decided that the value of the company after the BOAC-Cunard deal would be not more than £500,000 (£10.6 million in 2020 prices) admitting that "this is a sheer guess". The magazine added that it was understood that Bamberg had financial backing, for his reborn airline.

Bamberg's first task was to financially reconstruct his company and change the airline's name, and he had the original management team to help him. The resurrected Eagle airline was to become British Eagle International Airlines Limited (BEIA), but not until September 1963. Cunard Eagle Airways' emblem would be retained for BEIA.

Flight speculated at the time that Bamberg's Caribbean plans would not be taken any further for the time being. Instead, the renewed Eagle Airways would pay special attention to UK domestic routes. The airline had new licences for the major trunk routes from London to Edinburgh, Glasgow and Belfast. In *Flight*'s view, Eagle could view itself as the "major alternative UK domestic carrier". Ambitious Bamberg never made any secret of his intention to compete on the domestic trunk routes with the state-owned domestically focused British European Airways. Bamberg also wanted to target the business market with "businessmen's flights".

With the change of ownership came another change of offices with a move to Conduit Street, Mayfair, a short walk from the old Clarges Street address and passenger check-in services were moved from the Marble Arch Air Terminal to the Knightsbridge Air Terminal. At these central London Air Terminals passengers could drop off their luggage, check-in for their boarding passes, and take their seat on the coach that would take them to Heathrow; a 30-minute drive.

At times, Bamberg was questioned by the media about any possible merger with British United Airways, the other major UK independent managed by Freddie Laker. Bamberg always said no and repeated this negative answer when asked after he took back Eagle. Being the ambitious competitive airline owner he was, *Flight* expected Bamberg to reapply for more frequent domestic flights to make the network more of an economic proposition; but the application for exactly that would be rejected in 1964. A brighter option was the continental routes across Europe.

Eagle possessed licences for Copenhagen, Stockholm, Venice, Dublin and Nice. Bamberg was the owner of two of the UK's biggest travel agents Lunn and Poly, and they were expected to be valuable in generating passenger demand. *Flight* speculated whether any of these continental destinations might be "traded" in return for more UK traffic. Another source of revenue for Bamberg was the maintenance contracts he had with, of all airlines, BOAC-Cunard and Ghana Airways.

That engineering revenue could also be increased with new Heathrow based airline customers. *Flight* also speculated as to whether the continental destinations could be traded for better UK routes.[116]

Bamberg said in February 1963: "I am confident that we have an excellent future. Despite the low returns currently offered by investment in aviation, there is a vast international market which is growing steadily. The profit-making record of Eagle Airways in the past shows the company's spirit of enterprise: with the background of this record, coupled with the enthusiasm and experience of the staff, we are going ahead." Bamberg's move came at a time of turbulence at the top of UK aviation politics. While Bamberg was promoting his new venture, Smallpeice and Slattery were engaging in a public relations campaign with Labour politicians and the media.

The accountants' BOAC report was given to Amery in May and at the end of July Amery told the House of Commons that a White Paper would be his response. A White Paper is the first step in the UK's legislative process. Amery had kicked the BOAC debate into the long grass of the autumn. Come October and Smallpeice and Slattery had heard little from the Minster, they certainly had no answer about the £70 million. The end for the two of them began in November. Slattery had seen Amery on Friday 1 November and he was told that Sir Giles Guthrie would be BOAC Chairman from 1 January.

Smallpeice saw Amery on 5 November. In his autobiography, Smallpeice recalls that Amery asked for his resignation and the Minister made it clear that writing off debt of £70 million was not easy and a new Board of Directors was needed. Smallpeice did not want to go, his contract was until mid-1966, but he agreed to resign on 7 November. There would be no new Managing Director. Guthrie, who had been a part-time non-executive director at BEA since 1959, would hold that role and be Chairman.

On Wednesday 20 November, Amery told the House of Commons of the BOAC Board change, but it had already been reported in the press earlier that month. Amery also published the White Paper on the day he made the announcement. Smallpeice described its description of BOAC's finances as half-truths. In an example of the tortuous relationship between Amery and Slattery and Smallpeice, it later emerged that the two BOAC men had refused to provide the agreement it had with Cunard to the UK Parliament. The US government's Civil Aviation Board (CAB) and its airlines, Pan American, TWA and Seaboard, had all seen the BOAC-Cunard agreement; though the airlines had been asked by CAB to not divulge the agreement's details. It was because the Americans had seen it that Amery decided to ask BOAC to agree to the publication of the agreement, which was a £30 million deal (£642.2 million in 2020 prices). BOAC's management refused on the grounds that it was "commercially confidential", a large part of the reason that Amery forced the resignations of Slattery and Smallpeice .[117]

On 2 December 1963, Amery told the House of Commons: 'I think that he [Frederick Lee, Labour party member of Parliament for Newton] was on to a rather strong point when he said that the submission of the agreement to the CAB rather changes the situation. I have therefore asked BOAC and BOAC-Cunard whether they would agree to my putting a copy of the agreement in the library of the House [of Commons].'

Flight reported in its 26 December edition that it had asked a Ministry of Aviation spokesman whether Amery would, "now do something more than request BOAC to publish the agreement." The spokesman said: "The Minister is still discussing his request with BOAC," and five days late Slattery was officially replaced as BOAC Chairman by Sir Giles Guthrie, who had known Amery when they were both at Eton.[118]

On 1 January 1964, Guthrie became the new BOAC Chairman. For Smallpeice, his involvement with Cunard would continue in another form in 1965. After he resigned from BOAC, Smallpeice became an Administrative Adviser to Her Majesty's Household, Buckingham Palace in 1964 — a post he held until 1980 — but in 1965 he was appointed Chairman of the Cunard Steam Ship Company; the shipping side of BOAC-Cunard.[119]

Slattery would go on to join the National Bank of Ireland and even wrote a history of the bank, *The National Bank 1835–1970*, which was published in 1972. The bank had been acquired by the Republic of Ireland's central bank, Bank of Ireland, in the late 1960s. Slattery would also be involved in Irish aviation, of a sort, namely the Northern Irish aircraft firm, Short Brothers and Harland. He became a consultant to the company at a time when company was subject to parliamentary debates because of its financial situation.

In 1965, Slattery revealed to a Parliamentary select committee, why BOAC were so adamant Bamberg would not succeed in the Caribbean. He told the Select Committee on Nationalised Industries, that the BOAC-Cunard tie-up and subsequent reduction in competition in the region helped the BOAC subsidiary Bahamas Airways reduce its losses from £592,000 in

1961–62 to, "a figure for 1963–64 which is not likely to exceed £150,000" Slattery said on page 146 of the Select Committee's Nationalised Industries report: "It avoided wasteful and very damaging competition in the Caribbean area and we thought that the sales effort, the joint sales effort of ship and sea, would bring benefit to us, as they have in fact done." In 2020 prices, £150,000 in 1963 is worth £3.2 million.

Despite this elimination of competition, BOAC still could not make a profit in the region. On 22 November 1965, Liberal Party member of Parliament for Orpington, Eric Reginald Lubbock MP, said: "I think that Bahamas Airways made a loss of £229,000 in the year [1964] just passed, but that was mainly because of fare-cutting by competing airlines on those routes. Competition has not been removed altogether, although the effect of it had been reduced."[120] Harrow School-educated Lubbock, who was Orpington MP from 1962 to 1970, and became the 4th Baron Avebury on the death of his cousin in 1969, did however, support BOAC.[121]

Cunard would eventually abandon its venture with BOAC in 1966, selling its $268 million (£229 million July 2021 USD/GBP rate) share to the state-owned airline. Cunard needed the funds to keep its shipping line going which had financial problems of its own. In 1967, Cunard had to sell ships simply to stay solvent.[122] The Cunard deal with BOAC ultimately failed and BOAC's competitor, Eagle, was back. *Flight International* referred to the ill-fated venture as, "the misbegotten BOAC-Cunard".

This misbegotten corporation however was able to annex Eagle's western routes which it had built up, "painstakingly over four years. It was a bitter reverse [for Bamberg]," *Flight International* said at the time. The world's oldest weekly aviation magazine would speculate in 1968 on what could have been: "What would be the British position today on the North Atlantic if Eagle's licence had not been revoked, and if the BOAC-Cunard deal had not been done? Who knows — Eagle would almost certainly be operating a dozen [Vickers] Super VC10s, and Britain's share of the [transatlantic] traffic would be increasing."[123]

9 Independence

The 'Fab Four' of The Beatles stepped down the airstair to a torrent of screaming fans, bulb popping photographers and jostling newsreel cameramen on a warm cloudless Monday, 13 July 1964. The most famous pop stars in the world had flown home to Liverpool in a British Eagle Britannia aircraft, landing at what was then just Liverpool Airport — since renamed Liverpool John Lennon Airport in 2001. The reason for their return to the old port city was the premiere of their first film, *A Hard Day's Night*. The airline capitalised on the high-profile flight by selling *Beatles On British Eagle* branded bags.

Merchandising on the back of a pop culture event was just another of the innovations Bamberg and his British Eagle would bring to the 1960s airline market. Bamberg's escape from the suffocating clutch of BOAC and its misbegotten Cunard tie-up left him with a Europe-only airline and many of the problems he had faced before with state-run competition and the many upper-class figures who ran the state sanctioned enterprises; Lord Douglas of Kirtleside, Rear-Admiral Sir Matthew Slattery, Sir Gerard d'Erlanger and others. To distinguish British Eagle from BOAC, BEA and BUA, an association with glamour, and fashion, was one of the marketing tools his management team deployed.

Bamberg would need every management and marketing trick up his sleeve to survive the summer

The Beatles arrive in Liverpool on a British Eagle
Britannia to promote their film *A Hard Day's Night*.

season. Of the eight aircraft in his fleet one, a Douglas
DC-6, had been lost in a crash. In August, Bamberg had
some luck, the ATLB gave permission for scheduled
services from Heathrow to Belfast, Edinburgh and
Glasgow. It would be the first time an independent had
been allowed to compete directly with BEA on domestic
British routes. In September, Eagle Airways Limited was
renamed and registered as British Eagle International
Airways.

With his newfound independence came a small change
with a new livery for Bamberg's few aircraft. Much was
retained from the Cunard Eagle Airways livery, the

flying Eagle symbol in white on the vertical tail fin, the white fuselage with a red cheatline. But the fuselage now carried, in black, the name British Eagle. The remainder of 1963, however, saw Bamberg fight to keep the new name for his reborn airline. The name British Eagle International Airways, or BEIA, had previously been the name given in March 1960 to Bamberg's airline that flew in the Caribbean. British European Airways (BEA) took no time in 1963 in opposing its reappearance, suggesting that BEA and BEIA could be confused.[124] In an omen of what the future held, Bamberg lost and was unable to keep the name. In early November, the simply named British Eagle, made its first UK domestic flights.

Much of the last five years, 1958 to 1963, had been a game of cat and mouse with BOAC, but now the enemy was the other state-owned airline, BEA. On the evening of Sunday, 3 November British Eagle inaugurated a daily service to Glasgow. On Monday, 4 November daily services between London and Edinburgh and Belfast started. Bamberg's fares were the same as BEA's and genuine competition on UK main internal air routes had begun. BEA's declared policy was all-out competition with the independents, despite the state-ownership advantage.

British Eagle's Belfast services were very popular, especially for those holidaying in the off-season and returning home for Christmas — there was even a flight on Christmas day. Glasgow also saw strong traffic but Edinburgh was not as popular a route as the other two, but British Eagle's domestic network would increase through an acquisition.

Eagle's economic planning unit had concluded that more flights should be carried out of provincial airports outside London in order to stop the bottleneck

148

at Heathrow and the other London airports. The ATLB had taken the view that there was nothing to be gained by adding flights to provincial airports to allow them to carry more passengers and reduce the Heathrow bottleneck — a view shared by BOAC and BEA.

While the ATLB remained inflexible, Bamberg and his managers went ahead and offered direct flights from Birmingham, Manchester and Newcastle as well as other provincial airports. This strategy would be further helped by Bamberg's package holiday companies, Lunn Poly and Everyman Travel. By offering holidays with direct flights from airports across the UK, British Eagle made it more convenient and removed the added cost of getting down to London to make a trip. The marketing for this wider market included, the "slender purse plan".[125]

When the London, Glasgow, Edinburgh and Belfast proved popular he applied for permission from the ALTB to fly more often. BEA would alter its winter timetable to increase competition with British Eagle. New departure times would deliberately sandwich Bamberg's daily flight. For example, a 15:00 hrs flight to Edinburgh would have a BEA flight at the same time and then another BEA flight just 10 minutes later. BEA released its winter schedules to travel agents before British Eagle's 16 September announcement about its own wintertime timetable.

Somehow BEA had known beforehand about British Eagle's Edinburgh schedules. Airlines could have timetabling agreements but not at this point between BEA and British Eagle.[126] BEA would go on to amend its winter timetable again and again, so that a BEA flight would coincide with, or be very close to, a British Eagle flight. To stop this kind of predatory practice, Bamberg had previously asked the ATLB to limit BEA's capacity. The Board's reply was, "there is little or no evidence that BEA would engage in either of these practices (swamping and sandwiching a competitor's services)" yet they clearly did.

And the ATLB continued with its anti-competitive decisions. Turning down Eagle's application for more flights on the London, Glasgow, Edinburgh and Belfast trunk routes. Bamberg warned that the decision could make operating on those routes unviable.[127] To attract passengers, despite the ATLB-condoned sandwiching, Eagle was expected to offer seat-selection facilities, trickle-loading so passengers can wait on the aircraft not in the airport lounge and a full meal service, for example a bacon-and-egg breakfast from Glasgow to London.

In November, British Eagle already had 2,000 passenger bookings for its London, Glasgow, Edinburgh and Belfast flights, which was, "an encouraging response, the airline feels, before the service has actually started," *Flight International* reported. The flights included a meal service which used real glasses and cutlery and, in the first-class cabin, Wedgwood china. The airline was also introducing trickle loading where it was possible with an airport's infrastructure. At a news conference about the new services, Bamberg said: "We deplore the three alterations that BEA have made to their timetables just to duplicate our flights. This is wasteful duplication."

Bamberg had been speaking at a news conference he

gave in the British Eagle terminal at Renfrew Airport, Glasgow's domestic airport until 1966, for the launch of the trunk route services. At Renfrew, British Eagle already conducted trickle loading and the airline had adopted seat-selection more widely. Bamberg was asked about BEA's recent adoption of trickle-loading and seat-selection on most of its Belfast, Glasgow and Edinburgh flights to London. He said: "Well, I think I can say that it would never have happened but for us. It was certainly high time."

Bringing innovation to the passenger experience was not going to ensure that Bamberg's independent airline survived against the rigged market in favour of BOAC and BEA. British Eagle was doing well enough that Bamberg could expand through acquisition and he bought the small Liverpool based airline Starways in late 1963. The airline's 19 November announcement about the acquisition was careful in its language saying that the two airlines had, "reached an agreement to provide for an analysis of their positions in such a way as to produce a better integrated [route] pattern."

In winning Starways, Bamberg had beaten his domestic route nemesis, BEA, whose associate company, Cambrian Airways, was also trying to buy the airline. Cambrian already operated on the London, Liverpool route and acquiring Starways would have made BEA and Cambrian dominant. In its 18 July 1962 edition, *Flight International* had speculated that the price for Starways was up to £500,000, which is £10.7 million in 2020 prices. Ultimately no price was made public when the deal was done. Bamberg also announced at the time that three aircraft would be purchased to expand the combined British Eagle Starways fleet.

The agreement came into force on 31 December 1963 and the first flight of the Liverpool London scheduled service started on 1 January 1964.[128] Starways operated more than just a Liverpool-London service though. The airline also flew to Glasgow and Edinburgh and Cork, Blackpool and Hawarden in Wales and it operated inclusive tour charters from Manchester. Starways, however, continued to operate as a separate company to avoid any interference by the ATLB regarding route licences.

The intention was to closely integrate the two airlines' routes under British Eagle's overall direction. Liverpool was the hub for British Eagle/Starways London services for Glasgow, Edinburgh and Ireland.[129] Most importantly, a major presence on the London to Liverpool route was expected to strengthen British Eagle as a major UK domestic operator in competition with BEA and its associate company, Cambrian Airways, which also flew London, Liverpool.

As 1963 came to a close, Bamberg may have read in *Flight International* that Sir Matthew Slattery, still then officially BOAC Chairman, was having talks for a route deal with independent airline BUA's Chairman, Sir Myles Wyatt. BUA would eventually gain UK government protection as a "second [airline] force" in 1970 as its finances collapsed, while Bamberg had been allowed to go bust.

Nonetheless, the year of 1964, was a boom time for Bamberg's British Eagle. There was plenty of work and the vast majority of Starways' staff had been retained in the take-over. Seven aircraft were leased to make the most of Starways' routes, almost doubling British

Eagle's fleet. The London-Liverpool route soon grew and by May there were three daily flights between the cities. The fleet expansion also saw aircraft come from unexpected quarters, including Saudi Arabian Airlines. Eagle operated pilgrimage flights, but not to Mecca.

Bamberg must have thought Christmas had come early when in March 1964, the US authorities gave British Eagle open permission to operate transatlantic charters for three years. This meant Bamberg's aircraft could fly between any two points in the UK and USA. The only limit was that charters from the USA to the UK could not be more than one third of the number from the UK in a year. Even with that restriction, which came a year after Bamberg had escaped the Cunard, BOAC nightmare, Eagle would be once more crisscrossing the North Atlantic.

Eagle saw more success in Europe with flights to Stuttgart increasing their daily number and strong demand on the Luxembourg route. With almost 15 years airline experience Bamberg had long since learned the value of good aircraft maintenance. As the supply of ex-RAF engineers slowed, Eagle Aviation Services, Bamberg's engineering wing, started a four-year apprenticeship scheme to train new aircraft engineers.

In July 1964, British Eagle began a service from Glasgow to Tarbes, France for pilgrims going to Lourdes, but the vast majority of summer flights were simply for tourists seeking the sun. Barcelona, Palma, Perpignan and the Italian Riviera were popular destinations as the sixties got swinging. While Biarritz, Genoa, Naples, Varna, Venice and Basle were added to the network. British Eagle was stretching its wings and reached beyond Europe to North Africa and even the Caribbean with inclusive tours. While some partied, the 1960s also saw the depths of the Cold War. The UK was developing a ballistic missile called Blue Steel in the Australian outback and British Eagle flew personnel out to Adelaide to work on the missile system.

While Adelaide was a new government destination for the Blue Steel programme, Australia was also to become a source of revenue for British immigrants to the country. The £10 Poms were flying to the other side of the planet to start a new life in Australia and British Eagle flew them under contract to Qantas. The £10 Poms were British citizens encouraged to emigrate to Australia under an assisted passage scheme which saw the emigres only spend £10 for the paperwork to travel the 9,000 miles from the northern hemisphere to the southern hemisphere. The first flight was 9 October 1964 from Heathrow. Over the next three months, 48 services would operate between Heathrow and Brisbane, Melbourne, Perth and Sydney. British Eagle would keep flying the £10 Poms until their closure in1968.

Overall, 1964 would see passenger numbers increase by 254% over 1963, to 540,000 and miles flown jumped by 134% to 9.2 million. The revenue for the year was £8.5 million with an operating surplus of almost £900,000, £18.6 million in 2020 prices. British Eagle's number of employees had grown to more than 1,700. Bamberg's market innovations of seat selection, trickle loading, and in-flight meals combined with his merger with Starways had paid off.

With this solid financial foundation, Bamberg had many plans for his airline. He wanted to operate transatlantic group charters from London, Manchester and Glasgow Prestwick to New York from the end of May until September. He had appealed against the ATLB's refusal of inclusive-tour rights to Bermuda and the Caribbean and if he had won had hoped to start the inclusive tours in September. With the rapidly growing mileage flown and passenger numbers, Bamberg wanted a new engineering base at Heathrow's number two maintenance area and a dedicated passenger terminal on the airport's north side.

The new engineering base had been proposed to the Ministry of Aviation some time ago. But British Eagle could not finalise its plan because the Ministry had not made its own decisions regarding access and facilities at Heathrow 'Area Two'. Bamberg's request for a passenger terminal on the airport's north side had been refused because it did not fit with the Ministry's plans for the London airport, although Bamberg was prepared to build the passenger terminal in the maintenance area if need be. Among these new developments, however, there were still some serious problems.

"Losses on the domestic routes have been very heavy and it is unlikely that international scheduled services have shown much better than marginal profits," *Flight International* reported in its 21 January 1965 edition. The magazine also speculated that a significant portion of profits were likely to have been made on inclusive-tour, charter and trooping flights. For 1965, trooping flights were expected to be up to

40% of British Eagle's activity, UK domestic scheduled services another 30%, charter's 20% and finally 10% on inclusive tours.

Bamberg admitted during the 1965 January annual results press conference that traffic on the domestic schedule services had been poor. BUA's sandwiching strategy to steal British Eagle passengers was working. *Flight International* estimated that the London, Liverpool service, operated by the merged Starways and British Eagle, had the highest seat occupancy, and it represented 57%, of Bamberg's domestic routes. At that press conference, Bamberg stressed the need for an unequivocal statement by the new Labour government on its policy for the nationalised and independent airlines.

The previous October had seen a UK General Election, which Harold Wilson's Labour party had won. In November the independent airlines had asked the new government what its civil air transport industry policy would be. In January, the airlines were still waiting for a reply. *Flight* commented in its 21 January 1965 edition that "British private airlines have been waiting on and off, during most of the past 20 years [for an unequivocal government statement]". Bamberg said in his January press conference that any statement, ideally, would provide an assurance that the level of competition independent airlines wanted would be allowed.

In Bamberg's view, such competition would require long term (10-years minimum) licences for scheduled services and inclusive tours. And full competitive freedom for the independents could only exist if they had the rights to unlimited frequencies on domestic services. Bamberg considered that three daily services a week on the domestic routes was the minimum frequency for potential profitability. He added that a domestic traffic-growth rate of 20-30% a year more than justified additional services from other carriers.[130]

Unable to return to his old hunting grounds of the Caribbean and mid-Atlantic, Bamberg went in search of new foreign markets and international routes and in doing so achieved some industry firsts. The very same month that he set out his agenda for UK airlines, a British Eagle Bristol Britannia flew 38 passengers, less than half its maximum number, on a world first. It was a direct flight from southern Africa to South America. Its departure from Africa would be from Luanda International Airport in Angola. In 1965, it was a small single runway airport with the name, LUANDA, in large capital letters atop its single terminal building.

The ten-hour flight was unremarkable apart from the fact that no one had done it before. After landing at Recife, a city at the eastern most tip of Brazil pushing out into the Atlantic, the passengers would fly south to the country's most iconic location, Rio de Janeiro. The next half of the commercial aviation first would not be back to Angola but from Rio to Windhoek, Namibia. A journey of 3,995 statute miles. The final leg would take the Britannia back to where the inaugural flight had begun on 18 January, Johannesburg's then Jan Smuts Airport; now known as O. R. Tambo International Airport.

February saw tragedy strike again for Bamberg's airline, and this time with worse loss of life. It was

Bamberg's third fatal accident — the second had been in 1961 when a party of school children were killed in Scandinavia. Approaching Innsbruck, a British Eagle aircraft had encountered clouds at 11,000 feet and during the pilots' attempts to evade the weather they had descended to 8,000 feet, at which point they flew into the Glungezer mountain. The crash started an avalanche which brought the wreckage down the side of the mountain but made it harder to locate. Nothing was found until the following morning, when it was discovered that all 83 people on board had been killed. While airline demand was growing and more and more people took to the skies for their foreign, and domestic travel, accidents were still too common.

Despite the safety record of air travel in the 1950s and 1960s, flying was still seen as glamorous. Bamberg knew how to maximise this for publicity and the city of Paris and the world of fashion were perfect bed fellows for marketing aviation as glamour. For a trip to the 1965 Paris Fashion Show, four beautiful smiling women would look out from a British Eagle branded airstair at another throng of newspaper men, photographers and news cameras. Wrapped in fur coats and topped with fur hats, the four young models who shined on the airstair would board the Vickers Viscount 701 airliner and turn its. The publicity stunt, filmed by British Pathé News, saw three of the four: Trudi, Joan and Angela, walk the aisle in mink coats worth up to £1,800, a sum now worth more than £35,000.

The final three years for Bamberg's airline endeavours really began in the previous October of 1964. It saw an election that changed the government after 13 years of continuous Conservative administrations. During the 20 years in which Bamberg ran airlines, the Conservative party was in power for 13 of them: 1951 to 1964.

After Churchill, who retired in 1955 due to poor health, there had been Eton-educated Sir Anthony Eden, who resigned, following the Suez crisis. His successor, Harold Macmillan, would also resign citing poor health, but he had been greatly weakened by the Profumo scandal involving spies and call girls. Macmillan's replacement, Sir Alec Douglas-Home would lose the 15 October 1964 election to the Labour party's Harold Wilson.

Harold Wilson's Labour party manifesto for the 1964 election made no mention of aviation, its references to transport were wholly concerned with canals, roads and rail networks.[131] Wilson called an election again in 1966 because his parliamentary majority after the 1964 election was only five seats, and that had sunk to three seats following the Leyton by-election in January 1965.[132] The 1966 manifesto made no reference to airlines or aviation either, its transport references were concerned only with public transport.

Wilson never made a speech or referred to aviation in Parliament during his first term in office, but his government did reform airport legislation and passed the Air Corporation Bill in late 1965. Bamberg would again be disappointed — it was not what he had hoped for. "The main purpose of this Bill is to give effect to the financial settlement with BOAC which I announced in the House on 1st March this year. The need for the settlement arose out of the troubles which afflicted the Corporation under the previous government," aviation Minister, Roy Jenkins MP, told the House of Commons on 22 November 1965.[133]

Roy Jenkins was the first of three aviation Ministers Wilson's government appointed from October 1964 until Wilson lost to Sir Edward Heath's Conservative party in 1970. After Jenkins, came Frederick Mulley and John Stonehouse. It was Jenkins, whom the UK's independent airlines had asked in November 1964 for the government's air transport policy. In February 1965, the airlines got an answer from Jenkins, and it was not good news. *Flight International*'s Leader article said in its 25 February 1965 edition: "Such is the power of aviation Ministers that without reference to Parliament the air transport system can be radically changed to conform with a political ideology."

Flight International goes on to point out that the Minister's actions could almost be illegal as "his [Jenkin's] new "guidelines"… effectively repeal the 1960 Licensing Act." That Act created the ATLB which had been so biased in its decision on BEA's sandwiching practices and the Labour party was leaving that board in place. Jenkins claimed independents could apply to the ATLB for scheduled service routes, but Labour party doctrine was that scheduled services were for BOAC and BEA only. Jenkins, his Labour party and government, seemed to be unaware that in the name of "nationalised industries" they were prioritising companies managed by Conservative party aristocrats who had installed themselves as the executives — often having no aviation experience — after a Conservative government forced the merger of airlines.

BOAC was created in 1939 this way, as was Imperial Airways 20-years earlier under Labour party's first ever government. Sir Eric Geddes, Deputy Chairman for BOAC, had been Imperial's Chairman, with no aviation experience. Born in India, educated at Merchiston Castle public school in Edinburgh, he was a Conservative Parliamentarian from 1917 and knighted in 1919. Imperial was the result of a Conservative government forced merger of four companies.

They were, Instone Air Line, started by the sons of a poor German immigrant; Handley Page Transport, the brainchild of Frederick Handley Page a self-made man whose company produced the Halifax World War Two bomber; Hubert Scott-Paine's flying boat airline, British Marine Air Navigation Company, which he started in his twenties after buying aircraft maker Pemberton-Billing Limited in 1916; and Daimler Airway, created in 1921 by public school-educated Frank Searle, from the merger of his Daimler Hire Company and the airline he bought, Air Transport & Travel. Labour party off-the-cuff arbitrary policy decided by personal whim was a dark cloud for the future of the independents and set in train events that would lead to the descent of Bamberg's airline endeavours. For Bamberg, the toughest years were yet to come.

10 The Toughest Years

Despite the government backed competitors' efforts, British Eagle was making industry records traversing the world, expanding its routes, at home and abroad with acquisitions such as Starways. Bamberg left no stone untuned seeking new opportunities. What he could not have known is that despite his marketplace successes, the ruinous currents that would bring his airline's successful flight to an end were flowing through the British halls of power.

On 17 February 1965, Labour party Prime minister Harold Wilson's then Minister for Aviation, Roy Jenkins MP, told the House of Commons that: "So far as scheduled services on international routes are concerned, I am not convinced that the national interest is, in general, served by more than one British carrier operating on the same route." Jenkins added that he would not accept increased competition on domestic services either. In another ominous sign, British Eagle and BUA were only shown Jenkin's policy speech for the first time the morning of the statement. Neither had the ATLB been consulted on the new policy.

Jenkins opposition to the private carriers was underlined in his response to a joint independent airlines' statement sent to him before his Commons statement. Jenkins said that government policy would not be "determined" by "memoranda of this kind". What little light there was, was Jenkins' readiness to encourage and support new services and inclusive-tour charters. The support for inclusive-tour charters was not a generous act for the airlines' benefit, European nations had already agreed a policy of "licensing liberally applications by reputable [inclusive tour] operators of each other's countries," Jenkins told the Commons.[134]

Jenkins held out an olive branch of giving airlines licences on non-trunk routes, but if airlines could not be profitable on trunk routes what hope was there for others? Jenkins also announced a "study of the co-ordination of the transport system" to be undertaken by Lord Hinton of Bankside, who had been given his peerage in the 1965 New Year's honours. Lord Hinton was an engineer with no aviation experience, but he had worked within nationalised transport, having begun his career at the Great Western Railway. The University of Cambridge-educated engineer joined the UK government's Ministry of Supply in 1940 and in 1946 became Deputy Controller of Production for nuclear power.[135]

Appalled by the arbitrary decision to oppose, what the Labour party called, "unrestricted competition," and not encouraging domestic competition, Bamberg shut down domestic flights to Scotland and Northern Ireland. Jenkins had warned that "unrestricted competition" could see an operator eliminated from a route, but his actions had already created that situation. Jenkins also said that unrestricted competition would lead to higher fares because numerous operators on one route would not make a profit. Yet with no

163

competition, state-owned BEA was arguing for higher fares at the ATLB meetings held just a week later from 23–24 February.

Interviewed on British television after his Commons statement, Jenkins expressed surprise that Bamberg would stop services on domestic routes. Jenkins may have been equally surprised when BEA, now knowing it had a monopoly on many domestic routes, demanded that the ATLB allow it to increase fares.[136]

BEA Chairman Sir Anthony Milward's February 1965 demand for increased fares came less than a year after he took the job of Chairman from Lord Douglas of Kirtleside, and Douglas had been BEA's Chairman for 14 years, almost since the airline's inception in 1946. *The New York Times* reported in its 27 March 1964 edition that: "Lord Douglas said the airline expected a record profit of $8.4 million [£3 million] in the fiscal year, that will end on March 31." The US Dollar to Pound Sterling exchange rate in April 1964 averaged $2.79 for £1.[137] And in 2020 prices the "record" profit of $8.4 million is worth £62 million. Yet still, Milward was demanding higher fares.

Milward had been BEA Chief Executive since 1958 and became Chairman on 1 April 1964 following Lord Douglas retirement at the age of 70.[138] Milward was a former Royal Navy pilot, from its Fleet Air Arm, and he would be BEA Chairman for six years until 1970. When he was appointed to the BEA Chairmanship by the then Conservative government, he also became a part-time BOAC board member. Milward appointed by the then Conservative aviation Minister, Julien Amery MP. During his 21 November 1963 speech, announcing Milward's appointment, Amery also said he had considered merging BEA and BOAC. Prophetically this would happen ten years later.

Bamberg, who boycotted the ATLB February meetings where Milward made his pitch for higher prices, had planned to attend them to argue for lower prices before Jenkins' speech made the Board almost pointless for independents. The disappointing turn of events with Labour's ill-conceived policy followed an ATLB success for Bamberg, he was allowed unlimited frequencies on the London-Chester-Liverpool route. However, this generosity may have been because neither BOAC nor BEA bothered to operate to the UK's third largest city.

After Jenkins' Commons statement that led to the exact reverse of what he intended for his policy, the British Independent Air Transport Association (BIATA), the trade body for British Eagle, BUA and others, published its own agenda for civil aviation. Called *British Air Transport Policy* it had been given to Jenkins' Ministry on 1 February. BIATA's President, Cambrian Airways' Wing Commander L. B. Elwin would only say at the Policy's press launch that they "agreed to disagree".

However, independent did not always mean independent even for BIATA members. Founded in 1935, Cambrian had sold a third of its shares to BEA in 1958 and in return Cambrian was able to operate on certain routes.[139] Perhaps this is why Bamberg had his own policy report which he handed out to journalists at the BIATA press conference. Bamberg's report demanded a competitive marketplace which would also benefit UK aircraft manufacturers because of the inevitable growth in passenger traffic.

Bamberg wanted, long term, 10-year, route licences; unlimited frequency competition; inclusive-tour charter traffic that would not be hindered by BOAC and BEA; a Chamber of Air Transport formed with BOAC, BEA and the independents as members; an Air Transport Advisory Committee (ATAC) for government aviation policy development, and the transfer of trooping contracts delayed until ATAC had studied the new contract policy. *Flight International* reported at the time that the BIATA and Bamberg policy reports only differed slightly with no reference in BIATA's report to "unlimited frequency competition".[140]

Ignoring the BIATA and Bamberg policy reports, the Labour government gave BOAC monetary aid a month later on 31 March, at the end of the UK financial year. This is despite the airline being profitable for the fiscal year 1964/65. The problem was that previous years had not been profitable, and BOAC had an accumulated deficit of £82.5 million (£1.6 billion in 2020 prices) and debts of £176 million (£3.5 billion in 2020 prices). One source of that debt was interest on the government loans and advances given to BOAC which had made up most of its capital structure over the years. The government loaned BOAC £31 million and the government was credited with an equity investment of £35 million.[141]

In April 1965, British Eagle had 1,775 employees and a fleet of 14 aircraft.[142] Looking to expand their fleets and workforce, Bamberg and the other independents had hoped for a better aviation policy from Harold Wilson's government following 13 years of Conservative rule. But within six months of coming to power the Labour administration had disincentivised the airline industry and the public had lost services between major cities. Jenkins may have felt some justification for his policy come June when Bamberg reversed his earlier decision and restarted the domestic flights to Scotland, Northern Ireland, Glasgow and Belfast.

Starting with London to Glasgow on 5 July, Bamberg tried to head off an application made in late May by Gatwick Airport-based BUA for those once abandoned domestic licences. BUA wanted to fly from Gatwick, which was considered a "London" airport, to Glasgow, Edinburgh and Belfast, replacing the services that Bamberg had suspended from Heathrow, but they also demanded British Eagle's Birmingham and Manchester licences.[143] Bamberg said: "I was rather angry when this happened, though I have cooled off a bit now. Surely, we independents have enough common problems without fighting each other. The fact remains that these routes are not profitable without an increase in flight frequency."[144]

The year was turning out to be one of consolidation, at best, for the gains Bamberg had made since his 1963 departure from BOAC-Cunard. While the battles with the new Labour government were ongoing, there were some charters flown to Bermuda from Heathrow and Manchester and Bamberg was back in the Caribbean. One bright area was catering where Bamberg announced the construction of a 10,000 square foot facility for flight catering services. It would be built on the north side of Heathrow airport.

An activity of British Eagle's that saw more than just consolidation was its contracts to send troops to the Far East and Australia. They were still in place and British Eagle found itself transporting more troops because of possible Indonesian aggression against Malayasia. In the UK, British Eagle services out of Liverpool were doing well with a growing domestic network to London, Glasgow, Newquay, Blackpool and Leeds. International routes from the port city also did well with services to Barcelona, Dinard, Malaga, Ostend, Palma, Pisa and Tarbes, for the Lourdes pilgrims.

One great reversal for Bamberg when he left BOAC-Cunard was that the rump of Eagle Airways that was left had no jet aircraft. That did not change until 1965 when in September Bamberg was able to announce that three British Aircraft Corporation (BAC) 1-11 "Superjets" had been ordered with an option for three more. By December, Bamberg was able to announce that two more BAC1-11 aircraft would be acquired. The first of the new jets would arrive in April 1966, but not from BAC.

The British Eagle, BUA route dispute was not decided upon by the ATLB until 1966. In a bitter lesson, Bamberg partly won his dispute with BUA over licences but lost the Belfast and Edinburgh routes and would face competition for London to Glasgow. On the plus side, the ATLB Chairman, Sir Harold Kent, decided that the schedule sandwiching and other anti-competitive practices by BUA that the ATLB had previously allowed, had to stop.

After Roy Jenkins adamant comments about trunk routes being only for the state-owned airlines,

A British Eagle BAC 1-11. Image Steve Pyle.

Glasgow was now served by BEA, BUA and British Eagle. In another contradiction to Jenkins' claims about competition, Kent said he considered: "that British Eagle have shown that the competition of their services with those of BEA produced an improvement in the latter's services which was not maintained after British Eagle's [February] withdrawal. The evidence on this was convincing and was not contradicted by any evidence produced by BEA... I accept that this competition benefits British civil aviation."

Kent also commented that there was a need for domestic competition, again apparently contradicting Jenkins' view. In a final sting, Jenkins ruled that Eagle's licence for Heathrow to Glasgow services would lapse if the monthly minimum frequency of 36 flights was not maintained. Bamberg's reaction was that he hoped: "in the fullness of time, we shall be allowed more frequencies on the route in accordance with the application which has been lodged with the ATLB and which has been pending for some months".[145]

169

Despite that harsh start to 1966, *Flight International* had speculated six months earlier that British Eagle would have a good 1965 predicting a net profit of more than £500,000 (£10.7 million in 2020 prices), compared with the airline's £101,000 in 1964.[146] British Eagle's 90 North Atlantic charters and 91 emigrant flights to Australia for Qantas were the basis for the positive assessment.

March 1966 saw the airline announce a plan to buy two Boeing 747s for delivery in 1969. They would be used mainly as freighters. Bamberg was buying the latest airliner, the Jumbo Jet, for the very business he started out in in 1948, freight. By 1969, British Eagle expected to have five Boeing 707-320C airliners along with eight British Aircraft Corporation One-Elevens, also a jet aircraft, and ten Bristol Type 175 Britannias.

The transatlantic charters the US authorities had approved were a great boon to British Eagle and along with the growing inclusive tour market saw Bamberg's businesses heading for another successful year of growth. In a show of confidence, British Eagle became the UK sales agent and provided training for Air Spain, a charter airline. Although the Spanish carrier could be a competitor to British Eagle, there was money to be made from training flight crews and ground engineers.

As confident as British Eagle was with its European charter services, the UK government contracts were still playing a major part in Bamberg's business. The trooping flights, and other government work, contributed very positively to the British Eagle balance sheet, but this revenue stream was now the largest. It was a dependency on

A British Eagle Boeing 707.

one customer that would take a heavy toll in two years' time.

In April, the first of Bamberg's jetliners arrived, but not from the British Aircraft Corporation where orders had been placed a year before. Zambia Airways and Kuwait Airways were divesting themselves of BAC1-11s from their fleets. Four BAC1-11s were obtained from the two airlines and the first of them to be freshly painted in British Eagle colours was rolled out of the Heathrow hangar on 30 April. Used initially for the necessary crew training, the first aircraft, named *Swift*, took fare paying passengers to Glasgow on 9 May 1966.

By August the other three BAC1-11s were in service. Customers could now fly on a jetliner with British Eagle to Tunis and Djerba in Tunisia, Luxembourg, Palma, Perpignan, Pisa, Rimini, Stuttgart and domestic destinations such as Liverpool and Newquay. The British West Country was a popular destination for domestic tourism and British Eagle flew people to Newquay from Birmingham, Glasgow, Liverpool, London and Manchester. British Eagle did not just fly people in, it provided coaches to take them the last few miles to their final destinations across the region. Such was the goodwill generated by Bamberg's service for the southwest England economy, the Chairman of Newquay District Council pronounced British Eagle as: "The Best of the West".

In September 1966, a year after announcing that British Eagle would be re-joining the jet age, one of the airline's BAC1-11s went on display at the Farnborough International Airshow. It was there as part of the British Aircraft Corporation's participation and was in the flying display for three consecutive days of the weeklong air show.

BAC's 1966 Farnborough Air Show demonstrator was British Eagle's BAC 1-11 G-ATPL. Photo: Richard Goring (Transportraits).

In January 1967, the aviation media reported that Bamberg's new holding company, Eagle International, had complete control of the airline having bought back the remaining 40% from Cunard.[147] For the next stage of Bamberg's fight back against the state-owned airlines and government intransigence, he was reorganising his business.

"I remember when it came to be renamed and they bought it back from Cunard [BOAC]," said Eric Tarrant, an electrician who had worked for Bamberg since the airline had been Cunard-Eagle, before the BOAC buy out. "Cunard had just come up from Blackbushe [Airport]," when he joined the company. Reflecting on Bamberg's new fight as an independent, Tarrant said: "in a way it was quite exciting because it was a new venture. I know some staff were made redundant. He had to cut back to a certain extent until he rebuilt it again. [Harold Bamberg] was a guy that looked after his staff."

Tarrant has no such positive memories of BOAC-Cunard. "I have to say, I have a great dislike of Cunard. You have to admire Harold Bamberg because he was constantly being kicked in the teeth by the licensing authorities and BOAC and BEA for licenses."

Tarrant remembers Sir Basil Smallpeice in an equally negative light. "He was very anti-Eagle and Harold was on the board, of course, of BOAC [Cunard] and in the end he resigned because he found that there were so many restrictions and the management weren't managing the airline as he thought it should be managed."

Eagle International would now control British Eagle International Airlines, the charter arm Eagle Aviation,

British Eagle (Liverpool) which was previously Starways, Eagle Aircraft Services for maintenance and engineering and Sky Chef, Bamberg's in-flight catering firm.

Sky Chef served aircraft bars as well as carrying out in-flight catering. In time, Sky Chef would operate airport restaurants at Liverpool and, oddly enough, London Air Traffic Control Centre headquarters in West Drayton, just North of Heathrow Airport. British Eagle also operated a sort of terminal in Knightsbridge in West London. Used by five foreign carriers, Knightsbridge Air Terminal, which was also one of Bamberg's registered companies, allowed first class passengers to check-in and drop their luggage off before being ferried to the aircraft in 45 minutes.[148]

As early as December 1965, before the Jenkins airline policy was known, Bamberg decided to order two Boeing 707-320C airliners. It was the 707's greater payload and range, compared to the other candidates, which made it more attractive for the charter operations Eagle Aviation had planned. But a big obstacle to buying an American aircraft was the 14% import duty.[149]

Bamberg intended to negotiate with the British government for a waiver, after all, a similar concession was allowed for BOAC and its earlier order of two Boeing 707-336CS aircraft. Bamberg's 707s would be delivered in early 1967 and would be put to work immediately carrying passengers and freight on the Far East and Australia routes. But when the aircraft were delivered, the government refused to waive duty for Eagle as they had done for BOAC, once more putting Eagle at a serious disadvantage.[150]

The purchase of the aircraft had always been a gamble, but when Bamberg had applied to the ATLB for scheduled services to the Caribbean, New York, and in the other direction, to Hong Kong he had needed to show that he had aircraft which could serve the route. The wheels of the ATLB bureaucracy turned slowly and their criteria forced risky investments upon the airlines.

For once, the ATLB decision came relatively quickly: it was another no. Despite the US authorities giving British Eagle almost a carte blanche to fly freight across the Atlantic, the Labour government would not help Bamberg. There would be more disappointments from the ATLB regarding domestic routes later in the year. With the import duty and ATLB application rejections Bamberg had sold off the first British Eagle Boeing 707 by early February. It would have been delivered that very month, but it was sold to the United States firm, Airlift International, care of Boeing.

The first 707 British Eagle would receive would now arrive at the end of the year in December. The Boeing aircraft were still central to Bamberg's plans and while he sold off and deferred his first two 707s, in February Bamberg started negotiations for another to be delivered in mid–1968.[151] Bamberg's delivery problems and government obstacles would not stop British Eagle's other plans for the long, hot summer of 1967 and beyond.

As the year progressed, British Eagle was largely carrying on as usual, despite the hindrances. Charter flights were flown out of Liverpool Prestwick, Manchester, Belfast, but mostly from Heathrow.

Liverpool had charter work which took the airline to Istanbul. The trooping contracts continued and saw flights to the RAF Gütersloh airfield and the city of Hannover in West Germany. British Eagle even took work from other airlines, carrying out ad-hoc holiday charters on behalf of Transglobe Airways to destinations including Rimini. British Eagle also carried Canadian tourists between Niagara Falls and Manchester.

Transglobe Airways was another example of the shipping industry's interest in aviation. Its shareholders were the Ocean Steam Ship Company and Bolton Steam Shipping Company, owning 27% and 38% of Transglobe's shares respectively. Transglobe had applied alongside other airlines, including British Eagle, for transatlantic licences from the ATLB in the 1960s. Like the other independents it had been rebuffed by the Board. Although Transglobe applied for British Eagle routes after that airline's November 1968 closure; they would fold unexpectedly a few weeks later.

A root cause for British Eagle's end, and very probably, Transglobe's demise also, had been a Labour government budget decision in 1967 to bring in a £50 (£928 in 2020 prices) per head personal spending limit on overseas holidays. The £50 limit on taking money abroad, which equates to thousands for a family holiday at today's prices, would significantly harm the inclusive tour market. A further decision by the Harold Wilson government, devaluing the Pound Sterling against the US Dollar by 14% in the November, would be a contributing factor to British Eagle's descent.

In May 1967, British Eagle had leased two aircraft

from the Zambian government for the airline's Heathrow-Glasgow route which at the time was Europe's busiest. While it was introducing new aircraft onto UK routes, that summer also saw British Eagle expand its domestic services to include Newquay to Liverpool, Glasgow, Manchester and Birmingham. For Europe, on 12 June a Liverpool-Manchester-Frankfurt service began, and other new services that summer were, Birmingham to Palma; Liverpool to Pisa and Rimini; and Manchester to Pisa and Rimini. Continental European holiday traffic was becoming more and more popular throughout the UK.

North Africa was also served with London-Tunis and London-Djerba services which began in May and by July the flights there were increased to two frequencies weekly. British Eagle was operating its British Aircraft Corporation 1-11 jetliner on this North African route as well as some of the other Continental services.

Bamberg had recognised the value of travel agents early on and the previous year he had created Travel Trust. It brought together his travel agents, Lunn, Poly, and Everyman. Combined they made the UK's largest private travel organisation able to cater for the complete range of inclusive-tour promotions. Bamberg's Travel Trust held major holiday contracts with Cosmos, Global and Cooks. Such was the extent of this side of the business, British Eagle introduced a room-filling computer. The new International Computers ICT 1901 computer installed at British Eagle's Feltham, Middlesex offices was used for travel bookings by Travel Trust and the airline.[152]

Despite all this expansion and hard work, the

summer of 1967 was not as good as had been hoped and was ultimately one of foreboding for Bamberg's airlines. A drop of about 20% in summer holiday traffic hit hard and British Eagle made 48 crew redundant as part of a major cost-reduction scheme. At that point British Eagle had employed 246 pilots. Inclusive tours, where the airline usually made a lot more profit than other services, had seen a 15% fall in demand. Paradoxically, British Eagle had been forced to make pilots redundant at a time when there was a general pilot shortage in the airline industry.[153]

As well as redundancies, Bamberg instituted a cost-saving scheme where employees were encouraged to cut waste to reduce the airlines' costs. The cost saving target for 1967 was £250,000, which is £4.6 million at 2020 prices. Two of Bamberg's BAC 1-11 Superjets were also leased to other airlines during the year because of the depression in the inclusive tour market. Eagle also stopped operating on routes that were not profitable, including the Liverpool to Cork route; originally a Starways service.

By December, British Eagle started inclusive tours to Africa which was the result of a rare victory of Bamberg's against BOAC. The state airline had appealed against the ATLB's decision earlier in the year to grant an Africa licence. Now Bamberg was allowed to sell his £150 (£2,800 in 2020 prices) two-week Kenya inclusive tour holidays through his chain of Lunn Poly travel agency branches. Despite that decision by the ATLB, in 1967, British Eagle, and the other independents, would soon have another battle on their hands with the ATLB.

Sadly, this time it was going to be the last struggle

Bamberg would have with the Board, which was now overseen by the Labour government's President of the Board of Trade, Anthony Crosland MP. The fight with the ATLB began for Bamberg even before the summer was over. In July, British Eagle was informed it would not be allowed to increase its Heathrow-Glasgow frequency from 12 to 15 return flights a week and that its second appeal for a Liverpool-Paris licence had failed.

In July Cambrian Airways, soon to be a BEA subsidiary and not just an associate company, was given the Liverpool-Paris licence that Eagle had been refused. In August, there was more bad news for Bamberg. The ATLB approved Cambrian's application to operate the Liverpool-Dublin route and revoked British Eagle's licence for that service. Cambrian had to operate at least 24 return flights per month in the summer and 16 in the winter or lose that licence. Eagle had stopped their own Liverpool-Dublin services in February when they failed to find an agreement with Ireland's airline, Aer Lingus on timings and capacity. Nonetheless, the licence also had to be cleared with the Irish authorities and British Eagle could appeal.

On Wednesday 9 August 1967, the UK's two biggest independent airlines, BUA and British Eagle, announced their applications for North Atlantic services. It was a broad attack on BOAC's sacred cow at the moment that the government's independent inquiry into British air transport was about to start.[154] British Eagle's plan was a scheduled London-New York service which would begin, prophetically, in 1969, a year British Eagle would not live to see. BUA's proposals included services for London-Canada in 1968, London-Belfast-New York in 1969, and an extension of its South American service to Tahiti and New Zealand in 1970.

The ATLB applications were long haul services in direct or indirect competition with BOAC. Starting 1 April 1969, British Eagle was asking for the London-New York passenger service it had received approval for, briefly, in 1961 when it was Cunard Eagle. After the approval was rescinded by the then Minister of Aviation, due to an appeal by BOAC, Cunard Eagle and British Eagle only operated North Atlantic charter flights. Now, British Eagle was arguing that since 1962 there had been a decline in the British share of the UK-USA market.

According to British Eagle, the data showed that during the preceding five years, 1962—1967, US airlines had increased their market share by 10 percentage points, while the British share had shrunk seven points. As with the previous 1961 North Atlantic licence, British Eagle was asking for 15-years at a frequency of 14 services a week from April to October and seven services a week from November to March. The number of flights would also be increased during those 15 years according to demand and their Boeing 707-320C aircraft would be used.

Gatwick Airport was BUA's base of operations, and its application was more comprehensive than Bamberg's with unlimited frequencies for the North Atlantic. It envisaged a UK-Canada service; operations from Gatwick to Belfast to New York and Boston; a Gatwick to Montreal and Toronto service; as well as an expansion of its South American network from Santiago to Lima and Auckland via Easter Island and Tahiti. Belfast was included as there were no direct services between Northern Ireland and North America at the time. Passengers would travel via Dublin, Shannon, Manchester, Prestwick and London.

The Auckland, New Zealand destination was one BUA had introduced with Concorde in mind. The airline saw the mainly Oceanic route from Gatwick as very suitable for supersonic services to avoid nations' noise restrictions. A route to Australasia, over the Atlantic, the Amazon basin and the Pacific, BUA told *Flight International*, could be a typical supersonic operation of the 1970s. The plan had four phases starting in 1968 and concluding in 1971. But BUA itself would not last that long, merging with Caledonian Airways in November 1970.

Both BUA and British Eagle made the argument that Britain's declining share of the UK-USA market would benefit from another airline, as well as BOAC, operating on the North Atlantic. BUA said it saw no possible detriment to BOAC with its plans and only wider economic benefits for the UK. It was the sort of argument Bamberg had made many times in the past, along with Cunard Eagle's short-lived leadership, and it had all come to nothing on the altar of state-owned airline supremacy.

In addition to the early August applications by BUA and British Eagle, Bamberg had requested Atlantic cargo licenses. Late in August, British Eagle asked to operate an all-cargo service between the UK and the US eastern seaboard and beyond to Detroit and Chicago. The service would start on 1 April 1969.[155] Bamberg also made applications for a mid-Atlantic and Caribbean cargo service which would fly London-Bermuda-Nassau-Jamaica. Perhaps stung by the ambitiousness of BUA's applications, in early October Bamberg submitted further requests. These were Heathrow to Montreal, Toronto, Los Angeles and San Francisco, all of which were planned to start 1 April 1970.[156]

Smaller and younger, Caledonian was snapping at BUA and British Eagle's heels in 1967, announcing on Thursday 10 August that it was applying that week for North Atlantic services. And Caledonian went one stage further, by October it had filed objections with the ATLB against BUA and British Eagle's North Atlantic applications. Bamberg had already filed an objection, but only against BUA. Caledonian, notionally a Scottish airline, criticised BUA and British Eagle's applications for ignoring northern England and Scotland. It also criticised BUA for a Belfast, North Atlantic proposal that "cannot guarantee non-stop transatlantic operations". Caledonian also claimed the two other airlines would negatively affect its own transatlantic charter operations.[157]

To detail Caledonian's application, they wanted scheduled services, starting in 1969, from London, Birmingham, Manchester and Glasgow Prestwick to New York, Toronto and Montreal and Los Angeles and San Francisco. The proposed BUA routes it had opposed were London-Montreal and Toronto starting in 1968 along with extension of South American service to Lima. In 1969, BUA wanted to fly London to Belfast to New York with further South American extensions to Australasia. These would operate from Santiago or Lima to Auckland and Sydney, via Easter Island and Tahiti commencing in 1970. Also in

1970, BUA wanted London-Montreal and Toronto-Vancouver routes.

Transglobe were also seeking scheduled transatlantic services. They operated mainly from London and their application was for flights from London, Manchester and Glasgow Prestwick to Los Angeles or San Francisco and Vancouver, the latter of which would start in 1969. British Eagle's application was similar, Bamberg wanted to fly London to Los Angeles and San Francisco in 1970 and also London to Montreal and Toronto that year. Bamberg wanted his principal long haul route, London to New York to start in 1969 and a London, Bermuda, Bahamas, Jamaica later that year.

The ATLB's hearings for all these applications and the objections were to be held on 9 January and expected to last until the end of that month. Bamberg would have been anxious about the outcome because this time it was not just about the routes he wanted. It was knowing that the Boeing 707s he had bought could finally be added to the fleet and not sold off, as Bamberg's first 707 had been back in February. Neither Bamberg nor the other airlines had to wait until January for what would be an arbitrary bombshell decision making by the Labour government.

Flight International's last edition of 1967, 28 December, reported on the early decisions of the Roy Jenkins MP, Anthony Crosland MP, Sir Daniel Jack, coterie. The article was entitled: "The ATLB is Directed to Refuse…", and the first sentence was: "No doubt the President of the Board of Trade, Mr Anthony Crosland, would have liked to have killed all the independent-airline applications for new

North and South Atlantic routes." Before the January 1968 ATLB hearings had even taken place for all these proposals, the government had struck many of them down. Announced in a 4 December House of Commons written reply from the Minister of State for the Board of Trade to Joseph Percival William Mallalieu MP, Crosland had directed the ATLB to refuse substantial parts of the BUA, Transglobe, British Eagle and Caledonian applications.

The written reply, Mallalieu wrote, also cast doubt on what was left of the applications for the ATLB to deliberate over because, "the work of the Edwards Committee may lead to some changes in existing policies". The government's Edwards Committee, or as it was formally known, the Committee of Inquiry into Civil Air Transport, would produce a report, *British air transport in the seventies,* for the Labour party administration. The Committee Chair was a Sir Ronald Stanley Edwards, a Professor of Economics at the London School of Economics and Chairman of pharmaceutical giant, the Beecham Group.

However, Crosland could not tell the ATLB to refuse everything, despite it being in BOAC's interest, as the international agreements past UK governments had signed up to allowed for more than one carrier. The Bermuda agreement between Britain and the United States made clear that there could be more than one carrier. The US had three airlines in that North Atlantic, Caribbean market. Pan Am, TWA and Seaboard. For the Labour government's Minster for the Board of Trade, Joseph Percival William Mallalieu MP, to recommend a total rejection would have easily been challenged in a court of law.

So, Mallalieu was unable to halt completely the independent bids for New York, Chicago, Los Angeles, San Francisco and other US destinations. The Montreal and Toronto bids were also not entirely refused but the UK government knew it could let the Canadian authorities be the bad guy for these applications. The Anglo-Canadian agreement designated one carrier for the East coast destinations of Montreal and Toronto, so the chances were virtually non-existent that the applications would be allowed by the Canadian government. While the Anglo-Canadian agreement was not so restrictive for Vancouver, Edmonton, Calgary and Winnipeg, so Crosland wanted these refused.

In case the independent airlines were in doubt of the contempt the Labour government held them in, the carriers first learned of the ATLB decisions in the newspapers. The ATLB had told the carriers the decisions were forthcoming, the minimum the Board had to undertake. Under the US system for its CAB, airlines would be consulted prior to the public decision to discuss it. In the UK, the airline industry was afforded no such luxury. In an act typical of the Whitehall Mandarins' arrogance and their elected socialist bosses, friendly journalists were briefed first.

If that was not bad enough, in December 1967, Sir Ronald Edwards announced he would be visiting airlines to see for himself how they work.[158] When published, the Edwards Report would ensure BUA's future for a few more years but would end British Eagle's.

As January 1968 rolled around, the independent airlines' applications had shrunk and they could not be confident that any of the surviving proposals would progress. The Board of Trade's December ATLB directives had had an immediate chilling effect on the airlines' plans. British Eagle dropped its Los Angeles, San Francisco and Toronto, Montreal proposals and BUA abandoned the extensions to its South American routes.[159] This was a heavy blow for BUA as they saw their ATLB application as the first major development for South America since it had been given those routes by the previous Conservative government. In 1964, BOAC had wanted a subsidy to operate in the region.

The South American application rejection also impacted on BUA's hopes for flights across to New Zealand and Australia. BUA was interested in operating Concorde in the 1970s and saw a South Pacific route for it. The maximum damage that could be done to its plans had been done by the ATLB. The December 1967 announcement, that much of what the independents wanted had been thrown out by government diktat, came at the same time BUA changed its leadership. Helicopter entrepreneur Alan Bristow became BUA's Managing Director after Max Stuart-Shaw was promoted to the position of Vice-Chairman.

During Stuart-Shaw's tenure the airline had racked up debts of millions. Bristow had been on BUA's Board since its formation in 1960 and he had previously been Chairman of his own business, Bristow Helicopters, which had been bought by Air Holdings group at the time of the merger that created BUA. Seven years later, Stuart-Shaw's new Vice-Chairman role would make him responsible for getting the airline's plans through the ATLB hearings.

Caledonian, which would in future merge with BUA, was not so badly hit by the ATLB's decisions. Their applications to serve New York and Montreal and Toronto from London and the UK's other three centres, Birmingham, Manchester and Glasgow Prestwick still stood. Caledonian was also able to apply for flights to Chicago from the same four UK cities, and they had also applied to fly to the US West Coast but only from London. The smaller outfit, Transglobe Airways, which had applied for rights from London, Manchester, Prestwick to Vancouver and Los Angeles and San Francisco was left with London to either LA or San Francisco, but not both. Like Caledonian, Transglobe was also offered the opportunity to apply for Chicago flights from London, Manchester, Prestwick.

While the ATLB had eviscerated the scheduled passenger service applications, Bamberg knew how to make the most of a bad situation. He applied for all-cargo services from various points in Britain to New York and six other points in the USA, including San Francisco or Los Angeles, and these were almost untouched by the Ministers directives to refuse. While the ATLB had been offering Chicago to Transglobe and Caledonian, Eagle was refused the same city. Jamaica also had to be dropped by Eagle, even as a cargo destination. The powers that be were not going to allow him to get any sort of foothold in the Caribbean again.

So, the ATLB would have much less to discuss at its hearings when it met on its first day, which was now to be 16 January, a week later than planned. The broad attack on the BOAC dominance of the transatlantic routes had been repelled by the government and its ATLB. Perhaps sensing the outcome, Bamberg decided to lease the second Boeing 707 he had ordered, which was arriving that month. After a British Eagle crew had completed a month's training at Boeing's Seattle plant the 707 was leased to another airline. Bamberg had also bought two 707s from Qantas. The first was expected in mid-January and the second in March.

The plan was for these aircraft to be used on British Eagle's proposed inclusive tours to Bermuda and to the Bahamas which were planned to start in February 1968. As 1967 came to a close, British Eagle appeared to be doing well. Its fleet numbered 27 aircraft and domestic and international services had hit new highs in punctuality figures. The expected introduction, long delayed, of the Boeing 707 aircraft for the long haul charter market; meant that an African licence would have been very welcome but — despite the ATLB setbacks, depressed inclusive tour market, and a reduced level of profits —1968 did not look like a year to be feared.

As tough as the regulatory and competitive environment was from 1965 to 1967, Bamberg could be confident, but he would not have known how precarious his position would become. Eagle would have existential challenges ahead of them in the next few months and by November Bamberg's airlines would be no more. And all because of a single decision made by Harold Wilson's government in the first month of its administration. On 25 November 1964, the then five week-old Labour government's new aviation Minister, Roy Jenkins MP, made a speech in the House of Commons.

Jenkins told the Parliamentarians that the state-owned airlines would be allowed to tender competitively for troop transportation contracts from 1965 onwards.[160] BOAC and BEA were already able to tender for ad-hoc charters of whole aircraft for troops. Jenkins had also agreed to BOAC and BEA offering seats on scheduled services at reduced prices for ad hoc troop movements. This major source of income for independent airlines would be Bamberg's Achilles heel.

Harold Bamberg CBE. Image courtesy of *Flight International.*

11 Jet Setters

The Jet Age was going to shrink the world in ways no one could have conceived when the de Havilland Comet arrived followed by the Boeing 707, Douglas DC-8 and other jetliners and ultimately the conqueror of Oceanic travel, the Boeing 747. Making the change from propeller, or even turboprop, driven aircraft to jet powered airliners was the biggest development in aviation since the advent of heavier-than-air powered flight itself in 1903. All of the airlines had to rethink their business with new aircraft that could fly faster, further and carry twice as many people.

Harold Bamberg's airline was no exception and the transition from propeller and turboprop driven airliners to the jets was a substantial step, mired with problems. Writing the foreword of the 2001 book, *The Eagle Years 1948-1968*, Bamberg stated: "The transition from piston engine aircraft to turbo props and then to pure jets was a major step in terms of finance and technical skill. We achieved all these, but the British licensing system was not and could not be in favour of private companies and the state airlines were protected."

British Eagle used second-hand British-built aircraft for the first ten years or so. Their first aircraft was a Handley Page Halifax leased in the same year, 1948, that the world's first turboprop airliner, the Vickers Viscount, had flown. Turboprop powered airliners still operate today but only for regional services.

The world's first pure jet airliner, the de Havilland D.H.106 Comet 1 had flown from Hatfield by July 1949 and the Comet entered full commercial service in May 1952.[161] Powered by its four de Haviland Engine Company Ghost 50 Mk 1 engines, embedded in the wings, the D.H.106 Comet 1 cruise speed of 460 mph was more than 50% faster than the equivalent piston engine aircraft. The Ghost turbojet engine had been developed by the de Havilland Engine Company which was formed in early 1944 and it was the first jet engine approved for civil transport by the UK's Air Registration Board. For a few years, British aircraft manufacturers would lead the world.

The Comet 1 could carry 36 passengers, cruise at 720 km/h (450 mph) and had a range of more than 4,000 km (2,500 miles).[162] In its first year, the Comet flew 168.3 million kilometres (104.6 million miles) and carried 28,000 passengers.[163] Her Majesty Queen Elizabeth II, her sister, Her Royal Highness Princess Margaret, and their mother, the Queen Elizabeth the Queen Mother were all guests on a special flight in June 1953. In their first year, D.H.106 Comets carried more than 30,000 passengers with at least eight flights departing London each week for destinations such as Johannesburg, Tokyo, Singapore and Colombo.

The first fatal Comet accident led to the type's grounding and redesign when on 2 May 1953 43 passengers and crew died after the aircraft disintegrated at 10,000 feet. The second fatal accident that led directly to the grounding came eight months

191

later when on 10 January 1954, another Comet disintegrated at 26,000 feet in Italian airspace. The second fatal break up of a BOAC Comet 1 grounded the fleet until an investigation found the cause which would be metal fatigue. This fundamental design flaw would stop the Comet from becoming the world leading jetliner it could have been.

The developer of the Comet, de Havilland, was left with £15 million (£420 million in 2020 prices) worth of unsold aircraft, along with jigs and tools it could not use and would have to replace. The UK government would partially bail out de Havilland with £10 million (£280 million today) and orders for the improved Comet 2. Ultimately, the true price of the Comet design flaw was commercial delay in developing a fully transatlantic version of the Comet, the Comet 4, which could have beaten the Boeing 707 and Douglas DC-8 into service by many years.[164]

In the years that de Havilland had to modify the Comet's design and retool for its manufacture, Boeing, McDonnell Douglas, General Dynamics, France's Sud Aviation and the Soviet Union's Tupolev all introduced jetliners. Russia's Tupolev Tu-104 first flew in 1955.[165] The Sud Aviation SE 210 Caravelle took off the same year, and the Douglas DC-8 entered service in 1959, months after the Boeing 707 first flew passengers in 1958. The 130ft wingspan Boeing 707 could fly 181 passengers at 600mph, with a range of 3,000 miles flying up to an altitude of 41,000 feet.

The 707 was a huge gamble for Boeing. In the wake of the metal fatigue disasters of the de Havilland Comet, the airlines had to be convinced that the 707 design was sound. With smaller windows, the

707 had a more pronounced sweep to its wing than the Comet and swept horizontal tail fins. Although it lost the race to be the first commercial jetliner in service, the 707 was a huge commercial success and is credited with being one of a handful of civilian designs which literally changed the world, making long haul flying faster, cheaper and safer than it had ever been before. The 707 dominated passenger air transport until the advent of wide-bodied aircraft in the 1970s, and established Boeing as a dominant airliner manufacturer. The 707 would be Cunard Eagle's preferred choice along with BOAC Cunard.

Boeing delivered 725 of the aircraft for commercial use from 1957 until 1978. While the speed and range were dramatic departures for the passengers, the interior would not have held any great surprises for anyone who had flown on the Britannia or Viscount. An overhead rack, climate controls above the passenger's head, bag space under the seat, the 707 inside followed the standard forms of compact convenience seen in airliners ever since. While the 707 flew with Pan Am in October 1958, the Comet 4's first passenger service was inaugurated on 4 October 1958.

While the Comet 4 had the range (thanks to prevailing westerly winds) to fly nonstop from New York to London it needed to make a refuelling stop when going from London to New York. The 707, however, could operate nonstop in both directions and could carry substantially more passengers, while being up to 100 mph faster. On 27 May 1960, BOAC started operating 707s on the London New York route replacing a Comet.[166] With Cunard's investment in Bamberg's Eagle in March 1960, Cunard Eagle ordered two Boeing 707-400 jetliners with an option for a third.

Bamberg's airlines only began operating US aircraft, namely Douglas DC-6s and Boeing 707s because there were no comparable British aircraft that could match them for range. By 1960, the United States' airlines and their jetliners were dominant in Bamberg's most important market, the mid-Atlantic and Caribbean. Pan American (Pan Am) dominated North America to Bermuda services with a market share of 46% during the peak demand months of April to September in 1959. Pan Am had introduced overseas flights on its Boeing 707 aircraft just a year earlier in October 1958. American Airlines started using 707 aircraft on domestic services in January 1959. The DC-8 was Douglas' first jet and it entered service simultaneously with United Airlines and Delta Air Lines on 18 September 1959. Powered by four turbojet engines, the DC-8 could fly faster than 600 mph.

Bamberg's Cunard Eagle became the first British independent airline to operate jetliners when it inaugurated the Boeing 707 service between London and Bermuda in May 1962. On 5 May, a twice-weekly Boeing 707-420 service from London to Bermuda and Nassau began. One of the two flights terminated in Miami, the other ended on Jamaica island. From 5 July, a second 707 joined the route to provide a three weekly flight service. Two of these ended in Miami and the remaining service in Jamaica.

However, Bamberg would lose his second Boeing 707, reregistered as G-ARWE, to BOAC when it took over Cunard Eagle in mid-1962. 'Whisky Echo' would be a welcome addition to BOAC's fleet but would bring no luck to the state-owned airline. While on a transpacific flight the aircraft developed technical problems and was forced to divert to Wake Island from where she was ferried back to London for repairs. On her first flight following an overhaul she developed an engine fire and had to return to Heathrow only minutes after taking off. Although the crew performed a successful emergency landing, the fire claimed the lives of 4 passengers and 1 stewardess. In a bitter irony, British Eagle staff helped passengers to evacuate the burning plane. Queen Elizabeth II awarded the fatally injured stewardess, Barbara Jane Harrison, a posthumous George Cross (GC), the only GC ever presented to a woman in peacetime.

It would not be until 1965, after Bamberg had bought back his airline, that a newly profitable Eagle would decide to order two more Boeing 707s for international routes. Bamberg had been offered the Vickers Super VC10, a British built jet aircraft but he had calculated that the greater payload and range of the 707-320C version was a better choice for British Eagle's planned charter operations on Far East and Australia routes.

In September 1963, Bamberg had said that he did not have any plans for domestic jet services explaining that they would be "completely uneconomic" on sectors like London to Manchester and London to Birmingham. But he subsequently acquired BAC 1-11s which Eagle operated to Glasgow in competition with BUA and BEA.

March 1966 saw Bamberg announce a plan to buy

two Boeing 747s for delivery in 1969 which would be used mainly as freighters. Bamberg was buying the latest airliner, the Jumbo Jet, for the very business he started out in in 1948, freight. By 1969, British Eagle expected to have five Boeing 707-32OC airliners along with eight BAC1-11s and ten Bristol Type 175 Britannias. The 747s never arrived as British Eagle went bust months before their delivery. In November 1968, British Eagle flew its last flight; it was not a jet, but a propeller driven Bristol Britannia. By the time British Eagle ceased commercial operations, the airline and its sister airlines had a total of 163 aircraft.[167]

Harold Bamberg pictured at the 75th anniversary of Blackbushe Airport, which took place at the airport, in 2017. Image: Philip Johns.

12 Troops, Blue Streak & Suez

Throughout the 20 years that Bamberg owned and managed airlines, trooping contracts would be a vital source of income. When the Berlin Airlift (which had been a gold mine for the independents) came to an end it was trooping flights which kept Bamberg profitable. In 1968, the sudden loss of those contracts would be Eagle's *coup de grâce*.

In 1950, £250,000 (£8.7 million in 2020 prices) was spent on trooping charters. Bamberg's relationship with trooping contracts began in October 1950 when Eagle Aviation was chartered by the UK's Air Ministry to fly Navy, Army and Air Force Institutes (NAAFI) personnel to Iwakuni, Japan on 14 October.

Data from the 1966 annual report of the British Independent Air Transport Association (BIATA) shows that in 1950–1951 4,926 trooping passengers were carried but ten years later, in 1960–1961, that number had increased to 171,138.

By 1955, Trooping accounted for 67% of the independent airlines' total miles flown and even in the mid-1960s was still, on average about 45%. The Conservative government essentially excluded the state airlines, BOAC and BEA, from participating in the market. This would continue until the Labour government of the late 1960s.

The trooping contracts were, in essence, a subsidy to the independent airlines which may otherwise have found it difficult to remain in business when so many of the domestic passenger routes and international routes were monopolised by the state backed airlines. It may seem strange for a Conservative government to encourage subsidies. But, those independent airlines would buy UK built airliners from aircraft manufacturers who also built fighters and bombers for the RAF and the Berlin air lift had shown that in a war-like scenario, or even during wartime, the civil air fleets became invaluable payload capacity.

On 1 May 1954, Eagle started another military contract, the Canal Zone Troops Leave Scheme. A special summer leave scheme had been created to allow all those who were half-way through a year-long deployment in Egypt to take 10 days leave in Cyprus. The scheme included regular soldiers and those on National Service, which was an 18-month period of military training for all 17–21-year-olds. National Service ended for UK youths in 1963.

The RAF bases around the Mediterranean would also be a source of ongoing work for Bamberg. The "Med Air" contract's first flight was on 1 October 1955, and Eagle would base three Vikings outside the UK. They would make Nicosia, Cyprus their home for a while and the aircraft would be altered with RAF colours. They were used for ferry flights to Aden, Baghdad, Benina, El Adem, Malta, Mombasa and Tripoli. Those Vikings would be regular visitors to the many UK military bases in and around the

Mediterranean from Idris and Benina in Libya to Fayid and Abu Suier in Egypt. The flights would stop off at Marseilles and Biarritz. The aircraft stayed at Nicosia for several years until the base was moved to Malta.

In 1956, the Universal Company of the Maritime Canal of Suez was still a Franco-British enterprise 81 years after the Franco-British buyout. British soldiers were still garrisoned at bases on the Canal; despite the 1954 agreement that specified all British troops out by June 1956. That year, Bamberg did not have too much difficulty in getting more trooping contracts from the government. Initially these were ad-hoc contracts for the Mediterranean, West Africa and again Egypt's Canal Zone but the Med Air contract continued during 1956.

In May 1956 Bamberg secured another trooping contract for West Africa, which previously had been an ad-hoc arrangement. Now it was a one-year contract with a potential 12-month extension. The West African trooping round trip was supposed to be for eight days but often took longer with some of its more exotic stopovers. They included, Cisnerios and Agadir in Morocco, Banjul, Gambia, Abidjan on the Ivory Coast and Lagos and Kaduna in Nigeria.

In September 1956, a month before the Suez crisis erupted, Eagle was awarded a £1.25 million two-year contract to transport troops and their families to Cyprus, Gibraltar, Malta, Tripoli, and Fayid, which is located towards the Canal's southern end. The first flight took place in October when the Suez crisis began. The contract, like the Canal Zone leave scheme, required more of Bamberg's aircraft than a normal trooping contract.

Bamberg's British Eagle would continue to fly in the Mediterranean area for years after the Franco-British withdrawal from Egypt. Bamberg still had three Vikings in Nicosia, Cyprus for the Med Air troop flights contract. The year of 1958 saw further progress with the trooping flights. That year would see contracts for trooping flights to Aden, Khartoum, Benina, Nairobi and Nicosia. However, Bamberg had to invest in new aircraft to secure the work. government policy had changed, more modern aircraft were required and Bamberg bought two Douglas DC-6A aircraft from the US carrier, Slick Airways. The only drawback was that the two aircraft were freighters, so a lot of conversion work had to be done by Eagle Aircraft Services.

In May 1964, British Eagle was also awarded trooping contracts for five flights a week for two years to Hong Kong and Singapore which involved flying about 28,000 passengers, servicemen and their families, each year. From Adelaide to Malta the Med Air work continued despite Bamberg's change in companies, and the military needed British Eagle for the Far East again. Singapore and Hong Kong were not unfamiliar to Bamberg's crews, but this time round the destinations included Malaysia's Kuala Lumpur, Kuching and Labuan.

In 1965, trooping flights were expected to be up to 40% of British Eagle's activity, UK domestic scheduled services another 30%, charter's 20% and finally 10% on inclusive tours. That year, British Eagle's contracts to the Far East and Australia were still in place and British Eagle found itself transporting more troops to Malaysia's Kuala Lumpur, Kuching and Labuan.

In March 1968, Eagle's Australian migrant contract

TROOPS, BLUE STREAK & SUEZ

ended. A double blow with the cancellation that month of the Far East trooping contract. The end of Eagle's Australian migrant contract meant no more £10 Poms for Bamberg. But British Eagle was still flying to Australia, for the Woomera rocket work. In compensation for the loss of trooping, now being carried out by RAF Transport Command, British Eagle was contracted for six weekly flights to Ascension Island, in the middle of the Atlantic, just below the equator. Today, there is still an RAF air base there and a NASA listening post.

The end of the trooping contracts was foreshadowed by a Labour decision four years earlier. On 25 November 1964, the newly elected Labour government, in power for just five weeks, announced that the state-owned airlines, BOAC and BEA, would be able to bid for troop transportation contracts from 1965 onwards. BOAC and BEA were already able to tender for ad hoc charters of whole aircraft for trooping. The first of the existing trooping contracts to be renewed were to be re-negotiated in 1965. The following year would see the remainder of the government's trooping contracts reach their renegotiation time.

Labour government aviation Minister, Roy Jenkins MP, made the trooping contract policy change statement to the House of Commons on 25 November 1964. After the statement, Conservative member of Parliament, Angus Maude, asked Jenkins if he intended to, "reassure the independent operators that this is not the first move in a campaign to get them out of the business altogether." Jenkins replied: "I assure the House that there is no question of putting the independents out of business," but these were

201

weasel words.[168] The ending of government trooping contracts was a death sentence for Eagle, and would force others into bankruptcy or mergers.

One of the men who had been a Hungarian refugee in the 1950s, flown out of Vienna to the UK by Eagle Airways after the Soviet invasion, attends the 75th anniversary of Blackbushe Airport to meet Harold Bamberg. Image: Philip Johns.

13 Crisis after Crisis

As 1968 began, it looked like it was going to be another year of promise. January had seen good news from the ATLB, no doubt another surprise for Bamberg. The Board had approved licenses for inclusive tours to Bermuda and Nassau as well as Nairobi and Mombasa. The ATLB had also approved flights to Athens, Constanta, Istanbul, Izmir, Malta, Tenerife and Rhodes, amongst others. The British Eagle network was growing again, it just needed the tourists to fill the planes. The ATLB had also received Bamberg's submission for his "North Atlantic project" in January, for scheduled services to the USA.

As Bamberg told *Flight International* in an interview in April. "I think my greatest satisfaction has been to see the rebirth and development of Eagle since that very difficult period in 1963 after the formation of BOAC-Cunard. The reconstruction and development of the company since that time has been so successful that it gives me and my colleagues the greatest satisfaction and pleasure. It has been difficult, but worthwhile; it is most satisfying to fight back from a very bad position to a period of growth and vitality." *Flight International* also asked Bamberg if his airline would be the first British independent to become a public company. Bamberg's view was that: "It seems to me that we have a long way to go in Britain before we have created the right conditions under which it is possible to attract public investment on a long-term basis and on the scale required... I would like to see British Eagle go public at the right time." His immediate objectives were to make more of the international routes. In March, Bamberg had invested in a new Swiss charter airline, Tellair, taking a 30% stake.

A few months later, British Eagle would be dead and Bamberg out of the airline industry for good. Twenty years of dealing with successive governments, combating the skulduggeries of his competitors, and pushing for freer markets, would end in failure. The shrunken Australian traffic and the loss of the Far East trooping flights had been the final nails in Eagle's coffin.

There was still, however, cause for some optimism. February had seen the President Lyndon Johnson's administration approve British Eagle's application for an extension to a previously approved charter permit. Now it would include other European cities. March had seen the very first charter flight to New York. This very competitive market would see British Eagle offer round trip tickets to the US East Coast of only £64 including in-flight catering.

While Bamberg still believed he could win, the second half of 1968 was to bring new and insurmountable problems. Despite all the apparent success, the early months of 1968 had actually seen traffic down on previous years. The £50 travel limit had caused a drop in inclusive-tour business and the wider economic problems due to war in the Middle East were starting to weigh heavily. By October, Eagle was facing a perfect storm.

Bamberg was forced to announce the redundancy of 418 employees, more than 10% of British Eagles' workforce. The job losses were mostly in London, which took most of the pain, and Speke in Liverpool. Only 81 of the 265 Speke employees would keep their jobs, retained for routine aircraft servicing. Speke had been used to convert British Eagle's Bristol Britannia airliners for freight and that work had by then ended.[169]

As November came around, BOAC achieved one of its last victories against British Eagle when its application to the ATLB to revoke Bamberg's London-Bermuda/Nassau inclusive-tour charters licence was granted. Earlier in the year, June and July, BOAC had submitted its application alleging irregularities in the conduct of British Eagle's tour services. BOAC had also renewed its interest in the Caribbean, having invested in Bahamas Airways along with Cathay Pacific. Bamberg responded with a statement that the ATLB decision: "once more highlights the protectionist attitude of the present system in favour of the national airlines." He also complained about the limitations on the number of flights imposed on British Eagle's routes.

The attitude of the ATLB towards British Eagle and its decision of revocation was foreshadowed by the Board telling Bamberg earlier in 1968, that British Eagle was undercapitalised for the conduct of even the airline's existing operations, let alone the transatlantic schedules.

In passing what would be its terminal judgement regarding the Caribbean licence, the ATLB stated that, "the evidence tendered by BOAC left us in no doubt that British Eagle International Airlines Limited have evaded the terms and conditions of this inclusive-tour licence by representing the service, particularly in Bermuda and the Bahamas, as little different from a scheduled service operated by themselves, and by selling carriage on the service on this basis, thinly disguised as an inclusive tour by the provision of some limited hotel accommodation in London."

By late October, Bamberg was negotiating the sale of his travel firm, the Travel Trust group, saying that the sale of Travel Trust would allow him to devote his entire attention to his airlines.

In a further blow, America's Civil Aeronautics Board recommended against British Eagle services from Nassau to New York and Montreal to Toronto. The decision was based on the legal ownership of the subsidiary, British Eagle Aviation, and the question of whether its workers were genuinely employed by the company. In truth, all of British Eagle Aviation's management and staff also worked for British Eagle, and many of its aircrew were British Eagle employees.

On 6 November, the final blow came. Hambros Bank, who were Eagle's principal creditor, withdrew their support and the company ceased trading, going into voluntary liquidation two days later. At the time they operated 25 aircraft and employed 2,300 people including 220 pilots. British Eagle's debts totalled £5½ million; roughly equivalent to £106 million at today's values.

Eagle electrician, Eric Tarrant, recalled, "It was very sad actually. Yeah, it was a very sad occasion. There was a kind of hope, the crew members were talking about donating their pensions to keep the airline going and there seemed to be a kind of an element of hope that that might happen, but of course it never did. It was a very sad occasion because it was a great airline. Yes, it had its kind of problems, but it was a great airline. I enjoyed working there. [Bamberg] showed his appreciation to everyone and the support we'd all tried to give.

"I never thought that this [British Eagle's closure] was going to happen. I had gone into work that day on a late shift and we had gone over to the central area to do the flights because I was on line maintenance and [after] a couple of hours or so we were all called back to the hangar and there was the notice on the board saying that the company had ceased trading."

No buyer for the failed company was found, and many of Eagle's aircraft and routes were eventually taken over by other independents, notably BUA and Laker Airways.

The political fallout from British Eagle's demise quickly followed and in the week of 16 November the war of words heated up. That week, the National Joint Council for the Civil Aviation Industry, on which both unions and employers sit, strongly criticised the way in which Eagle suddenly ceased trading. After a meeting, the Council passed a resolution that said it regretted that the 2,300 employees were not told earlier about the airline's situation and that it deplored the "lack of consultation and breaching of agreements" by British Eagle. The Council also called for an inquiry to be set up by the President of the Board of Trade.

British Eagle's failure had many components, and poor decisions by Bamberg and his managers were among them. But the single overriding cause of Eagle's bankruptcy was the aviation policies of all the governments, both Conservative and Labour, which had ruled Britain between 1948 and 1968. Each administration, to a greater or lesser degree, had hamstrung Eagle and other independent airlines with policies that favoured the bloated, inefficient, state-owned carriers. This situation would not change until the European Union introduced "Open Skies" policies in the 1980s.

Harold Bamberg CBE in 2004.

14 Harold Bamberg

U nlike so many captains of British aviation industry, Bamberg never got a knighthood he never returned to civil aviation. He reflected on his 20-years as an airline leader in the book, *The Eagle Years 1948-1968* written by David Hedges and published in 2001. For the book's foreword, Bamberg wrote: "British Eagle International Airlines was formed after World War II, originally as Eagle Aviation in 1947 and was registered on 14 April 1948. I participated in a great many para-military operations like the Berlin airlift, Suez Canal Evacuation, Hungarian Refugee Airlift, Korean Ambulance Evacuation, fixed trooping contracts to Singapore, Hong Kong, the Woomera Rocket Range and to flights to Christmas Island in the Pacific for the nuclear deterrent.

"It was a popular airline with the British public and had an extensive network of civilian charter and scheduled services to 30 destinations in Europe and I was virtually the creator of the package holiday business… A tremendous amount of credit for our successful operations goes to the staff who were 100% behind the company and deserve my most grateful thanks for their effort, their humour and their full support. It was a great blow when we had to close down because of the revocation of a licence.

"This was done under the socialist government, and it was thought that further revocations might follow. The situation has changed today with a much more liberal Licensing Board and a totally different outlook about protection for state enterprises. Indeed, the nationalised airline that was, has now been privatised and we wish it every success, although it was hostile to us."

It was not only the nationalised airlines that were hostile, the UK government, under a Labour party Bamberg considered socialist as well as under Conservative administrations, was usually hostile. "It was the establishment that screwed him in the end, you know. He'd got all the financial bits sorted out. He'd got all the planning done. He was meticulous in organising all that. But what he couldn't organise was the objections from the state airlines. You can't be granted a licence to fly, go out, find an airplane and then somebody [decides] 'actually we don't like this because that's going to create competition,'" Hedges commented.

The utilisation factors of Bamberg's airline told the story. Utilisation factors is airline industry speak for what percentage of total possible flying time an airline's fleet flies for. Bamberg's airlines, with all the restrictions they suffered, achieved about 78%, while the State airlines of BOAC and BEA were about 46%. Bamberg's experience on the BOAC board was telling. He would thump the BOAC board table and the other directors would react badly to their new Board member's ideas. When Bamberg first joined the BOAC-Cunard Board in he had hoped to influence it from within.

Instead, Bamberg found the Board frustrating because they rarely made a decision about anything. The Board would muddle along and if they concluded that the airline was running out of money, the response was: "Well, we'll just go to the treasury. They'll give us more." That was the mentality. The BOAC Board was regularly bailed out of its difficulties. When Cunard-Eagle came into existence, BOAC decided that buying its competitor was the answer. After BOAC was able to get the ATLB to stop the Cunard-Eagle transatlantic licences, BOAC's Chairman Sir Giles Guthrie took no time in contacting Cunard's Chairman Sir John Brocklebank and negotiating a buyout behind Bamberg's back.

Bamberg loved horses and polo and in the circles of the British polo community, he found acceptance and friendship. But in business he was never going to be allowed to upset the rule of the aristocrats who made sure their interests were served and that even under Labour governments and within nationalised industries they still benefited. Bamberg today lives quietly at his home in southern England, a 98-year-old, still showing the determination and persistence that gave the airlines he ran the fortitude to survive a hostile environment. He has lived to see the airline market become the space of free competition that he wanted. He has seen small, innovative low-cost airlines displace those national protectionist airlines and offer the very low fares that he pioneered, opening up air travel to everyone.

15 Epilogue: Laker, Branson & BA

When Richard Branson went up against British Airways (BA), Lord King of Wartnaby was BA's Chairman and he was another man with no aviation experience. Born in London in 1919, King had no university education but became the head of his first business by marrying the owner's daughter in 1941. By the end of World War Two his company was the third largest UK ball bearing maker. In 1949, King became master of the Badsworth Foxhounds, then in 1958 master of the Duke of Rutland's Foxhounds and in 1972, the Belvoir Hunt Chairman. His love of hunting brought King into aristocratic circles and in 1970 he married a daughter of Viscount Galway, after his first wife of 28-years had died in the preceding year.[170]

Sir Colin Marshall was Lord King's Chief Executive and Deputy Chairman and he had joined BA from the world of car hire, or rental cars as they are called in the US where Marshall had had his career success. Marshall, who would become Baron Marshall of Knightsbridge in 1998, had one slight career connection with the UK aviation industry's past; he had started work on a shipping line. Marshall left his public school, University College School, in north

London at 16. He became a cadet purser for the Orient Line which would become a P&O brand in 1960.[171][172]

This second British Airways had come into existence in 1974 through the merger of BEA and BOAC and a host of smaller subsidiary airlines. In the wake of British Eagle's descent, other airlines also fell before Edward Heath's Conservative government created the second British Airways. The BEA subsidiaries Cambrian Airways and BKS Air Transport were absorbed into BEA by early 1970, perhaps in preparation for the creation of BA. In March 1970 the UK's largest independent airline BUA was about to be sold to BOAC by its owners, British & Commonwealth Shipping, for circa £9 million.[173] British & Commonwealth Shipping had bought BUA in 1967 from Air Holdings for £6 million.[174]

Caledonian Airways announced at the time it was applying immediately to the ATLB for BUA's licences to take over the scheduled routes operated by the for-sale airline. A £9 million purchase of BUA would make British & Commonwealth Shipping a tidy profit and would be a generous valuation for an ailing airline. After the proposed sale of BUA to BOAC there were immediate demands for the sale to be referred to the Monopolies Commission, but the Board of Trade responded that it saw no case for such a move, unsurprisingly.

The sale to BOAC was stopped and instead Caledonian would buy it through a convoluted hire-purchase like scheme. In due course, Caledonian, after it became British Caledonian in 1975, would be absorbed by the new British Airways in an uncompromising way in 1988. British Caledonian and Laker Airways would be victims of BA's actions and its connections, but Richard Branson would evade the behemoth's grasp, aided by the exposure of Lord King and Sir Coin Marshall's actions.

Long before Branson arrived on the scene, knowledge of unethical actions by BA's predecessor BOAC, had been suppressed. In 2013, a detailed account of the years 1946 to 1974, of BA's main legacy airline, BOAC, was published two years before its author's death. The author was a Professor Robin Higham. Born in the UK, Higham served as a Flight Sergeant Pilot in the Royal Air Force Volunteer Reserve from 1943-1947. He graduated from Harvard College, a school of Harvard University in Boston, Massachusetts, in 1950 and later it was where he earned his doctorate in 1957.[175]

Higham would go on to visit the UK in the 1960s with a view to writing a detailed official account of BOAC's first 25 years, 1939–1964. Smallpeice explains in his autobiography that: "Giles Guthrie [BOAC Chairman from 1964-1969], I was told later, considered it contained matters that were controversial and decided to suppress it. Higham's manuscript lay for many years in the archives. But... I had it resurrected in 1975 after the merger of BOAC and BEA into British Airways. Robin Higham was then commissioned to extend it to cover the whole 35-years of BOAC's existence from 1939 to 1974."

Almost 40 years after Higham finished that manuscript his book *Speedbird: The complete history of BOAC*, was finally published in 2015. Did of any of that original controversial content remain? While BA's privatisation in 1987 went ahead, its legacy company's way of working, strong arming smaller airlines, was not far behind it. Laker had had to announce the closure of his airline in 1982 when Clydesdale Bank would not provide the necessary funding. The fallout from this collapse was a legal dispute with BA about price fixing. It would see the defunct Laker Airways continue to haunt the flagship airline six years later when Branson would sue BA in 1992. In 1993, Lord King would resign.[176]

Like the BOAC and BEA of old, key people in BA in the 1980s were executives with no aviation experience. King and Marshall's Director of Marketing and Operations in 1988 was Liam Strong. A psychology and philosophy graduate of Trinity College Dublin, Strong had worked for Proctor & Gamble and UK household goods firm, Reckitt & Colman, before joining BA. Later on, Robert "Bob" Ayling would become Director of Marketing and Operations. Ayling, like Strong, Marshall and King had a non-aviation background, working as a lawyer in the UK civil service, at the Department of Trade and Industry.[177] BA's Chairman of its non-executive board members, Sir Michael Angus, was a former Unilever Chairman and another senior executive with no aviation experience. Angus was a key figure in the BA, Virgin fight.[178]

Angus would not escape the quagmire of the BA, Virgin spat unscathed. Commentators on his life point to the dirty tricks scandal as the reason why Angus did not get a peerage, unlike Marshall. Another reason given why Angus did not become a Lord is that Lord King's friend and fellow huntsman, Lord Hanson, blamed Angus for King having to resign, although Angus denied it.[179]

Fourteen years later the full story of what brought Laker Airways down began to emerge. In 1983, Laker Airways' receivers, the accountants Touche Ross (now known as Deloitte), began an anti-trust predatory pricing case in the USA with a demand for $1 billion from 10 airlines including BA. Pan Am, TWA, Lufthansa, BA and six others accused of loss-making pricing to drive Laker out of business. A few airlines had also sandwiched Laker Airways schedule, just as BEA had been allowed to do against Bamberg. McDonnell Douglas was even told by some airlines they would not buy the company's aircraft if the airliner maker did business with Laker.

Laker had achieved what Bamberg had never been able to, a successful scheduled transatlantic service, not just charter flights. The Bamberg strategy of, become vertically integrated with tour operators to maximise charter bookings, focus on the lucrative North Atlantic and use Caribbean routes to quickly start serving the US market, had finally worked; largely thanks to Jimmy Carter and his administration's readiness to liberalise.

Laker Airways went bust in 1982 owing £35 million (£126 million in 2020 prices) to creditors, staff and passengers. His costs had been in US dollars and his revenue was mostly in pounds, whose value had shrunk. In comparison with Bamberg's British Eagle, Laker's £35 million of debt in 1982 would have been worth £7 million in 1968 prices; more than Bamberg's outfit had at the end. Oddly, Laker also owned a horse stud farm, Woodcote Stud.[180]

It was 22 June 1984 that Virgin Atlantic's first flight took off from Gatwick Airport. Branson's airline ambitions began with a lawyer, Randoph Fields, who had applied for the transatlantic slot left vacant by Laker Airway's collapse two years earlier. Gatwick to New York. Fields' airline, British Atlantic, needed an aircraft, and money. Branson decided to jump onboard, and British Atlantic became Virgin Atlantic. The new airline had one thing in common with BA, neither Branson nor Fields had any aviation experience. British Caledonian opposed the transatlantic application at the CAA hearing but somehow Branson and Fields were awarded a Gatwick to Newark licence. The successor to Laker lived.

Branson would win where Bamberg and Laker did not because it was a different world. There was no longer a government commitment to a state monopoly in aviation. The aristocratic families who had made their wealth in shipping and rail in the 19th century had long since faded away. While the waning years of that era had led to the likes of Lord King and Sir Colin being given the reigns of aviation power; the weapons of political policy, influenced regulators rules and whims were simply not options anymore, but anti-competitive practices like schedule sandwiching were still around.

British Airways repeated the old anti-competitive practices of sandwiching and swamping against Branson's US routes. These essentially involve scheduling lots of flights and capacity to arrive or leave from an airport at the same time as the rival airline's service. It also repeated the practice of spreading rumours about financial problems, which BA had used against Laker. Laker had advised Branson to sue BA and he did exactly that. BA went further with

Branson than it did with Laker, trying to implicate Virgin Atlantic in a surveillance operation against the flag carrier using private detectives. It all blew up in the faces of BA's leadership and in January 1993, Branson won his court case against BA.

Like the many airlines that had gone before it, including the first British Airways, ultimately it would be the fate of the second BA to be merged with another airline to form a new airline business. Two years earlier than the Delta, Virgin deal, British Airways and Spanish airline, Iberia, formed International Airlines Group (IAG) which is based in Spain. Originally a merger between BA and Iberia, today, BA is simply one of a number of brands within IAG alongside Iberia, Aer Lingus and Vueling. British Airways was a success, for a while, after its 1987 privatisation, but its long history of privileged individuals who were given the job of running the airline despite having worked in other industries was its downfall.

In comparison, the history of UK airlines had seen — again and again — men, often pilots, who had used what little money they had to invest in one aircraft, would build up their fleet and then be side-lined when their company was acquired or driven out of business. From Imperial Airways, formed in 1924 from airlines which were mostly run by self-made men, to the first British Airways which was formed in 1935, the British airline industry had always had a history of forced mergers and bankruptcies.

In March 2005, Willie Walsh, Aer Lingus CEO, was announced as British Airways' Chief Executive Designate to replace Rod Eddington who would retire at the end of September. Walsh then became CEO and nine months later in June 2006, BA announced it was subject to an Office of Fair Trading investigation into alleged passenger fares and fuel surcharges cartel activity. In 2007, BA would plead guilty to price fixing and pay a $540 million fine to UK and US authorities. Virgin Atlantic was granted immunity as it had given full details of the cartel conduct to the authorities.[181]

Half a billion-dollar fines, tough competition from the likes of Air France and Lufthansa, a balance sheet with too much red, ongoing cabin staff disputes and strike action, and the seemingly never-ending market share loss to the low-cost airlines. Twenty plus years after its privatization, British Airways needed a route to stability and future growth. With Spanish Iberia, BA had a carrier facing similar problems but with a network which did not overlap to any great extent with its own. Walsh saw the 2011 Iberia merger into IAG as a way to fight back against the low-cost airlines.[182] At the time, Walsh would not have known that his move would help protect BA from the biggest event for UK airlines since his own carrier's privatization.

While British Eagle is a name that has passed into history along with Skytrain, BOAC, Pan Am, and TWA, pilots hear references to Bamberg's airline even today. Air traffic controllers still refer to the taxiway that runs parallel to Heathrow's decommissioned runway 23 as Eagle, because it runs past what used to be the Eagle hangars.

Harold Bamberg was an outsider — not a public schoolboy or Oxbridge graduate — nor even British, but a Jewish refugee from Germany. There would be no knighthood or peerage for him, unlike so many other airline leaders, however badly they mismanaged their companies. Demobbed from the RAF after years of flying dangerous missions in World War Two, Bamberg could hardly have guessed that his new enemy would not be his commercial competitors, but the successive Conservative and Labour governments that he would look to for support.

Now Boarding by Trevor Mitchell.

References

1   Thaxter, J. R. (1990). BCal Sir Adam Thomson Interview 1990. Retrieved from Youtube: https://www.youtube.com/watch?v=wiT7T8ZY8Bs

2   No 138 Squadron. (2013). Retrieved from Royal Air Force Museum: https://www.nationalcoldwarexhibition.org/research/squadrons/138/

3   Handley Page Halifax II. (2020). Retrieved from www.rafmuseum.org.uk: https://www.rafmuseum.org.uk/research/collections/handley-page-halifax-ii/

4   Bowman, M. W. (2012). Bomber Command: Reflections of War, Volume 2: Live to Die Another Day June 1942-Summer 1943. Pen & Sword Aviation.

5   Watson, C. D. (2013). British Overseas Airways Corporation 1940 - 1950 And Its Legacy. Journal of Aeronautical History, 136-161.

6   Hedges, D. (2001). The Eagle Years 1948-1968. The Aviation Hobby Shop.

7   The Earl of Longford. (2001, August 6). Retrieved from https://www.independent.co.uk: https://www.independent.co.uk/news/obituaries/the-earl-of-longford-9162237.html

8   William Beveridge (1879 - 1963). (2014). Retrieved from https://www.bbc.co.uk/: https://www.bbc.co.uk/history/historic_figures/beveridge_william.shtml

9   Lange, K. (2018, June 25). The Berlin Airlift: What It Was, Its Importance in the Cold War. Retrieved from U.S. Dept of Defense: https://www.defense.gov/Explore/Inside-DOD/

Blog/Article/2062719/the-berlin-airlift-what-it-was-its-importance-in-the-cold-war/

10   John Brocklebank. (2021). Retrieved from www.espncricinfo.com: https://www.espncricinfo.com/player/john-brocklebank-9407

11   Mr Bamberg's Big Jets. (1968, February 15). Flight International, p. 216.

12   Glasgow, T. U. (n.d.). Sir Daniel Thomson Jack. Retrieved from www.universitystory.gla.ac.uk: https://www.universitystory.gla.ac.uk/biography/?id=WH0080&type=P

13   Eagle retrenches. (1968, October 10). Flight International , p. 557.

14   The Eagle Close-down. (1968, November 14). Flight International, p. 767.

15   British Eagle (Cessation Of Operations). (1968, November 7). Retrieved from https://hansard.parliament.uk/: https://hansard.parliament.uk/Commons/1968-11-07/debates/2e7ca80a-ba16-458a-9f5b-

16   Farmer, H. (2018, March 1). The history of Imperial Airways. Retrieved from The Industrial History of Hong Kong Group: https://industrialhistoryhk.org/the-history-of-imperial-airways/

17   Halford-MacLeod, G. (2014). Born of Adversity Britain's Airlines 1919-1963. Stroud: Amberley Publishing.

18   Higham, R. (1959). The British government and overseas airlines, 1918-1939, a failure of laissez-faire. The Journal of Air Law and Commerce, 26(1).

19   Turner, M. (2019). BOAC and the Golden Age of Flying 1939-1974. Burnt Ash Publishing.

20   Lange, K. (2018, June 25). The Berlin Airlift: What It Was, Its Importance in the Cold War. Retrieved from U.S. Dept

REFERENCES

of Defense: https://www.defense.gov/Explore/Inside-DOD/
Blog/Article/2062719/the-berlin-airlift-what-it-was-its-impor-
tance-in-the-cold-war/

21   Stroud, J. (1989). Annals of British and Commonwealth
Air Transport 1919-1960. Putnam Aeronautical Series.

22   Williams, A. M. (1950). A Report on Operation
PLAINFARE (The Berlin Airlift). Headquarters British Air Forces of Occupation.

23   Turner, M. (2020). Britain's Airline Entrepreneurs:
From Laker to Branson. Burnt Ash Publishing.

24   Humphreys, B. K. (1973). The Economics and Development of the British Independent Airlines since 1945. Phd Thesis. University of Leeds.

25   (1950, August 31). Flight.

26   Mr Arthur Henderson's Statement. (1951, March 6).
Retrieved from www.hansard.gov.uk: https://hansard.parlia-
ment.uk/Commons/1951-03-06/debates/

27   Tarrant, E. (2017, 10 8). The history of Eagle Aviation
Ltd 1948-1953. Retrieved from www.britisheagle.net: http://
www.britisheagle.net/History-Eagle-Aviation.htm

28   Dix, A. G. (2019). Laker: The glory years of Sir Freddie
Laker. Recursive Publishing.

29   Internal Workings of the Soviet Union. (n.d.). Retrieved from Library of Congress: https://www.loc.gov/exhibits/
archives/intn.html#reps

30   Tarrant, E. (2017, October 8). Routes Belgrade, Yugoslavia. Retrieved from www.britisheagle.net: http://www.britis-
heagle.net/Routes-Belgrade.htm

31   Žarković, P. (2016). Yugoslavia and the USSR 1945 -
1980: The History of a Cold War Relationship. Retrieved from
YU historija: https://yuhistorija.com/int_relations_txt01c1.html

THE RISE AND FALL OF BRITISH EAGLE

32   Tarrant, E. (2017, October 8). Routes Belgrade, Yugoslavia. Retrieved from www.britisheagle.net: http://www.britisheagle.net/Routes-Belgrade.htm

33   Corporate history. (2017). Retrieved from Belgrade Airport: https://beg.aero/eng/corporate/about_us/history

34   The Crooked Sky. (n.d.). Retrieved from Internet Movie Database: https://www.imdb.com/title/tt0050274/?ref_=fn_al_tt_1

35   The Hungarian uprising. (n.d.). Retrieved from https://www.bbc.co.uk/: https://www.bbc.co.uk/bitesize/guides/zghnqhv/revision/3

36   Watson, C. D. (2013). British Overseas Airways Corporation 1940 - 1950 And Its Legacy. Journal of Aeronautical History, 136-161.

37   Humphreys, B. K. (1973). The Economics and Development of the British Independent Airlines since 1945. Phd Thesis. University of Leeds.

38   Klarmann, N. G. (1978). Entrepreneurial design possibilities of the private banker in the 19th century. In H. H. Hofmann, Bankherren und Bankiers. Limberg: Starke Lahn.

39   Tenkotte, P. A. (2016, February 22). Our Rich History: Erlanger and the d'Erlanger and Churchill families — unraveling a historical puzzle. Retrieved from https://www.nkytribune.com/: https://www.nkytribune.com/2016/02/our-rich-history-erlanger-and-the-derlanger-and-churchill-families-unraveling-a-historical-puzzle/

40   Roth, A. (1999, August 24). Lord Orr-Ewing. Retrieved from www.theguardian.com: https://www.theguardian.com/news/1999/aug/24/guardianobituaries

41   The Blackbushe Viking Accident. (1957, May 10). Flight, p. 643.

REFERENCES

42   Aviation Safety Network. (n.d.). Retrieved from www.aviation-safety.net: https://aviation-safety.net/database/record.php?id=19570501-0

43   Woodley, C. (2006). History of British European Airways 1946-1974. Pen & Sword Books Ltd.

44   1958 , April 18. Flight, p. 527.

45   Challenge to BOAC —1. (1958). Flight, p. 956.

46   Ibid.

47   Ramsden, J. M. (1960, January 29). Blackbushe to Bermuda. Flight, pp. 147-149.

48   Challenge to BOAC —1. (1958). Flight, p. 956.

49   Cunard and British Eagle. (1960, March 25). Flight International, p. 425.

50   Cunard and British Eagle. (1960, March 25). Flight International, p. 425.

51   Air Fares. (1960, April 5). Retrieved from Hansard: https://hansard.parliament.uk/Commons/1960-04-05/debates/4295aad4-0d36-4787-

52   Britain goes it alone. (1960, April 15). Flight, p. 543.

53   The new pattern takes shape. (1960, May 27). Flight, p. 741.

54   Humphreys, B. K. (1973). The Economics and Development of the British Independent Airlines since 1945. Phd Thesis. University of Leeds.

55   Caricom Caribbean Community. (n.d.). Retrieved from www.caricom.org: https://caricom.org/the-west-indies-federation/

56   To sort out the Caribbean. (1960, June 3). Flight, p. 773.

57   Ramsden, J. M. (1960, January 29). Blackbushe to Bermuda. Flight, pp. 147-149.

58   His early life. (n.d.). Retrieved from The Michael Manley Foundation:

59   Cunard Eagle Western. (1961, November 30). Flight, p. 860.

60   Turnill, R. (2003). The Moon Landings: An eye witness account. Cambridge University Press.

61   Ibid.

62   Cunard Eagle Bounces Back. (1962, April 5). Flight, p. 501.

63   Ibid.

64   Cunarder Jet Challenge. (1962, May 17). Flight International, p. 770.

65   Mr Bamberg and Eagle. (1963, February 21). Flight International, p. 251.

66   Holloway, J. C. (1983). The business of tourism (3rd ed.). Prentice Hall.

67   James Bryce, Viscount Bryce. (n.d.). Retrieved from www.britannica.com: https://www.britannica.com/biography/James-Bryce-Viscount-Bryce

68   Sir Henry Simpson Lunn. (2021). Retrieved from famoushotels.org: https://famoushotels.org/news/lunn-sir-henry-simpson

69   Civil Aviation From 1919-1939. London: London School of Economics.

70   The Eagle Close-down. (1968, November 14). Flight International, p. 767.

REFERENCES

71   Travel Trust signs with Dan-Air. (1968, December 5). Flight International, p. 924.

72   Travel Trust - no sale? (1968, December 19). Flight INternatoinal, p. 1019.

73   The Founding of IATA. (n.d.). Retrieved from www. iata.org/: https://www.iata.org/en/about/history/

74   This is Skycoach. (1960, October 7). Flight International , p. 559.

75   Humphreys, B. K. (1973). The Economics and Development of the British Independent Airlines since 1945. Phd Thesis. University of Leeds.

76   The Eagle Close-down. (1968, November 14). Flight International, p. 767.

77   Viscount Watkinson. (1995, December 23). Retrieved from Herald Scotland: https://www.heraldscotland.com/ news/12056190.viscount-watkinson/

78   Humphreys, B. K. (1973). The Economics and Development of the British Independent Airlines since 1945. Phd Thesis. University of Leeds.

79   Economic and safety enforcement cases of the Civil Aeronautics Board. (1961). In Civil Aeronautics Board Reports Volume 33 (p. 173). US Government.

80   Air Fares. (1960, April 5). Retrieved from Hansard: https://hansard.parliament.uk/Commons/1960-04-05/debates/4295aad4-0d36-4787-

81   New Earnings Survey (NES) timeseries of Gross Weekly earnings from 1938 to 2017. (2017, October 26). Retrieved from Office for National Statistics: https://www.ons.gov.uk/employmentandlabourmarket/peopleinwork/earningsandworkinghours/adhocs/006301newearningssurveynestimeseriesofgrossweeklyearningsfrom1938to2016

82   Hedges, D. (2001). The Eagle Years1948-1968. The Aviation Hobby Shop .

83   This is Skycoach. (1960, October 7). Flight International, p. 559.

84   Frugality in Scotland. (1960, November 30). Flight International, p. 860.

85   Ibid,

86   History of Hunting. (n.d.). Retrieved from www.huntingplc.com: https://www.huntingplc.com/about/history

87   Roger Eglin, B. R. (1981). Fly Me, I'm Freddie!: Biography of Sir Freddie Laker. Futura Publications.

88   Sir Alan J. Cobham. (n.d.). Retrieved from Encyclopedia Britannica: https://www.britannica.com/biography/Alan-J-Cobham

89   Our heritage. (2021, October 4). Retrieved from Cobham.com: https://www.cobham.com/our-heritage/

90   Turner, M. (2020). Britain's Airline Entrepreneurs: From Laker to Branson. Burnt Ash Publishing.

91   Dix, A. G. (2019). Laker: The glory years of Sir Freddie Laker. Recursive Publishing.

92   Ibid.

93   Mills, J. (2020, October 30). Come fly with me. Retrieved from hagerty.co.uk: https://www.hagerty.co.uk/articles/come-fly-with-me/

94   The company. (2012). Retrieved from silvercityairways.com: http://www.silvercityairways.com/the_company.htm

95   Fleming, I. (1959). Goldfinger. In I. Fleming, Goldfinger (p. 138). Vintage.

REFERENCES

96   Frugality in Scotland. (1960, November 30). Flight International, p. 860.

97   Civil Aviation Bill. (1971, March 29). Retrieved from https://api.parliament.uk: https://api.parliament.uk/historic-hansard/commons/1971/mar/29/civil-aviation-bill

98   Cunard and British Eagle. (1960, March 25). Flight International, p. 425.

99   Explore our past: 1950 - 1959. (n.d.). Retrieved from www.britishairways.com: https://www.britishairways.com/en-fr/information/about-ba/history-and-heritage/explore-our-past/1950-1959

100   B.O.A.C. Board (Appointments). (1960, June 20). Retrieved from https://api.parliament.uk/: https://api.parliament.uk/historic-hansard/commons/1960/jun/20/boac-board-appointments

101   Henry Francis Slattery. (n.d.). Retrieved from www.natwestgroup.com: https://www.natwestgroup.com/heritage/people/henry-francis-slattery.html

102   Humphreys, B. K. (1973). The Economics and Development of the British Independent Airlines since 1945. Phd Thesis. University of Leeds.

103   House Of Lords Offices committee. (1961, January 31). Retrieved from https://hansard.parliament.uk: https://hansard.parliament.uk/Lords/1961-01-31/debates/c8ea6391-e0d7-49ff-bb5b-7a111564039f/HouseOfLordsOfficescommittee

104   Glasgow, T. U. (n.d.). Sir Daniel Thomson Jack. Retrieved from www.universitystory.gla.ac.uk: https://www.universitystory.gla.ac.uk/biography/?id=WH0080&type=P

105   Cunard Eagle Wins. (1961, June 29). Flight International, p. 907.

106   Smallpeice, S. B. (1980). Of Comets and Queens. Airlife Publishing.

107   Air Transport Licensing Board (Appointments). (1960, July 26). Retrieved from https://hansard.parliament.uk: https://hansard.parliament.uk/Commons/1960-07-26/debates/e068cb12-7494-428b-9c53-567c05605577/AirTransportLicensingBoard(Appointments)?highlight=wilson%20air%20transport%20licensing%20board#contribution-70492fe0-ef36-4c47-956e-d92b8a90f1bb

108   Editor, A. T. (1961, April 13). Britain's New Board. Flight International , p. 471.

109   Public and Private Images. (1961, May 18). Flight International, p. 683.

110   Smallpeice, S. B. (1980). Of Comets and Queens. Airlife Publishing.

111   Houterman, H. (n.d.). Royal Navy (RN) Officers 1939-1945. Retrieved from World War II Unit Histories & Officers: https://www.unithistories.com/

112   History of Cunard. (n.d.). Retrieved from www.northpalmbeachlife.com: https://www.northpalmbeachlife.com/cunard----travel-by-air-and-sea.html

113   Cunarder Jet Challenge. (1962, May 17). Flight International, p. 770.

114   Humphreys, B. K. (1973). The Economics and Development of the British Independent Airlines since 1945. Phd Thesis. University of Leeds.

115   Lloyd, B. (2018, July 19). British Eagle flying against the odds. Retrieved from www.key.aero/: https://www.key.aero/article/british-eagle-flying-against-odds

116   Mr Bamberg and Eagle. (1963, February 21). Flight International, p. 251.

REFERENCES

117   Bishop, E. (1992, July 16). Obituary: Sir Basil Small-peice. Retrieved from https://www.independent.co.uk/: https://www.independent.co.uk/news/people/obituary-sir-basil-small-peice-1533712.html

118   Higham, R. (2013). XI. Beginning the Last Decade. In R. Higham, Speedbird: The complete history of BOAC (p. 441). Bloomsbury.

119   Election-labours-big-win-50-years-ago-this-month. html

Bishop, E. (1992, July 16). Obituary: Sir Basil Smallpeice. Retrieved from https://www.independent.co.uk/: https://www.independent.co.uk/news/people/obituary-sir-basil-small-peice-1533712.html

120   Air Corporations Bill. (1965, November 22). Retrieved from hansard.parliament.uk: https://hansard.parliament.uk/Commons/1965-11-22/debates/74eaf47e-3f52-4cce-8e52-479de63a7afa/AirCorporationsBill?highlight=air%20transport%20licensing%20board%20appointments#contribution-29778e7d-33c0-4482-b260-72c52c94495d

121   Perraudin, F. (2016, February 14). Liberal Democrat peer Lord Avebury dies aged 87. Retrieved from www.theguardian.com: https://www.theguardian.com/politics/2016/feb/14/lord-avebury-lib-dem-peer-dies-aged-87

122   Cross, C. F. (2011). The Cunard Story. The History Press.

123   Eagle Western Again. (1968, March 7). Flight International, p. 324.

124   Stronger Eagle. (1963, December 26). Flight International, p. 1019.

125   Hedges, D. (2001). The Eagle Years1948-1968. The Aviation Hobby Shop .

126   British Eagle. (1963, September 5). Flight International, p. 417.

127   Postscript to the domestic decision. (1963, October 24). Flight International, p. 682.

128   Stronger Eagle. (1963, December 26). Flight International, p. 1019.

129   British Eagle and Starways. (1963, November 28). Flight International, p. 855.

130   British Eagle 1964. (1965, January 21). Flight International, p. 84.

131   The New Britain: 1964 Labour party manifesto. (1964, October). Retrieved from www.labour-party.org.uk: http://labour-party.org.uk/manifestos/1964/1964-labour-manifesto.shtml

132   Baston, L. (2016, March 11). The 1966 election – Labour's big win, 50 years ago this month. Retrieved from www.conservativehome.com: https://www.conservativehome.com/thecolumnists/2016/03/lewis-baston-the-1966-election-labours-big-win-50-years-ago-this-month.html

133   Air Corporations Bill. (1965, November 22). Retrieved from www.parliament.uk: https://api.parliament.uk/historic-hansard/commons/1965/nov/22/air-corporations-bill

134   Civil Aviation Policy. (1965, February 17). Retrieved from www.hansard.parliament.uk: https://hansard.parliament.uk/Commons/1965-02-17/debates/8ac56f10-1a16-4dba-969a-7a35f7808d18/CivilAviationPolicy?highlight=hinton%20aviation#contribution-57bf5b5d-8bec-43da-a71c-6b11c197f8ef

135   Royal Academy of Engineering. (n.d.). Lord Hinton of Bankside OM KBE FRS FEng. Retrieved from www.raeng.org.uk: https://www.raeng.org.uk/about-us/what-we-do/40-years-of-the-academy/past-presidents/hinton

REFERENCES

136   Independents and the New Policy. (1965, February 25). Flight International, pp. 278-280.

137   Historical Exchange Rates. (n.d.). Retrieved from https://fxtop.com/: https://fxtop.com/en/historical-exchange-rates.php?

138   Woodley, C. (2006). History of British European Airways 1946-1974. Pen & Sword Books Ltd.

139   Humphreys, B. K. (1973). The Economics and Development of the British Independent Airlines since 1945. Phd Thesis. University of Leeds.

140   Independents and the New Policy. (1965, February 25). Flight International, pp. 278-280.

141   Congress House of Representatives. (1974, June 25). The role of Government capital in BOAC. Hearings before the Committee on Interstate and Foreign Commerce , pp. 272-275.

142   World Airlines Survey, 1965

143   BUA's Domestic Challenge. (1965, May 27). Flight International , p. 819.

144   UK Domestic Competition Again. (1965, June 10). Flight International, p. 896.

145   Three Operators for London-Glasgow. (1966, January 6). Flight International, p. 5.

146   UK Domestic Competition Again. (1965, June 10). Flight International, p. 896.

147   Eagle Buys Cunard Shareholding. (1967, January 12). Flight International, p. 47.

148   Eagle Holding Company. (1967, January 12). Flight Internationl, p. 52.

233

149   British Eagle 707-320Cs. (1965, December 30). Flight International, p. 1101.

150   Sensor. (1967, January 12). Flight International, p. 43.

151   Eagle Defers 707 Deliveries . (1967, February 9). Flight International, p. 193.

152   British Eagle's One Eleven Operation. (1967, June 1). Flight International, pp. 886-887.

153   British Eagle Cuts Back. (1967, August 10). Flight International , p. 204.

154   The Independent Challenge . (1967, August 17). Flight International , pp. 246-247.

155   Eagle Applies for Atlantic Cargo. (1967, August 31). Flight International, p. 325.

156   Eagle's New Atlantic Applications. (1967, October 12). Flight International, p. 595.

157   Caledonian's Case. (1967, October 5). Flight International, p. 554.

158   Sir Ronald Edwards. (1967, December 28). Flight International, p. 1055.

159   Independent Withdrawals. (1967, December 28). Flight International, p. 1057.

160   Airways Corporations (Trooping Contracts). (1964, November 25). Retrieved from www.hansard.parliament.uk: https://hansard.parliament.uk/Commons/1964-11-25/debates/5d33985f-a7b0-49b7-bc5d-

161   De Havilland Comet 1 & 2. (n.d.). Retrieved from baesystems.com: https://www.baesystems.com/en/heritage/de-havilland-comet-1---2

REFERENCES

162   Comet Enters Service. (n.d.). Retrieved from RAF Museum: https://www.rafmuseum.org.uk/research/archive-exhibitions/comet-the-worlds-first-jet-airliner/comet-enters-service/

163   Pushkar, R. G. (2002, June). A Comet's Tale. Retrieved from Smithsonian Magazine: https://www.smithsonianmag.com/history/comets-tale-63573615/

164   Hayward, P. K. (2018). Government and British Civil Aerospace 1945-64. Journal of Aeronautical History.

165   Tu-104. (n.d.). Retrieved from Britannica Encyclopedia : https://www.britannica.com/technology/Tu-104

166   BOAC's 707s in Service. (1960, June 3). Flight , p. 772.

167   Hedges, D. (2001). The Eagle Years1948-1968. The Aviation Hobby Shop .

168   Airways Corporations (Trooping Contracts). (1964, November 25). Retrieved from www.hansard.parliament.uk: https://hansard.parliament.uk/Commons/1964-11-25/debates/5d33985f-a7b0-49b7-bc5d-32c586675381/AirwaysCorporations(TroopingContracts)?highlight=trooping%20contracts#contribution-306f0695-ada2-472c-9934-196b9c193389

169   Eagle retrenches. (1968, October 10). Flight International, p. 557.

170   Lord King of Wartnaby. (2005, July 13). Retrieved from www.theguardian.com: https://www.theguardian.com/business/2005/jul/13/britishairways.obituaries

171   Calder, S. (2012, 7 7). Lord Marshall: Executive who turned British Airways from a sleeping giant into a world leader. Retrieved from www.independent.co.uk: https://www.independent.co.uk/news/obituaries/lord-marshall-executive-who-turned-british-airways-sleeping-giant-world-leader-7920614.html

172   Orient Line. (2016). Retrieved from P&O Heritage: https://www.poheritage.com/our-history/timeline

173   BUA for sale to BOAC. (1970, March 12). Flight International, p. 366.

174   Towards a British Aeroflot. (1970, March 12). Flight International, pp. 365-366.

175   Smithsonian National Air and Space Museum. (n.d.). Prof. Robin Higham. Retrieved from www.airandspace.si.edu: https://airandspace.si.edu/support/wall-of-honor/prof-robin-higham

176   Gow, D. (2005, July 13). Lord King, saviour of BA, dies aged 87. Retrieved from www.theguardian.com: https://www.theguardian.com/business/2005/jul/13/britishairways.obituaries1

177   Davidson, A. (1995, October 1). UK: The Davidson interview - Robert Ayling. Retrieved from www.managementtoday.co.uk: https://www.managementtoday.co.uk/uk-davidson-interview-robert-ayling/article/41006

178   Gregory, M. (1994). Dirty Tricks: British Airways' secret war against Virgin Atlantic. Virgin Publishing.

179   Adeney, M. (2010, April 15). Sir Michael Angus obituary. Retrieved from www.theguardian.com: https://www.theguardian.com/business/2010/apr/15/sir-michael-angus-obituary

180   Dix, A. G. (2019). Laker: The glory years of Sir Freddie Laker. Recursive Publishing.

181   U.K., U.S. fine BA for price fixing with Virgin Atlantic. (2007, July 31). Retrieved from Business Travel News: https://www.businesstravelnews.com/More-News/U-K-U-S-Fine-BA-For-Price-Fixing-With-Virgin-Atlantic

182   Press Association. (2010, November 29). BA and Iberia agree £5bn merger. Retrieved from The Guardian: https://www.theguardian.com/business/2010/nov/29/british-airways-iberia-agree-merger

Index

INDEX

INDEX

Also from SunRise

DE HAVILLAND COMET
The plane that changed the world
James Carlton

Wings Over Time

See Jane Fly
Feminism in Aviation
PETER PIGOTT

SOME PILOT
NIGEL HARRISSON

The Golden Age of Flying Boats
Peter Pigott

Sky Talk
Stories from flying's Golden Age
Philip Hogge

BOAC AND THE GOLDEN AGE OF FLYING
Britain's iconic global airline
Malcolm Turner

THE CONSTELLATION
Lockheed's Graceful Masterpiece
Alexander Clifton

IT'S PULL TO GO UP
From Lancasters to VC10s
A pilot's tale
Jeff Gray

Britain's Airline Entrepreneurs
From Laker to Branson
Malcolm Turner

Comets and Concordes
The pilot who flew the first and the fastest of all jet airliners
Peter Duffey

Ari, Jackie & Maria
The Pirate, The Princess & The Diva
Onassis, Kennedy, Callas
The Love Triangle of the 20th Century
Malcolm Turner

www.SunPub.info

Printed in Great Britain
by Amazon

85267281R00139